God is an Apricot

The main object of religion is not to get a man into heaven, but to get heaven into him. —Thomas Hardy. *The Woodlanders*, 1887.

Published by the Buon-Cattivi Press, 2025
Adelaide, South Australia

ISBN (PAPERBACK): 978-1-922314-15-4
ISBN (EBOOK): 978-1-922314-16-1

Book and cover design by Andrew Crooks.
Editing by Cameron Rutherford.

God is an Apricot

A metaphysical tour de forceps

Robert Moore

Buon-Cattivi Press
Adelaide, Australia

Dedication

For Cameron, Frances and Jennet.
He swims through the air and she flies through the water.
Until they all reach the narrow door.

Contents

Acknowledgements

This work is a product of desperation, determination and desire.

When I was diagnosed with HIV in 1999 my immediate reaction, apart from shock and carefully selecting the people I would tell, was to get on with adding an extension to my creative path.

Time would run out. I would soon die.

And in a strange kind of way, given I often hid my sexual preference from other people and even myself. I had to draw on extra reserves of that same secrecy to deal with the diagnosis.

This situation couldn't last. I had to open up. I had to talk about HIV.

My HIV.

I'll never forget the support and counselling from Bill Gaston who saw me the day after I was diagnosed. A couple of words from Bill assured me there could be, should be and would be an addition to that path.

A few days later I opened up to Roger Zubrinich, the coordinator of Professional Writing at the Adelaide College of the Arts.

I'm sure with each of these decisions to discuss HIV I was formulating ideas for *God is an Apricot.* Who and how to tell was rehearsed endlessly. I never told my elderly mother. The real me also had to be the pretend me until she passed.

And I was still living.

There's much talk about the health system in South Australia but I want to acknowledge the exceptional medical and dental care I have always received in this state.

That's why I'm alive and kicking and extending my path to connect with a yellow brick road.

Several organisations have assisted with *God is an Apricot.* I'm grateful for both the input and sponsorship of:

Suppository International.
Scurf Australia.
Cloaca Inc.
Tall Orders Pty. Ltd.
Cygnet River Dairies.
Lamington Council for the Arts.
Grow Up
New Directions Mt Compass.
University of Gibberoidia
Bantam Breeders of Lilliput

I'm especially appreciative for all the support and enthusiasm that Dr Alex Dunkin and Buon-Cattivi Press have given me.

Finally, there are two people who have helped me from the very beginning to ensure that my manuscript would bear fruit.

To David Lewis, a huge thank you for all your re-reading, edits and suggestions over the last decade and the eradication of gummosis in the manuscript.

And to my partner Cameron, who has cared for my grafted Moorpark, non-dwarfing, rootstock apricot for the last twenty years, your attention to all punctuation conventions has ensured that apricot freckle has not taken hold and created a blight of unnecessary full stops.........

Preface

The afternoon of Friday the 17th of September 1999, I was diagnosed with HIV.

The family-friendly doctor I saw in Blackwood told me I had AIDS.

The following Monday I went to a LGBTIQ-friendly clinic in the CBD. The doctor I saw contacted the 'family-friendly' doctor in Blackwood. There was an altercation between the pair.

'Why were you seeing someone else and not me?'

More tests were advised. It was suggested I have my bloods rechecked before any decision was made to begin drug therapy.

King Fear took over. He looked over all aspects of my life and made some big decisions.

Around this time my creative restlessness intensified, combined with the conflict in accepting my sexuality. I plunged into the future and enrolled in an Advanced Diploma in Professional Writing. It was during the first weeks of this course I learned I had HIV.

Well-practised secrecy was taken to another level.

If I were to tell anyone, who would it be and how would I do it?

One of the first people I confided in was Roger Zubrinich, coordinator of Professional Writing at the Adelaide College of the Arts. I'll not forget the support Roger afforded me and, apart from a brief extension on my assignment load, I completed an Advanced Diploma of Arts with no issues.

My head was full of all kinds of thoughts. I remember thinking since I had HIV, I didn't have to worry about getting it anymore. Concern about catching the virus was replaced with management of my new predicament.

Gay beats and saunas were out. Alternative therapies were in. I resisted going on medication.

It was part denial and partly a belief I could rid my body of any intruder.

While studying I had my first children's book published and a month later a second. Creativity was fed by urgency, or maybe it was the other way around. I wrote a play, *Brewing,* as part of my studies. The Richard Llewellyn Trust of Arts SA funded creative development of the play with the late Geoff Crowhurst, professional actors and a dramaturge.

But fearing time was limited, I desperately wanted to initiate a work incorporating multiple artistic disciplines.

I needed a character whose entire life was built on the dream of exploring artistic limits and pushing the boundaries of what might be deemed socially acceptable. This character had to be resilient and committed to initiating and producing an inclusive event despite the challenge of his deteriorating health.

I decided that a conceptual artist as the protagonist in a stream of consciousness novel was the best way to convey the freedom I've always sought to embrace, express and, most importantly, share.

Gabriel Dorset is the protagonist in *God is an Apricot.*

He has been immersed in a variety of artistic disciplines his whole life. But now he must juggle the demands of his failing health with the pressure of staging a huge theatrical event.

Gabriel and short-statured dancer Marcia Font apply to the Lamington Council for the Arts for a grant to present Tchaikovsky's *Swan Lake* with 500 short-statured people on Shepherd's Hill Recreation Park in an historic amphitheatre.

Swan Lake is renamed *Cygnet Waterhole* and is the centrepiece of *God is an Apricot.*

Moses, two kelpies, Thomas Hardy, Mother Teresa, Liberace the cat and Golda, the transgender salmon, all assist Gabriel and Marcia with the production.

But as opening night approaches, Gabriel is desperate to prevent the public and private threads of his consciousness from joining as one.

This is something he's been sweating on for a long time.

1: LOAVES AND FISSURES

IT'S taken ages but I'm comfortable. So much so I'm comfortable being uncomfortable. Well at least from head to heart and left toe to right testicle.

A sweaty thought ripples. It surfaces in the centre of a large relief map of psoriasis. An archaeological dig is unearthing a lost artefact. Someone skims a stone across my holy water.

I pray that time is on my side.

I need to keep on going.

Northwest of the Murray Mouth I drive up Shepherds Hill Road, discarding the flat of Adelaide. I'm a body without a head. This allows me to feel something yet nothing. It's not a passing whim that's finding circuitous routes in my brain. I'm finally listening for freedom.

I have no other option.

Time is running out. An inner voice repeats, 'This is it and this is the only way.' It synchronises with the gear changes of my manual. What should be in my head is of secondary consideration. Feeling removed is part of the discomfort.

My acceptance is ongoing life support.

The river isn't flowing.

My head sits in the passenger seat. I've relegated it to observer status. To witness the truth and to tell the truth faster. Now and then I glance at its eyes and mouth to see if they're still mine. I can't be fined for inattention or operating a mobile device. I'm reassured.

'Honestly I was watching with my eyes,' I would say in my defence.

My car converts to automatic transmission. The dislocated voice still responds to what my body says. The raging fever I've been fighting for some days hasn't abated. Cast aside, my head knows it must allow the truth to be spoken. This liberated communicator is both referee and overseer. Clutch and crutch interchange. Sounds and words find reason to continue the ripple as my mind flicks through the pages of an old manuscript.

My head is on autopilot. A clot is forming on the blotter as I try to write.

The letter I've promised to post for Louise is underneath my head. She says it's important. All about my numbers. I know there's a post box somewhere but I'm not sure of its exact location. My eyes blur as I'm forced to rise above the sweat which drips from my face and causes my hands to slide around the steering wheel of my dodgem car.

I'm being rained upon from the inside and I know I should see a doctor because the multiple doses of Panadol over the last week aren't working.

The blur of an Australia Post box is a red mirage that blinks on the footpath in front. The clot has shifted. I slow down and indicate I'm about to stop. The bike lane is my lane and I need it for better judgement. There are riders in front and behind. Stereo curses surround me bumper to bumper. I'm overly cautious as everything now requires second grabs from steering wheel to gear lever, to indicator.

And yes, I'm glad I'm still comfortable about feeling uncomfortable. The sweat rivers away. I wonder if I'll boil dry and stick to the seat like overcooked rice in the shape of a couple of arse cheeks.

The car bucks as it stalls to a stop. The handbrake and second gear fight for stop start. I peel out of the car in an uncontrollable shiver. The bike riders are now in front and give me a final look of contempt as well as a couple of fingers with a smelly history.

I see nothing but letter box. I feel nothing but sodden letter and curse the fact I've smudged Louise's carefully written address to her brother in the US.

I should see and hear but I shiver the truth about myself to the passing cars that suddenly slow both sides of the road. I really don't know what I'm doing. I really shouldn't be driving but somehow I need this trip as a test.

A head start perhaps.

It could be my last.

I've opted for a challenge, had the required self-talk about getting to Louise's and back to bridge the gap between the private me and the person I present to the rest of the world. I want that same person to be available all the time and right now the desire is being put to the test. How easy it would be to be the same person all the time and in every situation. A sense of urgency dissolves wishful thinking. Reconciliation is necessary. There's no time for more yearning.

The artefact must be quickly uncovered before I boil dry.

I have a leaking radiator.

I eventually find the chute for the letter. I convince myself all I want is total frankness. With other people and myself. I wonder why this thought is driving me and why I try to dismiss it. The rivers of sweat demand an answer. The continual hiss of passing vehicles insist I shelve this kind of thinking.

But I've posted the letter and it's time to move on.

Home beckons but I don't see what I should see. Home is not all that far. I ignore the seat belt. It's already slipped out of my shaking hands twice and I can't find the buckle. It's playing hide and seek around the hand brake. I start the drive slowly and stick to the bike lane for a few metres.

Wear your helmet. Where is my helmet? I put my head back in place as I move off. I practice swallowing to see if I've successfully reconnected the tissue.

The transplant is a success.

The flashing light of a police car travelling in the opposite direction is eventually red and blue drizzle in my eyes courtesy of the rear vision mirror. The car does a U turn and races in front and indicates for me to stop. I'm not going all that fast and pull over.

I'm riding a bike, aren't I?

Have my helmet on.

Get ready to crash into Jupiter. I'm in an induced coma for the long journey. HAL is checking me. I see stars. I'm not sure whether it's fire, ambulance or police.

I'm suffering from rocket rash.

A policeman gets out of his car and comes towards me. Time lapse kicks in as a protector and rallies with its earthly gravity. This is not an emergency. Goodbye fire and hospital. Seconds become minutes become hours of contemplation. I have a lifetime to live before the cop gets to my car and questions me. I rehearse what I want to say. I have an alibi.

That voice insists on the truth again.

You've been rigidly socialised away from the real you all your life.

Again, I'm flooded with the nagging wonder of why at this moment I opt for an ultimate 'don't care' attitude. For fifty years I've been silent on the constraints of gender and sex. Continual unexplained strep throats have been the consequence. Make believe answers to satisfy the questions of others has been my only way of avoiding domestic violence.

Survival.

It's always been an act I've had to rehearse while playing dumb. Powerlessness now needs a coffin. The original egg requires a stronger shell.

I must speak what's on my mind or I'll crack.

Truth and dare drive like never before. I panic. Will what I say be what I want to say? Have I ever really known what I've wanted to say? The expectation of others' expectations pulses. I'm sick of hearing about empowerment. My rights to my free speech. I know my body language can be read the way it's meant to be read. The steering wheel slips continually through my fingers like oil that's just left a bottle.

I am the bottle.

The artefact to be preserved for Ali Baba has been delivered via the sketch map of the Middle East in my Sunday palms.

The policeman practices a conciliatory walk towards my car. He exudes recent training in dealing with the public but I can see beyond this veneer. He's nothing more than muscle. He's just completed a course in safety in the workplace. Still he wears awareness well. His costume almost fits.

But will he outgrow it in time?

'Good afternoon, sir. I see you're not wearing a seat belt. Do you have an explanation?

'I was thinking about my next production of *Swan Lake*. It's with midgets. Suppose it should be *Cygnet Pond*. My head is full of tutus and whether it would be best to have Odette and Prince Siegfried on stilts.'

'Could you repeat that?'

'So, they'll rise to the occasion.'

I try to mop my brow with a buttonless shirt sleeve. Sweat drops onto my groin and trickles uncomfortably into an underground spring full of steamed anus. The policeman's crutch pumps the Festiva window. I think about rocking the car to reciprocate.

'Sorry, I forgot. Not feeling well. Do *you* think Prince Siegfried should be on stilts?'

I eye the cop's crutch. He backs away from the window, in anticipation of a standard response, but notes something hurriedly in his records.

I watch him for roles as I watch myself for a final dream come true.

I can't turn back a page as I get out of the car, dragging the clothes of a drowning man still seeping and sodden across a bitumen shore. Rice trickles down my legs in a syrup of colitis.

'Those cygnets have been a problem for days. I don't want them elevated. This is what happens when I downsize everything. Midget choreographer, midget musical director. I'm the only tallie in this show.'

I could opt not to have eye contact but seize a death-defying moment and look the cop square in the eye. I've used up all my expectations, the sight, sound and smell of normal behaviour.

This is my world.

I continue unabated. Although the sweat pours away, I pretend it's not happening. Those midgets are here. The cop is still here. And the infringement is being issued. Out of my car I shadow the cop back to his, in an ungainly squelch.

It's the return to the sea that has breast stroked millennia for my saline sanity.

'Do you issue smaller fines for midgets? The co-director is vertically challenged too. She was grabbed for loitering in an elevator in the mall. Said she was getting futuristic ideas about Princess Odette's castle. I know I should have been more attentive. I just posted a letter. Not feeling well. On my way home.'

With both hands shaking I take the infringement notice and shiver back to my car. The biro is already running. The print indecipherable. I fold it and open it. An irritated fixation takes up residence on my recently realigned face. I fan the notice around my head, hoping the spontaneous design work is acknowledged by the issuing officer.

'Just like the forest by the lake,' I say, raising my voice above the glares from cars that slow well before the sign for the speed limit.

The policeman stares at me and I wonder if something more needs to happen. I remain on the side of compliance. He comes back towards me as I get inside the car. It's obvious he's not met the director of a midget ballet before. He calls for backup but I assure him that all is normal.

It's only a tiny matter of detail.

'I'm not well. I need to get home. You're in my face and I'm not in your world,' I say in a reassuring manner which results in one confused cop. He's forced to respond seriously to my ability to play it straight irrespective of the free rein I've allowed my tongue. I dial my own number on my mobile out of sight of the law. I answer the phone.

'What?' I say into the speaker.

I turn to the cop.

'I need to get home. Must work out a new rehearsal schedule. Three of the cast have rung in sick.'

The cop opts for a cautionary lecture about wearing a seat belt at all times and how to deal with an expiation notice.

'Cygnet syphilis. Can you believe it? Three midgets down with the pox?'

I wait for the cop to leave, unravel the seat belt from the hand brake and latch it into the passenger's side. I need to secure my head in the passenger's seat again.

Anyone could be watching so to speak.

Walls Have Eyes Too.

WET me and my head receive our welcome from the walls of home. It's a relieved hello to the Frontal Lobe filing cabinet inside the front door and it's so nice to be with my floor to ceiling family again.

My only family.

The files of the past are ready to slide into my mind. There's no knowing how the eyes hidden in the plaster sheets will seduce me into considering the importance of family. I breathe freely or pretend to breathe freely allowing relatives witness to my current malaise. I praise the walls but will not go down on my knees in their expectation of total surrender. The other part of the house beckons me to a state of straight comfort.

I deadlock the front door and acknowledge the eyes that follow me like a tribe of optical Jesuses. There's an overload of halos but I need the protection of a solitary heavenly force. I know there could be a halo fight but I'm also confident there is no pecking order where halos are concerned.

Jungle juice sweats from pores to the applause of a mushy dermis. I'm all Amazonian from delta to forest. The eyes covering the plaster could possibly sheet over old asbestos as I cough uncontrollably and correct my balance to find gratitude in solace.

This is all there is and this is how I've planned it.

Different eyes eagerly plead for attention en route to the back door. They bow in praise and hallelujah to the rear entrance which I could open to the outside world. For them I am Messiah but the tropical body needs the miracle of more Panadol working. Liberace, my cat, demands attention and the talkative bird population is busily fox proofing itself for the night.

Must I go into the outside world again?

Finally, I close the back door, close everything, plead and praise simultaneously, think about eyes from Frontal Lobe which incorporates a piano and a wall of yet to be read books. I haven't the strength to remove clothes and yet I want to wash the remains of men right out of my hair this cum-enchanted evening.

I want the power to fine people for using the word family. Thanks to the carriers of the Conformity Virus I'm always looking out for the family. Louise says she's in this world but not of this world. That she was born disconnected. Had no rights according to her adoptive mother. And was not family. I wonder why she says this, repeats this and remembers this.

No, I don't wonder. I know exactly why she says what she says. I'm curious about her letter. She says she has a feeling about my life lesson. Her US brother is a famous numerologist. She wants to find out if her intuition is true. That my numbers will tell her something definite, but the sceptical side of me resists her numbers' game.

The eyes are watching from the front again. I can see them shooting out their requests blink after blink with their secret drawers. I wouldn't know they were here if I didn't allow them to be.

Police files, midget files, ballet files.

They're near the ceiling and slide in and out making the overhead fan rattle with their familiar delirium. Louise hides from them though. Nothing is familiar for her.

I call for the quill, biro and the keyboard all in one. I'm travelling centuries, decades and the latest updates. The three files in contention trickle as the sweat fills a dam of soiled clothes. The phone rings and rings. I stagger to the shower and turn on the water. I can't tell the difference between hot and cold. I search for reason and meaning with my current predicament. The now or never scares me to death but the demands of eyes in walls, which have usurped the reason for ears, urge me on to complete an unknown journey.

'Thirty-three, thirty-three,' the eyes whisper in unison having learned lip service as a matter of urgency during the death of Jesus. I'm still unable to speak of how I feel, what to say or ask and importantly who to go to for help with the total truth on and off my chest.

Too much time has been spent saying the right thing, being the right person, thinking the right thoughts. It's choice, all choice and it's up for grabs now. I want to be contrary much, much more than Mary, Mary. I want to be liked for hate. I need to speak about my hate, what

I hate, who I hate, the vast cemeteries needed to bury all the people I hate and want to kill still.

There's an inner death, a killer at work inside that has attracted such strong feelings, or is it the ease of writing such clear-cut words that enables me to say anything? To know that shit massages as it escapes to the sewer disguised as indelible ink.

Again, the eyes of plaster surface to see for me and to beg to drive me senseless into an ego pool of contradiction and goose bumps. My family asks that I backtrack and return to the source via a tortuous route, to immerse myself in Frontal Lobe while meditating in a cocoon of barbed wire.

The water burns and freezes. I slip on soap and imbibe mildew that's multiplied in the last days. The smell has married stench. My dribbling nostrils cling to the flooding odour. I see the files in Frontal Lobe with an out-of-date computer sanctioning that those files need further insight, thought and physical work.

There are files for the building of livers, table biting and fence licking. There's a file labelled, 'How to explain these thoughts to ordinary people'.

As I scrub my slippery body rebellion drives me to the outside of crematoriums where bulldozers congregate waiting for their cue. I need to revisit my plaster family and sit with them for a while to ascertain which thoughts need immediate action.

Still conscious that eyes have ousted ears I wonder what has happened to the other senses in this lime war.

I wet three towels trying to get dry. I turn on a gas heater and a wood fire full pelt but still I shiver. I stagger about wondering if all I am is thought. The physical body seems far away from me and I'm asked for a custody order to reclaim and detain it as part of safe survival.

Away from the intrusion of plaster on the senses in Frontal Lobe I listen naked and dripping with ears that have sought refuge from warring eyes. I can hear the slide and roll of the files as they jostle in and out of their designated cabinets to position themselves somewhere near police and midgets, ballet dancers and cyclists. The hate files are moving in and out fast. There're several of them. There's been an attempt to call them dislike files but hate seems a truer fit. I can hear their fast shuffle like underground trains stopping at every station and wasting time for passengers who neither get on or off. The cops and the midgets are keeping them in place.

Cygnet Pond is now definitely *Cygnet Waterhole*. It's murky, full of algae bloom and the bloated bodies of the people I've just killed. I've searched for them, or have they drifted into my line of fire? Unfortunately, they all had the Conformity Virus. Main symptom of the virus is fear. Correction. Was fear. There's no treatment for those afflicted because all they can do is spit out one calcified word.

Fear.

That's why I'm sick. I don't belong to a word. I have to belong to this word to be in this world. So, in this world I propose that families should be discriminated against. That prams be turned into coffins. Retiring footballers retrained as family hate therapists. Dingoes get invited to set up boutiques selling matinee jackets and they're also given grants from the government. People of every current gender rally with the same placard which reads, 'Gay men make the best heterosexuals'. I replace the Union Jack with these words.

But I have to watch out. The Christians are after my blood.

Yet they might not if they knew what I *should* know.

Using supportive ears, I placate this fear and listen as I dry covered in wet words and letters. The filing cabinets slow their tracks. Frontal Lobe wants its ears back. It's gone too far. I listen intently. There's a slow rumble of a heavy file. I know it's close to the floor. It's so basso continuo. The treble files clef shrilly at the prospect of cops and midgets drowning in waterholes. I don't want them to drown but I want them to change.

I delete their sentence.

The phone rings again but I elect not to hear it. I accuse it of being an agent of the basso continuo. A sauna of used towels saturates my polished floorboards. The freedom to be near death so often doesn't run through my mind. It runs it permanently from within.

My hearing is uncluttered. I hear the words. I see myself seeing the words. Old basso keeps plodding on attempting to move up the scale. He sings to me. He slows the information in the file down so I get a chance to read what is written on his most recent manuscript.

I forgive myself totally. There is nothing that love can't heal.

Midgets and cops call helplessly from *Cygnet Waterhole*. They lose their notation but manage to crawl exhausted onto the bank, a series of semibreves sustaining common time.

I start coughing uncontrollably.

All I can think of is waltz of the swans with TB.

Bed Jobs.

I CONTINUE to dry the wet only to be wet again. The room is warm. In Frontal Lobe where the air is iced with imminence I scan the files while relegating them to temporary sleep. I fall into bed coughing nonstop. The rasp of lung fluid clings to every alveolus as trees of phlegm try to outgrow their chesty restriction.

I turn on my side, grateful that most of the files are locked by a desire for security. The coughing continues, the sweating starts again and I shiver to every death's door urged by a beckoning Jesus who is trying to solicit me for unknown purposes. The relentless coughing forces me to sit up but now I fear that parts of my lung will make my nostrils emit wind. If I worked in a Thomas Hardy dairy I'd be pleased with my ability to produce clots. In times gone by a Madonna caring for a sick child was happy to see thickened mucus while puffing on her tailor-mades.

I lived in terror that my mum would accidently set fire to me and the manger.

Exhausted, I fall to one side again using my whole body as a suppressant. It doesn't work. I pull last Saturday out of an unfulfilled and reluctant file. Relative ease of access lightens as I wheeze. This file rattles, suspended in rooms away, the loneliest file in my universe. *Do not disturb* whispers about like an air conditioner on night watch. Now and then spiritual sentry duty starts as I instruct those three words to routinely check the contents of Frontal Lobe.

Do not disturb.

I'm at the front door of the sauna. Jesus is already inside but within is only a question God can answer. I open the door and listen to the sound of my footsteps echo in the entranceway. I commit the sound of the steps to memory, conscious of a past habit wanting to recall normality as I re-enter the outside world at a later date. I roll back onto the broad of my back. The wheezing continues as I undress, check out the tackle of guys dressing or undressing. Fantasy and hunger always leave me unsatiated. The ritual of a wraparound towel followed by a hot shower then steam followed by a sauna has begun to suck. I cough again. Thomas Hardy is demanding. The cows are dry and so is the sauna but the tits full of male milk are easy on the eye and in search of numerous mouths.

And not the hands of dairy maids.

Somehow, I'm carried aloft and away to the ultimate sauna. I toss and turn between coughing, irritated that the bedsheets are soaking. Jesus is beckoning me again and I can't fathom why this poor crucified cunt is featuring so strongly in my life. I follow his finger up sodden stairs past cubicles to a tongue rotisserie. The Lord points me in the direction of a skin and saliva waterbed. There are tongues everywhere and I'm in the middle being gently tossed and turned by dozens of taste buds.

Like a trust exercise I give into weightlessness and the support offered by moist licking.

The tongues force themselves into follow the leader and, as excited as maggots, reveal the rest of their bodies which kiss and suck me all over. So many tongues in and on my arse, armpits, cock and balls I want to explode but take this continual baste in my hands piled with cocks, my face sat upon by arse after arse, to be reciprocated with additional succulent lips.

I crash through the barrier with all that's ordained.

Praise the Lord.

Filled with slut guilt and fear, I allow cock after cock to dissolve these feelings and redesign my rectum. The coughing hasn't abated and Jesus is still watching. A mother and a father had me. A mother and a father unloved on the inside bred me. My rectum pulsates with the birth of pleasurable guilt. I'm overcome with these feelings. An undiscovered mum and dad attracted all the accoutrements of family and plunged on into the unknown with their own guilt placing boundaries around how much filth to allow into their lives.

And I chose these parents?

They were bawdy up to a point but there was always a curfew. Whispers were in their genes. Open talk was not. Derision and put downs of anything abnormal were what they breathed.

They were expected to breathe and breed.

So why did I choose them?

I sit up in bed again. My heart thumps evenly. The wheezing continues. Jesus winks at me. Men float by naked and searching. Erections force flimsy towels from waists. Some reach for me but it's I that needs to reach for myself. I want the ride of my life again, to feel the men of now in, on and around me because there's no going forwards or back. The men of now are responsible for present pleasure. They have brought their wants to this place with a fervour that no religion could understand let alone sanction.

Stained glass windows depicting cock sucking men are in my cathedral. I cough deep and uncontrollably and fear there is no end.

Or perhaps this is an end?

Light-headedness takes hold and I fall back onto wet pillows dreaming of a conversion into a human pie with scrolls of cocks holding the uncooked pastry sheets together. I see the pie cooking and the cocks expanding in the oven. By a design of genius, the deft placement of fingers beforehand ensures the cocks have grown foreskins.

I'm born again complete this time.

I get out of bed, shivering uncontrollably. The rush to the light is necessary, has been necessary and has to be revisited again. Jesus wants me back in bed to finish matters. I'm stalked by the disciples who've just seen my stained-glass windows. I notice they're all smiling and would like to guess what for but those blessed genes passed on, passed on and keep getting passed on without correction are interference. I know there'll be no passing on of genes as far as I'm concerned. There'll be no marriage. No next generation. I want to scream the ultimate fuck off to all those who can't accept diversity and that is why I try to sleep in my own way, as restless as it has been for many long nights and days.

A monsoonal build up of sweat is a sidekick to swooning and is once again firmly established in Frontal Lobe.

Waiting to be Doctored.

'CONTACT person.'

'I have no contact person,' I say to the receptionist who fails to lift her head up and away from the computer screen.

'I need a contact person in case of an emergency.'

'I have no contact person. I have no contacts,' I repeat to the receptionist who this time moves her head in a fashion not unlike the young girl in *The Exorcist*. I wait for the head to do a full rotation. And some filthy words.

'Family then. Friend.'

'They're all dead.'

'I need a contact person otherwise your details can't be processed. Surely there's someone.'

The receptionist pretends calm but I'm not giving in or giving her what she wants. Her computer is a shield. Her life force. I'm still wet enough to be a fish but out of water. A higher power is pushing me into the light.

'Thomas Hardon. Thomas is spelt T H O M A R S E.'

'Address?'

'Durbevillia Way.'

The receptionist is pleased that she can be lulled by convention and wants to type quickly.

'How do you spell Durbevillia?'

'Ur as in turd. Villia as in Grevillia.'

'What number?'

'5050.'

'That's a postcode.'

'Sorry I don't remember.'

'Take a seat. Doctor will see you shortly.'

I turn in search of a seat. The slippery fish is out of control. Drugged mothers littered with out-of-control progeny sprawl from one end of the waiting room to the other. The migrating salmon has to hurdle the rapids of spilt Lego to find a place to spawn. I slump wet on vinyl that farts with any movement and this discovery makes me wriggle all the more. Some of the progeny not yet aware of personal space invade mine anyway as if I'm the most interesting thing that's happened to them since their conception.

'Bradley, watch you don't hit the man with your helicopter.'

A voice from the other end of the waiting room is only half full of concern yet a keen sense that mothers and children in this place and most places have more rights than anyone else. Out of sight of the Mama Cass, I growl like a dog and make a contorted face which is half monster and fully retarded. The child drops the helicopter, screams and runs back to the Cass Converter while I continue to fart and look and feel for that special place to spawn. I stare ahead pretending and yet seeking oblivion while the drugged Mama soothes the upset child who by now has snot tributaries cementing a crusty dummy.

More patients check in with the receptionist. Now and then the Mistress of Conformity glances at me in a disapproving manner, mired by the superficiality of her important communication skills. I don't belong here but she does. I consider supplying her with the same face meant for snotty toddlers but opt for a façade which some might think ice induced or belonging to a mentally challenged soul.

In this space I pause to consider if my reaction might be different if the receptionist was male. I concede this is not a gender or sex issue but more the effect of those intent on spreading the uniformity of the living dead. The waiting room is populated with the powerless, those not taking responsibility for their lives, those who unwittingly bemoan the choices made.

Me?

The receptive magnet partially hidden behind sliding glass digs for a suburban smile expecting that whoever she is dealing with will recognise her sincerity and respond appropriately. Everyone does. I wonder if I'm the only exception. Or if I'm just kidding myself with tunnel vision arrogance.

I'm already the true face of the Conformity Virus?

Bradley has returned to the Lego box with a new-found friend, Teagan from the other end of the waiting room. Together they make hybrid helicopters for the US air force. The US President needs special protection in the Kenyan waiting room. The Cass Converter has replicated and sprawls in Ultra Panavision. Mamas One and Two watch their children still oblivious to the rest of the people waiting for one of six doctors and the potential injury caused by flying rotor blades.

Desperately I search for that special spawning place. There is no chance with the obstacles placed in the way of natural rapids and waterfalls that are easily negotiable. The vinyl sticks like plaster. I try to peel it as discretely as possible. I need to keep up the façade to extricate myself away from the overriding compulsion to belong. I have Parkinson's Disease and for one long minute I shake and contort as I let the vinyl rip from my sodden body.

Heads turn in my direction. The helicopters cease to hover but I continue shaking thinking I might mutter some expletives or speak in gibberish as an explanation for salmon side-tracked by vinyl. Genuine shaking replaces the Parkinson's tremor and facial contortions. The salmon arrives in a scoop of water fitting for a holding pattern for spawn. This is despite the reflection of overhead rotors via multiple golden ponds. Bradley and Teagan hover between the legs of respective Cass Converters. Their rotors continue to spin creating a downdraft. While waiting for a landing site Bradley is summoned to surgery as Teagan is left to land his craft alone on the flooded mid New South Wales coast.

The receptionist looks up from her screen, drinks coffee without holding the handle. She casts her eye around the room pretending not to afford me any extra attention but her power seat ensures she thinks she is at the controls of everything including the life cycles of salmon and refurbished choppers.

'Gabriel Dorset.'

Still contemplating a world of salmon hovering and waiting for lift off from vinyl I extricate myself one last time and shadow Doctor Gloria Love into what I hope is her open-heart surgery.

You've got to love Doctors.

I SIT facing Doctor Love. The hellish journey although short is peppered with what-ifs. I fear my tongue has been swallowed by someone posing as me. Signposts collected from the past day desperately help me understand why I'm here. All I can see or remember is Louise and her world soggily conveyed by a letter. Louise's words spring around the surgery and settle on charts and diagrams. Doctor Love has preconceived ideas I decide. She is a woman of this medicated world.

All I see is family, couple, children and an upper middle-class celebration of the boredom of life in a professional fast lane. There's a negotiation to drift into an even faster lane but only if there is a tangible and materialistic reward. Two mobile phones and a tablet are having tantrums while trying to communicate with one another. Doctor Love asserts the need for non-verbal recognition of her role and to apologise for the interruptions. She expects me to fill in the gaps and acknowledge her busy life.

'So, Mr. Dorset what seems to be the problem?'

In the back of my mind I know to draw on my resources and tell the half-truth. I know I have to apologise for being single and not having a partner. The world of Thomarse has to be reactivated as protection. I have to both hide and reveal. Say and be silent. Present an image as continual fear expects me to traverse the same well-trodden path. My fast lane has a speed limit imposed by me. It's both a chase and getaway.

'Been sweating a lot for a couple of days now. Panadol doesn't seem to be working. I guess it's a bad case of flu.'

The good doctor examines my throat, takes blood pressure and temperature and suggests I need a course of antibiotics. I sweat on another plane. A nervous energy has slotted in replacing that which has been present for the entire world to see these past days. She hasn't asked any more questions. She looks at the notes made by the receptionist and cages herself.

Am I some escaped beast she has to tranquilise?

I'm in a rejoicing mood already. I have something that can be treated and fixed. I'm head over high heels. Rouge over rectum. I smile at the continuing tantrums between tablets, phones and a desktop computer. I can't wait to rush back to the sauna to meet Jesus again. To be massaged by the Messiah is all the spiritual comfort I want. I have plenty of sweat.

'You seem to be perspiring a lot.'

Back to Earth I plummet. The mocking Messiah points at me. I've been hit by a thunderbolt. Dr Love reddens. In fact, her beetroot face looks as though it's to become a permanent fixture. I think Dr Redden rather than Love. A name change might be a means of saving face. I don't want any more questions. I want strength again. I can feel and see the next question. It's coming like the birth of something I'm not prepared for.

The mocking Messiah breaks wind above as the tired salmon, eggs now loose, splashes lazily in her after-confinement. The blurred words of Louise slip and slide around the room. The salmon dives back into the journey from where it came.

'Enough to fill a pond or waterhole?'

Dr Love smiles reassuringly and seems grateful for my words.

'You should be better by the end of the week.'

I let each of us off hooks. I look for contempt in the doctor's package but I sense nothing quite so extensive. I look again and this time it's for awareness of a bigger picture of what drives fear.

Who drives fear?

I appreciate that there is no reference to family, partner or next of kin. Yet I know it'd save a lot of problems for everyone if deep within my salmon grounds I could easily throw out a line past the sauna queues of never lasting lust to find family, friend and future.

Oh, the need to spawn.

The mood for rejoicing establishes once more as I squish out of the surgery into the rest of what I believe to be a Monday morning. The waiting room has been repopulated. The Bradleys and Teagans have gone to be replaced by a coughing cardigan brigade of male oldies propped up by their angry womenfolk.

All along I have planted the seeds of knowing. It's the seeds of death that have now been propagated But I have no capacity to embrace all that at this stage. How convenient it is to go to a local family doctor and receive a part truth when I know if I were to visit a gay friendly clinic, I'd be encouraged to have blood tests. But for today, this precious believable Monday, I step out into the late winter sunshine shielded from the world with a prescription and breathing in and on for dear life. So treasured is this unmeasured breath of mine.

I jump in and out of several apparitions as I make my way to the car. I can't quite remember how I got here. I can't remember which part of me I brought along for examination.

The salmon is making it downstream. The rapids are lessening and the river becomes a steady churn of floodwater, scum and melting snow. The prescription is a fan. I'm hot still. I notice a Community Hall nearby. I think about a venue for the ballet. No, aim for the best, I tell myself again and again. Something much bigger.

Time is short.

Jesus sees me get in the car. He winks and beckons. I have to follow his directions. Is he a policeman this time or is he trying to lure me into further pleasure? I piss him away as I start the car. I turn the motor off and sit for a moment, bathed in a mix of bitter lemon sun and sweat.

Louise shouts in my ear. She shouts in my face. Her spit stinks.

'There is nothing love can't heal.'

I see Dr Love and then Dr Redden. I see them both in the rear vision mirror accompanying Jesus as they walk towards me. They keep walking and into the car via the locked hatch back. They lift me up and fly with me in a figure of eight that ties itself around the Festiva like a giant Christmas present. I'm wearing the prescription on my head. I dance from Hills Clinic to City Health Practice.

While the lone salmon goes to school once more, I'm desperately mindful of rehearsing a corps of cygnets.

Time is too short, my heart says once more.

There's enough sweat to fill a waterhole.

And just enough time to fill a prescription.

IMMEDIATELY I'm home I drop everything. Frontal Lobe screams. There's a file waiting. It slides in and out of its gyprock compartment, teasing the old asbestos. It's diorama time. The file grows wings and chases me to the back of the house where I double dose on huge antibiotics, the first cousins of elephant suppositories. The diorama takes shape somewhere but I catch my head before rummaging through a stack of cardboard boxes to build the real thing. Felt pens, glue, Stanley knives are flung across the kitchen table. The cat wants to play with anything that moves. I pull out my sketch pad. My mind's eye. I turn the pages in Act One and Two. My other eye.

Goodbye theatre chasing. I can't afford the rent. Hello outdoors.

I press the rewind button and go back home to a childhood waterhole. The one that's chockers with frogs and slime. I draw on this as I hurriedly sketch. I want the music to be the same, the storyline somewhat similar but the dancers will be very different. The waterhole is perfect. Behind it is a steep gully. I get my father, a lover of bulldozers and tree felling, to level the ground above the waterhole. He's good at raping the environment but with his Caterpillar plaything, it's called progress.

It's not just set design but a whole experience for audience and players. Now I've got it. The audience will be the other side of the waterhole. The cygnets will dance their life away on hallowed ground. I've got Jesus on the guest list and hope that he'll run his finger over the performance and give it his blessing. I'll have to advise him not to walk across this water. Budgeting reveals that public liability doesn't cover Messiahs contracting tinea. I've rounded up the sheep so they may safely graze in the hill behind the audience. So what if they've shit all over the edge of the waterhole and need to be shorn after all these years? I've cordoned off the performance area. No cloven hoof will tread on this territory. And the sheep shit will dry in time anyway. I leave the real ducks so that people will say, 'Really?'

I wonder if they'll quack at Siegfried or Odette. Then there's that castle. What will I suggest to my partner? I need to get in touch with her straight away. That's if she's not been arrested for protesting in another elevator.

I scribble a note to ring Marcia Font with the idea.

Kind of what I'm thinking is Stonehenge colliding with Cradle Mountain.

My note to Marcia commingles. The pen ceases its might. There's too much activity. Gelignite has been planted in Frontal Lobe. I hold the detonator between my teeth. The midgets are to arrive on bullocks or horseback. Elements of a rodeo. Their changing rooms are above the performance area. A series of wagons. I think a semicircle might work as a backdrop.

A lone salmon soars out of the waterhole. It alerts the Cass Converters. They move back and forth on both sides of the waterhole, quacking for their little ducks Bradley and Teagan. They drop their guard down as hysteria builds. Two ducklings emerge from the waterhole choking with umbilical cords of slime. They slip on fresh sheep dung and are humanly transformed as the sun sets. Odette has an eye for the Cass Converters and knows how they feel. A spell of humanity is required. She urges them to collect their brood and flee. Sorcerer Von Rothbart feels his way into this picture and can see the obese Indian Runners waddle through their painful crutch rot with their grizzling young crying tears of downy mildew.

I know my father will lend a hand if I give him certainty about my sexual orientation. The lie I tell myself most of the time is the lie I allow him to share. He wants to pass the farm onto me but I'm not in love with bulldozers. But at this point of time and the amount of rain there's been and the degree of moisture in the air, bulldozers are just the thing to tow two disused chook pens to the performance area.

And so it happens with chains and strain. The marshalling yard bellows and neighs. The changing rooms arrive. The tiered seating is set up. I can see it. I can feel it. I watch the chook pens being towed into position side by side. The bulldozer drags a mountain of eucalypt stumps and positions them hard up against the back of the chook pens.

Marcia Font has already discussed an Aussie type palace for Prince Siegfried.

I wonder if she'll like my ideas.

Sitting back from the diorama I lift a rigor mortis coffee cup of memory to swallow. The beginnings of fermentation hits my guts. I'm shivering again and must look like I'm caught in a downpour. The lone salmon backtracks in search of the correct route, trapped in the waterhole. It can smell old chook shit, fresh cattle breath and the virgin earth terrorised by my futile father.

In his twilight years he's given himself an eight-hour day to contemplate a future to naively disturb nature by his torture. The salmon seeing this swiftly scuttles back into an ongoing Russian conflict of entrapment and decay.

It will try to flee later.

The Cass Converters stand atop a rise halfway between heaven and the waterhole. Teagan and Bradley are taken by the snorting and bellowing of the horses corralled nearby. Dust tries to fly from ploughing hoofs, yet buries within a squelch of clay icing, creating surreal gingerbread men which grow out of faecal matter.

Cattle fed on hay during a drought I assume.

I get up from the chair but it gets up too. I hunchback around the kitchen before unshackling the unwanted parasite, which lands with a stabbing thump of four legs on linoleum thanks to the creative genius of dance guru Pina Bausch. I believe it's still Monday and want to travel back to my prime spot at the waterhole. Years of calendars from the beginnings of dust are stacked in any order. The ideas are here and there but the diorama is still just a collection of materials.

The application to the Lamington Council needs to be filled. I'm waiting for Marcia Font. Things can't happen fast enough. Can I sell my thoughts to her? Will feelings take shape?

Morning has become late afternoon too quickly. I panic. This has happened too much in the last few days. And then I realise it's been like this since the sweating started. How many days now? When did it first start? How much did I tell the family doctor? The pileups continue increasing pace. How long have I been like this? How truthful am I?

So, you want to wed fear and give birth to more fear by forceps then?

I wonder if I belong here in this place which I call home, but is it?

I've lived here for years but something is saying I've never been here and that I don't fit the mould. I've never belonged. The sweat goes on and on. Homes. Families and all kinds of belongings both physical and metaphysical are up for grabs and explanations.

I float and reform.

All of me is plasma or a newly defined energy that I have to come to grips with soon. The frog spawn slips through my fingers and the slime follows. The salmon hovers, pretending it has found its home but knows this is totally unfamiliar territory. There has never been a home. In the dark it must decide not to look for rapids. There's little moonlight for it to practice what is second nature and instinct. It looks to me for the cues. I suggest cross dressing.

A transvestite salmon. No. Get it right. This performance is contemporary and inclusive. They hide at least two? Transgender. They want to be she, her and they. That's their journey too.

I move to the furthest part of my kitchen and curl up in the light in a foetal position. The sun picks me out and I wink at Jesus. He winks back. The disciples join him and they start dancing on a shaft of light flicked with glitter. It seems to be something from *A Chorus Line*. But there's constant practice and positioning on the well-lit stairway from heaven.

The Cass Converters carry their kids on their shoulders and waddle into the sunlight pursued by Dr Love. Into cars they pile but are reprimanded by my favourite policeman from whenever. And all this is happening now.

For their own protection the Cass Converters are told to backtrack.

A safe house has been created for them around the waterhole.

I'm forced to think Now. The fear gripping me is the sweat leaving me. There's never been a time like this but I've been playing Russian roulette for too long. There's a real reason for Now. I don't want to see the logic.

I contrive an illness or am I really ill?

I want a cure – one that is delivered by nice family doctors who read from the script of their lives, diagnose me, and in their antibiotic haste thrust part of their rehearsed script in my hands to cure all ills forever.

I'm a puddle of myself. A shivering and uncontrollable malleable form of amoebic ectoplasm. Jesus dances with his merry men half naked via the sauna to their holes in heaven as the salmon searches for just one of her kind in the great lake of creativity, the *Cygnet Pond or Waterhole*. She's still waiting for my cue. I reach above and flick a packet of Panadol from the kitchen bench into my lap. Like unfinished laundry I ooze onto my feet wishing I could spin dry. The need for lightness drives me. It's unattainable. I seek recognition of this space but a voice is urging me to push through boundaries and to ride out the turmoil I'm experiencing.

Liberace is uneasy. He purrs and circles for attention. This is his home but he's dissatisfied, unable to discover diamonds in his home brand salmon. Why then is this place not home? Nine lives entwine my shaky legs as I swallow more than the recommended dose of Panadol in twenty-four hours. I'm not sure anymore that an hour is a measurable unit that is familiar.

Those seconds, minutes and days are all flashing expiation notices.

I open the back door. It's the past. All the back doors in my life assume a personality and leer at me. Suddenly I stop. Frontal Lobe is calling out. It wants immediate attention. It's witness to all back doors. I rush to the front of this house and hope to redefine it once more as home or at the very least a familiar place to analyse my next breath. Filing cabinets are shunting back and forth, shackled souls restrained in an asylum. There is little room for storage. High on the treble clef above my piano a tune screams. I don't recognise it but Victor Borge is playing. I look at the piano. It's become a pianola and plays Tchaikovsky's famous Piano Concerto in B minor. Australian folk songs compete for space along with the Overture from Disney's *Snow White and the Seven Dwarfs*.

What about the music from *Swan Lake*? Get ready for Marcia.

Back doors are angry. They are not being remembered or acknowledged for the part they have played in my life. They believe themselves to be the arteries to happiness. I go to return to the rear of this house once more but Frontal Lobe urges me to stay. I slump on the piano stool.

Clogged.

Tchaikovsky screams again. My mother peers around the door as I lunge into that concerto. I slip on the keys barely distinguishing black from white. The sun shafts in on me from all angles. Its lemon bitterness lingers. The salmon in desperation has grown rudimentary legs and hobbles into the mud to watch my father on his D9 clear a space for the stage. She searches for saintly intervention in the watery threads of her cross dressing.

Swan Lake *must come out on top. Play it by ear but know it off by heart.*

The Little People begin arriving. Hugely talented, I will require them all in the grant application to the Lamington Council. But at the moment the protestation of the files in Frontal Lobe is a number one priority. These cellular memories are desperate for survival. I let Jesus in through the manhole but the disciples curse because they are not part of the audience. Files quiver, wondering about the intrusion. Matthew and John lift the cover to sprawl at my feet. The others fall onto the carpet lolling about trying to re-create another last supper. Twelve egos all want to upstage one another.

Frontal Lobe is a hummingbird. I smell of sweat and the stink of Russian cholera. I see every back door again. The files are mesmerised. Unhinged, they've been flown in to bear silent witness and have strict instructions to behave themselves yet serve as a reminder. They're on parole. Numerous suppression orders accompany them. I've a visual feast, a soundscape and the taste of trickling vomit as I try to keep the Panadol and the antibiotics down.

Togetherness.

Tchaikovsky sends his fantasies into my fingers. I want to kiss his music. It's soppy but kissable. From groin to epiglottis the concerto tingles inside a series of concert halls either destroyed or yet to be re-built but there's an audience. They want my essence. I remain in Frontal Lobe observing the discomfort of back doors, the negative relegations of a past life. My forehead could burst.

Bandage it with bandannas, I'm told by another man called Peter.

I the foetus wriggle on the piano stool, a just born salmon. The slippery ivories entice my fingers. I apologise to a great master but I need to satisfy a father and release a mother. Dr Love has put none of this on my prescription. Luke and John offer me wine but I brush them aside and smile at Jesus who's sitting on top of the piano. His robes dangle just above my head. I take a peek underneath. He's definitely Jewish. I hope I don't get my fingers caught in a frenulum as I motor up and down the keyboard in an unholy manner.

How Old Testament can you get?

Liberace has come into the room unaware that just the day before he became part of Frontal Lobe. 'How up myself,' I mumble as I castigate myself for thinking that the cat hasn't got me worked out already and will become the favourite plaything of the cast of little ones. The concerto fades and the great master tells me to play Australiana folk songs in his style. But I have to desperately recycle to find the road back to Peter's Russia.

The music from *Swan Lake* is bursting at the seams. *Gundagai* and *Waltzing Matilda* interpose concertos. The keyboard is awash as in a MONA gallery waterfall. The activity in Frontal Lobe has accelerated. Marcia Font is calling me. Lamington Council is calling me.

And Dr Love is watching me as Dr Redden.

THE phone rings in Frontal Lobe. I have to answer it. I unstick from the piano stool. Where is it? I knew where the phone is but now I don't. Where am I? All sweat and fear. Which of these artefacts did I uncover? This has to stop. Faith needs to be employed but faith hasn't been a consideration to date. The phone keeps ringing. Frontal Lobe rests in readiness for a viewing.

Remember it's Monday. I hope so. Remember it's day not night. I think.

I'm a body. But I have to learn how to pinch again. So I pinch. Yes, I'm a body. I rush for the phone. Two hands grasp it. Panic thumps. Can I still walk? I did. Can I talk? The explosion of gross motor doubts and fine motor ignorance is incalculable. I lift the phone from the cradle. It's a foetal attraction. Is this what I do in this world? Eat it, smell it, look at it and swim onwards, upwards and out. What is this? Memory planning and unpicking. It's in my hands. I hear a voice. Should I listen or swallow? Smell or view?

The diorama lies dishevelled, incomplete on the table. I wonder what this is and when this will be. The cat is content to figure eight between my jelly legs. I want him to purr down the phone. The receiver is in a psoriasis snowstorm.

'Hello. Is that you Gabriel?'

I hear a voice. I know the voice. I can't respond. I've forgotten the name. The cat stills then becomes the usual demanding number one. Figure eights have brought no response.

'Gabriel?'

'Who is it?'

Panic and frustration have tied a knot. I have to recalibrate. A journey rushes from five months to fifty. Where am I on this timeline? Where is my timeline? It's a punishment just to breathe. I'm not allowed to breathe. I have no entitlement to live. That's why I'm living now and dying now.

But dying to live is the hardest.

It's a phone.

'Marcia?' I murmur from a deathbed of strength.

Back doors and front doors open and close in a lottery of exits and entrances. The diorama springs to life and beckons the Stanley knife. The murder of cardboard and the slow poisoning felt tips are waiting to spring into action by me their guide.

'Gabriel, are you ok?'

'I feel so.'

'Feel so?'

'Yes. Feel so.'

Steam rises from my shirt. Groin rot rejoices in its spread. I move uncomfortably, preferring to conjure up past consorts. I see from the past to the future. Sight becomes urgent, another guide for me to use in my predictions. It's more sensory perception than real sight but I know I must stick with this gift even though it courts affliction. The joy of nervous neurons in Frontal Lobe are energised by me giving in. The classification of files according to creative need, scramble up the gyprock. I see more doors. More front doors than back doors. I look again for confirmation. More front doors than back doors. I smile briefly but only allow enough time to speak with Marcia from the heart.

It's seconds but they could be light year trips beyond this solar system and back. Jesus and his disciples are entangled in a crown of thorns multiplied sixty niner. Returning from the manhole in Frontal Lobe they splash their jellied eels heavenwards, mindful of me interrupting their last suppers. Jesus winks as usual and invites me to join but somehow in all this moisture I know thirteen is definitely an unlucky number.

Jesus the overseer or the conjoiner?

As I calm on fourteen the salmon jumps higher out of the waterhole, this time landing on the performance space. The Cass Converters converge with their snotty progeny on a hillock and rip up tufts of clover to wipe nostril drizzles. There's a crash from the chook pens as they're lowered onto the clay tarmac. The bullocks and horses hear the noise and snort and whinny in a dusty circle.

'Marcia, I've been thinking.' I'm ready to talk and listen. Monday is now one layer.

Buried deep is the memory of yesterday's policeman acting better than a judgement day. The salmon temporarily transforms into a lungfish and lunges about the performance area as my father assembles the chook pens for Siegfried's castle. The dressing rooms are hauled into place through a bog above the dusty stage. Climate change is here and now. Everything dries fast. There's no lingering seasonal shift from season to season. Ten inches have fallen a metre away. Nothing has fallen on the stage.

'I have it,' I say both excitedly and with a measure of desperation.

Time is of the essence. It is measured and I haven't much left. The disciples all mop up and loll about on cumulus cushions. Their job is to make it rain everywhere. Cloud seeding is their final cum shot. They watch the salmon. She wants to return to water. It's too hard to breathe and it's raining tadpoles.

'Sorry I haven't been in touch earlier,' I add. 'Been a bit crook.'

'It's me that should apologise,' says Marcia. 'You've been on my mind all weekend. Got a good behaviour bond. No conviction recorded. Not allowed to protest in elevators. Have some thoughts about the set design.'

'So do I. We should get together soon. Lamington Council applications are due next month.'

'Outside?'

'Make it different but the same. Load it with contradictions. Keep the original score.'

'You definitely were on my mind.'

'I know all about difference so let's exploit difference. Big time.'

'None of your midget put downs. It has to be Little People from now on.'

'*Cygnet Waterhole* or *Cygnet Pond*?'

'*Pond* sounds more universal than *Waterhole*. But if you want that Aussie feel.'

'Know just the place. Waterhole, castles, sheep, cattle and a cast of Little People dancing to the music of Tchaikovsky. All we need are the performers.'

'Publicise Australia-wide. We'll get the numbers. I know heaps of people who're really good dancers.'

'So, no tallies at all.'

'Only Little People. Affirmative Action for and by Little People.'

'Make it next Sunday.'

All the pain of intrusion hits hard. Producer, director, originator is a shared experience for one headspace. Marcia's voice resonates. The disciples unpick the thorns from the crown and from their comfortable cushion spear them at me. Dr Love flies in and out of the hatchback trying to ward off the thorns. Now they're after her like a swarm of wasps. She rushes back to her morning clinic apologising for keeping people waiting.

It's 3pm everywhere on her Earth.

The salmon reverts to tears in the waterhole and tries to soothe the gashes in her rudimentary fins. She finds a blackberry covered channel that leads out of the waterhole and courses downhill. It rains here. Solidly. A nonstop dripping curtain wholly apart from the rest of the world. With joy she leaps in the air and sees the chook palace being assembled for Siegfried. But there's no turning back. I can't turn back. Onward and forwards I must go. The rain shimmers on the salmon. The disciples are unrelenting with their spears, so gentle in nature so softly seated, yet now so cruel with the crucifying of emotions.

I pray for the salmon under the cover of thorns and in a channel, that's now widening at 3.05pm.

In her desire for a true identity she's transformed into an A380 taxiing on an inferior tarmac and happy to find the end of a runway just commissioned for its heavy first load. The salmon is a flying fish free from entrapment and ready to begin a new life as a refugee in a creek full of trout.

Dear salmon is still a fish out of water.

Jesus grooms the disciples. They're up for it but as for a diorama? It's not stained glass. History has recorded them differently. Cathedrals have been their home and homes away from home. As they walk the shores of the Sea of Galilee they wonder if they might have to throw their master a lifeline. What if he doesn't feel like walking on water today? Monday is prescription day.

If he takes my tablets then what will happen to the salmon?

The one that threshes about in the local creek ostracised by rainbow trout organising a rally for same sex fishers.

The salmon's joy is short lived. Past memories of lungs are revived. This fish is more out of water than ever. Jesus sees her. The conniving Messiah has stolen bread from The Rainbow Bakery in the Adelaide Hills and now the flying fish has wings. The shock of lungs to seaplane to a scaled-up version of the A380 swims through the sky procreating en route. Seeding the clouds over Israel, the salmon spawns by mistake in the Dead Sea and finally drops exhausted into the Holy Sea just as Peter pulls up the last of his nets. Someone has told him there is a ban on drift netting and he believes the others in his group who say it's because their master might get tangled when he does one of his walks.

I glance again at the diorama and see its completion as I want it. But finished yesterday. The waterhole is calm. The orphan salmon has been redeployed. I regulate the search for her and invoke support from Mother Teresa and the cop I spoke to when the diorama should have been finished. I ask them to search for her but persuading them is not easy. I grab a slice of Shepherds Hill Road to chew on as I drive through an Indian orphanage. Now part plane I soar over the Middle East avoiding spawn that's turned to hail. The cop and Mother Teresa hold me aloft. Below in Galilee, Jesus and his men furiously rip open packets of sliced bread. Thousands of starving refugees suddenly appear while thousands of future salmon spring from the Holy Sea to flip flop as *John West* sardines between slices of sourdough.

Jesus skis on Galilee, the surefooted Christ and supervisor to a million Mother Hubbards.

Meanwhile Mother Teresa and the cop head skywards and grab slippery me for a hasty exit west over Kibbutz Ein Karmel and the Mediterranean. The salmon and Jesus have words over who has miracle rights.

'I did the dividing,' the salmon says.

'I did the divining,' Jesus cuts in.

A million mouths chew. Jesus estimates the number of crowns of thorns he can make with arms and legs the size of knitting needles. Meanwhile the disciples pig out on the leftovers from the Rainbow Bakery.

The waterhole is flat. Silent. Sun dries the hardened clay of the bulldozed stage. The Cass Converters look on with bovine bewilderment, their eyeballs on Serapax. Bradley and Teagan roll up and down the hill behind the stage. Dry and not so dry cow pats make green patterns on their tracky dacks.

'When can we go home? Teagan grizzles.

'I want to go home too,' Bradley adds.

I have another look at the diorama. In Frontal Lobe the files shift about as the daytime Cinderella hour approaches. Soon it will be afternoon and soon all parts of me will have to be reintegrated. I have a massive panic attack. A massive manic attack. I want to go flat out forever and never stop. Eat all the time, drink all the time, laugh all the time, have sex all the time. But I must divert any sense of me and perception of wicked thoughts to another time, place and headspace. The diorama still presses.

I'm glad I've spoken to Marcia. She seems to be on the same page as myself at 3.10pm.

So it must be afternoon?

There has to be a big clean up. Clean up my act. I've heard the words. I am the words in multiple eyes. I hide everything in Frontal Lobe. The files are deadened. The coffins are not willing to go to the crematorium. Their prayers for life after death and life after life after life are heard and have been heard. Jesus has no access to my manhole this afternoon though. Perhaps I should drug the files? Put them to sleep for that journey beyond Jupiter to that yet to be discovered planet I'm destined for.

But I must have access to them before the application to the Lamington Council is due.

'Please remember me,' I feel like crying to the plain gyprock, the piano that swallows and gulps clefs, bars and notes. 'I'll be back soon.'

The inner life of Tchaikovsky has to be unimagined for now. Liberace reminds me of circadian rhythms and the value of all that's in the metaphysical realm. He again resorts to figure eights, sensing he will gain my attention soon. I close the lid of the piano and from Frontal Lobe stare through the house at the diorama to be.

The mania and the panic fight. It's ugly. The 'to be's' and the 'has been's' feed their respective sides. I take comfort for my tentative union with the outside world and remind myself I am in this world and not of this world. I shadow Louise and like a puppet unravel and attach myself to her vocal folds.

I break free from the puppeteer, the paedophile sent by God to keep me attached and always his. I peel off my clothes and leave them in the doorway to the bathroom like lunar craters. I shiver uncontrollably again and for the first time in days catch a glimpse of myself in the chattering mirror. The ghost that looks back alarms me. I know something major is wrong. But I urge myself forward while hanging onto the thoughts and words of Marcia Font. Although she's the tiniest person I've met, she has the biggest heart and a soul that's ageless.

I reassure myself again that she seems to be on the same page as me.

I turn on the shower. In the past a waterfall, for hours of sweat and fears, but now an unwanted desperate swim back to reality for a few necessary hours.

To pay the bills.

I wish all clocks were waterproof.

Work from Home.

Sorrow.

I bid farewell to Frontal Lobe for the time being and welcome my work from home. It's an act and not a good feeling. Quickly I borrow thoughts and emotions for the words I need to soon speak. The diorama is on hold but still I mull. The first thing I have to do is curtail the sweating. Towel after towel following the shower can't dry the seep. I dare not look at what's happening. Thoughts rush through like fast trains automatically programmed on a network of tracks. There's no stopping. No end and no start but it's going fast. Platforms pin pricked with patient people slide into buildings into country with a rush from Japan to the London Underground.

Preparation of interacting with people is being prepared. Oh, how I wish for Marcia Font to pop up now and curse the world she lives in. But the reality is hitting home. My family of walls has shifted into neutral. There's no pretending they are anything but walls. Gallant gyprock gazes on with glazed expressions. Reality has had a quick renovation. The files have been gagged with double thickness masking tape. The piano opens and closes its own lid in preparation for a final musical defaecation. They're coming. They'll soon be here. Nazi knowing and flushing fills a void. Could this be the *Diarrhoea of Ann Frank*?

Good riddance is palpable and necessary.

I dress and then undress. My clothes are already saturated. True I've always sweated a lot but there's a tap that needs turning off and I can't find it. Three changes of clothes and I'm ready. Watching my watch and wishing it backwards doesn't work. Ready to face the real world. Louise's words ring loud again and again, 'I am in this world but I'm not of this world'. I grasp at every letter in those words hoping they will plug the hole in my dam. Should I receive her manipulation again?

I cover myself with the contents of a dictionary. I'm A to Z from head to toe. Navel is where it should be yet naval is not far away. A flotilla of boats has replaced the train and I'm nothing but a caught wave, a relentless ebb and flow of water washing through my spongey mesophyll. I try desperately to assert the time and day by counting seconds. My life is driven by events. A train reverses slowly past a platform. Any notion of night following day is foreign but a plucked hour has to be devoted to one-on-one tutoring of a boy requiring help not only with reading, but life.

I raise an eyebrow.

I walk and turn through every room, bumping out an old show and readying it for a new one. Liberace is preparing for strangers. Marcia Font is a friend. The salmon, Mother Teresa and the policeman can be tolerated. Even Dr Love, Teagan, Bradley and the Cass Converters can be stomached, if not with staples. In his anxiety Liberace lands on the kitchen table and plays with the diorama. I'm far from the waterholes of my past but I'm sure I'm greater than part of a solution.

I raise an eyebrow again.

Convinced I'm ready to receive clients, I place tissues and towels at strategic points and don a jacket to hide the paisley sweat patterns forming relief maps of newly discovered lands and the artificial lungs on my body shirt. I can't remember when I last ate and decide on being a gastronome when clients have been and gone. Trains interchange with flotillas. I confirm to a diminished part that I've locked down everything in Frontal Lobe. I run my fingers along the keyboard as if to rid any thought of a choleric Tchaikovsky sweating on me.

The doorbell rings.

Suddenly I'm well, healthy and totally 'of this world.'

Warren has arrived with his dad. I'm pleased his mother has opted not to come on this occasion. She finds my idea of working with the entire family confronting and would rather I perform a miracle to propel her son into the rest of his life. Always there's a doubt on my part about my ability to engage with the young but it's what I've been trained for in this life and I put myself through the painful process of cutting through the crap and making sure the kid gets on with it. I sense that Warren cops it from home quite a lot. He has an older sister with aptitude and a younger brother with both aptitude and attitude.

And so I sit around the table with Warren and his father. His father wants to be involved and I encourage him. I observe Warren. I observe myself but pretend I'm not doing this. Some files have worked the masking tape adrift. Fuck the sweat. I can't afford any naval gazing. The binoculars are misted over and anyway where is the horizon? Warren doesn't want to be here anymore than I do. But his parents want something different and have come to me with Warren for the past four years. I try to engage the boy in a variety of activities. Sight words and sounds. Sounds and sight words. Reading for meaning. Reading words and not understanding a thing about what they mean together or apart. Why should words have meaning? Whose meaning? I've got him interested in writing. He wants a decent motor bike. I wonder what an indecent one might look like. I force myself back into the present applying more gags to files.

The steamy heat rises from my paisley torso and I pull my jacket across to hide everything including the artificial lungs.

Warren wants to ride from Adelaide to Darwin on his motorbike. He's got a couple of mates who want to go with him. They want to get pissed and do drugs and speed all the way up the Stuart Highway.

And so Warren's story begins. For once he has a smile on his face. His story has momentum. It has a beginning, middle and end. He yawns. I yawn. He's plotted this well. He can talk about it and now he wants to write it down. Part of him wants to shock but the shock is a cry for help, for the entrapment of not being able to communicate about the things that interest him. His father shifts the energy in the room and moves into the lobby around the corner. He senses that Warren is about to come into this world amongst men and needs his privacy.

His father says 'fuck' to everything and about anyone and while immaculately dressed in a business suit is fighting to roll up his sleeves, expose his tatts and lay a few bricks. He has immersed himself in a book. Warren wants a reaction. I smile uncomfortably at first but then relax. The boy desperately wants his voice to be heard now. The boy wants to write his words his way and who am I to be telling him anything else?

'They all buy beers, Jack Daniels and get marijuana from friends in Alice Springs.'

'How many days will this take?' I prompt.

'Probably ten days. They might stop off for a few days in other places.'

'Where do the bikes come from? How much do they cost?'

Warren is resentful. I've tried to use tact in getting him to write more but it's got his back up. There's going to be too much to write. He only wants to write a short story his way.

Remember.

Around the corner Warren's father coughs and turns pages. He can hear the narrative unfold and I wonder what he might say about me allowing a Year 7 boy the liberty to write a story about drugs and alcohol.

'Sounds like a good story, Warren. You should try and make it longer like Gabriel suggests.'

I appreciate fatherly intervention. Warren thinks about this.

'Can I storyboard it first?'

Of course I agree. This is the first time the boy has attempted something by himself. I bless the Stuart Highway for dissecting a continent and providing a dictionary to a boy who's never liked anything to do with reading or writing but now wants support with his journey.

Back the Present into a Corner.

WARREN and his father can't leave fast enough. Another lie makes Atlas and Sansom argue over load sharing. I cut Sansom's locks and offer to trim Atlas's pubic hairs. Merkin mayhem abounds. Where previously it's been loaves and fishes Mother Teresa helps to hand out, she now blesses shaved rent boys and gives them her consecrated pubic regions in exchange for their lice. A legendary nit-picker, she's caught onto the protein source espoused by those wanting to serve fleas and cockroaches as part of a staple diet while feeding the starving and saving the planet.

Frontal Lobe rockets awake unmasked, its tapes hanging strewn and tasselled like sticky Rapunzel's.

The files argue and slide. Gyprock dust flies everywhere. Files off tracks are any trains in any country. My itchy navel ruptures at sea in search of the golden salmon that has quite a reputation now. As a conduit to the Blessed Mother's healing powers the newly proclaimed Golda the salmon has separated from the A380 and flies skywards as supervisor of global protein deficiency. As she dives through the heavens she writes in air and water, 'Lice is nice'. The hungry clamour with outstretched hands and gather the sundried crabs while feasting themselves into last minute survival and sterility.

Abortion clinics are as close as a wish for every last family. Yet desire and compulsion still fight for all available oxygen to procreate misery.

I can't terminate Monday, whichever one it is. I try to place Marcia Font at the centre of everything. There's urgency to get the application finished for the Lamington Council. There's so much research still. I've got everything built according to Frontal Lobe but the diorama will have to start again thanks to Liberace. All the tools for model making have their own personalities.

I wonder what tool I was in a past life.

Probably a bastard file.

Golda dives and swoops in the slipstream of the A380. Now a converted cargo plane the A380 leased by *NunAir* is packed with aircraft meals of cockroaches, locusts and lice. I know Mother Teresa is working overtime with her crutching but her bevy of giggling postulants maternalise the masses like Friesian heifers raising adopted calves. Some lap up the rent boys while others cluck about their merkin making and wing their way to the good Mother for 'in the field support' when required. Sister Deferential at the controls of the A380 snips and tucks the great silver goddess from Galilee to Lobethal, Kolkata to Canberra and any place in-between.

Millions of hands stretch and tickle the polystyrene packs that parachute earthwards from the belly of the A380.

I have to talk all this over with Jesus at some stage, disciples permitting, but for now I want Mother Teresa to perform miracles closer to home. The Cass Converters have settled on their bank and with spinning wheels coerce some Dorset Horns to safely graze close by. They smile contentedly as they connect with a wider world which is far preferable to current domestic arrangements. They unravel, chat and join with a new history which informs them they are safe but not as safe as their own houses yet. As the ewes graze, single skeins of wool loosen from the rumps of each to be relentlessly spun.

When there is enough wool they will soon dye.

The cygnet costumes will be soaked in elderberries. Golda swoops by, confirming her roots and struggle in the famous waterhole.

Teagan and Bradley are happy to gambol with the lambs. The cop scratches his forehead and writes more notes on the bonnet of his car. 'Male person spoken to' is written with pressure. The only thing that makes sense for him is 'male person'. His biro runs out. He calls for backup.

In Frontal Lobe there is a growing restlessness. All references to a Warren and a Dad are quickly removed and stored. I will the watch backwards. An imprint of the wristlet band makes furrows in my forearm. Add a touch of red and I'm legally someone's Poll Dorset. I remove the watch slowly, taking hairs. The Dorsets don't mind. They bleat and mumble to their lambs while contentedly ingesting one end and defaecating the other. Apart from where the Cass Converters are spinning, the hillside paddock is a paragraph on a giant smartphone display with full stops everywhere, the product of punctuation never taught properly to sheep.

Meanwhile Thomas Hardy contemplates an English reissue down under hoping the current strain of aspiring Dorsets have remembered to check the typesetting.

Frontal Lobe rumbles. Mood changing files fling their cabinets open wide. If I were thicker skinned this would be the perfect place for a massage. The piano groans an invocation for pianola days and slowly tinkles a tune. It has a certain style but the melody is not recognisable. Liberace, sensing extra effort on his part not to be ignored or perhaps being the centre of his universe, negotiates the thrust and shove of information which might have him as the focus of attention.

I ask the cop if I posted Louise's letter but surely Dr Love or her partner Redden would have told me so. I wonder about Louise. How she is? What could be in the letter for me?

About me?

Dates and times continue blurred in a poor translation of the Bible but I consult my watch and check the numerous clocks in Frontal Lobe. Some have stopped. The others show different times. I listen. They tick. I listen again. My heart thumps with swallowed clocks which I aim to use to keep time. Salvador Dali has just discovered toffee clocks. I still think it's Monday although any thought of a yesterday is clutching at straws.

The racket in Frontal Lobe increases. I want to calm it but don't know how. Liberace, disgracefully fallen from a hot tin roof, treads the ivories and attempts to play with a piano still obsessed with being a pianola. He tries to flick notes away with one paw only to have another tap his tail. Such is the opening to the Piano Concerto I'm still hanging onto.

I flee to the back of the house deciding whether to open or close the door on Frontal Lobe. I close it at first but then open it. I check more clocks for correct times. None are working in the back. This worries me because my life has always been guided by time right up to the last split second.

On the kitchen table the tools of some creative pursuit stare in a mess. Cardboard, glue, felt pens, Stanley knives are strewn from a former time. I can't remember what they're for or what my intentions might have been. I wonder if I've used up all my memory to live in the present. I start walking backwards. The clocks are ticking now. Frontal Lobe sounds like a disco. I'm frightened by the noise.

I take a deep breath, reassured that this is a function I'm aware of and open the door on Frontal Lobe. There is a certain mindfulness that fuses and confuses all the *NOW* energy. Voices and files scream, 'Choose me!'

Mother Teresa rides Golda the salmon. Jesus and his disciples are mud wrestling on the shores of the Dead Sea. The Cass Converters are spinning contentedly while their progeny play hopscotch on what they assume are the last dried cow pats in creation. The cop writes a report while consulting Dr Love naturally disguised as Dr Redden who suggests that she and the policeman swap prescriptions for reports.

I'm convinced I'm still who I think I am. As a cake of conditions, I allow hundreds and thousands to freely sprinkle ASD's, bipolar and ADHD all in one hit as an additive to life if I want to believe a past diagnosis.

I'm the one Gabriel Dorset selecting the right files for *Cygnet Waterhole*, preparing for my meeting with Marcia Font and preparing our application for funding to the Lamington Council.

I can't wait for Marcia to arrive.

She's the one person in my life who'll never tell me to grow up.

This Saint Doesn't March.

GOLDA uses her many guises to convert the A380. This time it has the capacity to land on water. On instructions from Mother Teresa I've chosen Goolwa as a rallying point. The huge seaplane lands adjacent to the barrage. Just what am I thinking as I dissolve the last of my crystals to form a runaway jelly? The salmon slips into the brackish water of Alexandrina. Carp terrorise salmon but with the assistance of Mother Teresa and Jesus, Golda's ability to fly protects her from the rednecks of the river. The transgender fish places a sign on the Goolwa end of the bridge to Hindmarsh Island.

The sign reads, 'NO CARS OR BOATS ALLOWED ON IS-LAND'.

As far as the eye can see cars are bumper to bumper. The never-ending sound of horns is deafening. All I feel is frustration increasing to anger.

The Altered Boys have arrived and hand out infringement notices on behalf of the Alexandrina Council and the advice of Mother Teresa. The notices read, 'Because you've used your car horn more than once in the last seven seconds you are fined seventy dollars and seven cents. You need to pay this fine in coins. Please be advised that exact tender is required as there is no rounding up or down.'

The horns stop but serious connections of Dr Redden make unconscious decisions about surviving heart attacks. SUVs rev, roar and reverse. Pelicans glide past smiling with Golda lookalikes singing 'We Shall Overcome' from their earthmoving bills. The Altered Boys in all seriousness confer and procreate more Altered Boys on the spot to deal with the growing aggression. They record the registration numbers of cars, boats and trailers. Exhaust fumes combine, challenging a persistent smoke haze.

In the middle of this night packaged in unknown days I try to see what happens next. A whirlpool of the same towels trip me as I slide into bed. I want Marcia but question why I need to unfold the salmon's journey. The slippery conduit linking physical and spiritual swims to a joyful Jesus and some not too discerning disciples.

Now known to both spawn and fawn, Golda is consciousness expressed in fillets. Mother Teresa will soon arrive and Golda has decided that as coordinator of my life's Earthly thinking and all that has meaning she has a responsibility to inform me of what transpires.

I wet the bed's wetness. I dive through hoops of fire which are quickly put out by the wet coils of a rusty mattress. My skin sizzles as if in the aftermath of visitations from relinquishing dragons. The opposing sides of water and fire fight a war to extinguish one another and are not inclined to reconcile. The towels are multiple nooses. I haven't the right neck... yet.

Someone removes my heart like in a good Jesus picture and lies it upon my chest. I watch my heart beat before it's returned to its rightful place to thump with extra vigour. The chatter in Frontal Lobe rings in my ears. A whole room is about to explode in my head. There's growing urgency for the meeting with Marcia Font.

Mother Teresa is ferried ashore from the A380 on a pathway formed with the backs of compliant pelicans. They have been trained for this occasion and the selection process has involved last minute visits to the nearest pelican vomitorium. Mother Teresa has insisted that there be no carping amongst members of her well-trained security. She's also insisted on keeping a low profile and has resisted the inclusion of heads of government to meet her.

'I go where I feel the need. I do not need the alms of government.'

The gracious birds frighten the last of the exiting vehicles by giving them the pelican eye. After saintly duties have been completed, they'll consult their own memory files and summon a workforce to further deconstruct the present and restore pleasant perpetuity.

But now they walk with trained gainliness. After watching numerous films on dancing elephants their choreographed steps grace the procession in a connected shimmer. Their mere presence flosses the dawn and removes bad odours. Mother Teresa dons her Velcro sandals as she alights from the feather ferry and walks to the Goolwa end of the bridge.

The locals come to smile and stare. Four-wheel drives, boats and trailers finger away from the coast to join a distant smoke haze. It's the noise of smoke and the sound of eye strain. The pelicans are confident in making their webbed waddle appear both professional and ceremonial.

What time is it? What day? I think it's Monday still. Is this a thought that has to be learned and is stuck permanently in all the calendars I've seen? Perhaps I'll be stuck on Monday forever. Two of me climb walls, huddled and small.

'What am I up to, Golda? Am I seeing this Jesus?'

He nods but Golda is slipping in and out of Lake Alexandrina to rally any lost relatives. My bed is now a waterbed. The squelch is back again. I'll soon be dust if I don't drink. The irony of a pissing body forcing me into drought, creates scabs. I implore the cockies in the Norfolk Island Pines screeching their enthusiasm for the soon-to-be saint to bring me water and wash my Mother's feet. It's good she's not wearing her Docks. It's a hassle with all the laces, washing feet all the time. She's got this down to a fine art.

I wonder if she learnt this in the orphanage.

The cockatiels are here and there in an instant. My crown of thorns from the unfinished ring of fire are now their beaks. They douse and quench me gently. I feel their hooked beaks slide across my parched lips as they fill me with respect, tradition and hope. I need more water to restore the correct fluid ratio.

I know Marcia will soon be here. Or do I? I try to remember what we'd decided on the last time I spoke on the phone. The Lamington Council grant application. When does that have to be in? What's the timeline for *Cygnet Waterhole*? Fuck. Where am I going to get that cast? Do I have faith in Marcia's connections? There's so much to do. I turn over and back again. I'm all pages from soggy sheets. Where am I up to? Frontal Lobe is going crazy. Files are running amuck. I'll have to give them extra attention.

Life is one continual edit.

The pelicans form a guard of honour. Mother Teresa begins her walk across the bridge. The tail fin of the A380 bobs up and down above the barrage. The pelicans shadow the good woman of Kolkata. The Blessed Mother stares into the lake from both sides of the bridge as she walks. She imbibes a Sea of Galilee that sweeps across the entire lake. The water teems with fish. She crosses and blesses herself, praying for abundance but not forgetting her current job as chief protein harvester and sensitive merkin maker for the rent boys of the world including those of the Great South Land. Fish jump the barrage from the open sea and joyfully play with Golda who has forgotten about looking after the security on board the bobbing super Jumbo.

More pelicans, seeing the saintly procession, are keen to join. Soon there are twelve birds, not randomly picked, but who have a knowing that doesn't require training. Golda sees a Tiger Moth performing acrobatics above the Goolwa airfield and replicates her own display for the gathering fish now turning the lake into a seething sea of swollen Emperor Moth grubs.

Mother Teresa walks and blesses in silence. The breeze spins her robes into a series of black funnels which then inexplicably turn white. Extra cockatiels swoop and liquefy the good mother's holy steps. She may not be walking on water but well-meaning cockatiel reflux is the next best thing.

Everywhere there are sodden rings, the volcanoes of past and present towels steam. Mr Policeman is still hanging around flicking through pages of his report book wondering what to write. He wants me out of his mind and he keeps looking for an exit line. Codes, learned speeches, authoritarian stances. Which one does he choose? Which one still restricts his decision making? Which one stops him moving on to the next job?

I can see him backtracking. He's definitely not out of my mind and I'm not out of his.

I text the cockatiels again relying on the inspiration and dexterity of Stephen Hawking. They bring more water but this time it's very salty. The lake is overrun with saltwater fish seeking brackish asylum. They are gathering to watch and wait for a sign from the Great Mother. I ask Jesus to intervene but he just smiles and tells me that we'll both get together later on.

I want him and he wants me.

Residents try to follow Mother Teresa over the bridge but The Altered Boys intervene and demand they wash their feet in the basins supplied. There is of course a cost of ten dollars per foot. All proceeds are to be donated to Save The Bakeries From Christians Fund, they whisper behind the Blessed Mother's back.

'We knead your dough,' the boys shout when Mother Teresa is out of earshot. 'See the light or remain unleavened.'

Reluctantly the residents remain on the mainland.

My mattress coils jut across Alexandrina as Mother Teresa reaches the island. Thousands upon thousands of coils catch the light and hula hoop a rainbow collection of fish that part the waters in a multitude of fountains as Mother Teresa steps onto island land. Wet fireworks work here when fish collaborate in permanent sunshine.

Golda zips past Mother Teresa as the elephant pelicans waddle to a stop, forming sealed envelopes with their wings and tails. They sidle to a wobble, shake and prop their heads. Their instinctive gullets, connected to fluttering bladders, play *I Spy* with the feast in Hula Lake.

Real estate agent Ray Devine walks towards Mother Teresa. He's heard that an Indian visitor will arrive and even though he's here, he's not quite sure if he has arrived. Like any Saturday, and every day is a Saturday for him, he's well suited for his special calling. Open inspections and enthusing prospective clients about living in *Disney on Hindmarsh* are both part of his belief system. He's heard some unsettling rumours about why an Indian investor should chuck in an orphanage, climb out of a grave and fly halfway around the world to inspect *Disney on Hindmarsh*.

I can still hear the hum of departing vehicles on the mainland. Golda ensures I have clear vision of what is going on. First I hover with her above the fish in the lake, and then I take a peek from behind the pelicans. The cop gets into his car and roars down Shepherds Hill Road. There's been a multiple pile up of SUVs and boat trailers in Happy Valley. Should I tell the saint-to-be or the original beings? How much pollution is there in *Disney on Hindmarsh*?

I swear that Ray Devine has been taking deportment classes from the policeman. Who else could walk like this? He carries his agency's A frame which reads, '*THE EXCEPTIONALS. OPEN TODAY.*'

Ray Devine speaks.

'Welcome, Mother Teresa. It's nice to have you in such a beautiful part of the world. I've always wanted to meet you. Are you interested in a property? Another orphanage perhaps? I assume you're exhumed.'

The fish drag their hula hoops to the bottom of the lake. Whales of clouds form dorsal fins as far as the eye can see. The cop gets out of his car and radios for backup.

'Wrong side of the road.'

'I thought for a moment I was on the lake.'

'Did you pay that fine?'

'What fine?'

'Who pays for all this?

'Who pays for just this?'

A head and someone else's body argue in a pool of mixed blood. Both have brought this accident on as an act of conciliation.

'I didn't have the right change. I couldn't round up or down,' says the head.

Shoulders shrug.

Exodus.

Mother Teresa smiles through Ray Devine.

'My God has sent me here.'

Ray squirms and is painfully polite. He steps from one foot to the other, sending his haemorrhoids packing to a much hoped for cushion of comfort. I move from pelican to pelican. Golda hovers, creating joy with every flight through parting clouds.

'Thought it was a council initiative.'

The Cass Converters wipe their brows. The spinning, tying and dyeing is tiring. Braden and Teagan are asleep with lambs. All are stained with elderberries.

'I go where there is wrong to right. Your council came up with a community development proposal which was compelling.'

'*Disney on Hindmarsh* is made for you. Can I show you some properties?'

'I'm here for the masses. For feeding the starving and healing the wounded.'

'There's no wounded here.'

'Allow me to be the judge.'

The eyes in the back of my head support those in the front. I watch the two trek across the newly laid bitumen. '*FOR SALE*' signs dominate the landscape.

The Cass Converters are thrilled with their efforts. Half-naked sheep oblige, stare and listen as yarn is spun in conversation. Dorset by name and nature, The Lord's My Shepherd imprints more full stops on the hill of paragraphs. Durbevillea is the way.

'The lord's the shepherd I badly want in green pastures,' I murmur so that my current amphibious body feels grounded.

But it isn't.

The cockatiels bring more water. They liquefy my retinas so my vision can swim again. Golda busily takes photos. Posterity starts as the clouds un-dorsal. Mother Teresa and Ray Devine reach the first of the cut-out houses. *Disney on Hindmarsh* has never looked so real. Cruisers bob on artificial inlets longing for seas they'll never see. Cut out number one has been stolen from *Hansel and Gretel*. It's all Tim Tam and custard. The *'FOR-SALE'* sign matches the decor.

It reads, '*THIS ORIGINAL PROPERTY IS FOR THOSE DESIRING TO ESCAPE CITY SAMENESS. IDEAL FOR ENTERTAINING AT HOME. THE FULLY EQUIPPED KITCHEN IS TO DIE FOR.*'

'I thought people liked living here. Why are so many properties for sale?'

'People come and people go. Good time to buy.'

'Good time to goodbye.'

'What do you mean?'

'I feel the residents need help.'

Mother Teresa summons Golda. My eyes are melting moments encouraging the fish to return. The A380 has swung around on its moorings.

'And you need help.'

Blessed Teresa leaves Ray Devine to his many devices and daintily steps along Callistemon Crescent. Towering houses jammed together with no consideration of colour and shape are an insult to rainbows. No one is seen or heard. No voices. Cruisers rub on personalised jetties in unpleasant friction. More pelicans arrive seeking service and restitution. They eye the former orphanage nun hoping she'll notice them but mark the sealed surfaces with droppings the same colour as their plumage. Mother Teresa thinks long and hard about a solution.

'I know why I was asked to come here but I'm afraid my afterlife demands that I heal this place first,' the Blessed One says, returning to confer with the real estate agent.

'Heal? I have open inspections.'

'Good timing. I'll be able to meet with some of the vendors before they leave?'

Ray Devine sources help from God knows where. Mother Teresa takes out her tablet and scrolls to find her latest app. Golda swoops and gleefully photographs Callistemon Crescent with the born-again nun and Ray Devine. A real rainbow bleeds in the sky at the end of the street. Multiple hands part vertical drapes which open onto the deserted street of a bombless Syria. Inclined heads peer from upper storeys. Golda swoops up and down more streets busily recording images on her phone. Symmetrical stares abound. Even street numbers reveal heads that lean to the right. Odd numbers have heads that lean to the left.

Drapes hang at obtuse angles.

The pelicans pair off and stand at the end of every street. More arrive and confer. The untrained birds try catch up and impersonate. Golda promises protein all round. Mother Teresa scrolls through her app and inserts her password. The sullen fish in the lake spring to life again. The Altered Boys armed with megaphones walk up and down every street shouting, 'In the name of God let go of your Disney! It's time to be little!'

Their words echo across the island and a series of mini tsunamis rock yachts and cruisers. I toss and turn, give in to levitation and muddy recoil on my mattress where life has had unthinkable beginnings. Now a recall is imminent.

Meanwhile the Holy Mother's support crew of nuns giggle across the bridge armed with their shaving equipment. They've climbed every mountain and have been given paddle boards to reach Goolwa from the A380. There are no pelicans to escort them in the shadow of their Holy Mother but the locals make way for the strange throng carrying their walk-on water emulators. Still upholding their supposed virginity, they daintily sidestep pelican afterthoughts and are immediately serious seeing the disciplined bird security unravelled and unruffled, waiting for the return of their Mother from fact finding contemplation up and down Callistemon Crescent.

If he could split in two or disappear the latter would be the desire of Ray Devine. As he puts out multiple open inspection signs which read, *'THE EXCEPTIONALS. OPEN TODAY FOR A BETTER TOMORROW'*, he is painfully aware of confusion and anger. He questions why he put his hand up at council to show an Indian visitor over the island. A strong supporter of community development on the island, he has wanted glossy *'SOLD'* stickers plastered on billboards instead of the weathered *'FOR SALE'* signs. Something is burrowing under his skin and he is sure the unexpected presence of the Holy Mother is the reason.

Real estate Ray arrives back at the bridge. Mother Teresa follows.

The Altered Boys blare away. There is an air of encouragement and the expectation they'll deliver more fines. Golda rejoices and soars from water to sky writing loops reading '*love*'.

Front doors slam shut. The Altered Boys issue instructions, 'Repeat again. In unison. Anyone not banging in unison will be fined for not banging properly. One last time. Everyone bang together.'

The sonic boom travels across the lake. Jet vapor trails wriggle in the sky overhead and inscribe the words, '*SICK CUNTS*'. Golda zooms over her rellies as the carp continue their fireworks. I sit up in bed quickly in this night of days and nights. The sweat is drying and the dust is coming. The cockatiels are now well practiced in keeping me hydrated. They're working well with Golda, I think. The birds squawk as they circle Happy Valley and see the everlasting cop and his body parts. They flush the blood and drop a wreath of pine needles on a head which still spasms.

I wait with the trained pelicans dying to perch on jetties again. The nun support crew still giggles. I watch Teresa and Ray. Ray appears as though he has to start looking again. I admire him for stepping outside his comfort zone and wonder if he has family on the mainland. Family trekking back to the city via SUV and boat trailer. But my preoccupation with his plight is muffled by the sounds of megaphones and the vision of exiting inhabitants. Cruisers and yachts ratchet up the rumble and noise and break free from their moorings.

Strange, as the water is quite calm.

While keeping my distance I feel an extraordinary quiet descending. The hula fish continue in silent joy. Golda is working her energy on this giant document, ensuring the pagination is correct. A slight breeze gathers. On the other side of the bridge a large crowd swells. I feel a lilt and a wave then a curl with my head between the cervix in my pillows. The cockatiels cry on my crown leaving stigmata.

Slow turning on the spot has started. Pelicans and nuns. Real estate agent and a soon-to-be saint. The whirling dervishes of *Disney on Hindmarsh*, like mute wind generators, mesmerise. Untrained pelicans copycat on jetty pylons. Cruisers and yachts, having collided with the barrage, spin into the middle of the lake rudderless but whirling in their own loops. The hula carp wriggle closer to the island and taking their cue from Golda, dive high for closer scrutiny of Blessed Teresa and her spiritual mob.

I pull the pillows either side of me, leaving more maps and archaeological digs on the linen. I signal the Cass Converters and their children. They move closer to the waterhole and stand by stacks of recently dyed tunics. The boys climb on top of the woollen Corinthian columns and stare into the waterhole.

Lovely Dr Redden jumps up startled from her desk. Her mobile phones and tablets begin a whirling dervish on her desk blotter. There's a bit of hovering. The letters on her eye test chart start circling too. The good doctor turns one way and then another. She pirouettes out of her surgery appearing to be pissed and definitely more flushed than usual. Patients in the waiting room are whirling. Zimmer frames spin alone.

They are moving tributes to those who have just died while waiting for a Dr Carousel.

'Walk down the centre of the roads,' the Altered Boys repeat. Residents of *Disney on Hindmarsh* thicken on the asphalt. Some carry '*FOR SALE*' signs like backpacks. All are furiously texting on their mobiles unaware that dervish momentum has caused a drop out in signal strength.

'Stay in the centre.'

The whirling dervishes continue spinning themselves into an ecstatic trance. Pelicans and nuns are culled from concentric circles to audition separately then re-join the heady mix. I want to join in but know that any untoward movement will ruin what I can see. I allow my mattress to be doused and blessed in lake water. Like a flat dog it shakes itself dry before slumping somewhere familiar for me to rest. Whirling pelicans catch the spray and replicate a drying mattress.

Blessed Teresa and Ray Devine keep nuns and pelicans together as they complete a rotation on the circumference. As they do, birds and nuns separate to form an opening for the drugged amalgam exiting Callistemon Crescent for a final walk as citizens of the island. The hula fish sing a medley of popular Disney tunes while Dr Redden peers into her desk blotter still fighting out of control electronic devices.

The Cass Converters hard work has come untied. They spin and wobble on the edge of the waterhole, tying themselves in knots and desperately trying not to undo their hard work. Curious Dorsets, some half spun and half shorn feel the need to entwine their yarn spinners. Some get their legs tied in knots while fighting off an old memory of live sheep exports. Teagan and Bradley try copying their mothers on top of the Grecian columns.

Two men untidily dressed in Yakka overalls and safety vests arrive at the waterhole gate.

'Hello, Dad!' Tegan and Bradley call out together. The men go to place their hands on the universal gate which is locked to the outside world and in doing so are flung back into deep tyre tracks where they hula out of character. The Cass Converters in their temporary safe house are unable to communicate exactly how they feel or what to say. They're caught up in their French knitting not wanting to return to suburban lives.

Their good hard-working husbands pull wrenches from their Yakkas and hold them threateningly over their heads. The wrenches grow dumbbells and with each revolution the tools of trade get heavier.

'What are you lazy bitches doing?' they shout as they strain under the weight of lost tools.

The Cass Converters say nothing. The lack of reaction infuriates the men clutching the tackle of their livelihood.

'Why aren't you cunts at home with the kids?' the revolving dads groan.

'Look, Dad!' the infants on the columns shout. 'We're on top of the world!'

The pelicans click get me to the chiropractor on time as buried heads in smartphones file past silently and attempt to walk onto the Brigadoon Bridge. Now hundreds of residents from *Disney On Hindmarsh* walk on the spot where the asphalt and a layer of gravel greet. Nuns and pelicans combine to form a wall of habits and feathers. Single fingers tap displays, scroll and repeat the process. Out of muddy times past, some kind of Creator has made faces and moods from the same clay. The sound of feet walking in unison continues. The average age of the controlled stampede is sixty. The pylon pelicans are now joined by their mates determined to twirl the day away.

Mother Teresa and crew cordon off the bridge just metres from the throng. They maintain equilibrium by rocking back and forth on their feet. The unmanned yachts and cruisers appear to be part of a dressage event on water. The joyous fish never to be caught steers them in immeasurable trips around the sun. Ray Devine who is still unable to comprehend what is happening continues to turn on the spot. A number of pylon pelicans flock to his rescue. Ray tries to catch '*FOR SALE*' signs but the encumbrance of '*THE EXCEPTIONALS OPEN TODAY*' sign like a rotor on his back bothers him deeply.

Cockatiels screech in crowns of thorns above anything that whirls. Norfolk Island Pines have transcended into bird heaven such is their manna. As the wind generators slowly un-whirl the stampede continues.

Polystyrene meal cartons from the A380 are collected by a cooperative swarm of pelicans and cockatiels. The nuns prepare themselves with shaving gear. Blessed Teresa is ready with her tablet. The Disney singalong gargles above the lake. A version of *When I Wish Upon A Star* is heard above everything else. The Altered Boys stand at the rear reinforcing the blockade. The walking on the spot is unrelenting.

'Life blessings to you, my gathered ones. The Universe has requested that I assist where it is humanly possible. I was not counting on there being a group of people with such pressing needs.'

The Holy Mother defers to the pelicans in her party. They giddily walk and stand at the sides of the island residents.

'The Akashic Records have been prioritised on request from my point of rest. It is said that a transformation of energy must be enlivened in this animated place. For that to occur all mobile devices must be surrendered herewith. Praise be to Albania.'

Un-flapped, the pelicans wander through the rows of residents. Mobile phones are dropped into their throats where they automatically SMS countless address books in their bladders.

I'm replete on my travelled bed. Fish and boats bob at my back. Golda suddenly appears after her absence. She seems tired. Too much flying and too little swimming she says. I agree. *Disney on Hindmarsh* is about to experience a miracle. It's all so exhausting. But then the fish is off again to check the A380, her brethren on land, water and me. A single cockatiel drops potable water on my lips.

The restorative properties like nitrogen laden rain allows my cells to dog paddle in their mitochondria.

I'm concerned for the Cass Converters who are carefully unravelling themselves in their final escape while a tirade of abuse continues from two weightlifters who've elected to journey back to dust through a misery of nicotine, grease and BO. The Cass Converters suddenly lose weight and weep with joy. The heavens open and connect them via intimate channels to witness the consultative work of the Akashic Records from times past, worlds present and a future free of fear.

Dr Redden receives a call from the cop. She scrambles to placate her devices, spins to her car to render assistance alongside epileptic paramedics on a corkscrew bend in Happy Valley.

Performing CPR on a head is a tall ask. Stopping legs, arms and trunks from bleeding requires a special bond. But she is God and Dr Love combined.

A stitch in time saves more brine.

The residents form a single file and move towards Mother Teresa. Neanderthal stances stare with nothing, at nothing. The walking becomes a shuffle. A sea of hands is at work removing the last garments of *Disney on Hindmarsh*. Pelicans waddle through the shuffling throng eyeing human remains they may not normally view. A huge flock fly from Corinthian pillars to pylons and nestle next to nuns who are ready to shave and save. On the other side of the bridge the crowd is still growing. There seems to be a festival of sorts or a celebration. Thousands of fish form lines either side of the bridge gargling obscene versions of their last Disney refrain. '*When You Fart Upon A Star, Don't Leave Your Stools Inside The Car*', echoes across the lake.

The cop walks over to the doctor. He starts spinning out of control. The paramedics, now recently signed up members of the St Catherine's Wheel of Fortune, hover life, death and roadkill into driverless ambulances being trialled from Volvo Sweden. Dr Love argues with the paramedics.

'This arm goes here. This head doesn't belong.'

Ambulance doors spin open once more and flying body parts wanting to meditate on higher meaning get to choose the ambulance ride of their lives.

The novice nuns although novice in time served but not as devoted assistants to the Blessed Mother quietly restrain the colony of pelicans that are totally gobsmacked by the collection of cocks, cunts and contemporary choreography.

Golda is re-energised and sails through the sky checking all water and land routes. The A380 is a giant beach ball. Sometimes the tip of one wing appears above the barrage resembling a metal dolphin wanting to separate from the fuselage and to frolic with the fish of the day. The unscrewed yachts and cruisers continue to sail in pointless circles having spent restricted hours attempting to impress a lost colony of animators.

Ray Devine finds himself locked between The Altered Boys and the vendors he's surrendered. Never sure of what label fits and what to wear he pretends to be unruffled. In a lonely world of his own he stops and restarts his whirling dervish hoping that this will afford him protection from all he can't comprehend. He thinks about convening an on-the-spot meeting of the Alexandrina Council but realises that access to and from the island is currently denied. The Altered Boys would have targeted infringements for corporations. Ray's ratepayers would incur the costs.

'Join them, Ray! You're one of them!' the Altered Boys declare via megaphones.

So Ray strips. Totally naked he attaches '*THE EXCEPTIONALS. OPEN TODAY*' sign to his back once more and saunters in a half spin to the end of a row. He stumbles while completing a final whirl and starts pounding the earth. Like a bull, he is keen to solicit the attention of the flock he wants to protect but has probably screwed the day '*FOR SALE*' signs were attached to their *Tomorrow Lands*. Two pelicans stand either side of Ray eyeing his crutch which he's covered with his hands and mobile. Without waiting, two beaks knife and fork across his groin ripping the mobile phone from his grasp. Other birds are stirred to retrieve the final device. Mother Teresa needs a clear connection with the Akashic Records.

'Please no damage. Bring this one. Do not swallow.'

The mobile phone is in pieces but is still operable. Mother Teresa scrolls and presses. Her tablet confesses. She has the right app. Her universal link is established. She scrolls for greatest need and want. The Earth's navel swells with desperation. Turkey has closed its borders with Syria. Frantic hands grab and pull nothing out of thin air.

Mother Teresa knows there can be no more hold ups as the scratching in front of her is creating dusty potholes. Pairs of hands start scratching groins and not necessarily their own. The happy nuns giggle and ogle as they test their shaving equipment. All the pelicans peer inwardly from the sidelines. The spell of restraint continues. The sound of muffled texting can be heard masticating in bird bladders. There is new grit in the crops. Someone is sending multiple messages.

A SINGLE line forms and walks past Blessed Teresa. The Reverend Mother places her hand on the frontal lobes of the passers-by. She whispers quietly to her congregation.

'Thank you for giving so freely. You're helping to feed the starving and defend a lifestyle I wouldn't normally tolerate.'

The Blessed Mother explains how she had a vision. The planet's current malady made her turn in her grave and she was given the opportunity to perform a trial run to counsel rent boys and supplement new protein sources for the world's hungry. She was exhumed to speed up her beautification.

'They gave me their lice and I supplied them with coiffured merkins. My daughters here had a lot of fun getting the right fit. Hands on experience is always best.'

Ray Devine dares to look skyward. He sees hungry hands dying to create manna while having an epiphany with the staples in his abdomen. He approaches Mother Teresa confused by his transition. He has to believe this saint-to-be. He's been trained to believe and sell. But he is at war with himself and his known world as he tries to fathom the kind of transaction he needs to make. Nothing is for sale. All is a given. '*THE EXCEPTIONALS*' display sign slips from his back and drags behind him like a road grader providing a smooth path to Christ knows where.

Dozens of battery-operated shavers sting the air like aggressive insects. They attract the mosquitoes. The insects are netted by the nuns, euthanised, and placed in the food packs. Bald pubic regions face the next group of nuns. With tweezers, crab eggs and adults are given the mosquito treatment before resting cunnilingus in the polystyrene food packs.

'This one's from a guy called Bartholomew. Try it for size. Or there's a Peter, James or Judas at the bottom of the basket. Yes, I think a Judas would be very fitting. It's had a good innings.'

Ray Devine fastens the blond merkin. He scowls privately remembering his slick overdyed jet-black toupee.

'How can I disagree with this lot? Listen to your client even though I look like a fucking zebra.'

Lice freely given, merkins fitted, and a variety of insects collected, the cockatiels oblige by vomiting over the contents of the boxes. Golda, now the collector of catgut, encircles the boxes and lifts her cargo skywards towards the A380. She repeats the process several times. Her water brethren look heavenwards as if this is a sign for their own rapid development or acceptance of their environment which will soon buzz with a traditional source after decades of rape.

New beholders of merkins twist and turn in pubic technicolour one last time this side of the bridge. Like the good Earth, the beholders rotate and revolve around Mother Teresa as they move towards the bridge.

Dr Redden speeds back to her delayed surgery, trying to forget the buckets of mince that have been rushed to the nearest medical centre. She flings open the door to the surgery waiting room, acknowledges patients and admin staff with a necessary smile. She plans a quick break, dumps her satchel and spins on her chair towards her desk with her eyes closed for a minute of necessary relief. She opens her eyes and screams. Other doctors and support staff rush to her surgery.

A thick jungle of pubic hair has grown on her desk blotter.

No one has come to the aid of the cop who is busily trying to piece everything together. Witness statements are taken. The road is blocked in both directions by SUVs and boats. Several have jack-knifed.

'Don't know what caused it?' one witness asks, standing with his arms folded as if preventing the free flow of information through his conventional body.

'I know what fuckin' caused it,' another witness says, overhearing what is being recorded in indelible ink. 'Those people from the council who fined us.'

'What people?' the cop presses.

'I don't know,' witness number two continues. He too has taken to folding his arms as if disallowing the feeling and discussion of what has happened at this end of the Hindmarsh Island bridge.

'These cunts fined us all for making a noise.'

'What kind of noise?' The policeman is inclined to yawn but part of him is enlivened by a conversation which could be the dawn of a new era. 'What were you doing?'

'We wanted to cross the bridge and they turned us back. On the spot fines. Seven dollars and seventy-seven cents all in coins. Who has that fuckin' kind of money these days?'

'And so you all had to leave?'

'Right.'

'So why weren't you allowed to go across the bridge?'

'Fuck knows.'

Through my navel my heart this time climbs out and pumps me in the eye but I stare above and blink back in blood. The heart returns quickly and reminds me with a thousand other hearts rallying to keep me alive still. Tchaikovsky gets taken to his final bath. I see his agony as the cholera lesions sizzle a last resort.

In Frontal Lobe files attempt a sideways movement. I want to get back to the piano and the diorama but I decide to wait for Marcia. I'm further agitated as to when she'll come.

Have I made a time?

When did I last speak with her?

The Cass Converters paddle in the waterhole. I'm glad they've become self-appointed custodians of the performance space. They need shelter and protection. The world is still not a halfway house for them. Golda interrupts her cartage contract and flies back to some of her beginnings.

Cockatiels once more come to the rescue and lace a shelter beneath a dense stand of Tasmanian Blue Gums. As frogs croak, woolly ones eat and bleat, the so called loves of their former lives turn to dust ready for calcification as an impending departure of a lost spirit prepares for her return to Kolkata.

The sisters of pluck and tuck pick up their paddle boards. They hold them aloft and twirl in a circle. The former residents of Disney on Hindmarsh attempt to raise their heads. Yachts and cruisers increase their speed once more to sail in meaningless circles. Fish swim furiously either side of the bridge wanting to hula again but are prevented from doing so. My eyes are drawn to them as if by intuitive necessity. The fish are experiencing a range of emotions. Their stop-start behaviour concerns me. I want to ride on Golda's back but she's still busy packing polystyrene boxes into the hold of the A380.

As the nuns whirl, their paddle boards become chiropractic tables. The boards spin around in their own energy field, large magnets continuing to divide and occasionally splitting hairs and iron filings.

The Cass Converters take shelter under the Blue Gums. Two pregnant Dorset ewes stamp their hooves at the women nursing their sleeping young. The women lay their children to rest and allow the ewes access to the privacy of the hastily made aviary. The sheep drop healthy twins in unison and then confused by numbers but not scent nuzzle and chew afterbirths as their progeny stand up in a new life for the first time.

I sit up in cervix land with pillows either side of me. The fish are making another attempt to align themselves either side of the bridge. I hope Golda sees this but there appears to be celebrations either end of the bridge now. Golda removes the last of the boxes from the aeroplane. The chiropractic tables are laid out in a semicircle. The Altered Boys begin to tango with each other while managing to blockade any thought of retreat by the recently realigned residents.

Dr Redden grabs her blotter and personally dumps it in a wheelie bin for recyclables. She doesn't hear one of her phones trapped and suffocating in the human bush. She returns to her surgery via the rest room and warily looks in all directions. She checks under her desk and examination table, empties her rubbish bin, forgets her protective gloves and repeats the process. Two mobile phones text her simultaneously.

She reads each of the messages which are the same, 'I AM LOST IN A HAIRY WORLD.'

The letters on the eye chart are still spinning.

The cockatiel district nurses are to die for. They continue to check on me and moisten my lips with increased frequency. I tell them that I'm okay and that Golda might need their help. The pelicans might need their help. In fact I think there is need for assistance both sides of the bridge.

The fish scoop and whoop in half-hearted hulas. The Altered Boys stare into each other's eyes.

'Will you be my Valentine?' Peter whispers in Thomas's ear.

'With beaks and scales,' Thomas replies.

'I could do this forever,' Andrew sighs grabbing Matthew's crutch.

'Careful,' Matthew murmurs holding Andrew's wrist. 'There's no merkin. I'm all me.'

From pillar to pylon, pelican to postulant there is friction in the air.

Blessed Teresa places her hands on each of the chiropractic tables. Her nimble nuns gather around her and steer the mute residents into a single line. The pelican army has grown in anticipation of bigger things to come and the possibility of a higher mission.

'My lost lambs. Your transformation is almost complete. After a final adjustment from my girls you will be ready for your new life. You will not feel as though you're an island anymore.'

The Holy Mother steps back from her chiropractic barricade and holds her palms towards the heavens.

'Aren't you pissed off that she's stealing your thunder?' I ask Jesus. 'This is something you should be doing. Why dig up a nun who's against contraception and abortions to heal the masses? The planet's fucked. If you breed you pay a pollution tax. Simple.'

'Let her have her way. She's doing more good than you give her credit for.'

'I don't understand.'

'I will explain when we meet up again.'

'Feels like I've never met you sometimes.'

'Absence makes the heart grow fonder.'

The cockatiels wet me from head to toe. I think there's a Norfolk Island Pine close by that Golda organised to be transplanted. Frontal Lobe vibrates. Everything shifts and moves. An earthquake is happening all around. The piano is up the wall and a merry mix of files is a tongue tornado as desperate as the heaven held hands. Skeletal boas of infant malnutrition hang around the half dead necks of war weary women and men. Tchaikovsky screams in agony. '*Swan Lake. Cygnet Waterhole.* Don't drown.'

His music lives on.

A rat drops out of the piano and looks for corners to hide but there are none. Frontal Lobe keeps turning and spinning. The cockatiels increase their visits. The Cass Converters milk the ewes and feed their boys Dorset colostrum. Golda has secured all the protein boxes. Delivery needs to happen quickly. Frontal Lobe, on a tilted axis, spins one way and then another. Pelican security is lost in a world of continual whir. A colony of bird dervish is mesmerising. The energy draws flocks from the inland to the island. A ceiling fan in Frontal Lobe is on the floor or perhaps it's still on the ceiling which is now the floor. The files are in agony desperate for attention. A life of continual plight numbs every living soul and every living soul needs a cellular rout.

The Altered Boys keep dancing and barricading, brushing off old and new readings of their own testaments. Maintaining contact with the Akashic Records they allow their souls to be drip fed their most recent identities. Easily confused as disciples they have been told they are descriptors.

And it's they who keep buried nuns alive until time runs out.

The nuns start to manipulate the naked residents who have already started to exhibit an inner smile. The clunk of neck vertebrae complete, pelicans deliver back massages up and down the naked bodies. Ray Devine is reluctant to relinquish. He still carries '*THE EXCEPTION-ALS OPEN*' sign on his back like the shell of a deformed tortoise. It only emphasises his nakedness. His original sin is eye catching. But once convinced he no longer requires his props, he accedes to two sets of pelican feet that ply him from neck to coccyx.

'I've just the house for you, Mr. Percival,' he groans in pleasure. 'It's slap bang on the southern flank. A good fishing spot.'

The pelicans eye each other, ruffle their feathers and continue to ply their recently well-trained trade.

Mother Teresa moves from the chiropractic amphitheatre to the bridge entrance.

'Alight in the name of the Lord,' she commands.

The pelicans fly from human bodies and earnestly waddle towards the Blessed Mother.

'The time of change is about to begin,' she continues raising her hands heavenward. Golda dives and swoops parallel to the bridge. The hula fish are sucked into her jet stream and swarm in a mist of dry ice across the chiropractic tables. Halos of fish buzz like the cylindrical heads of whipper snippers. They hover up and down the naked residents who still have their heads peering through the holes in the tables.

Meanwhile The Altered Boys walk in twos, arms around each other to join Mother Teresa. They've prepared for the mist which has thickened into a fog. Celebratory noise from the mainland increases in volume. The busy postulants work devotedly checking their clients. Text messages continue in pelican crops. Those that have just finished a massage fight to keep their mobiles down to prevent an outbreak of a communicable disease.

The flip flop of fins slippery with brine swim in columns. The sky has sucked from the water and now the temporary amphibians drill through multiple auras while consulting the Akashic Records. In the dense fog, the air swimmers change direction multiple times as heaven's workshop coordinates not only the realignment of physical, mental, and emotional bodies but the metaphysical as well.

Before the fog starts to lift Golda escorts her brethren back to the lake whereby well-schooled fish learn the ropes of water knots again and rehearse all available gill gatherers for the final exodus.

The Holy Mother and her postulants raise their hands palms upwards and direct their eyes first to the skies and then to the bridge in front. Pelican security unravel their wings and eye the sky as well. Behind them the loving Altered Boys count their numbers and separate to form a third tier of blissful contemplation. The fog forms a snake the length of the bridge. The sun filters through as bleary-eyed Golda senses a moment in her life when a nanosecond is fed bliss for eternity. She swoops silently alongside the fog, dives over the other side and checks the A380.

The Cass Converters welcome the lifting of the mist. Their boys have changed overnight.

'What's happened to them?' they say in unison.

They search the Hill Paddock as a crinoline of fog gets tucked unevenly into the broccoli trees.

'They're just so happy. Free of something.' Cass Converter One allows a relieved smile to soften her face.

'Them?' Cass Converter Two questions.

Cass Converter One points over the locked gate. Cracks have appeared in the road at right angles to the tyre ruts.

'That's the best hash tag I've ever seen,' Cass Converter One adds.

Lambs of God hoof towards the women. Those still waiting to give up their fleece make sure they queue at the front.

'We're about halfway there. Should be able to make good progress now we won't have unpleasant interruptions.'

Cass Converter One turns away from the gate.

'What are we going to eat? It's not safe to leave here yet.' Cass Converter Two seeks reassurance.

'Come over here.'

The women find a ewe that's cast giving birth. A dead lamb veiled in afterbirth lies at the rear of its dying mother. Maggots wriggle in their hundreds to hasten the dying and the decaying.

Cass Converter One wrings the ewe's neck.

'Should have done this to you know who.'

Cass Converter Two is perturbed.

'What do we do with it?'

'The wool can still be used. The mutton should be okay and the maggots are protein for the new age.'

'We can't eat them.' Cass Converter Two displays a reluctance to accept the rapid changes confronting the boys and the growing confidence of Cass Converter One.

'Thousands are dying for them. Dry 'em or fry 'em. You won't go hungry.'

The women look at each other and swap feelings without saying anything.

Meanwhile Bradley and Teagan have created the old world of hieroglyphics from dung.

They seem fascinated by fish in particular.

Pelicans and postulants step from side to side. Yachts and cruisers continue in lazy circles reflected in the sky. Ranks are soon to be broken so it takes more effort than usual to maintain eccentric concentricity with crewless pleasure craft. Little waves send a pleasurable pulse into every hearing ear. Fish ring either side of the bridge in ordered discs and are able to fully execute water to air funnels in an immediate fog free future. The fish sing again. Word has got out about the insects in the polystyrene boxes. Now that everything Disney is being eradicated, they begin a final practice of a popular insect song. The final metamorphosis is about to start. The cockatiels have been informed of the latest shift and hover above the fish replicating screeching loops. The Akashic

Records are not serving their purpose so it's a harder job getting them to mimic creatures that are not so deep.

Mother Teresa raises her hands for daughters and birds to cease movement. The Altered Boys stand pillar to post, the essential sentries not on duty.

The Blessed Mother moves forward as the last veil of fairy floss crystallises. Suddenly the chiropractic tables whirl in the air and become paddle boards once more for the tired nuns.

'The Lord welcomes you to a new world,' the Holy Mother announces.

'Why is she speaking on your behalf?' I say to Jesus. 'Don't you ever get sick of other people quoting you?'

'I let the dead speak for themselves. It's likely to be the only chance they'll have getting people to listen to them.'

'I guess you'd know all about that.'

Dr Redden cautiously opens a desk drawer and retrieves a bottle of Scotch. She drinks straight from the bottle. She opens another drawer, removes papers and files and scratches around for a broad-spectrum antibiotic. She takes two of the tablets, has another swig of Scotch and realises that she is not wearing protective gloves. She puts tablets and Scotch back in their rightful places, slides on a pair of gloves and decides to repeat her immediate past actions. She lifts out the bottle of Scotch and pretends to drink then takes out the box of antibiotics and makes out she's removing two tablets. She convinces herself that everything is back in synch as she replaces pills and alcohol. Wanting to save time she opens both drawers simultaneously. To her horror the drawers are full of pubic hair. Again she shrieks as Dr Love. Scotch and antibiotics spill over her blotter.

I prop myself up on my pillows. My head is a planet off spinning to determine an equinox. Everything rotates and revolves. The circuit training is swapped so I get a feel for lightness in the light. I can hear nothing but arguments and counter arguments from Frontal Lobe.

Liberace scratches the door of Frontal Lobe then checks me out, demanding to be fed another diorama he can play with. I reach to pat or grab but everything is turning. I listen for Marcia Font. I see Marcia Font. I want her here and now to place more full stops where the sheep graze, to oversee the work of two homeless infants playing at making words but still deep in dung and experimentation.

I slump on the broad of my back. A grey and white feather floats down and then decides it's the master of gravity and dances across the room pulled by whimsy. My dry eyes beg for fluid as Tchaikovsky is lifted from his bath and placed at the piano dead. So called friends slap his cheeks and prop him on the piano stool which is off the floor and at right angles to the wall. The rat runs across the keyboard. I want Liberace to catch it but he's more interested in the feather and the message it brings. I'm forced to read the feather. It's an infringement feather. Discarded by a pelican and a policeman at the same time. A cockroach walks across my cheeks in search of food.

I eat the cockroach.

The policeman sits down at the kitchen table.

'Where have you been, Dad?' a small girl asks.

'Will you fix my ambulance?' the girl's brother asks. 'It doesn't go anymore. There's red oil coming out of it.'

'Later, my boy. Much later.'

The policeman's wife massages her husband's shoulders.

'Hard day, dear?' she enquires.

'You could say so.'

'You must be starving. We've already eaten.'

'What's for tea?'

'Spaghetti Bolognese. There's a new butcher shop in Happy Valley. They had prime mince as an opening special you know.'

'Yes, I do know.'

'Rise up again, my precious children. The Lord commandeth you to go forward.'

The eyes of birds and beasts marvel at what they see. All look in the one direction.

'Remember from now on Small is Tall.'

The fish of the lake, the birds in the sky, postulants, pelicans and Altered Boys all chant continuously, 'SMALL IS TALL! SMALL IS TALL!'

500 naked midgets with heads held high are marching on the spot.

One has a board on his back.

In Frontal Lobe the files are out of control. I try to console them but there isn't time.

What are these tablets?

I must remember it's still today.

Memory again. Train yourself for clues.

Monday?

Antibiotics?

I tell myself, because the good doctor told me, that the tablets will help.

Will they?

Are they?

It must be Marcia Font and the Lamington Council grant and nothing else. Nothing else but *Cygnet Waterhole*.

But how can I stop the sweating and the shivering? I'll have to pretend that everything is ok. If Marcia comments, I'll tell her it's male menopause.

To lie again until I'm dry again.

Can someone dump some rubble over my Niagara?

I am two threads. Two threads will be me from now on. One public and one private.

The Lamington Council thread must come out on top. It must come first. I wish those files in Frontal Lobe would be still.

It's hard to stop them.

Will the threads become one?

Hide the one you don't want anyone to see and pray that the Lamington Council grant for *Cygnet Waterhole* will stop all intruders.

THE midgets mark time. Quite unexpectedly the march turns into an ungainly lurch towards the bridge. As the former residents approach the crossing, the pelican security group around Mother Teresa. Texting can still be heard as several of the birds dry retch on receipt of messages. The postulants carry the paddle boards under their arms.

Surfies in drag are entered into a new file in Frontal Lobe.

The holy women slide in front of the marching midgets and succumb to the pattern of hundreds of tiny feet joining the forward thrust. Blessed Teresa and her gurgling bird security follow with the Altered Boys bringing up the rear. Now the entire group marks time. The postulants guide the midgets to the front while everyone else re-forms behind them.

The small fry radiate genuine joy. There are no false smiles or a wait to see who smiles first with this little lot. They are looking up for the first time and the Teresa vibe has begun to work through them. Not knowing what lies ahead, the fearlessness of these Little People shines through. The bridge is metres away. It's a lure that draws them.

Overhead hysterical cockatiels screech in disorderly circles. Fish not suffering from an atmospheric version of the bends flipper triumphantly in hasty rings singing *Bare Necessities*. Golda swerves and dives between water and air making sure her role as conduit to the Akashic Records is realised. She maintains a holding pattern for the important walk across the bridge.

The smiling throng of naked midgets are not looking back, nor are they surging forward. Mother Teresa keeps a watchful eye on those in front of her. Occasionally a pelican shovels up a phone and then swallows it again. The procession moves on, everyone looking directly ahead. The gathering on the mainland is growing larger and louder. From a distance it appears like a human muster. The bobbing heads of the dusty mass are bunches of red grapes.

The first feet hit the bridge. Arms swing from side to side. Genitalia not scaled down during the makeover flop any which way to be wacked by swinging arms. The midgets burst into song:

> *We all lived in a broken lavatory*
> *A broken lavatory*
> *A sewer by the sea.*

Their singing drowns out the *Bare Necessities*.

Behind the party a continuous rumbling builds. Bitumen and bridge start to crack and break apart. Whole sections of cement girders lift into the sky, rockets destined for *Nowhere Land*. Above the island rows of houses magic carpet away into the stratosphere for a Disney death. Yachts and cruisers break out of their circle and float aimlessly towards the mainland. Fish fly over them. Cockatiels inspect and hover above but the commotion on the half bridge ensures that both birds and fish occupy their respective elements in parallel to the party leaving the island forever.

The midgets march on continuing to sing their version of *The Insect Hymn*:

> *We all lived in a sewer by the sea*
> *A sewer by the sea*
> *A broken lavatory.*

Mother Teresa's party continue their chant, 'SMALL IS TALL! SMALL IS TALL!' The effect of this mantra behind the midgets, propels the Little People forward with gusto.

The crowd on the mainland swells. They marvel with delight at the daytime fireworks of a well-lit bridge and upmarket houses disappearing into infinity. Some dive into the lake and take control of the yachts and cruisers which they steer towards the wharf.

'Lake cruises for seven dollars and seventy-seven cents!' the enterprising boat operators call. It's no surprise there are a number of takers. The folk here have the exact tender.

'This is better than *Titanic*!' voices shout via loud hailers.

'Be the first to see the last of this bridge before it lands on heaven's doorstep!'

'You'll never see the likes of this again!'

The all dancing all singing fish are hoarse. They form a single line from part bridge to barrage shedding a sophisticated light on synchronised swimming. A considerable percentage of carp have Tourette's Syndrome. They contribute to the joyful occasion singing *Bye Bye Arse Licker Disney*.

The A380 swings about on its moorings responding to the underwater vibrations of frolicking fish and a dismantled bridge.

Tireless Golda spreads her energies between the gravitational pull of her mission to Earth and always consulting the Akashic Records. Relieved all is going to plan she swoops low along the bridge eyeing everybody. Pelicans blink back. Nuns smile adoringly. The Altered Boys blow her a kiss. Mother Teresa appears a little more restrained and watches her fledgling converts puppy step the last few metres to the mainland. She bows to Golda unaware to this point and contrary to her teachings she has been liaising with a transgender salmon.

The mighty midgets stare straight ahead. Some have learned to blink again. Others try to break ranks by sneezing, scratching and arse gargling, but the power of the group, the intention of combined souls is seen, heard, but more importantly felt.

At last the party reaches the mainland. The midgets dizzy with joy are applauded loudly. They stop abruptly on the spot then mark time idling, a flesh machine of several moving parts. The cockatiels reoccupy the Norfolk Island Pines as a canopy of feathers. The Altered Boys assume their work is done, embrace the midgets and nuns then disappear in pairs into the crowd of curious well-wishers to their strategically planted SUVs. They need to make a hasty escape but word has it the roads are blocked in Happy Valley. They must detour.

I look again and am not quite sure what I see. I search for Mother Teresa and Golda and am happy they are on their way again. The convivial group of mainlanders intrigues me.

The diorama that was, is hastily reassembled. Liberace tiptoes through the confusion on the table. Pens roll and fall. I hear them and know them to be pens. I try to place the other sounds but the cacophony which is Frontal Lobe drowns everything. The bridge in rewind rebuilds momentarily. I move it back and forth in my screen of sweat.

Who is it standing there with all these people?

I look again. Most of them are wearing red and white elf hats. Only they are not elfin physically. The midgets keep marching on the spot. Should I intervene now? It's not a place or time for midgets. I know what she said.

Little People.

But she isn't here yet. Or is she? Please Marcia. Where are you? Time is running out.

Blessed Teresa and her party walk along the banks of the lake. They stop and turn around to watch the last bridge pylon rocket heavenwards. There is a round of applause. Red and white hats are flung into the D-Day air. The synchronised swimming fish do one final waterworks and swim upstream to more tranquil waters. The cockatiels wave from the trees and lap across the lake, an uncertain tide of white screeching. The waves become smaller. Now the tips of the Norfolk Island Pines play host to white water.

Red and white hats go back on the folk who are feverish with joy. There is no place for those who see things differently. Mother Teresa's party arrive south of the barrage. Security pelicans rework their earlier journey. They flatten themselves two abreast on the edge of the ocean. The Blessed Mother removes her sandals and steps onto the birds' backs. Like a return to Avalon the water birds glide to the A380. The cheery postulants atop their water boards again try fooling those watching that they're next in line to Jesus. Their collective joy is the kind of mimicry seen and expressed by the red and white hat brigade on dry land.

Without warning the Altered Boys return hurriedly to the barrage. They run to the pelican cluster who are watching the procession making its way towards the aeroplane.

'Golda!' they yell into the sky repeatedly and in all directions. 'Where are you? Can you hear us?'

'One last job for you and us! There's a blockage! We were told to head back here to perform the septic miracle.'

Golda hovers above the starboard side of the plane. The bridge partially reconstructs itself from the mainland. Everything rewinds. Midgets walk backwards. The cheerful hat brigade of locals walk backwards. Joy to joyless expressions fight. Security pelicans, Mother Teresa and the postulants bob on a dead sea.

'Have you cleaned the aircraft lavatories? Have you got rid of the turds?' shout the Altered Boys.

Golda swoops and dives either side of the plane. She wraps the aircraft in a jet stream.

The Altered Boys keep yelling. 'Don't dump anything in the water. Attracts the sharks and there'll be no more walking on water. Your waste is at our disposal.'

A four-inch canvas fire hose unravels and spins through the air just missing the motionless composition still bobbing. The Altered Boys back their vehicles up to the hose. They take eskies from the back and place them close to the nozzle.

'Thanks, Golda.'

The jet stream loosens from the A380 and the holy party slip across the salty meniscus to the aircraft. Meanwhile, the community of coloured hats move towards the Altered Boys. Pelicans thinking they might get a free feed are bitterly disappointed when the Altered Boys steer the nozzle across the tops of the eskies like old hands positioning pre-mixed concrete for a slab.

The holy party climb aboard the A380. The assembled community turns towards the plane. The immediate desire is to hold both nostrils between unsoiled digits. As heads turn and fingers tweak noses the Altered Boys arm themselves with tongs and serviettes as well as a holy shit detector.

'Line up now. Free shit sizzle. Be part of history. All proceeds to the global treatment plant.'

The mighty midgets are still content to mark time, to bring forth a blink followed by another. They are starting to see. The cockatiels above them screech nothing but joy and abundance. Slowly the midgets turn south and start the slow move towards the red and white crowd and the Boys. They are computerised creatures just off the production line. Their movements seem hesitant until repetition makes it appear more intuitive than counter intuitive. They are as yet unaware of what lurks in the shadows as they start stepping out on their own. But in the unclear is their future. In the past was another life.

A memory.

They think collectively.

A memory.

What is memory?

The door to Dr Redden's surgery opens. In the crowded waiting room, a fearful number of patients wait with folded arms. Their anger and frustration is more palpable than the original ailment that has brought them here. There is a loud rumbling from the doctor's surgery. Everybody looks down the corridor or guides an attentive ear to the long stretch of disinfected vinyl. The noise becomes a roar.

The first patient to see what emerges from Dr Redden's room screams and implores everyone to leave.

'Get out! Get Out! Go!'

The waiting room empties but not at the speed recommended by the first witness. Zimmer frames are not in this race. They get knocked over in the process. The receptionist barricades herself in her office and backs against the wall.

A gorilla stands in the hallway with a stethoscope around its neck. It beats its chest and delicately removes fleas which it eats.

'There's nothing like being self-sufficient. There's no need for doctors,' it announces in a guttural rumble. 'Bring on the protein era.'

'First prize is the Blessed Mother's turd. You can dry it or fry it.'

A red and white hat person calls out.

'How do we know it's the real shit?'

'It'll glow in the dark.'

The remaining Altered Boys circulate amongst the crowd tearing off raffle tickets. Eager hands count and recount the correct coinage.

'Seventy-seven cents a ticket. No refunds. Runners up get postulant poos. They won't glow in the dark. Just a flicker. If you're epileptic suggest you buy a ticket for someone else.'

There's a lot of clamour. The Altered Boys sing joyfully:

> *There was an old lady who raffled her turd.*
> *How absurd to raffle a turd?*
>
> *We're undeterred to raffle her shit*
> *She'll be dust again in just a bit*
>
> *We raffled her turd to appease our Lord*
> *He knows there's a problem with sphincter*
> *fraud.*

The last of the tickets is sold. An Altered Boy borrows a hat from the red and white brigade. The ticket stubs are emptied into the hat.

*   *   *   *   *   *   *

*   *   *   *   *   *

*   *   *   *   *   *   *

Jet engines roar as the A380 creates sufficient waves for its take off. It does a final turn in front of the barrage and with the effect of a thousand fountains sails into the sky just as the pelican security lob back onto the mainland, ruffle their feathers and assume the status of birds with no special power other than the glorious insight of all creatures great and small.

Through all this I hug the pillow, the walls of the uterus determining that a curette is required. My placenta bed so wet with the break of fluids, dyes the sheets and blankets red. Skid marks of blood and shit are inextricably linked in a linen crown. In Frontal Lobe there's moaning. I attempt to get out of bed and stub my toes in the process. Drunkenly I fall against walls and crawl on all fours towards the front. The moaning intensifies.

Should I check out what is going on?

I reach the door. I'm all headache. My whole body is a head over heels headache. I want the top of me removed again to sit as a passenger. Go for another drive. No letter this time. Sit in silence. Separate and contemplate. When did this last happen? A day ago, or tomorrow. I'm all tomorrow and I've been all yesterday. The soothing caring cockatiels no longer come to me. Am I better? Have I changed? What is the reason they don't come anymore? I try to watch the pelicans but they're not having anything to do with me. I crawl backwards to my bedroom where I can see the plane through the skylight in the ceiling.

Remember your priorities. Lamington Council. Time for more antibiotics?

The A380 climbs steeply and then does one last dive over the shores of Lake Alexandrina. Fish, birds and homo sapiens receive and garland the plane. The pelican security has a twinge not covered by its collective instinct and peers skyward. The cockatiels mimic the fish and spout water funnels into the air behind the jet stream. Golda encircles everything that offers spheres. She rings the A380 and ensures her union of water and air is everlasting. The Altered Boys look above with hands across their hearts. They cling to the hat containing the raffle stubs.

The thrust from the plane is cyclonic.

The midgets gain strength as they march on to join the rest of the coastal community. They know there is a celebration and an interruption to that celebration. They see the red and white hats and that visual cue inspires them onwards. Occasionally they stop, start. The red of the hat wearers and traffic lights from an old world confuses them. However, their stilted walking appears controlled. The novelty of a new life occupation makes them tread a careful path. Instinct, balance and confidence is all theirs but years of trauma means these positive skills need to be relearnt.

I get back to my bedroom. I'm still on all fours. I rock back and forth. Past and future only. There is no present. There is no ability to yearn. I can't entertain this kind of loss.

The A380 climbs high in the sky and heads west. A faint vapour trail wriggles in white. It reads:

'THANKS FOR THE CRABS.'

Golda scales to great heights and sails in the jet stream. She disperses the vapour trail so that it can be read by birds and fish alike. The tablet in the sky yields to a cloudy screen saver as the great Southern Sea of Galilee teems with happy fish. Native fish swim in their reclamation having evolved a forgotten treaty with the settler carp. The songs of Disney, while not banned, are no longer necessary.

Everyone wishes upon kelp or sea grass.

And while the rapid changes fall into place there is still alertness for the rewind button to be activated. Embracing the new is remembering the past and all its traits and customs. The personality of the environment must be found, enacted upon and implemented. There is no time for reaction.

'The winning ticket is number A380!'

The information is repeated.

There is no response. The communal reaction is to look around and above. Golda does a last swoop with the vapour trail.

'A380! Who has ticket A380?

The midgets are making good time with their progress towards The Altered Boys. Now almost all 500 of them are walking naturally, still nude and naturally. The sustained flip flop of body parts excites the cockatiels still making a final adjustment back to stripping Norfolk Island Pines of their embryonic cones. The pelican security forms arrows that firefly up and down lakeside. Members of the contingent grace the sky and offer reflective thought to the fish colonising lost waterways. Their eyes tilt skywards to the A380 defaecating a trail of white sausage meat. Pylons, jetties and the backs of SUVs have a particular intrigue for the birds that sense and eye a foretold future. The folds in their gullets continue to reflux messages.

A call from past servitude keeps texting them. They try to interpret with true grit but are forced to crop an unpalatable swallow. Heightened instinct fights the memory of usefulness. Another arrow formation takes to the air, wings above the water. Pylons, jetties and SUVs are interchanged. This tide of disruption to normal pelican pleasure is repeated time and time again.

The Altered Boys are impatient.

'We'll have to draw the other tickets!' one announces. 'Hopefully the recipient of the winning ticket will turn up soon!'

'Winner of the two-kilo pack of postulant poo is ticket number A350!'

There is a shriek from the hat wearers. A wave of red and white parts, letting the ticket holder through the buzzing throng. The eager hands reach up to catch the glad wrapped stools from an Altered Boy.

'In time you can mount this as a wall plaque. Mind you with this kind of exhibit, plaque does take time to form.'

'Thank you!' The ecstatic hat wearer removes her hat and catches the covered squelch.

'What will you say to your children when they ask what you were doing the day you got the shits?' the head Altered Boy asks.

'I don't know, shit head. Do you?'

The red and white hats applaud loudly and wolf whistle. They frolic in what appears to be a vague resemblance of a Morris Dance. Bells and whistles magically appear to be replaced with pipes and bongs but the dancing continues and for ticket holder A350 so does the squelch.

'Winner of the one kilo pack of postulant poo is ticket number A330 ER.'

The dancing is frenetic. Red and white hats become bunting and brief costume pieces from different eras. The joyous celebration turns to a clap as the holder of the winning ticket receives his delicate prize which again is neatly folded in glad wrap to contain both odour and shape.

'As I think we said eons ago to another group, Small is Tall. In your case no job is too small. Do you have any idea what you'll do with your poo parcel?'

'I have a month-long mentorship with Gilbert and George. I have a tactile function I wish to complete.'

Prize caught in his hat and returned to his head for security the third ticket holder re-joins the throng of celebrants and dances away scanned time with postulant poo MRI imaging beneath his hat.

'Don't shake it too much!' the Altered Boys all chorus. 'You must allow it to settle. One last call for the holder of ticket number A380!'

The celebration temporarily subsides. The tight community look about them, at one another and to the sky. The pelicans continue repeating their gentle arrows and choose different landing stations each time. In the background a shrill chorus of songsters is heard approaching.

> *We all lived in a broken lavatory*
> *A broken lavatory.*
> *A broken lavatory.*

And in between the singing the sound of pitter patter footsteps pummels the words.

> *We're all free from the broken lavatory*
> *The broken lavatory.*
> *The broken lavatory.*

Now the mighty midgets are marching in unison. With military precision they pass beneath the garlanded Norfolk Island Pines completely whitewashed with cockatiels. The birds screech non-stop and increase the volume when the midgets are not singing. All surfaces from grass, bitumen and gravel thump with pounding. The hat people resume their celebratory exploration of manmade history.

Some correct each other and call it a people past.

The cop is halfway through his spaghetti Bolognese when he pushes it aside.

'Fix my train, Dad.'

'You're not looking well, dear.'

'I'm fine. Haven't the stomach for this today or the head and shoulders for that matter.'

'My train won't go, Dad. Will you fix it for me please?'

'Leave your dad alone for a while dear. He's had a very busy day.'

'That's ok. Shouldn't have eaten so much. You feed me too well. Midget size next time.'

'Midget?'

'Small portion.'

The Cass Converters ply their cottage industry. Eager Dorsets line up to be spun into antiquity.

'You know, with all that is happening I feel like a new woman,' Cass Converter Number One remarks. 'I can't remember a time when I've felt as content as this.'

'You took the words out of my mouth,' Cass Converter Two replies. She straddles a ewe with a seven-year growth of fleece. 'Just look at how happy our kids are now. They're not living in fear like we were every moment of our lives.'

Cass Converter One steers her fleece free sheep back towards the rest of the flock and sits above the waterhole and begins to spin. More columns begin to stack. Their children resume fossicking for elderberries.

'Not many more to do now. We should be halfway. The costume designer is coming here soon.'

'How soon?'

'Don't know exactly but I feel it'll be soon.'

'How do you know all this?' Cass Converter Two starts to spin the fleece from the last ewe. Her fingers are soft and slippery from the lanolin so much so that the occasional blackberry prickle fails to register any reaction.

'Suppose I could say people in higher places.'

'Higher places?'

'I'm not sure yet but I know something, or someone is watching us. Guiding us.'

Freshly clipped sheep flicker and adjust to their close shaves before joining sheep with their fleece still intact. Before and after is something that the snow white Dorsets can't contemplate yet the rugged ones laden with lanolin dripping coats look upon the new order with disdain.

'I had a dream last night. At least I think it was a dream. I received a letter. I opened the letter. The contents flew about the place in a gust of wind and I had to grab the loose pages.'

'I can't believe you're telling me this.' Cass Converter Two wipes her hands across her apron and goes to wipe a final time but instead stops and stares at Cass Converter One.

'I had a dream too. I had that dream.'

The women face one another wide eyed. In the distance they can hear their children picking and throwing the elderberries. The perfect counterpoint of sheep bleating and dropping full stops in all the right places on the paragraph encourages a closer look for words and meaning. The green paddock slips down the page. Neither woman knows who will speak first. Familiar fear surfaces. Both have voices that can speak for them. The unravelling of the past takes time but they persist with the complementary feelings they're experiencing.

A feeling that can take more than one breath away.

'Did you read the letter?' Cass Converter Two prompts cautiously.

'Did you read the letter?' Cass Converter One hastily responds.

'Yes,' is the joint reply.

'From today you shall be known as Mary Magda. That's what the letter said.'

'Mine said today I'll be known as Mary Virgo.'

Teagan and Bradley arrive with buckets filled with elderberries.

'No full stops in this I hope,' cautions Mary Magda.

'No, all berries,' the boys reply having quickly grown up overnight.

'Good. Then we can turn a new leaf,' Mary Virgo says with her hand held gently across her heart.

'Yes, we can, dear sister. It's from the same book.'

For now there appears to be less activity in Frontal Lobe. I think the files understand they have to queue if I'm to give them extra attention.

Know that there's one file that has priority.

I'll have to create a way to lock that thread in place so it's immune to any upset. I'm worried about time again. How can I stop it from running out?

Where are you, Marcia? We haven't much time left. Are you watching?
Can't let her see me like this.
She's bound to say something.

Golda's Connective Tissue.

ABOVE, the speck of an A380 flies west. Golda takes an instant dive from her stratospheric duties to inspect the welfare of those forced to shelter by the waterhole. She halos the two Marys and cocoons the children in a golden light. She revisits her spawning and fawning ground, the waterhole, and enters the required dimensions for a performance area at a later date.

Her internalised smartphone has many crossed connections which throws her into a spin. 500 smartphones are not so smart and keep messaging the same number. Golda temporarily loses her connection with the A380, those aboard and the Akashic Records. She spins out of control and crashes into the waterhole. She switches off all connections bar one.

The A380 is sound only. No speck is discernible to the earthly eye. Mary Magda and Mary Virgo help steer Golda back towards the heavens where she continues her guidance of an exhumed nun and her bevy of pretty postulants.

And I watch the plane in the sky. Watch that Golda is safe. The roof over my head is off my head. Is it the sun or a full moon? A rooster crows and crows waking up the suburbs. I yawn for dawn but lengthy slumber is what I need most. By crawling backwards I pick up from where I left off. I can manage to leave stuff behind. But Frontal Lobe is as clear as day in my mind and I hear all its sounds and voices. There is a funeral to attend. Peter Ilich has gone. I watched his torment for too long. That awful bath he had to have as a last resort.

It's that shower I must have soon.

I'm cockatiel droppings, man sweat and dick cheese in search of the first light and the latest version of *The History of the Scab* – the chronic psoriasis is acute.

It's painful to move. On the floor and going backwards is a necessary rewrite of my life since I was fifteen. The lesions are less inclined to tear open. I'm all crutch. All crutch rot. Nothing soothes. I'm alone and wanting. Wanting but not needy.

I clarify this for myself.

This is a time to fall in love. To embrace both threads. To fall deeply in love with sequences.

Remember Lamington Council must come first.

The energies scattered in Frontal Lobe must now rest. I try to block out all their pleas. Do I pick the baby up if it cries? I'm under its birth bed now. Flat on the floorboards beneath the mattress I dose up on claustrophobia and x-ray the mattress protector. My scales have been left behind. The blood of my biggest organ is patterned like a giraffe jigsaw puzzle. Still the rooster crows pushing dawn into a fast dusk and back again. Still I crawl backwards to a place where I can't terrorise myself. I want my heart but I haven't one so I've been told time and time again.

But here in this timeless moment if I lie still, very still, I'll be able to listen in my childproof pen. I really will wear one beating organ on my sleeve.

I roll onto my back and breathe in mattress dust and the faint whiff of polyurethane used to seal the Oregon pine floorboards. Peter Ilich Tchaikovsky is finally lowered into his grave. Golda rests on top of the A380 as it descends low over the border between Turkey and Syria. I hope there is enough to feed the masses. I can't see inside the plane and I'm not sure if I'm meant to or that some higher force is forbidding my ease of access to witness the Blessed Mother being reinterred.

And I'm pleased with my life so far. That I can be both here and there. But as I lie and lay low, as I wait for ascension to a more comfortable life I macerate cellular structures and float with relative ease back onto the top of the bed. I watch my liquefied body comfort itself as best as possible. The least amount of movement is essential so as not to set off an eruption on an eroded landscape. I find a nesting space where former fluids have capped. Where once there was convenience now there is the fold of memories written in the cotton sheets of letters.

And one of them is from Louise. Did I post a letter for Louise? That letter for Louise. The only letter Louise has ever given me to post. I am in this world but I am not of this world. Something is starting to make sense. The world under the bed and in the playpen. The place where I cut my first teeth and my lower jaw. From what were you hiding?

Is it *were* or is it *are*?

Now is an escape. My fingernails are still solidifying. Now needs escape claws. I have none.

Just quick.

I see Dr Redden as she has never seen herself before. Her gorilla uprising sees her wander through the waiting room with a kidney dish. A caring creature she wants to share her good news and diet tips with all in one. But there is no one in the waiting room and the receptionist is still hiding under her desk.

'That's strange,' she rumbles totally unaware of the great changes that have taken place in her life. 'Where is everybody?'

She dips her hand into the kidney dish and pulls out a dead grasshopper. She munches on it.

'Anyone for new age protein? Beats being a smiling vegetarian.'

At that moment Golda swoops and flippers on the door.

The door automatically opens and the salmon swims through the opening.

'Ah. Fish too I see. How terribly last century.'

'They're all here. They're all here. You've got them. One of them has grown upon you.'

'Am I seeing things correctly? Is this... Pardon, are you a fish?'

'I'm a transgender salmon. Rainbow trout to all my closet friends. Take a good look at yourself.'

'Me? Look at myself? You should talk.'

'Don't you realise what's happened? The pubic regions all disappeared from *Disney on Hindmarsh*. One of them has grown on you and is still growing. All over you. They've grown accustomed to this place.'

'*Disney on Hindmarsh*. Disappeared. Grown on me. What are you talking about?'

'Is there a mirror somewhere?'

'Why?'

'Take a good look at yourself before I say anything more. Mirror?

'Hold this Flipper. Follow me. There's a large one in the women's toilet.'

The gorilla in Dr Redden pauses.

'Wait outside please. This is ladies only.'

Golda juggles the kidney dish. She hears a loud roar and not the kind of noise expected from a women's toilet.

'This isn't me.'

'I'm afraid it is.'

'How did I become like this?'

'Do you have property at *Disney on Hindmarsh?*'

'Hindmarsh Island. What's this Disney thing?'

'There's been a glitch in Mother Teresa's app. I knew there'd be a problem working with the exhumed.'

'Mother Teresa? Oh, stop it. Stop it. How did I become like this?'

'You should have been there for the transformation.'

'Where?'

'On the island this morning. It appears after the shave, all the pubic hair went haywire and attached itself to the nearest resident not currently residing on the island.'

Dr Redden wails and roars.

'Is there any way out of this?'

Golda's left fin is starting to droop with the weight of the kidney dish.

'I don't want to be seen like this. I can't afford to let my patients witness this catastrophe.'

'Can we go into your surgery?'

Golda and a hastily plodding Dr Redden lock themselves in the surgery. Golda flings open drawers and cupboards.

'There were 500 pubic regions removed. And they are either on you or in this room. I've been in contact with my record keeper up yonder and he's fixed the Blessed Mother's app.'

'What a lousy thing to do.'

'You'd be grateful to have a feed of western fed lice if you were starving. Mother Teresa detected a lice infestation at *Disney on Hindmarsh* amongst other things. Now I want you to stand on that chair and sing.'

'Sing what? This is ridiculous. I can't sing. I'm tone deaf.'

'Don't belittle yourself. I'll sing along with you. You know *The Insect Song*?'

Golda dances around the surgery singing first.

We all live in a broken lavatory

A broken lavatory
A broken lavatory.

Reluctantly the gorilla in Dr Redden begins to sing also.

'What will my husband think about all this? He's at our island home this weekend.'

'Not anymore, he isn't. What's his name?'

'Ray Devine. He's in real estate.'

'Was in real estate.'

'What do you mean? What's happened to him?'

'He's had a change for the better. He's currently marching nude along the foreshore in Goolwa with 500 hundred other people from *Disney on Hindmarsh*. But don't you worry about him. You'll join him soon. But first let's get these pubic regions out of here. Keep singing. Louder.'

Like ungreased lightning Dr Redden's surgery and her person is cleared of pubic regions. Great wings of hair fly behind the flightpath of the holy A380. It forms a packaged parachute to enhance the landing of the big jet.

'This lot of pubic regions will become merkins for those on chemotherapy. You've no idea how great the need is.'

'Wrong. I do have an idea. What's happening to me?'

Now somewhat mute but with a happier disposition, nude Dr Redden is ready to be recalibrated so she can join the midget minority advancing on the cheery community gathered around The Altered Boys.

The A380 makes a steep descent over the northern Syrian border with Turkey. Anti-aircraft fire and drones whizz uncomfortably close to the *NunAir* jet. Thousands of desperate souls, with barely enough strength to raise their hands, nevertheless watch the giant bird fly at near-stalling speed over their cramped campsite tucked away in the mountains. Polystyrene boxes are released from the plane via parachute. The aircraft banks steeply and flies back over the campsites. Again, there is a further release of prepacked meals. The desperate animals clamber with paper skin covering their skeletal remains. Some are too weak to do anything and die just as sustenance is reaching their mouths. Everyone has mobile phones. Everyone who is mobile enough has just messaged somebody in the world about their plight. The need to communicate has replaced the death diet. People are either dying texting or dying to text.

As the polystyrene boxes are ripped apart, hands still clutching phones shovel mouths too weak to open. Emaciated babies are comforted with phones by mothers who are no longer able to produce breast milk.

The A380 repeats its flyby once more dropping more relief. Missiles of all kinds shower over the big bird but it deflects all these attempts to ground it. On the ground skeletal pigs scramble over rotting bodies to snout into the boxes. There is a birth and a rebirth here. There needs to be as there is so much death to balance. Gratitude would like to spread like wildfire but any appreciation is a mere smoulder. Fighting to stay alive, fear of death and an even greater fear of a living death is all consuming.

I can smell it everywhere. So many peoples' times are near. Those who can still breathe are grateful they may have another dose of energy to find shelter across the border and a place to charge their mobiles.

Boxes are licked out. Bits of polystyrene are chewed. Someone has a mobile signal. Cadavers gather in their stink to peer at some history on a Samsung tablet before it explodes. The Warner Brothers' logo appears first and then a film title.

It reads *How the West Was Lost.*

Zap. A tiny crab has defied rapid freezing and has emerged from its induced sleep. The fingers in a bony hand shatter as the crab is squashed and eaten. The chewed insect is spat into the mouth of a two-year-old.

Later the child is heard singing 'When I Wish Upon a Star.'

No one serves coffee with this after dinner mint.

Golda has slipped inside the aircraft as it climbs over the Mediterranean and heads south to Palestine. The postulants have more duties to perform. Blessed Teresa has embraced her death again. Her Eminence is about to prepare for her last resting place. Golda swims through the cabin and enters the cockpit. She reminds the captain to retract the amphibious floats and ensure the wheel housing is in place for a ground landing. The plane glides over all lands deemed holy, the Dead Sea and the Sea of Galilee. The salmon slides out of the wheel housing, smiles at her team in the Sea of Galilee and sends these vibrations to the Great South Land and those in the water or on land around the southern Sea of Galilee.

There's a temporary shudder as the Middle East scissor kicks in the sky above Goolwa. Shadows are rained down. Water spouts shoot up.

Smartphones snap the occurrence but all images are lost. Only those who allow themselves to be present can feel the shift, the beautiful cataclysm experienced in the imagination of those with open hearts and souls. Golda now on autopilot nestles in the slipstream on top of the aircraft fuselage. The plane takes a south easterly turn and heads on its final leg towards Kolkata.

The purposeful postulants are busy embalming their Holy Mother in preparation for another end to her life. They place the comatosed saint back in her original coffin and watch for signs of her last visitation breath. As the plane touches down Mother Teresa sighs deep and murmurs, 'Small is Tall. Please put it on my afterlife app.'

The postulants are far from gloomy despite jet lag. They escort the body of their Blessed Mother back to her original burial site ready for reinternment. They sing softly as they slide Blessed Teresa to rest.

> *You don't live in a broken lavatory*
> *A broken lavatory.*
> *A broken lavatory.*

'Last time, you silly cunts. Who has ticket number A380?'

The looks, stares and exclamations from the pressing throng still reveal no answer. The Altered Boys are getting desperate. They want to hit the road again. The second and third place getters try to contain the squelch in the crush. An unpleasant odour of the putrid nappy variety wafts occasionally. Golda reappears. A black veil trails from her dorsal fin. She's on restricted duties but can still clearly read every situation that confronts her. She watches the midget army advance along the foreshore.

The former Dr Redden is out of kilter with the other small fry. She sees a small man with a board on his back and recognises the slug between his legs. She joins him, shares his emotions, thoughts and feelings. She is one with him, herself and the rest of the group.

But I know there's an overriding feeling of confusion and wonder as to where this group has come from. The cockatiels can offer no explanation. So too the pelicans who are busy shedding past interruptions to their natural roles.

And fish both native and introduced are preoccupied with the signing of ineradicable treaties in a special waterproof edition of *The Book of Moses* attached to the barrage.

'Ticket number A380! Is someone hiding it under one of those hats? Speaking of which, why are so many of you wearing those silly fucking hats?'

'Santa Christs. We're Santa Christs. Jesus is amongst us.'

'Well, Santa Christs, which one of you has ticket A380? Is Jesus amongst you at the moment? Has he got A380?'

Golda is in a flurry. Her dorsal veil is tied with a black ribbon. She swoops over the midgets, exchanges a fishy wink despite viral conjunctivitis and urges them on. The former Dr Redden is still out of step. As yet she cannot smile and worries that everyone can, and it seems normal. There's a canopy to the world and she is under it. She may never escape. She can't hold the group consciousness back anymore. Ironically a need to heal herself is greater than those around her. She still feels shame and embarrassment. The last vestiges of old thinking are like a series of roots that need to be worked loose and removed. She sheds a tear but everyone else is smiling.

There's a train coming and she must feel the smile before she crosses the track.

'Jesus is always amongst us. You just never know when he's going to find form and front up.'

A spokesperson for the Santa Christs edges to the front of the group and speaks with The Altered Boys.

'My guess is he could put in an appearance today. Tomorrow's his birthday and even though he's dead, buried and born again he still plays games. Kind of like hide and seek.'

'Do you think he's with those Little People?' another Altered Boy questions the spokesperson, sensing the exasperation of his fellow Altereds.

'Your guess is as good as mine. I helped them flee the island. Wasn't Jesus involved with their repatriation?'

The Altered Boys glance nervously at one another. They go into a huddle and whisper.

'I thought you said no one knew.'

'Our cover is going to be blown.'

'We need to get out of here.'

'What about first prize?'

'Christ only knows what we should do.'

'And what if he doesn't know?'

'He's an elusive cunt.'

'He's probably undercover with them. Those bogan Santa Christ freaks.'

'Impossible.'

'If you can walk on water you can also fit through the eye of a needle.'

'I tell you, he's close at hand.'

'You wanker.'

'We're going to make one last call. Ticket number A380!'

'Look, it's turning to dust.'

'The Holy Mother has just been reinterred.'

'This is your chance to have a slither of history.'

'A mind-altering moment that'll have you reinterpreting *The Book of Job*.'

The cop is fetching up his guts. It fizzes in his nose. By the strength of his contractions he feels he'll soon spew shit. He examines the partly digested pasta shells and thinks if he were a cat he would probably start looking for kitty litter to bury this death in his guts.

I'm a police officer. Can't have weird thoughts like this. They'll probably think I'm on ice.

The random thoughts keep coming and so does the rainbow-coloured vomit. He hears his phone. Somebody has sent him an SMS.

'Darling, are you alright in there? Someone has just sent you an SMS.'

'Be there in a moment.'

The cop staggers out of the little house. The acid smell of vomit chases him into the lounge where the ceiling fan circulates it everywhere including the family room.

'Pooh, dad! You stink!'

'Darling, you look dreadful. I'll get the air freshener.'

'I'm ok. I'll just sit down for a while.

Lavender air freshener and the smell of vomit is not a good mix. The cop grabs his mobile phone and rushes for the toilet again. With one hand leaning on the cistern, his volcanic guts talk Esperanto once more. It sounds as though a dinosaur is snared, is in pain and trying to escape. As he gathers his composure, he flicks open his mobile phone to check the SMS which reads:

> *We all live in a broken lavatory*
> *A broken lavatory*
> *A broken lavatory.*

He drops his phone in the toilet, slicing the rainbow. The toilet bowl is loose. There is a flood. He has to learn ballet quickly so he can join his lavender hill mob.

At this stage he is unable to walk on effluent.

In my original mud I draw my legs up to my chest. One at a time. Cracks open with every movement. My epidermis remembers *Kindergarten of the Air* and *Let's Join In*. But nothing is connected. Spare gyprock from Frontal Lobe might be the answer to paper over the cracks. I pray an internal seep will be prevented. That entrails will be contained. The trip to hell needs to be put on hold. Eventually I hug my knees but in doing so can feel and hear the tearing skin. My dry eyes nevertheless find the pain for just two tears. Life on Earth is to begin again but every movement forward and up is replaced with hesitancy and a recall from the source. Tired and thirsty, the scabs on my desert landscape attract flies. The energy and determination to go on gets washed ashore with the last visiting wave.

Its tidal pull is a pulse.

As I sit on the stains of my most recent crown of thorns Tarot, I read ahead. Dead seas are seeing seas again. The music of the ocean sings and cleans as selected corpuscles of acid collect all that's not natural for reconstitution. The churn of the discarded is working miracles. Me and my country are the beginnings of a clever pinprick. But there is work to be done as the multiple rivers of bronze serum clean, heal and reveal what lies beneath my fish, bird and reptile.

The balance of scales.

I'm lulled by a gentle stupor. A place of rest. The pelicans eye all that's human and the cockatiels are the bells of birth to be celebrated annually in the Great South Land. They are the snow of summer for families buried in tradition. The community of Santa Christs have acquired more hats. I try to walk among them but I'm forced to view them from afar courtesy of an overworked fisheye lens.

Where are you, Marcia?

The Altered Boys are more frenzied than ever. They have to work harder. Now without the support of postulant and saint they rely totally on their own kind. Great turds of history look as though they might become the birth of dirt.

I unfurl and lie flat on my prickly back. The mattress feels like needles. I go into the pain and relentlessly shed. From here I can see and feel, hear and smell. Marcia is somewhere close. Marcia is coming. We will get the application done. The hoops of thorns from head to foot are unrelenting but I breathe on and through it. The pillows cervix again.

A litter of me is arriving.

The midgets are making good time, I decide. There is a standoff between The Altered Boys and the Santa Christs. No one is going anywhere until the turd is claimed. Dr Redden has started to smile. Her new status means she is just in time to embrace Dr Love before her metamorphosis.

'One of you bloody Christians must have the ticket.'

'We're not Christians! We're Santa Christs!' the congregation yells. 'We're not like them!'

'Well, whatever you call yourselves, no more games or dress ups. That's for children.'

The midgets can now be seen. The Santa Christs stand back and create a pathway leading up to the SUV. The Altered Boys suddenly change. Clones of Conchita Wurst appear in their place all cock and frock. The midgets flop to a stop. A latecomer has joined the group. Golda bustles the former burly man who is still reducing alongside the former Dr Redden.

'Hurry up,' she says flicking her dorsal veil aside. 'Give me your phone. And your badge. No piercings are allowed.'

She rips the policeman's badge from his left nipple.

An inquisitive pelican snatches the phone and flies back to a pylon. It envelopes itself just metres above the water. The Santa Christs create an even bigger pathway for the midgets. All of them together are total group energy but not much more.

Mary Magda and Mary Virgo take shelter in their humpy with their children. They can hear thunder and although it is still quite light there is a flash of lightning across the paddocks surrounding the waterhole.

Sheep continue to nibble what grass exists between the variety of punctuation marks. The first drops of rain prick the stretched skin of the Earth. There is a rush to grab all the costumes and store them under cover. The Marys carry the costumes to the humpy while their boys collect fallen branches to cover them.

'Elderberry runs. We can't let them get wet,' Mary Magda urges.

The women slip and slide on the wet earth as they carry the Corinthian columns of clothes under cover. They reassemble the columns. The isolated spots of rain become a downpour. Huddled amongst costumes in their humpy the women and their children are unaware of two sets of fins pushing up through the earth the other side of the gate.

Emerging lung fish appear to comprehend their environment of transition.

Everything is in place and going according to plan. Just bear with it, I tell myself. I borrow the bird in Golda and fly to her side but out of sight. Golda corkscrews above The Altered Boys and erects a series of stages cushioned by clouds. I shadow the midgets and know this kind of reference is not politically correct. Little People, I repeat over and over. The person who'll put me in my place is nearby. I don't want to lose her.

I hope she's nearby. But do I want her to see me like this?

A blast of music erupts with a drum roll from a platform of clouds accompanied by a bolt of lightning. The Twentieth Century Fox logo heralds the beginning of 3D sky cinema. The postulants appear on the first stage and scratch out a blissful tune:

What the world needs now are lice, sweet lice. It's the only thing that there is so much of.

Above them Mother Teresa hunchbacked by a pyramid of halos, croons:

Look at me. I'm the louse who stole a merkin from a flea.

The tempo changes abruptly. The postulants dance wildly and join with the Blessed Mother in fountains of golden showers that staircase between both stages.

I'm going to tap on your groin, flick through your flaps shave all your pubic hair.

If you're not home tonight when the moon is right
Then I'll tap and flick and scratch you...

Hundreds of cockatiels can be seen preening and scratching their own infestations. My shadow is followed by their shadows. Behind me they trail after excess protein. Psoriasis scales. The pelicans prove how well-adjusted they are. They have one eye on the singing and dancing in heaven while balancing on a single webbed foot. They use the other one to scratch crops and heads. The sound of multiple muffled phones ring consistently. Pelican crops are battery chargers. The noble birds alight in a bunch at one end of the Santa Christs who remove their hats and hold them in front of them. The pelicans walk and face the Santa Christs. They place their bills in the hats and retch up every phone. In unison they step back and take their cue from Mother Teresa. The Santa hats vibrate. The Santa Christs can't control the vibration. They hold their hats with both hands.

What about the Marys? I ask myself, Are they safe in their humpy?

'They got no further than Happy Valley,' is the voice I've chosen as my seer. 'They never made the island. They are already in your future. The coordinators of good things to come.'

With that I lie back on my bed breathless and while dying of thirst the desire to live is the priority. The bed of nails has been upended. I'm lying on the heads of nails now. Frontal Lobe mumbles. Rumbles are spread out and become a series of hissing whispers. I walk sadly away from Peter Ilich's burial with a commitment that I will let his music live.

I just need the assurance that Marcia Font feels the same.

Blessed Teresa lights up the heavens with songs of praise for protein as all the lousy birds in Goolwa continue their avian screeching. The lousy Santa Christs also screech in time to the godly music. Some feel compelled to cross their legs but still manage to carry the rhythm. Many are not sure whether it's a case of infectious laughter or an infestation of physical theatre. You can't always laugh when to screech seems to be the consensus.

The Santa Christs remove the mobile phones from their hats. They wipe pelican spew on their clothes and shake as much residue from the insides of their hats before placing them back on their heads again. They open the mobile phones.

They all read the same SMS:

THIS PHONE IS THE PROPERTY OF MARCIA FONT.

A puff of wind sends a communal emission through the avenues created by Santa Christs and pelicans. Irritable snow flies chaotically from tree to tree screeching in new decorations. Bolts of lightning spin a Bethlehem stable around a great Southern Cross. Golda urges the holy choristers to ascend forever. Fish fly feverishly and attempt a scratch from the tails of others swimming in the opposite direction. The lung fish outside the gate blink in the pouring rain and see what is foretold. They see the A380 and its amphibious capabilities. They hope that a new adaptability has usurped ego, power and their dose of toxic masculinity.

Forked lightning illuminates the path of the midgets. Now it's the turn of the Santa Christs to move their heads like sideshow alley clowns. Some have to be restrained from swallowing mobile phones.

Pelican imprinting is a bug in the system.

The midgets have fully arrived. In front of them, leading the way like a drum majorette, is Marcia Font. She brandishes raffle ticket A380.

Thank God, she's here at last. Remember the Lamington Council grant must come out on top now. Pray that Cygnet Waterhole *stills all activity in Frontal Lobe. My sweat will become a drought breaker.*

'I heard this is a lucky number,' she says walking over to The Altered Boys.

'At last. You're lucky it's not chocolate.'

Marcia clutches the holy turds which flicker.

'I thought this was to glow permanently.'

'Bit of electrical interference,' the Altered Boys apologise. 'Once the weather calms down you'll have a permanent glow.'

To say that I'm somewhat reassured Marcia has fronted is an understatement. It wasn't a random phone call after all. I've talked this through with her. I want to rest but first I want the assurance that the cockatiels are safe. I send them a thank you. To the pelicans I award them medals that match their all-seeing eyes and to the fish everywhere I shed more of my scales just for them and to requite their inner amphibious cannibal. The holy party, beautifully indoctrinated in death as in life, I'm pleased I can recall and rely on.

And Golda, dear Golda, the life and soul of the party. Who would think that a transgender salmon could soar to such great heights, bring heaven down to Earth and allow 500 lost souls to find themselves happily lost and found as Little People ready to start rehearsing greatness?

'Believe that small is tall,' I say to myself. I thank Mary Virgo and

Mary Magda for holding the fort thus far. I know it's going to heat up again soon, I tell them. More printer cartridges, more paper and, yes, those sheep are editing really well. The pagination is right. We'll build better accommodation for you soon. Thomas Hardy will be happy. I'll have to learn both Tess's and Bethsheba's lines when his manuscript arrives.

Must remember this for the Lamington Council grant.

My breathing is shallow. The white light is soothing, I think.

Marcia Font turns to me and winks.

'Good one, Gabriel. Let's get on with the show.'

2: GOD, YOU'RE A DEVIL

As Long as You're Frank.

I TAKE the last of the antibiotics and cover myself from head to toe with *Caroline's Cream*, and salicylic acid. Every movement is another skin tear.

What will he think?

My face is almost blemish free. Will he read my face and concur about the rest of my body? And mind?

Psychotherapist?

I'm not visiting him in a professional capacity. I allow the intention of the meeting to filter through my body. I'm grateful I have both a destination and purpose. Point A to Point B is a relief. I can't detour. The effect of the antibiotics is a faint but bitter cud in the back of my throat. A universal sorrow for cows is considered as I slip into my car and fasten the seat belt.

Avoid milk.

Bathe in it if you like but don't drink it especially if it's from the melamine breed.

The excruciating agony of bending down and positioning myself in the driver's seat is beyond comparison to anything I've experienced. This outbreak over my body is the worst it's ever been. I long for the soft feel of feather after the scales of fish and reptiles drop off.

Will I evolve again? I can only hope.

Today I try to direct my mind along one track but the whys and wherefores as to the reason for my current dilemma lets rip with painful frequency. Some of the eruptions I brace for but most are unpredictable.

The slosh of the creams creates a buffer as I reverse the car. I'm a body inside another. A parasitic twin is my undercover. I try to do a quick rethink of how to drive with the least possible movement. A driverless car would be a wonderful choice right now. Somehow, I rise above the pain and measure my problem against the pain and trauma of others.

There's always somebody worse off, I remind myself.

Traffic lights that are familiar give me extra oxygen and a distraction from the pain. I drive on to meet the psychotherapist in the pub. As usual I'm doing everything to avoid being now centred. I'm driving there but I want to be there at this moment, have it over and done with and back home.

The outside world needs to be shunned. I'm no better than a leper. I daren't reveal my skin to anybody. Chronic and acute gets a fair exchange in my rabbly head. There is a reason for this and this is not the reason. The rush and flush of past behaviour inclusive of Russian roulette is part of the journey. What is out there is why I'm in here seems to be the entrapment I've opted for and remain shackled to.

But as yet I've avoided the tests which would give the definitive proof.

The final traffic lights on this epic journey shimmer in front. I pull up outside The Cathedral Hotel with the engine still running. I opt for a side street so that getting out of the car is not visible to passers-by. If I can get myself out of the car and walk a little the worst of the pain will have been dealt with. I can't imagine having to do much bending other than the elbow.

I reread the reply to my ad. It's been important to bring the hard copy. It means that my imagination will still be fed right up until I enter the pub and the Hyperbole Bar presumably tucked away at the back.

Specific words jump out. I wonder what the writer might have been thinking when he wrote them. There has to be something different this time. I catch a runaway thought again and focus on the cylindrical slosh of my body's grease gun rubbing against cotton. Cotton jocks, shirt and socks talk to my presence and translate the sodden body language so I can connect and feel confident. A soup of sweat and lotions trickles from my crutch to my feet to mirror the inside with the outside of my socks. My slip-on shoes carry the extra weight like something recently forged by a blacksmith.

Orthotics for a horse?

I grimace, hopefully for the final time, as I swing out of the car and allow my feet to take my weight. I'm early and so crunch away from the pub to kill the time. I don't want to be early and I don't want to be too late. The act of being, and in particular being outside, feels strange. It's a new world and a world I've just brought something extra into. I don't know how I've got through the last two weeks. I assume there's been days piling into weeks but all this measurement dulls in a haze of both loss and wonder. While the fever has gone the weakness is still palpable. There's something to think about now. But I half know a half truth and have been half treated for an illness which for all intents and purposes is a severe infection.

Mind over matter has juggled uncontrollably and continually with the mind winning most of the time.

But that's my diagnosis.

I turn to face the end of the runway and move towards The Cathedral. I don't rev up. Key words from the psychotherapist's reply refuel concentration. Measured steps try to pull my mind back into a steadier pace but any ability to sanction or curtail its march is impossible. I feel these two parts and fear that one of them will trip me up. The entrance to the pub looms. I want to retreat but it's my warts and all that has to be displayed.

There's no place to hide.

I wonder if I'll be able to speak, if I still have a voice. I've seen no one. There have been phone calls I think but the last days have been rather blurred and I can't quite recall who rang and who I spoke to but there is a sense of what I spoke about. It feels like salvation in a memory that has been retained or retrained.

Is it selective memory?

I push open the door with my right hand. Skin unhinges from my armpit and elbow. I brush and shake like a wet dog one last time before I enter. There is silence as the desiccated scales coconut the doormat and the sheen of the wooden floor is dusted white. No one seems to be around. A couple of bars open off either side of the foyer. I take some deep breaths and expect some kind of guidance to steer me in the direction of The Hyperbole Bar which is indicated by an arrow pointing to a narrow flight of stairs presumably leading down to a basement dive.

Expectation means that the current silence is noisier than real noise.

Standing at the top of the stairs I cast my eyes downward. My heart gallops. I brace for the pain of bending and stretching as I negotiate the steep steps.

Shouldn't there be a lift?

As part of this journey I've deliberately left my mobile phone at home. It's taken courage to rise from my bed but considerable guts to stave off the anticipation of clone fever. If I'm to speak with the psychotherapist I want to do just that without the intrusion of the avoidance mechanisms of the 21st century.

Eyes down, earphones in and tongues tied and swallowed. No.

It's time to breathe again. And I am here to speak. Not to have a conversation. Part of my general malaise is to do with meaningful people having conversations. I'm disturbed by those who have conversations but don't really talk. Don't say anything.

I wonder if they'll learn the art of speech again but this is not something that's talked about I often muse.

Holding onto the bannister I place one foot on the first step. It creaks its age and so does the next. The silence continues. Ahead are the bi-fold doors leading into The Hyperbole Bar. Through etched glass frames I can see shadows. The doors are loose fitting and rattle with my approaching footsteps. I'm relieved I'm down without too much pain though behind me is a trail of albino sawdust. I pause before placing the palm of my hand on the door to open it. I want to reread the response, to pick out the keywords to hang onto the turn of phrase, to do a final imagining as if planning the rest of my life from this pivotal point in time.

There's no going back. I have to enter.

Another world hits me.

It's a world of action and inaction. I reel from the contradictory sight. A number of tables and chairs are strategically placed around a small cabaret stage area. While most are occupied, not all the patrons are seated. No one speaks but for a moment I try to ascertain how the people here communicate with each other. A sea of dead pan faces swim in the shadows of a mirror ball. My eyes search the predominantly hunched over bodies for a face that registers the expectation of my arrival. My presence is ignored. Smartphones and tablets abound. They provide glue for the eyes of dead fish, and back and shoulder problems for the majority. Not to mention the preponderance of arthritic thumb and forefingers which resemble pig trotters.

I've walked in on a rehearsal. The movement of the patrons is stylised. My audience eyes pick out a couple seated at either end of a table. They text each other, having recently fallen in love with their new tablets. As I skirt the perimeter and head towards the bar another couple who at least are in an embrace, text each other over respective shoulders. They smile at the messages they send and receive.

Their fisheye lenses stare in developed death.

Around the walls of the dimly lit bar are a series of blown-up sketches of *Tom of Finland*. In these sketches Tom has discovered the *Narcissus Plus* mobile phone or for the most part his cock has. Advertisements for sales of *Viagra* are interspersed between Tom, his cock and his latest tablet or smartphone.

The tableaux formations drift and reform. Phone after phone discovers the latest version and draws the human forms in along for the ride. Lust is measured by the speed of a text message.

It's the new erectile tissue.

The lights dim further. A performer covered in smartphones mounts the stage. She starts lip synching.

> *Try to remember*
> *When I changed my gender*
> *And swallow, swallow, swallow.*

The sea of patrons stop and point smartphones and tablets at the stage. The phones covering Miss Communique light up and flash simultaneously. The queen of data picks a random phone and texts. She speaks as she texts. It's a relief for me that someone can speak. I look again and I listen. Alas her speech is lip synched too.

'I've just sent a text to one of you out there in Nowhere Land. Your treatment is about to begin in the Penis Punctuation Room. No phones allowed. Send your last text now.'

A young guy in a neck brace pulls out earphones and peers at Miss Communique.

'That's mine. That's mine. You called out my number.'

His voice sounds as though he's had a tracheotomy. Its amplification is accompanied by lights which flash around the Toms of Finland.

'Consider an upgrade to *Narcissus Plus*. Inconsiderate you and your selfies will not be outdone or your voice back.'

'Look, he can talk. Now that's progress for you. You'll enjoy your stay in Penis Punctuation.'

I wait for other verbal responses but Miss Communique continues her rendition of *Try To Remember* as smartphones and tablets light up and swoon. One by one she discards her devices on the floor in front of her to reveal a male physique covered in alluring tats and a cock to choke on. She straps a Narcissus Plus to her cock and whirls off the performing area amidst the applause of multiple flashes. The patrons slump in chairs and over tables. Furious texting starts again.

What am I to concur from all this?

Be less like them and more like yourself. Bet they're putting it on Facebook and Instagram. Narcissus Plus *has its work cut out.*

Still walking around the periphery, I realise that this brief distraction has prevented me from looking around and about me. For a mistaken moment I run my hands up and down my body checking for my own mobile but this action only serves to remind me of the tender skin in need of a complete repair job. I run thoughts through my body beginning with the top of my head and focusing on my toes as journey's end. I reverse the process as I edge towards the bar avoiding the amorous advances of a smartphone which attempts to massage my crutch. I'm filmed and messaged to everyone present. I feel naked without my own device, but Miss Communique with the last of her phones seemed more naked, I had thought.

The top of the bar bumps and supports my back. I wince, grit my teeth and ease around to face the barman who is plugged in to earphones. I point to a beer tap. I use my hands to indicate size, blush briefly thinking my hand gestures might be construed as a reference to activities in the Punctuation Room.

The desire to escape builds. Again, I think from top to bottom and reverse the procedure to calm myself. I can feel the occasional mix of broken razor blades and sugar fall from crevassed skin. The beer is slid towards me as the barman replies to the next request via text. I lift the drink and scan the bar. I wonder what a psychotherapist might look like. Now would be a good time to have access to a mobile phone but a true search and discover as in the old days is what I want and what I'm used to. This is not the time to change plans.

And definitely not a *Narcissus Plus* upgrade.

Someone has noticed me. There's no intrusion into my personal space by a device. The someone is sitting alone at the other end of the bar. My first impression is that this man knows this place really well. He seems detached from the activity in the bar yet connected to himself. He exudes 'my body is in this space and I allow it to be.'

A number of patrons swim by him lifting their heads in acknowledgement. He smiles at each individual but more often than not, the smile is not reciprocated as the owner occupier of the smartphone is drawn back into the crowd of disconnects. I don't want to stare but it's clear I've not been to this place before and so my search of the bar has been noticed the moment I stepped into this foreign territory.

The man looks at me in the eye from his relative distant space. He smiles at me and I return the smile. It's a smile I've always had but seldom has it been seen. I do a final run through of the mental notes and reread the hard copy in my head. I remember that perhaps I've just got to this day by luck given the last fortnight. That maybe I've borrowed a day, any day for the time being.

The desire to escape seizes me again but I've bought into this entrapment. All the embarrassing situations in my life have piled up and I want to unpick each one of them and resolve the feelings around them before I consider my next safe step. My heart beats solidly. The pump knocks the silt of flesh in outer arteries downstream. Bees, the carriers of pins and needles, have a double sting attached.

My ankles are concrete.

'Gabriel?' the man questions with appropriate volume for a private meeting in a public place. He gets off his stool and walks towards me. I think his voice conveys the sensitivity and awareness his profession demands.

At first, I'm taken aback that someone actually speaks to me. And I notice that the psychotherapist is unclad.

He's apparently without device.

'You must be Frank Ly. It's nice to finally meet you.'

I'm surprised how easily the words form and leave my lips. Again I allow one of my seldom smiles to shine. I pull my jacket around me and shake hands with Frank the psychotherapist as the patrons in The Hyperbole Bar continue their texting while ignoring their total being.

You Sure You're Being Frank?

I LET go of Frank's hand. A moment passes in which I quickly remember my lines before vocal calibration.

'I like what you said in your reply,' Frank says raising his voice above the constant replay of *Narcissus Plus* promos and blinking quickly in response to the ongoing flashes.

'Your ad stood out from the rest.'

I smile as if taking ownership of the feelings that allow a smile to settle on one's face and for Frank to see those feelings. I look away and pull my jacket around me tightly again. I press into the bar as I ease myself onto a stool. I try not to show the difficulty that this poses but am sure Frank has noticed. This man knows a lot, I think as I grapple with unbearable pain and reassurance at the same time.

'Suppose you wonder why I'm in a place like this?'

I attempt politeness while tenderly adjusting myself on the stool.

'Haven't had time to take it all in. Feel naked without my device.'

'I should have explained beforehand. I run a group for those with device overdose.'

'Device overdose?'

I listen intently and feel puzzled and Frank sees this.

'This is a workshop for those wanting to kick the habit of smartphone addiction. It's a six-week program where the participants are equipped with skills to reconnect with themselves again.'

'How long have they been doing the course?'

'This is their first weekend. Halfway through we block all phone signals.'

'Who thought of this?'

'I suppose you could say I was told.'

'Told?'

'Message from up above.'

I let the beer swill in my glass, give it a shake and stop just before it spills over the side. I want to hear more about this group but I want to talk with Frank. I'm taken by his presence and it feels as if I've met him previously. Perhaps in another life? Old souls meeting place? I want to know all about him, his past and his future. Part of me feels that this situation is a setup, that maybe he's dumped me in the deep end to see how I will react.

Do I want a control freak in my life?

'I'm sorry if this is a bit much for you. I think it eases the situation if there's a distraction. Makes first meetings easier. You can't say everything in a letter or a text.'

There's a cry for help deep inside. The ability to continually dull the pain is being challenged. I'm glad that there's an agenda, that for once it's being set by another person. I play with my drink again, take in as much detail as possible of the presence on my left. The clothes, the hair parted in the middle. A Modigliani portrait. He's not unlike Keith Urban, I muse.

I look around the room. The texting continues at a furious rate. The eyes of the dead fish occasionally blink.

This is an optometrist's goldmine.

'What happens in the Punctuation Room?'

Initially my question carries added volume but is more subdued as I lean in a little to share Frank's space. He smiles.

'I'll show you. Do you want to have a look?'

I nod apprehensively allowing Frank to sense my awkwardness. I follow him, gathering all strength to prevent more rips in my covered attire. Frank opens a door in a wall adjacent to the stage. I can smell incense and other fragrances. In yet another wall Frank slides a partition which opens into a dimly lit massage area.

Ricky, the winner of the Penis Punctuation is lying on his back. Warm oil dribbles over him to be rubbed caressingly by the tips of multiple fingers. Naked guys move around him kissing his oily body in between the touch type of fingertips. They link arms and with a wave of flesh move back and forth gently brushing against Ricky's body. Their stiff cocks are a conveyor belt which massage his impressive six pack. The glockenspiel of erectile tissue plonks. One of the masseurs stands at the front and manipulates Ricky's wrist which is clenched around his smartphone.

'Let go. Let go,' the masseur whispers.

The masseur's cock flip flops across Ricky's face. With every stroke a trail of pre-cum is left behind. I move around the perimeter with Frank who watches intently. The guys delivering the massage swap positions. They kiss each other and gently suck any cock that slackens. The plonk of well-oiled percussion resumes. Ricky moans. He drops his smartphone. *Narcissus Plus* blares frightening the shit out of me. My shoes are full of desiccated coconut but I'm aroused. The thought of a massage is an unbearable longing.

But no one would want to touch a body covered in scabs.

At the head end of Ricky, I peer in the dim light. His head is turned to one side. Pre-cum in the shape of a heart is on his right cheek. The masseurs begin a low chant. Individual voices echo around the room. The cock glockenspiel moves up and down Ricky's body. His own cock acts as a buffer to contain the melodic drone at its bass end while his nose supports the extent of the treble drift. Affirmations about love, forgiveness and acceptance accompany the slip, slop, flop.

Ricky is helped from the table. He is not fully cognisant. The masseurs kiss him all over and lead him towards an easel. He makes frequent grabs in the air. One guy holds his wrist firmly and massages his hand from the wrist to the tips of his fingers. Affirmations are whispered between kisses and sticky shafts. Pots of paint are manoeuvred next to Ricky.

'What's your favourite colour?' a masseur quietly enquires.

'Green,' Ricky replies.

Frank invites me to stand alongside Ricky. All I can think is that I'm confronting my pain. I've done everything possible to hide it but it's not working. The masseurs work their hands over Ricky's body. His rock-hard cock springs to attention. Affirmations continue. His left hand still searches for the familiarity of the smartphone.

Ricky's cock is dipped into a pot of green paint.

'Write what you feel,' another masseur whispers. Tongues and cocks steer Ricky towards the easel. *Narcissus Plus* screams the advantage of an upgrade as Ricky paints, draws and writes in legible cursive:

I am free to speak my mind.

Ricky is wiped, kissed and wiped again as masseurs unload on his relieved body. Frank looks at me and smiles. I can't look at him. The seed of my being needs a similar release but cracking clay disallows the experience of pleasure. Frank eases me back into the main bar where the texting continues. I edge myself up onto a stool unsure as to how I should feel or whether to say anything.

I indicate by gesture to the barman for another beer and almost repeat the same gesture to Frank. I'm still without words as if just culled from the patrons currently texting the bar. At the last moment a single word forms on my lips. I've lost the power of speech by means other than external devices. Well-practiced behaviour of listening, not speaking, and knowing my place in a frightening world is a time frame, thawing memory.

'Another,' I whisper as saliva moistens the petal softness of my lips. The fullness of both upper and lower are the blossoming indicators I want to reveal. The man on my left is a keen observer. He watches everything and misses nothing. He knows lots about me already. He draws me in close even though I want to slide away without him noticing, even though I'm not noticing too, it seems.

The rest of the bar is in deadly pursuit of predictive texts and mis-interpretations. An orgy is being planned as is another floor show with Miss Communique and her backing group, *The Dick Touchers*. Spotlights flash and dim, on lighting bars blurring the line between performers and spectators. The *Tom of Finland* posters are restless and spring to life blaring more information about *Narcissus Plus*. Secreted panels like stained glass windows either side of the posters reveal twelve well-endowed guys self-massaging with their smart-phones.

They're *The Dick Touchers*.

A sudden jolt shoots through my body. I prepare for the pain of more skin tears but this time there is none.

Frank watches Ricky at the bar. The other patrons dive around him desperate to communicate with him. The flash of multiple devices and the noise of texting challenges the piped music increasing in volume. Ricky smiles at everyone but doesn't respond in an expected fashion. I notice he pats his body and searches for his phone but then gives up. Frank notices this too. I feel as if I'm mirroring two people. That maybe I'm some kind of link to what is happening in this bar.

'There's been a shift already.'

Frank's words reverberate. They crunch in my head. Common anxiety surfaces.

Is he reading me too well or am I reading into what he says and sees?

That nothing is further from the truth is also close to the truth. I repeat Frank's words. They pulse and ripple deep into my body. Penis Punctuation is painting clearer pictures for me. The need to watch Ricky is compelling. I don't want to stare at him. But he's less desperate. I want to talk to him but I'm torn between Frank and Ricky. Provider and client clash.

Your thoughts are in tatters. It's all in your head now.

The weird feelings become realisations embellished in the metaphysical. The dual feelings offered by this thought must be embraced. I can't turn back. I itch all over. I want to scratch, to tear what's already torn with fingernails neatly manicured by contemplative chewing. The itching is unbearable. But it's a sign of healing. Things are happening fast.

Maybe my brain will tear. What's happening on the outside will rip into my grey matter? My head will turn into a coconut.

The desire is to get off the stool. I've left somebody seated at the bar. My shadow. The past me is still here and there. The last fortnight sends a pulse to remind me of apprehension about life and the ability to survive.

Even the desire to live.

The Dick Touchers alight from their stained-glass windows without a shatter. Miss Communique arrives on the stage once more resplendent in her devices. She starts singing Cole Porter's *I Get a Kick Out of You*. Every time she sings 'kick' a smartphone covering her cock lights up. The patrons flash their smartphones simultaneously. When Miss Communique finishes the smartphone addicts create an oversized vas deferens leading from the stained-glass windows. *The Dick Touchers* don hats with tails so that from the rear they appear to be a desperate pack of giant sperm. They pulse and force their way through the narrow path. Miss Communique rolls about on the stage using every available device to take multiple selfies. She starts into a new routine, bellowing *I Want to Be Felched By You*. The participants twist and turn along the outer skin of the vas deferens and they too take selfies as an adjunct to masturbation.

Frenzied, *The Dick Touchers* reach the stage and circle Miss Communique with their sperm headgear now resembling engorged quotation marks which flick furiously in all directions. They grab hold of each other's cocks and circle Miss Communique in something akin to a traditional Greek dance given the precision of the footwork and the movement of heads over shoulders. The music gets louder. Miss Communique springs up on the spot with her smartphones massaging texts all over her. Parts of words form smudged reflections on uncovered skin. She jiggles about the stage as *The Dick Touchers* break into groups of two or three to have sex.

I'm engrossed in all that's happening but still conscious of leaving part of me behind on the bar stool. Frank has moved closer to me behind my back. Miss Communique cartwheels amongst the cock suckers while the device overdose crowd disregard the vas deferens and bat away to their selfies' content.

Narcissus Plus screams every thirty seconds. Every Tom of Finland springs to ultra-life and showers the bar with scented cum. *The Dick Touchers* all want to be fucked. No one wants to top. Miss Communique grabs cocks and points them at arses.

'Take it or leave it,' her lip synch says as she removes a greasy smartphone from a Dick Toucher's flexible sphincter.

The headgear sperm flay about, their tails entangling in cords or pubic hair. *The Dick Touchers* not fucking perform a horizontal ballet and slide between the legs of those being screwed. Multiple orgasms, multiple selfies and hungry felching by the thirsty acrobats on their backs surround Miss Communique.

The twist and turns of the Greek dance resumes. Hands hold cocks. Tongues ravenously lap ceiling white sauce as it's expelled. Traditional Christmas puddings are forgotten. They're a thing of the past. The timing is spot on. Tops and bottoms kiss, lick and suck as they twist and turn in a crazed circle.

Miss Communique, now in the middle of this circle, has a prolonged ejaculation. She anoints all *The Dick Touchers* in a final communion. The last strands of *I Get a Kick Out of You* fade in as the troupe retreat to their stained partitions caressing the cocks of the participants as they exit. The tails of their headgear flick from side to side like dying snakes. Miss Communique throws a cum covered phone into the audience.

'Who's next for Penis Punctuation?'

With one hand holding his own phone a guy called Brian collects the slippery property of Miss Communique in his free hand.

'Take a picture of my phone with your phone. That's easy and convenient!' Miss Communique shrieks. 'How self-indulgent can you be? Go on then. Pump your stump. Enjoy your stay in Penis Punctuation.'

Everything seems to be over as soon as it has begun. The Toms of Finland play with their out of this world cocks in 3D. The *Narcissus Plus* advertisements are quieter, yet more suggestive and alluring. I turn back to the bar expecting the stool to be in the same place. I grab at an empty space. Frank smiles and shifts the stool back. There is so much to ask. There is still residual dread of asking the wrong question. I enter what seems a prolonged phase of castigation but there is lightness in my being. I send body detectives in search of tears and fissures, pustules and scabs. I wait for them to report back but in the meantime my eyes settle on Ricky who ignores the advances and directives of smartphones.

Although alone at the bar, he appears somewhat serene. My eyes turn back to the overdose participants. I wonder who might be next for the Penis Punctuation Room. More importantly, is there some kind of manipulation involved? Manipulation within manipulation. Frank Ly, the man to my left, needs to answer lots of my questions.

I feel he is hiding something.

Is this whole setup a ruse?

I'm unsure about what I feel.

I turn back to face Frank. The hum of phones and tablets is another world. So close and so far. The personal space between me and the psychotherapist is respectfully negotiated and agreed on. Frank smiles away. I go to return the sincerity that his smile seems to invite but at the last moment I look away.

'How are you?' Frank asks. His voice feels reassuring but I wonder if this is all part of the tools of trade that a psychotherapist would arm himself with.

'I don't know. I have lots of questions.'

'Of course you do.'

I recoil hoping that Frank hasn't noticed my reaction but he has and so this means I cease to fight further on this front. Frank shakes the hair drifting across his face and gently flicks it back over his shoulders. His trimmed beard looks the perfect fit for his face. I know the face. From where? I have seen it somewhere but it's a face that's hiding something. I'm sure he's hiding something. I want to leave and I want to stay. Suddenly I'm desperate. I want to find comfort in the past and freedom in the future. The present is too painful. There're too many cliffs.

'All this has blown my mind.'

'It's meant to.'

I look at Frank. My confusion is layered anger now. Do I want to reveal my real feelings? I think I've trained my face to show the pretentiousness of life and living but now as I recognise this, I want to show as I feel. The thoughts of years spin through my head. I want a real face connected to real feelings to be displayed. It might be the first time.

Frank waits for my reply. Frank has waited for me for a long time. It's a now or never encounter with the truth about my very existence. Frank is still smiling. Part of me wants to battle him. There's a power game being played. He has all the tools to win the game. The mind doctor has been doing it for years but I don't want to participate.

I put a face on top of a face and keep on moulding the contours so that what is seen by others is my supposed calm.

I forget what has happened to the rest of my covered body. The torture since the birth of dust over the last weeks. The agony of flesh separating from flesh. Of course I understand the layers of my face and facial expressions now. The crucifixion of emotions. It's all happening on my face as the division of cells shifts to the outside. I'm a prisoner of my face but this is what I show to the world. Soul, spirit and aura demand a channel to feed calm and knowing into my pores.

'Meant to?' I repeat as if resuming consciousness.

Frank looks at me. Long and hard. His eyes delve and discover me. I show him all I am. The pulse of texts and photos continues. I don't hear them now. They're mere background. I shift on my stool and look away. The incredible itching resumes. It spreads fast and returns as a faint contraction in my guts.

He knows too much about me without knowing me.

I look back at Frank with a face that's finally settled. I'm sure this is the one I want him to see. I'll play his game. This is the face I'll get him to analyse. To work out and comment on. To tell me all about myself. Am I expected to reciprocate? Will I feel confident enough to tell a psychotherapist all about him? Perhaps he is above all this kind of analysis. That it only works one way. That to work on others gives him sanctuary from others' views. I'm prepared to rewind. To look at what's got me to this point in this place. So that by being here, tomorrow and the following days will make sense.

'How do you know all this?'

'Your letter said it all. I read between the lines. You're suffering a fair bit at the moment?'

'I wrote that some weeks ago. I suppose you're right.'

I throw a querulous glance at the psychotherapist and consider that Frank is the wrong name for this person. The identity of this man feels not quite exact. Again, I have feelings of mistrust that I'm being taken for a ride, a long ride through new age supernatural explanations and opinions. My heart races. It has an uneven gait. The parasitic twin is suffocating. It has nothing else to feed on. I'll have to contain it within my own being. Dissolve and incorporate it into the preciseness of my own DNA.

'Was nice to receive a written reply. It felt genuine. You didn't have to say much.'

I allow the slide of a good feeling to create ease even though it's only temporary. I feel light. One right word at an appropriate time is all that's required. 'Genuine' sends rays, echoes, rings on the water and a gentle pulse.

Am I won over? Or am I playing a game? My game or his?

'It's a lost art. Too easy to text or email. I wanted to show I was serious. I need to take time. There's still a place for snail mail.'

Serious about my words I think quickly and want to grab them back and say something else. But I can't. A relationship has commenced, the kind that I want and have been longing for. My words will have to be my words and not analysed in so much depth. Set myself free. This is the journey I'm meant to be on. This person. This psychotherapist. This Frank character.

I glance behind me again. Brian has just finished his Penis Punctuation. He joins Ricky at the bar. The rest of the mob swarm around the two men, devices outstretched, wanting to capture moment after moment and not reliving the moment ever again. I estimate the number of people in the room to be about fifty.

Fifty men wanting to end relationships and start new ones.

The power of the mob frightens me. Everything is borrowed. Moods, emotions and thought patterns are a conglomerate. I search for an individual fire, a faint flicker, even the smoulder of anger. I can't see any.

Ricky and Brian smile and nod. The barman appears frazzled. Brian asks for a cider. The barman takes his earplugs out. He searches Brian's person for a device. Brian pats himself all over.

'I'm all lost,' he says. 'Have to use this from now on.' He sticks out his tongue and touches it.

The barman fills other orders via text. Brian points to the cider tap.

'I've heard this has quite a good taste but takes some getting used to.'

The barman nods but saunters about the bar with his head down and earplugs back in. He slides the effervescing glass towards Brian but his eyes and ears, unaccustomed to verbal requests, automatically search for the obligatory smartphone. I see all this and acknowledge the new discrimination.

Discrimination of the verbal.

The Coopers is relaxing me. A distant voice calls on me to be cautious. The bar is more like an aquarium. Everything swims. The dead fisheyes protrude more so. Some hang distended as if ready to drop on the floor. Slimy pearls to be squashed underfoot with the drying cum. I imagine the room filling with water and everything floating high, low or away. I try to make a brief list and categorise what and who should be in each category. I wonder if the Toms of Finland should be on the list but hope they'll cling to buoys and be rescued perhaps by Frank. He could do that.

I snap back into the reality of the Hyperbole Bar. Frank has turned away from me. He is talking with somebody and a couple of participants prevent me from seeing who it is. The barman readily serves the texted requests and scowls at me as he moves towards the other end. I swill the last drop of Coopers only to receive a smartphone up my front as I swallow. I want to knock the intrusion out of the way but instead smile and turn the other cheek.

Frank sees the infringement on my space and intervenes. It's then that I see who he has been talking to. Miss Communique is introduced to me as Adam Knight. We shake hands. I like this formal acknowledgement of another person. Less superficial than the email or texted 'hi.'

Adam's persona is in stark contrast to that of Miss Communique's. In the shadows of the Hyperbole Bar he tries to be as insignificant as possible. It's obvious he has a special connection with Frank.

'Adam is a pivotal part of the rehab program. He agreed to work on the concept from the beginning. We were able to get both health and arts funding to run the course.'

I'm all eyes and ears. I want to hear more about the funding arrangement.

'So what was the first priority? The health or the artistic side?' I ask, pretending interest but keen for clues for an obvious successful grant application.

Again, I try to reclaim spilled words. I know how important a community health initiative would be viewed by the Arts Council.

'Health. Programs that focus on device addiction are all the rage. Then we have to reach the target group in a novel and innovative way. The LGBTIQ+ community has special needs and anything that can be done to enhance the community's well-being is a positive.'

'Oh.'

Frank sends me a look I think might be a suggestion of minor irritation. I allow this feeling to wash through, mindful of including Adam Knight in the conversation.

'It's a one off at the moment. If it goes well we may apply for ongoing funding to run it again. Lots of evaluation to do.'

Adam downs the last of his beer and goes to move away from the bar.

'I'll make sure everything is packed up by midnight, boss.' He smiles making sure to include me in his parting glance. 'Nice to meet you, Gabriel.'

Smartphones hum and flash. An involuntary ballet over chairs and tables stops and starts. Now and then I observe that some of the participants use their other hands to operate their smartphones and tablets. Glued wrists free of sliding and texting are held in the air and tilt back and forth like origami birds discovering the freedom of unexpected flight. The birds flock in a circle with their device-less hands held high while opening and shutting in unison.

As if responding to a similar cue around the walls of the bar, the Toms of Finland stretch their hands behind them clasping their mobiles. They lean forward just inches above their throbbing cocks. Their mobiles flash and spark. *The Dick Touchers* are revealed concealed behind their stained-glass partitions. They too, irritated by their encumbrances, tie their tablets to the tails of enlivened sperm hats which spin slowly at first but gradually gather speed.

Gone are the circus girls with the multiple hoops for here are the men with sperm mobiles.

Neil Diamond starts singing *The Windmills of Your Mind*. While I watch and feast on the multiple images of devices challenging dicks, the lyrics of the song has a peculiar resonance. What I see and what I hear is hypnotic. I have received an implant. The sound and images spin through my own windmills. The Toms of Finland make sperm halo smoke rings. Their scented essence drifts through the bar. Miss Communique places herself in the centre of the origami birds. She gropes and fondles cocks and kisses the origami flights of fancy. The music volume is turned up as Miss Communique synchs. There is a combined sense of loss and beauty. Origami birds make a grab for their phones but the glue has been transferred to non-dominant hands.

Tears and tears.

The latter is mine and now the former is mine.

The pain of relinquishment is observed.

There are no dry eyes.

The walls of the Hyperbole Bar revolve. *Narcissus Plus* promos are desperate to perforate but an increase in Neil Diamond's volume means their message is almost inaudible. Miss Communique remains in the centre of the origami flight pattern. She continues kissing multiple birds encouraging them to keep on flying. She urges the circle to reverse while keeping the delicate birds in the air. As the music fades, the circle begins to break up. The birds limp back to tables and chairs taking their human puppeteers. Scissored arms flap and grab. Devices are punched back into dominant hands with the aid of dead birds. Toms of Finland resume individual poses and *The Dick Touchers* flaccidly resume neutral positions within the confines of their stained glass.

As if taking advantage of the silence, the *Narcissus Plus* ads scream one last time. Their citations are filled with trepidation and few options. It's a feeding frenzy for them. The vultures of communication are waiting to prey on the disempowered. Miss Communique watches this as she leaves the floor. She turns and looks at Frank. The look seems to suggest that there is still a lot of work to assist the participants beat the habit. I'm again mindful that I've allowed myself to be caught up in an act of healing. Time seems to know no boundaries. The emotions and feelings are everyone's. To disconnect so as to properly connect screams. My own journey has seen its direction. The signposts are everywhere in the bar.

I turn back to face Frank. He watches me but again I jostle with feelings of entrapment. Perhaps I really am part of this psychotherapist's experiment. Mind over matter does count.

'Would you like another?' Frank notices my glass is almost empty but the need to be alone is overwhelming.

'Thanks, but no thanks, mate.'

I'm pleased there's no analysis of the words that leave my lips and there's no recall. I've inserted 'mate' as part courtesy and part potential endearment.

'I think I might head off soon. Haven't been all that well lately.'

'I know.'

I look at the psychotherapist querulously. A hint of unspoken accusation rises inside me. I want to ask the obvious question and I do.

'How do you know?'

'You'll see in time.'

I'm about to continue asking the obvious to keep on continuing down the path of logic. I take a deep breath and feel all the space around the spoken and the unsaid. Eventually I speak.

'There's something about you. About all this.'

Frank looks at me again. 'And I know there's something about you. Something any bloke would die for to find out.'

'We'll meet again soon,' I respond hastily as if a rare moment might be lost forever.

I'M convinced I'm my normal self once more. I need to celebrate. I jump in the car, tear up the driveway and disregard anything on the footpath as well as the 50km speed limit. I hit Shepherds Hill Road and increase speed. This is my road and everyone else should look out. I change lanes frequently without indicating, wind down all the windows and scream. SUVs think it's their duty to overtake me but at 65km/hr they hold back to allow my affectionate rust bucket the right of way. I hit the Woollies roundabout. Both hands are off the steering wheel.

Woollies. Sheep. Sheep. Woollies. Of course.

Back down Shepherds Hill Road I speed. As cars pass me travelling in the opposite direction my arms are still dancing above my head. I pull faces and bleat. The great stare ahead with unblinking eyes is my favourite. I continue to chop and change lanes. My car is a pair of scissors. The bitumen a jigsaw to be cut and reassembled. A real live madman is at the wheel.

Or one who's had a mutton seizure.

At the bottom of the hill I'm forced to wait for traffic lights. I look for sheep. I continue bleating. Ewe to lamb and lamb to ewe. I've been a decoy for sheep many times. The perspicacity of me baaing is a testament to good memory. SUVs either side have drivers on mobile phones. Where are the cops when I want to round them up? I pretend I have a phone and speak in loud gibberish. The tone I convey is annoyance.

'Blendry forrobaound masitookla, Moses!' I yell into one hand as the other gestures above my head. My fingernails hoof the roof of the car.

I catch looks but I continue a heated rave, get out of the car while yabbering into my palm. I dance around the car, bending and twisting, kicking the rear bumper bar. I give frequent fingers to the horn blowers piling up behind me. One last circuit and I jump back inside. Quickly I change lanes and do a U-turn back up Shepherds Hill Road.

The queue of drivers left behind continues to sound their horns. The lights change to amber. Some vehicles spill across the intersection copping horn abuse from traffic that now has the right of way. I pull over to the side of the road, get out of the car and have another animated conversation. I attack the car this time. Bonnet, hatch and windows receive equal treatment. A few more dents and scratches ensures my own set of wheels now looks balanced. I bleat repeatedly. Ewe, ram and lamb get another practice run. The wether is overlooked but not for long.

It's wool orchestrated melancholy.

'Blendry forrobaound masitookla, Moses! Be Toyota's Dame Edna, Moses!' I yell while trying to mimic a jumping sheep up the race. 'I once pulled the wool over my eyes but now I see!'

Woollies. Sheep. Sheep. Woollies. Red Sea parting. That's it. Thanks, Moses.

Apparently there are roadworks. Cars are piled up both directions. I can't see what the holdup is. Drivers get out of their vehicles and ring and text. They all want to accuse the person in front. And now I'm stuck in the middle of them. The uphill traffic begins to move slowly. I can hear dogs barking and the whistle of commands. Impatient drivers take to horns again. The cacophony is unrelenting. Surely the police are here to see what's going on?

They should arrest those for disturbing the sheep.

Finally I reach the fresh food people. I avoid the roundabout and go to pull into the overflow carpark. But I can't. They're everywhere. The sheep. The SUVs. The not so happy people trained to phone. Trained by phone. Both car parks are full. Full of sheep and cars. People with trolleys. Sheep in trolleys. A truck with a cherry picker swings into action above the shops. A sheep farmer whistles several obedient dogs. Caramel and chocolate Kelpies run in and out of the supermarket and specialty shops anticipating the command to round up all the woolly ones. Traffic is at a standstill. All fresh food is tainted. The smell of the country has hit the suburbs. The green pearls from past foraging is loose shrapnel, the spent wisdom on cement and bitumen. Sheep are on boots and bonnets. In boots and passenger seats. Kids want to ride on the backs of ewes as they rush out of the supermarket in search of lambs. Marked down greens dangle from many woolly mouths. Rams demand the loan of trolleys and butt resistance.

But the stoic wethers lead the way. Their compliance is orderly although they balk at the supermarket's automatic doors. The doors leading onto Shepherds Hill Road are locked. Police sirens blare.

The dogs occasional barking is a rallying sign of earnest work. They watch their master overhead swing across the stationary vehicles high then low in cherry picker genuflect mode and wait for his commands. Around me the effects of sheep is seen and smelt. My car is the only unblemished one by woollies.

People are advised to stay indoors or lock themselves inside cars so the sheep can be rounded up. But more pour into the carpark from the opposite end. The sheep obey commands but not so the people who slip and slide in the supermarket which now resembles a holding pen. Sneakers claim the space where cloven hoofs trod, stilettos squash the currants. The farmer speaks with the police officers gathered below. The mob of sheep continues to grow. The gridlock of cars extends from bitumen back to paddock.

Away in the distance overturned semitrailers jammed with sheep block major roads. Some poorly cut wethers unfurl banners which read, '*NO MORE LIVE SHEEP EXPORTS! INGEST AN INSECT FOR CHRIST'S SAKE!*'.

Single lines of sheep work their way to Woollies. Megaphone diplomacy is vital.

And still the sheep arrive branded, refugees escaping drought, the holding pens and the abattoirs of the Great South Land. The farmer whistles his dogs. The faithful Kelpies begin to work the mob onto Shepherds Hill Road. A few stragglers rush to join the woollen sea, forming a tidal wave down both sides of the busy road.

Kelpies perform frequent miracles by walking on wool.

Moses now. Bring your staff.

I get out of my car. There's a rumble of thunder, and lightning cuts the black cloud dough choking the nearby hills. All around me people are clasping their hands together and staring at the cherry picker. Some are courageous enough to get out of their vehicles and fall on their knees in adoration. The cherry picker is lowered. There's a final whistle from the farmer, a gust of wind, but when I look again, Moses hops off the back of the cherry picker with his staff.

'My Lord. It's Moses. I don't believe it.'

The whispers snake through the praying crowd. For once I'm not afraid to listen to private words in public. I'm not prying. No one dares to flash or text.

'Then Moses stretched out his hand over the carpark, and all that day the Lord drove the sheep back with a strong east wind and placed them on the footpaths. The sheep were divided into two flocks and the SUVs went through the mob without further hindrance, with a wall of wool on their right and on their left.'

On the footpaths either side of Shepherd's Hill Road, sheep are standing on their rear legs. Some are knitting quilts. All of them are wearing red ribbons. It's the 1st of December of course. Several Dorset rams hold placards aloft.

Wool yes. Mutton No. Get Your Protein from Your Groin. Nourish a Nit-picker. Don't Press my Mutton.

The Kelpies assist the police with the movement of vehicular traffic and fence the flock by patrolling up and down the road. Although there is a speed restriction I manage the standard 60 km/hr. I wind down my windows and wave to the sheep.

Moses uses his staff to do a bit of pole vaulting and to direct traffic. I drive through the sheep sea. Everything is moving faster now. The tide has turned.

'They'll soon be back to relive the first invaders on Shepherds Hill Recreation Park,' I bleat softly.

Yes, I'm my normal self again, I remind myself.

I turn off the road leaving sheep to follow sheep.

I COUNT the days without antibiotics. My fridge is full of yoghurt. From today I will eat sensibly again forever. The all-yoghurt diet will dominate my life. The all-cake diet has failed and so has the breakfast with scalded cream and dinner with 500 grams of milk chocolate.

Out the back door I slip to confront all the jobs that have to be done now or never. The garden is a mess. Where is my magic wand? Shouldn't I be companion planting with every vegetable under the sun? Bugs have attacked everything. I consider feeding yoghurt to leeks and lettuce. Strange as it seems I'm looking at the garden for the first time. I've just moved here. I turn to look at my house. How did I get here? Familiarity cries inside me as does a sense of order and the energy to multitask and complete those tasks.

The thought of having the ongoing support and help of a partner crosses my mind and scales my body. Recent weeks have brought on a shift. I haven't time to fall in love, to use family as an excuse or reason at every moment, conscious or unconscious. There is no poor me. I'm alone in the world. I want my own life. I'm greedy for this life and not that life. The seesaw of existence is in my face. I've lost a lot of weight. Hooray. It's not the way to lose weight but I've lost it anyway. Maybe the all-cake diet can be resumed.

I have a bit of a sweat again. I remove my jumper only to put it back on moments later. I shiver. Something's not right still. I let this thought pass quickly but register its presence. Two sets of scales juggle. One is my clearing skin with all its pink newness, the other an unknown intruder.

The shivering continues in the shimmering of the sun. I go back inside. There's work to be done and a need to sift the confronting challenges so that I complete the most important jobs.

The diorama lies waiting on the table. It has a disability. It's fallen from grace just moments from completion and been played with by Liberace who now tiptoes on the piano either attempting or adding to my Russian blues. But I will rebuild it bearing in mind the importance of a balanced diet.

The urgency to focus is overwhelming. Within the confines of the all-yoghurt diet I hope I'll discover a rhythm and to confront the most important issues in life. But it's a day of daze. The flip flop of past, present and future is desperate for an anchor. I start to resurrect the diorama. Somehow what's important floods back. I seem to remember bits and pieces of the past two weeks but an inner strength has got me this far. The shivering continues to come and go. It seems to be a deterrent to a desire to ascertain a clear path. As I proofread my life sentence I can see an end point. It blurs and shifts but I can see it. This has never happened before.

And it urges me on.

Liberace winds his way around my legs creating seductive music with his asthmatic purring. He looks at me as I desperately try to reassemble the diorama. The agonising cry for the creative input that warrants attention to detail dominates. Windows, doors and walls are obstacles. I search for hidden truths. I redesign history and construct bits that work as I leave the diorama and strip my bed. I look for dates and times to confirm the present. My hard-working self would benefit from another pair of hands but I doggedly plough on cleaning the house. I lock down all intrusions and concentrate on one thought.

I hate the scattering of energies that has confused my *Hansel and Gretel* pathway home.

Sheets are shrouded into the washing machine. I bring on the noise of agitation. There is progress. Life is being created clean and new. Out comes the vacuum cleaner. It sings to the washing machine. I hear and feel dual vibrations as I suck up dry skin. The yoghurt diet should go. Dairy is bad for the skin. I imagine the scales turning to yoghurt as I vacuum and receive an electric shock. It's not the kind of therapy I require.

But what if I were to open the fridge and there was a cow inside?

I undo a tangle of vertical drapes to remind the sun to warm me on the inside. It does so. This house starts to look familiar. I'm an efficient family of one. I pray internal thanks for the skin that has healed and has been vacuumed up. Grandparent skin, parent skin, my skin, baby skin.

All my inherited epidermis needs acknowledgment.

Empty the vacuum cleaner on the clover. It'll get a kick along and the Guernseys won't feel ripped off in Mount Compass.

Half complete with physical tasks, I return to the table. I drink a litre of filtered water and contemplate the effects of bombs on my past creation. How many times will I have to rebuild my life?

To start again.

I wonder if in a past life I forced people from their homes, to flee their homelands in search of safety. All those families polluted with religion escaping others polluted by religion. Over the last few days I've had to confront and learn quickly. To know that all the answers in the wider world are the solutions I seek within me. I carefully glue and cut trees around a waterhole. The odd sheep grazes away from the main flock. Am I that sheep? The bulldozer is working hard clearing the ground for the stage.

Sense returns as a true partner to my unflinching desire to complete a bigger picture. Liberace further demands my attention. I demand my own attention. Lamington Council Grant Application. I search for it and find two hard copies. I read the closing date. It's in less than a week. What day is it? I freak out again. I don't know what day it is. Reluctantly I turn on my smartphone which I've had turned off for some time. The battery's flat. I do a recharge.

It's the 1ˢᵗ of December.

Why don't you wear a red ribbon?

There's a pile up of messages and emails. I don't want to read them. A thought gets in my head that I don't know how to use a phone. I've had one for...? My home phone is more real. It defines me. I want to communicate with anybody who wants to talk with me this old way. I, the master and mistress of scattered energies, wants no more smart technology. My idea of a clever country is not tied up with the distraction of the latest upgrades.

I choose an innovation of my psyche first.

I panic. What if I can't remember what I've done for years? When did I last do an upgrade? Was it when my skin took flight? The amber light shows my phone is charging. Lamington Council needs to be the main focus.

The washing machine has finished and I may need to vacuum again. On the table the temples on the diorama are being restored. The bulldozer has cleared a space for the stage. There's a dusting of coconut around my feet again.

But it's all or nothing for the Lamington Council grant.

Marcia Font is coming tomorrow.

A Manger Nearby.

THAT rare feeling of exhilaration has hit me. I take it all in as I climb Willunga Hill. To reach the top will be an achievement. I urge my four wheels towards Mount Compass. Names are pivotal. There's balance in them. Scales of measurement. Scales that have been discarded.

Is this the new me?

One who has finally chosen the right direction? Both fish and snake compete for land legs.

His voice had that immediate connection and reconnection after the Hyperbole Bar. I plunged into disbelief that he would ring. I didn't count the days or hours for him to make contact. I wanted to remove him from my mind. The 'been there and done that before' scenario was not something I wanted to entertain. I could have rung him but I didn't. But he rang because he wanted to and all I could think of was to rush to the reaction wardrobe and select the glowing all over feeling.

I was and I am ready for a new direction.

I stick to the left lane. I have so much to process. If there is an adjustable headscarf nearby, I'll grab it and put it on, so that things I need to discard can be eradicated easily, allowing the good stuff to settle.

The look will be part apiarist and a tad Katherine Hepburn.

I've watched the phone and hated myself for wasting the hours. Looked at clocks and calendars and confused myself with time. Little wonder that the old unresolved issues of past experiences still found a way to surface. The wishing and wanting, the waiting and hating was a wedge.

Is a wedge.

But I can see it now as I allow more of myself to represent the true me in the present picture. The drive helps.

Frank has given clear directions. Mount Compass, the delineation between town and country. The Murray Mouth filters my thoughts. I think how reality will be daydreamed when I eventually see it. Now as I approach my destination I try to piece together elements of the last meeting. It's important that he sees my best side, I repeatedly tell myself as if ongoing grooming will hide the blemishes I don't want to confront. I hang onto his voice, the smile and the Keith Urban image. I try to process everything from that day while in the company of the smartphone addicts.

I turn off the main road and soon I feel the rumble and crunch of gravel. Some of it hits the bodywork and windscreen and I curse the need to treat another outer shell.

Psoriatic duco.

A corps de ballet of Hans Heysen gums hold their position either side of a stretch of road. Light and shadows come and go so quickly that it feels as though day is yielding to night in the tropics. My eyes blink frequently adjusting to this eclipse. I'm on the watch for a turnoff. I need to look for a sign. I've memorised the directions. The last of the trees has passed. Daylight has resumed. There's a bend ahead and I'm starting a dip towards the coast. I catch a final glimpse of the stand of *Eucalyptus arabesque* in the rear vision mirror.

The psychotherapist has a property.

So he's not just into fixing minds?

That wardrobe of selections demands a final choice so I can arrive calm, orderly and with an ability to reciprocate what I've previously received from him. But it's still terror. I'm not good enough. It'd be easier to turn around and go back right now.

If there was a cliff ahead would I drive over the edge?

Do I deserve the pain of a constant rerun? I don't want to present failure when the frustration of an unrequited vision demands my delivery of the artistic goods. I do a final reconnoitre with the residue of agony and put up a wall. In doing so the garb of the apiarist and Katherine Hepburn floats away.

I look for shingles.

Some swing in the breeze, others are weathered and the writing indecipherable.

Ahead a large white sign jiggles in the breeze. I slow down. I look for other landmarks mentioned by Frank. The two Palomino ponies are on the other side of the road. Their galvanized shed shelter is attached to poles cut straight from trees. As I slow to turn into the driveway it's intrigue more than trepidation that fuels me now. I do a final quick comparison with the feelings of our first meeting.

I can't compare them. I haven't asked questions. I've just received directions and soaked up all the verbal information. I've left space for imagination and revisited the signposts as directed with my first Frank connection.

I'm going forward. That's what matters.

As I enter the scoria driveway the shingle waves me on. The words fly in my face as I try to fit all the pieces together.

A psychotherapist who does performance art to assist with smart-phone addiction?

A psychotherapist who raises chickens as a hobby?

I've arrived at Frank's place.

Through my rear mirror the sign '*CHEERFUL CHOOKS*' flaps back and forth.

A Matter of Cribs.

IT'S not quite the opening to *Gone with The Wind* but everyone is there to greet me. It's a perfect day and one just made for great camera shots. All that is needed is a branch of blossom to drop across the left of screen. I need an upmarket car but those gathered for my arrival are more concerned with the driver than the mode of transport.

Ah! Tantric Tara.

I get out of the car and cast my eyes over gardens and bushland. The delineation between both is unclear and the dozens of free-range chickens seem mindful of preserving the flow between native bush and a largely European garden. Frank is standing on the top step of a wraparound verandah. Several chooks rally around him while a rooster has no compunction about pleasuring a hen on the front doormat. Coition complete both ruffle feathers and wander off in separate directions to explore a world which although the same is new territory for a chook. Frank comes down the steps towards me. He flicks his fingers and two New Hampshire pullets are happy to land on his forearm expecting to be fed. Others alight on his upper body so I have to look through a boa of feathers to find the face of Frank.

The real Frank?

The sound of chooks can be heard from all directions. I hear them before I see them. A choir of egg layers increases its volume while rehearsing over and over. The chicken acapella is both arresting and soothing.

If the sun could have a voice Dr Chook would perform groundbreaking surgery to instal regulated clucks.

If only.

I wrestle as I referee a continual fight over conflicting feelings. Reality and imagination are poles apart. I'm trying to compare the Frank from The Hyperbole Bar with the Frank who has a shifting ruff of chooks eager for his attention. Frank speaks to the chickens as if giving a command to a dog. The chickens alight to explore their part of the Great South Land. Magpies and cockatiels screech in sufferance at those without a pact.

'Lovely to see you again, Gabriel.'

Frank grabs both of my hands in his and goes to embrace me but there is a special recognition of respective space. Instead he looks me in the eye and I reciprocate, knowing it's safe to do so. Roosters crow everywhere, trying to reassert order, dominance and acknowledgement of territory. Mock discoveries of insects by several cocks entice hens to rally around the male providers for sex and grubs.

'And you too.'

I smile at Frank after another quick appraisal of all that I can see and hear. I want to fit everything together. There is a moment of angst where I dip into the turmoil of the past weeks, the fever and the skin shedding. The challenge to my mind and matter. I can't believe I'm here and that a gentle quirkiness pervades everything.

It's all mirrors.

Part of me questions whether I deserve this experience. I want to escape into the past for the familiar and arm myself for hope. Somehow I manage to allow all this to either reside neutered or pass through me.

'Come in.'

Frank leads the way up the steps and inside. I turn around to take in the vista of undulation on one side and elevation on the other. Native birds can be heard carolling above the chooks. Some crows mimic the chooks.

Inside the sprawling mudbrick bungalow windows of all shapes are located in a variety of positions. Much of the hallway floor is glass. Chooks can be seen scratching underneath. Their beady eyes peer up as I walk through. I stop to assimilate all that surrounds me. Frank is aware I need to take time to gather myself. Part of me wants to race to his side and walk in unison. Another part is distracted by a series of pictures which have the same theme. Chickens feature in all of them but in a way that makes me think about not thinking at all.

Intrigue and disturbance makes me walk then balk.

The Hyperbole Bar floats back. I'm not prepared for other worlds. I'm in the deep end again and want to get out. But it's the light from every angle that floods into Frank's house. Flowers have been arranged in strategic locations so that their blooms are caught by the light and are refracted inwards. Unheard varieties of roses catch the light and splash both their colour and petal shapes. On the rooftop garden ferns and fuchsias partly shaded by towering eucalypts drain green and crimson splashes into an entertaining area where Frank is now standing. And above more chickens have birds' eye views of all forms of human movement housed below.

All this might be enough to absorb in itself but I take a closer look at the pictures adorning the wall. A first impression suggests that the paintings are old masterpieces. I look again. There's a similarity in all of them. I let Frank stand in the entranceway to the entertaining room while I peruse the pictures. I'm puzzled. Without close scrutiny the masterpieces could be any work of art walked past, seen and admired in private collections and art galleries all over the world.

I backtrack and examine the first picture. Three camels are drenched in starlight from the Star of Bethlehem. I look more closely. The centre of the star is an egg yolk. There are no wise men on the camels but on their heads perch roosters with brilliant plumage. All three carry embroidered sachets in their beaks for the Christ child.

'*Three Wise Cocks*,' Frank comments.

'Of course,' I reply allowing a smile to blossom.

More paintings catch my eye. Each depicts the birth of Christ from a chook's point of view. There are chook shepherds watching sheep. Angels deliver important messages to a Buff Orpington Virgin Mary resplendent with a halo over her comb. Buff Orpington Joseph and White Sussex Mary ride a donkey. An Australorp innkeeper refuses accommodation to a broody New Hampshire Virgin and her Cochin husband. I need an excuse to gather my senses so that I can absorb everything around me.

Frank lingers in the doorway. Above and below I can hear the sound of chooks clucking and the competitive crows of roosters. I feel safe in this environment. There is contentment everywhere. *I'm meant to be here*, is a good feeling that flushes through me.

I pray that it stays.

I catch up with Frank and slide past him to view the rest of the exhibits. A variety of sculptured objects are on tables and pedestals. All feature chooks in a variety of poses. But my eyes are transfixed on a huge painting that is strategically placed to catch the light filtering through a series of skylights.

Rembrandt's *Night Watch* meets Bethlehem chooks I think?

I almost trip because this painting seems more like a blown-up photo. Frank offers me a seat on a spongy comb red settee. Still transfixed on the image in front of me, I sink into the softness of the settee which slips and slops like a waterbed. I get up and walk towards the picture, stop and stare at the detail and turn back towards Frank.

'Who's that?'

'Me.'

'You?'

Is it a joke or disbelief? I question myself as to whether I really have fallen into a trap and am being taken for another ride. I don't look at Frank, instead relying on his response to become the soundtrack for an astonishing image.

'That's right,' Frank replies quietly.

Backing away from the picture I turn briefly to face Frank and allow my eyes to quickly scan the room for clues to substantiate the psychotherapist's claim. When and how are the first words of questions that are building inside. I sit back down in the settee feeling all the contours gently mould and shape my body. A couple of chooks peer through the skylight, acknowledge my presence and cluck a gentle request for me to speak to them. But it's the Bethlehem manger that has drawn me back to view its subject matter for further contemplation. The Bethlehem manger that has been given a surreal refit and photo shopped.

The Jesus story is being retold.

'My beginnings and my second coming all in one,' Frank continues.

Words are not sufficient explanation. The noise of chooks continues above and below. Their quiet interjections fit the picture. A larger-than-life black Virgin Mary Orpington fills the manager. Her halo sparkles. A white Joseph Leghorn looks on. He has just dropped some wheat in the manger. The Three Wise Cocks have alighted from their dromedaries and strut their stuff.

But in front of the Virgin Mary Orpington and recently hatched is a wet and slimy human Jesus. Part of the shell is still attached to his head and in time it will become a halo I suspect. I daren't look at the picture anymore, fearing it will come to life and the players might step out of the frame, wander around Frank's home and expect me to contribute something essential to their existence.

I'm not inclined to deliver or receive impending messages or explanations.

Restless from over stimulation I get up from the settee and walk towards the picture and peer at the Christ child. I look at Frank and turn back for an extended viewing.

'You?'

'Yep. Me.' Frank responds, watching as I try to comprehend everything. He brings out a couple of wine bottles.

'Rhode Island Red or a White Leghorn?' he continues. 'My own drop.'

'Oh, Jesus... Sorry. Red would be nice.'

I'm not inclined to drink a bit of Joseph.

My reply is rushed. There's no time for a double take to build politeness and mask an otherwise hasty response.

In the Beginning There was Marcia.

I'm wild and I want to be manic. The mania is to come later. The house is attacked from top to bottom. It's never been this clean before. I've got everything in place. There're a couple of stools nearby and a highchair. It's the little things that matter. I consider what part of me is doing all this. Is it the me that needs to impress? The me that's testing my health? The me that needs to feel comfortable with myself in order to be comfortable with other people?

She's little. I only need to work half as hard.

Immediately I castigate myself and set out to reclaim the last thought to enter my mind. An idea that's been floating for some time is about to be born. Five years of phone calls and coffees in the city and raves about life in general. Five years of meetings with funding organisations, asking all the right questions. Five years of getting knocked back. Five years of bitching about those who get the grants and five years of feedback that a computer spits out and tells you nothing.

And after all this time I feel as though I only half know Marcia.

Stop it.

I love her freedom. Her gutsy nature. The way she speaks up. Speaks her mind. And me. I've done none of that.

When did I last speak up about something that moved me?

It's little wonder that I should strike up a friendship with Marcia. I reflect on her stories about growing up in a small community.

Not again. Grow up.

Down the driveway I hear the earthy chug of a Kombi van. The dog next door starts to bark and this time it sounds as though it's never going to stop. The Kombi does a full circle and backs up to the front steps. I do a final rush around making sure that everything is okay for my little mate. I'm worried that some detail has been overlooked. I want to be discrete without drawing attention to the fact that a Little Person is coming to see me. I find a couple of foot stools and place one in the toilet and another in front of the hand basin. The table where I work has bits of the diorama, a couple of high-backed stools, cushions and chairs. I've positioned them in such a way they look as though they've always been there and are part of the furniture. CDs and the score for *Swan Lake* are on the piano.

The door of the Kombi bangs. There she is. The little dynamo struggles up the front steps like a puppy that's learning to explore the difference between heights. I reach the door before she has time to jump up and push the buzzer.

'Hello there, my favourite poofter madman.'

'Hello there, my non-lesbian midget.'

I bend down to hug and kiss. I want to pick Marcia up and hold her at eye level.

'Don't pick me up or I'll piss on your head,' she adds wriggling. 'Must use your loo. I'm too shook up with all the bends getting here.'

'The waterhole's this way.'

'That's right. I'll piss and drink like a cow at the same time. Better make sure I don't fall in. Waterhole is better than pond by the way.'

'There's a stool.'

'Step in or step on,' Marcia squeals as she butt kicks doors.

'On.'

I gather up the beginnings of the diorama and make my way into the office. Liberace is on top of the piano once more and alights like a Persian knight onto the keyboard. The sound of two people talking and not my own gibberish conversations with myself and the cat, disturbs his aural sensibilities.

'Coffee?' I ask as Marcia comes into the office. She climbs up onto a highchair and looks at the diorama.

'Please. Black.'

Liberace attempts to swirl around Marcia's chair.

'Are you okay, Gabriel?'

'What do you mean "okay"?'

'You sounded dreadful when I rang you last.'

I feel confused and panic. I can't remember.

When did she ring? What did she say? What did I say?

'Pretty crook a couple of weeks ago. I don't seem to remember much now. I had a fever. Bit delirious for a while. Fine now.'

I redden but nothing can hide the eventual whitewash of my face.

I break off to make the coffee. The beat of a hidden thump directs me to re-examine clocks and calendars without me knowing. I pull back and try and empty my head so I can fill it with nothing other than Lamington Councils and waterholes. Marcia calls out from the office.

'Almost got trampled to death by a horse yesterday!'

'Oh.'

Marcia comes into the kitchen as Liberace springs back onto the top of the piano to escape or adorn.

'Took the lift in the Myer Centre. No protest this time but this bitch with a pram as big as a horse float took up all the lift.'

You are making coffee and listening. You are not going to worry about your memory.

'I got jammed under the lift buttons with this bitch's arse in my face.'

This is a great story. Keep making coffee. Don't panic. You're getting better every day.

'I said, "Excuse me but is that a foal you've got there?"'

I place mugs, coffee and a plate of biscuits on a tray and walk back into the office. Marcia follows.

'I'm getting a bit sick of these people with prams who automatically have more rights than anyone else. Think I'll have to get one. One that I can do somersaults on the handles. I'll get pissed and fill it up with stubbies.'

I smile. Marcia is what I need. Is all I need. Her performance art is a tonic.

'You must do it.'

'Now where can I get some live cygnets?'

'Cygnets?'

'Publicity has to start somewhere and some time.'

'Of course.'

I pour the coffee.

'Just imagine the headlines. Midget gets arrested with a pram full of live cygnets on the second floor of David Jones. Fuck off innovation and the clever country. Disturb the dullards with *Cygnets Down Under.*'

'Biscuit? Try one of these.'

'Hands!'

'Just for Easter.'

Marcia turns the hand shaped biscuit over. The palm is filled with a raspberry jam crater.

'My God, what next?'

'Father. Into your mouth I commend this wafer.'

I settle down facing Marcia. Wild ideas fly around the room. Liberace washes himself on top of my sheet music. The laughter is contagious. The ideas get crazier.

'*Cygnet Waterhole* then?' I say trying to suppress a barking cough and mindful of Marcia's eyes all over me.

'Yeah. Pond is too European and a bit twee. Want the Aussie connection to be strong but without any *Waltzing Matilda* crap and Akubra hats.'

'We need to sort out roles. I think where possible LPs should be in the production team as well as the dancers. '

'So, who is going to direct all this?' Marcia prompts.

'You.'

'But what are you going to do?'

'I'm happy to assist as a conceptual artist but I think we need the best creative team to pull all this together. People who've done this stuff before. Besides you've been in *Swan Lake* previously.'

'As the fucking court baby or the token royal child. I think it'd work best if we both worked on the concept and production side.'

'Okay.'

I'm relieved Marcia wants to share the load in this way, but the vastness of the project and the ideas scare the pants off both of us.

'Keep thinking big,' Marcia chortles. 'Aim for the festival. It's not some bloody Fringe show. God forbid that I have to see another face puller advertising a show for the status quo. Fucking family shows. Why not anti-family shows. Let's have demented cygnets that attack babies in front of contented parents.'

'We need a cast of hundreds.'

'Don't worry. I've been working on that. There's a large refugee community of Little People not far from here. I've spoken to them. I'm sure they'll be only too keen to get involved.'

'And a full-scale orchestra.'

'Plus the staging, sound and lighting will be intrinsic.'

'And all Little People?'

I'm a mix of excitement and trepidation. The ideas are big. The scale phenomenal. Five years of ranting and raving with Marcia now has to take shape. I'm scared as hell. I look at my partner. She's going full pelt with the idea. There's no turning back with her. When she makes up her mind it's pull out all stops.

'We need to start costing all this. I don't want people doing this for nothing. No volunteers. Total professional commitment from all involved.'

'Agreed.'

'So where do we do all this?'

'Shepherds Hill Recreation Park. I know just the spot. I've been looking at it for some months now. Feels like home to me. There're a few cows and sheep grazing from time to time. It'd fit in well with the atmosphere we're trying to create. But the big plus is the pond. We'll go for a walk later.'

'Waterhole, not pond.'

'How could I forget. Must commit it to memory.'

Christ. My memory again.

THE sun's brilliance ensures I'm in squint mode. Marcia hurries alongside as we negotiate the driveway. I slow the pace so that she can keep up. I'm used to hanging back and half sauntering so she is just in front.

'What's it to be? Parkinson's or Tourette's?' Marcia prompts.

'You do the obscenities better than me.'

'Okay. Start shaking a leg.'

The walk down to the railway station and across the tracks becomes slower. I try to gallop ahead but the little pony behind me snorts as well as ticks. I do a slow half turn maintaining a permanent tremble of my right hand. I spill water from my bottle down my front then drop the bottle.

'Arts Council arse lickers. What do they know about fucking water sports?'

Marcia retrieves the bottle and presses it into my locked fingers. Her ticks and other involuntary movements are a bit too balletic but her words colour the day. The pair of us are about to cross the railway line. A goods train comes around the bend. Marcia rushes onto the railway line and lies across the track. She kicks her legs in the air while continuing to scream.

'See! I'm the perfect fit, Gabriel!' she shouts lying parallel to a sleeper. 'Fuck the shit out of Jesus. Mother of Godfrey. Come on, train! It's time to kill my fuckin' tick tocks! Freight train freight train going so fast! Freight train freight train cover my arse!'

People on the platform are watching. I'm in no condition to rescue a midget from the oncoming train as much as I would love to make a silent movie. My shaking must continue. I plead with the passengers for help. Instead they take pictures. Marcia hops up just in time and sautés gracefully to the other side of the track then resumes obscenities and violent contorted movements. The siren on the goods train blasts continually. I watch out for my mate and catch glimpses of her between the carriages. The people standing on the platform are having unexpected conversations. I hold a shaking right hand with my left and transfer the tremor.

'Is she with you?' an elderly woman asks who has just arrived at the platform.

'Yes, she is,' I respond allowing the tremor to punctuate my reply.

'She should know better. She might have been killed.'

'Really. She's a stunt artist. Very skillful. A famous stunt artist. Some say she's a cun-cun-cunning stunt artist.'

'Gabriel, I'm still in one piece!' Marcia sings out, momentarily controlling her tongue and tick.

'It's shameful. I bet she's on drugs.'

'Actually, she has Tourette's Syndrome. Have you heard of it? She says shock therapy helps control it.'

Marcia paces and shifts about on the spot. She plies and sautés before losing her body to random jolts.

'Come on, Gabriel. Which way, cock sucker? Swan syphilis.'

The elderly woman joins the other passengers on the platform, shaking her head. The normal silence of commuters continues to be interrupted by an embarrassing hum of people talking for once. I shake and stumble across the track as the suburban train rounds the corner. Marcia rushes back across the line.

'Dare you to lie down. Go on.'

I drag my little friend to the safety of the other side just as another goods train approaches. I've never heard two trains sound their sirens together for such a long time. I'm glad the platform is completely obscured.

Afflictions are cast aside as we hurriedly make our way to Shepherds Hill Recreation Park. Fortunately, the dip in the road helps to hide the view of trains and passengers. A police car drives past slowly, turns around and comes back.

'Help me. I'm going to vomit. I'm all shook up,' Marcia whispers under her breath.

There are two police officers in the car. The one in the passenger's seat winds down her window as the car stops.

'Are you okay?' the female officer enquires.

'Fine. Just a case of late morning sickness,' Marcia replies. 'I'm so lucky to have such a considerate husband.'

The police officer tries to divide her sympathies between midget and apparent spew.

Marcia stands upright and grabs a tissue from her shoulder bag. I hold both of her shoulders for support.

'Got to rise above it all,' she continues.

'Thank you. We'll be okay,' I add, wanting to move on as quickly as possible.

The police officer smiles, having extracted and assessed a measure of normalcy with the situation.

'Take care,' she says allowing a smile steeped with puzzlement and intrigue to temporarily dislodge her authority. The car moves off slowly. I don't look back.

'No more stunts.'

'Oh, Gabriel, you'd make a wonderful father.'

A goods train rattles above but the embankment soaks up most of the engine noise.

Minutes later we're in the middle of Shepherds Hill Recreation Park. Gulf St Vincent stretches in front as far as the eye can see. A long finger of polluted cloud is stuck on the horizon waiting for an artist to brush it away and perhaps some of the suburbs underneath. A stack of planes line up to land as others take off into the north. I walk slowly, aware that Marcia is taking everything in.

'I thought down here would be a good spot. Have to get my sense of direction right. It's a northwest southeast alignment with the mouth and Mount Compass.'

'Mouth?'

'The Murray Mouth.'

'Of course. That energy connection is so important.'

I lead Marcia down a gentle slope. Soon open bushland hides the creep of suburbia although the hum of traffic is still heard.

A young roo bounds off into thicker scrub. Eventually the sounds of the bush dissolve the city's hustle and bustle. An underground spring has been turned into a waterhole for stock decades previously yet its shape as a large muddy raindrop about to splatter is still evident. Reeds have sprung up one end and the continual plonk of frog noise is soothing. Native ducks have interbred with common domestic varieties and colonised the occasional sprawl of blackberries and cutting grass choking one end of the hole. A feeding frenzy of feathered arses upside down on the water suggests the duck population has become an unusual form of water weed that is spreading out of control.

I walk around the perimeter and Marcia quick steps in the other direction so that we both meet up on the opposite side.

'I thought this side would be just perfect for the performance area and over there the audience could take advantage of the natural undulation.'

'Gabriel, this is wonderful. It's like a natural amphitheatre. Why didn't you tell me about this before?'

'Just wanted to be sure we were on the same page.'

We spend some time watching, contemplating and imagining together. Paths trodden by foot and originally by hoof are still evident as trails off into the bush on the southern and eastern flanks. Rabbit droppings and condoms, shoelaces and a pile of decomposing kidney shaped horse shit tell the modern history of this place. The quietness is intoxicating and Marcia's ability to be quiet when necessary is appreciated.

The pair of us walk back up on to the rise to the sound of suburbia and the shifting fingers of pollution now forming intestinal tracts in the sky. The wind gathers speed as we reach the main access track. A couple of joggers and people with dogs go by.

'Of course, there's got to be lots of permissions to sort to do all this, let alone the staging costs. Hope you're not getting cold feet.'

'Me? Cold feet? Darling, I'm hot for this one. It's amazing how lost in another world you can become in just a few short steps.'

'I think if we go to all this trouble then no expense should be spared with the production.'

'Agreed.'

'I don't think the original storyline and Tchaikovsky's score should be touched.'

'The venue and the artists will be the drawcard.'

'And people can get here by train, bus and car from different directions,' I stress enthusiastically.

'I've been thinking a bit more.'

'Don't stop.'

'Seeing those planes why not chopper the Little People onto the performance area at the beginning,' Marcia says, dancing in the gravel on the main access path to avoid a brown snake which is moving at cross purposes to her animated movements.

'Gumnut babies descend from the heavens. Watch out, Gabriel.'

'And of course, there's going to be a huge public liability component with all this.'

We walk and turn on the spot back towards the railway line but the waterhole and the cygnets are taking shape and have to quickly.

'Tourette's again?'

'I suppose we must. It's a matter of keeping up appearances from now on.'

And Shepherds Watched The Ugly Duckling Too.

I CATCH my reflection in the second glass of Rhode Island Red. I allow the wine its own tide to rise and fall as I hold the glass on an angle. Frank's face is mirrored and lost above in a sea of crimson as the coming and going of overhead shadows creates petals out of refracted flesh. My body gives into the massage of the undulation of the red comb settee while I let a rare moment of relaxation fill me with red too. I muse on the sound of chooks cackling, crowing and informing the world of their presence. The wave of their chatter, their appearance above and below helps steady the unstable meniscus in my glass.

Frank, sitting opposite me in a large off-white recliner, says nothing. I eye him nervously when I'm sure he's not looking directly at me. The notion of a different world outside is hard to fathom. I feel both lost and found. My own world belongs to another era. Part of me has been sent to Frank and part of me has stayed at home in a familiar space. However, it's a lost in transit feeling that overrides. The need to let go of the old and bring all of me right into Frank's living room becomes a priority. Beginnings have ends and ends have beginnings, I keep reminding myself. The sliding scale that measures that journey forces me into the present. The glass of red reduces as does the effects of the coloured tide.

Black Orpington Virgin Mary and White Leghorn Joseph can't be ignored. I swill and stare. Stare and swill again. I get up once more, wobble forward and examine the artwork for more detail. I look at the shell still stuck to the head of the Christ child and then on closer examination explore the baby's face for signs of the adult Frank.

'I don't believe all this,' I eventually say, my back to Frank.

'I know it's hard to comprehend. Even I have difficulty in reconciling who I am.'

'So you really are Jesus.'

'Yes. To put it more accurately Jesus recast and reborn.'

'Why don't you announce it to the world?'

'Too difficult to explain. There's a history and a future to be considered.'

Frank pauses for a moment and looks away as I position myself to face him on the settee. The noise of chooks intensifies. Chooks under the house scatter and those free ranging flock on the roof and peer through skylights. Shadows and clouds are created with wobbling combs and wattles darting and flicking above.

'You do have human parents?'

'Did. They were poultry farmers. Also raised show birds. Dad was always experimenting with different breeds. "Got to get close to your birds," he apparently told everyone. It's difficult to talk about.'

I watch the change in Frank. The cool and collected individual is now struggling to hold it together.

'Why difficult?'

The chooks above shake and flick their heads. Roosters cackle aggressively. Hens and pullets are relegated under claw or to the upper circle amongst ferns and fuchsias.

'Bestiality with feathers.'

Frank sobs. My mind wants to rush but it's as if I've been handed the baton of compassion, detached compassion, from the man given to sort out others' problems.

'My father was a fowl fucker.'

I look back at Virgin Mary Orpington and Joseph Leghorn. The birds appear to move. Baby Jesus shakes his head. Part of the attached shell falls off.

'It's hard keeping up a facade with this kind of history,' Frank adds.

Any disbelief is difficult to consider as I attempt to process Frank's story. All I can do is look and listen. I don't ask any more questions as Frank continues to unload.

'So much for wanting and having a normal family. When Mary laid me, the egg continued growing to the size of an elephant bird's. Joseph gave the rest of mum's eggs to other chooks to hatch. Apparently, I have brothers and sisters who I've never met. They're probably all dead now anyway.'

'What happened to your real father?'

'In and out of psychiatric clinics apparently all his life. I was taken into care. However, I did manage to have clandestine visits with Mary and Joseph when I was older. They were pretty old then but it was good sharing their roost at night. I was always discouraged from having anything to do with chooks. I was reminded constantly by my Christian foster carers that I started life as a devilled egg.'

Frank appears relieved he has shared his story. In the background a little voice wants to grow. I listen to it while silently observing Frank. I wonder who else has heard this story. Who else has visited Frank and seen what I've seen? Felt what I'm feeling right now.

'I'm so grateful you're in my life. You probably don't realise what you mean to me.'

I'm ninety percent dumbstruck but one hundred percent determined not to react. I sit in the relative silence of the family room and contemplate the clucks and crows infiltrating the holy space. Out of the corner of my eye I catch the eyes of several chooks as they move and shuffle into positions where they can all see Frank. Chook heads tilt one way and then another. Combs and wattles flick, interrupting a temporary preen. But chicken eyes zone in on Frank, chicken eyes that indicate something astounding is about to happen. These birds are well rehearsed or have an instinctive knowing of what it means to be both part of an audience and a performer.

More chooks arrive as if the fowl word has gone out for a special gathering. It appears to be part protest and part celebration. Whatever is to occur is out of my control and Frank's too. The Mary, Joseph and Baby Jesus painting starts to swell and wither like a fade out in a cinema shot. The widescreen ratio expands to CinemaScope. The manger images blur while the focus is adjusted. A large Bethlehem star appears from nowhere and not out of place given the sunlight that gets eclipsed by the flowers and greenery. The star moves around the room with a soft drone like hum. It hovers above the holy poultry. The centre of the star, a large yolk, bleeds controlled tears of yellow and orange.

Frank runs his fingers through his hair, allowing for the natural fall to settle either side of the part in the middle. He avoids looking at me and I sense he doesn't wish to be confronted with what he's going through. I'm expected to take control of the situation which is difficult since I'm the guest. The host has beckoned but my unease must allow for a practice run of divided feelings whereby I dig deep for solutions, right words and raw empathy.

'You probably think this is a setup,' Frank says, as gloom and a half smile seesaws in the light of chicken combs, sun and vegetation. His words, while meant for me, echo in the shifting void as if part of a sermon. The Holy Bethlehem chickens ruffle the occasional feather and dote upon the Baby Jesus.

'Should I be calling you by your proper name? Jesus or Lord?'

'Good God! No, mate.'

'Mate?'

'Mate.'

'So where does Frank fit into all this?'

'I only really remember Frank. My foster parents called me this. Apparently, they had backyard chooks and had to get rid of them before I arrived on the scene. Human Services thought there might be some unwanted imprinting that could stir things up. Little did they know.'

'Why?'

'I was too impressionable. Or perhaps buried memory might be awakened.'

Frank gets up from the chair and goes for more wine.

'Another?'

'I'll just sit on this one.'

I startle myself, thinking that any chook reference might be deleterious.

'Just be yourself. Don't worry about any slip of the tongue. What is said needs to be said. Has to be said. I'm so glad you're here and that we found each other.'

Words I've wished for and the words I've dreamt of make my Cinderella heart thump. Prince Charming wants me and I want him.

But fucking with the Son of God is a massive freak out.

I allow the settee to swallow me whole. Out of the corner of my eye I'm aware of extra movement within the Bethlehem picture. The Three Wise Cocks have jumped from their dromedaries and proudly strut towards the Virgin Mary Orpington and her Jesus chick. I hold my head to one side and peer towards the skylight, shake my head, blink and soak in the atmosphere of a December night and a day thousands of years ago and thousands of years to come. Still more chickens arrive as the Star of Bethlehem bleeds more yolk. Frank comes across to me with the bottle of Rhode Island Red.

'Sure I can't tempt you?'

'Why not?'

I wobble the glass. Multiple wattles and combs flick and shake all around like uncooked pasta shells in Frank's intimate Omnimax. The assembly around the Christ child gather in closely as the picture swells further sending bubbles and cracks into the oil paint.

'Glad you're seeing this. It's meant to happen. I was told when the right one turned up, I could see myself again.'

A silence takes hold. Chooks everywhere respectfully hold their gaze. I use my glass of red as a control device to activate the wall hanging but also to offer the faintest distraction possible to anything that could be perceived as real or questionable. Virgin Mary Orpington and Joseph Leghorn begin to sing to the baby Jesus... and the person sitting opposite me.

> *Little baby Jesus nesting in the hay*
> *Feathers beaks and wattles*
> *Without them you're ok.*

There is a shrill crescendo of squawks and clucks as the choir of gathered feathers fluff into song to join the holy family in Sensurround.

> *Loo la loo la loo la lay*
> *Spread the word that Christ is gay.*
>
> *Little baby Jesus nesting in the hay.*
> *Feathers beaks and wattles*
> *Without them you're ok.*

The feather choir keeps singing as the Virgin Mary Orpington pecks at the remaining shell stuck to the emerging halo. Joseph Leghorn gratefully receives gifts from The Three Wise Cocks. He places three nifty sacs in a cushioned trinity at one end of the nest. Dromedaries, bellowing cows and two donkeys with mange gawk at the infant Messiah. Virgin Mary Orpington looks at Frank amidst a mix of pixilation and oily celluloid.

'Ork, ork ork,' she clucks.

Frank's eyes well with tears. I want to avoid him. I want to pretend that nothing of what's just occurred has happened. The well-trained part of me doubts the motives and sincerity of my host. The highest host it appears. The CinemaScope image resizes as the Holy Family enters into another still life phase. The chickens above and below begin to disperse to the four corners of their known domain as the sun's effects on this part of Mount Compass begin to wane.

I skol the last of the Rhode Island Red. The thought that the wine might be spiked jostles with slight inebriation. But I can't fight. So war weary am I dealing with self-conflict that I have to marshal all energy to prepare for what lies ahead.

Frank comes and sits close. He looks down and then turns to face me. We hold hands. I can feel the pulse of two bloods thump strong.

'I keep thinking about the ugly duckling,' I hesitantly venture to say. Relative quiet resumes.

Let Us Mate.

EVERYTHING swims. The Rhode Island Red is well and truly in my blood. I'm close to Frank. I prefer not to look at him but peer at myself from near and far. The grateful distraction of chooks high and low means I can pretend to listen to their soothing molestation of an otherwise silent space. As I continue to hold Frank's hand I can feel his pulse pump its distinctive rhythm across the barrier of his flesh.

I turn my head towards the nativity scene and Frank's parents. I look for signs of life as if dying seconds are to be reborn again and again but the Bethlehem setting is the same as when I first saw it.

I can't rely on chooks to supply the only noise. The desire for human intervention becomes a priority. To be a prisoner of the quirky, the unexpected and the unknown fills me with trepidation. But I suspect the freedom I want will come at a cost.

'So they're here looking at you all the time?' I say bluntly. The effects of the red brings on an insensitive candour which I'm aware of but can't be bothered correcting.

'I wouldn't say looking. They're more a presence. It's rare they come to life like they did for you.'

I let go of Frank's hand. The unshackling seesaws the merits of freedom over an intimate bond. The former has been well practiced and while I yearn for the latter, the momentary grab at another way of life yells incarceration to a cellular memory. I succumb to the physical situation I'm in and try hard not to analyse anything other than being with another man. Being close to another man. I allow my hand to be both the cup and saucer in Frank's palm.

'Will it happen again? I mean now. Tonight?'

The challenge of listening to another person is challenged by listening to my own thoughts and words. Apprehension is stopping me from hearing, when the ability to listen, so unpractised living alone, is what is required now. My whole body is an apology, a maudlin apology. My host deserves better. I try to relax but there is an alert button that can't be switched off.

'Who knows? Then, perhaps I should know because I'm supposed to know these things better than anyone else.'

Immediately my eyes dart to the wall nativity and the slimy egg child peering out from underneath the developing halo and to the outside world. I glance at Frank and feel the warmth of his hand. I look away and feel the padding pulses that are his individual fingertips. I put eyes there to see the feelings. My senses are on overload. I'm all eyes but I feign passivity, remembering to listen. Frank reaches across and strokes my cheek. Again the tips of his fingers touch and talk multiple dialects. I try not to react but I'm on the threshold of a tingling that rouses the dead to life.

The sun starts to relinquish its hold on the summer's day. The residents of *Cheerful Chooks* search for night protection. Frank closes a series of screens once the sun bleeds into black. The various pecking orders can be heard juggling assertiveness for favoured roosting spots. As the screens close, a series of dimmed lights reverse the previously departed shadows. The wall nativity is lit from above and below. The red wine has started to wear off. I think about making a move and realise nothing has been mentioned about this since I arrived. I net any over analysis as Frank resumes his seat next to me. I feel his leg in parallel to my own and again his hand searches gently for mine.

'I'll prepare something to eat.'

'I really should be going.'

'Really?'

'I didn't expect things to turn out this way.'

'And what way is that?'

'I don't know. I mean I do know. It's all happening so fast and so unexpected. Sort of so good.'

I prolong my eye contact with Frank. He gathers me in his arms and we hold each other close.

'You're free to go and equally free to stay. I'd love you to stay the night.'

Frank smiles but I can see it's both an expectation and a plea. I play the game of the carefully courteous one to the hilt, knowing full well we both want to be with each other. I look over my shoulder in part reassurance that the wall nativity has remained in place and isn't about to spring to life again.

'Don't worry about them. It's sleep time for chooks. Nothing will disturb them. That I have on word from above.'

I'm not sure if it's my heart or Frank's. The thump is unrelenting. There are extra beats and missed beats, perhaps the confirmation of relinquishing old habits driven by bad timing. Our cheeks touch. Both of us try to pull ourselves in closer than the space allows. I move my head from top to bottom, temple touching my host. The togetherness of minds and bodies matters.

I unleash from Frank and half turn away with my head lowered as he goes up a flight of steps to the kitchen.

'Make yourself at home. Wander around. Pour another drink for us.'

I fill Frank's glass and carefully gauge the amount I consume. The trickle of the wine equals the constant trickle of uninvited feelings. I panic, visualising the problems and possibilities of making it with the New Messiah. With both glasses refilled I detour past the wall nativity and carefully look for hints and signs. I look into the eyes of the Virgin Mary Orpington, White Leghorn Joseph and Baby Frank. I'm convinced the eyes are watching me, that I saw Baby Frank blink, smile and then look most holy again or as much as a human bird baby can.

I'm drawn by the sound of crockery and cutlery into Frank's kitchen. The occasional muffle from settling chooks can be heard as well as the intermittent downpipe of their droppings. Frank's kitchen is an internal orchard. Preserved jars of fruit and vegetables add subtle blends of colour crammed on a wall of shelves. The soft purr of a fruit dehydrator is a supplement to the larder of life beyond the confines of... His House.

Frank sees me ogle at the wall of preserves including larger jars of Jerusalem artichokes.

'That's all the work of chooks. They don't talk shit but drop it where it's needed.'

He tosses a gigantic salad generously interspersed with a variety of pulses and legumes.

'The chooks like this too.'

I stop in the middle of the doorway.

'In here with this,' he continues, leading the way into a dining area with a skylight that frames the Southern Cross.

I follow and place the glasses of wine on a long table. I wait for Frank who returns to the kitchen, opens and checks the shelves of drying apricots in the dehydrator and returns with a meat platter.

'Take a seat.'

Frank picks up a pair of tongs.

'I'm afraid this happens to be a Woolworth's special. Couldn't come at one of my own.'

I stare uncomfortably at the leg of cold chicken on my plate and wonder if it should be buried under coleslaw.

'The body of Christ,' Frank says lifting his glass.

WE walk as one back down into the family room. Our fused bodies slump into the undulating contours of the settee before separating. Temporarily apart, I adjust to a different space to take stock as my eyes blearily wander to the nativity picture hoping that more information will be forthcoming. I look at Baby Frank and the man sitting alongside me. Frank's eyes meet mine, over which I have quickly placed a film of calmness. For some time I soak in his pupils trying to dissolve any obvious trepidation and to finally discontinue cantering thoughts. Frank's soft smile ignites a coy reciprocation.

'How are you?'

I quickly search for the right words thinking that all I'll say will sound unconvincing.

'I think I'm fine. Things are happening fast but I'll catch up. I want to catch up.'

My caution is constipating.

Frank moves closer. My eyes dart around the room and then blur. I relinquish the fear holding me back and then snuggle into the balmy warmth of man with man. The eyes in the back of my head pick out the nativity and the judgement scene it might be playing out. Baby Frank is behind me but the adult in my arms is the real challenge.

Oh, Hell. I'm in the intimate company of The Son of God.

'I can't believe this is happening.'

'What is it that you can't believe?'

'All of it. Me. Your family. Your life.'

'What you see is what you want to see.'

'Who else knows about all this? About you?'

'You're the only one who knows the whole truth. The chosen one.'

'Me? Aren't you the chosen one?'

I unknot our laced limbs and stare at Frank without a word. He is unperturbed and waits for more questions. An extended pause becomes uncomfortably long, exacerbated by the lack of words. Frank gets up to refill my glass. I feel a sense of loss, abandonment and also reconnection, as if the few short hours in his company have been the final discovery of lost soulmates. I'm happy to see him return with more wine but also to resume the closeness of his body again. What I've missed and what I've just found takes some adjusting.

My still unstill mind is both the devil and protector, it advocates a constant lookout for any signs of deceit. I allow a measure of naivety as I insert cautious observation of my current predicament. The safety of detachment becomes less of an option as I entwine with my host and reciprocate his touch and kisses. As yet my lips and his have remained unsullied despite a growing desire to connect. My body salivates.

The irregular plops from roosting chooks continue above and below. I'm wrenched with weird expectation. The extraordinary birth of Frank pushes me to release and halt any more foreplay. I wonder if there are any signs of Frank's chicken life hidden by his clothes.

Is he covered in feathers? Does he have a cock? Perhaps it's just his pubic region. Will I grow feathers? If I kiss him will he peck?

The softness of long-lost lips worm together excited by the transfer of the products of two clitella. Frank extends the line of his lips towards my cheeks with soft kisses petalled in spit. My body bursts with the dual partnership of strength and gentleness.

There's no differentiation between the Son of God and this man of passion.

Frank unbuttons my shirt and slips one hand inside. I feel the miniature moss cushions softly burrow and finger towards my neck, under my arms and then circle and cup my taut nipples.

My heart pounds in competition with heavy breathing. I wonder at what point I might become active or remain passive. Thinking about this ascribed intrusion turns to tension as Frank's hand brushes over a lone psoriasis scale. Frank senses the reaction to this discovery and intervenes with reassurance.

'You don't have to explain. It's clearing up really well, isn't it?'

I indicate approval with these words and relax into the frantic frenzy of hands undoing buttons and belts.

Fingers dual with harmony and reticence.

Are there feathers or hairs on his chest? Will his fingers turn to claws?

We start to swim over each other. The tide and the waves afforded by the settee contract and expel with ease and unpredictable direction. Under the dimmed lights Frank's curls are long enough to plait. I nuzzle into his armpits for the true smell of man wondering if the Son of God would smell any differently to other men.

Thank God he doesn't smell like a chook.

'You've enough to make dreadlocks,' I cackle quietly to the Son of God.

Or is it the boy of hen and rooster? So much hair. Perhaps they're feathers disguised as hair. Do they become feathers overnight and hair again by day?

'We all need a cover of sorts.'

My antennae are erect. Is this a clue, a cue or both? I unravel and slink back into the back of the settee.

'I guess it's the Orpington from mum's side of the family desperately wanting to assert feather over hair. So far the hair has won.'

Outwardly, I feign concern as Frank grapples with something he has thought about a lot.

'It looks just right on you. I love hairy men. It's like taking a walk in an enchanted forest. Better than my "all over smooth as a baby's arse" body.'

We both resume the exploratory tangle of limbs and lips but this time I feel the turn to take the lead. The planting of kisses on exposed flesh is unrelenting. The swoons vibrate endlessly. I'm unaware of whose hands remove jocks and fling them towards the nativity picture. The fact that the man I'm having sex with is being watched by his mother and father and his own past childhood feels a bit too public but the assurance that this wall hanging is only hanging onto past glory and Frank's confirmation that previous appearances are very rare soothes the potential of multiple seeds of doubt.

'It's still a still life,' Frank affirms and in doing so insists any worry is not warranted.

I try to stifle a burp and in the sudden reflux I taste supermarket chicken.

'And this is trying to remain still too.'

I need two hands with which to create a new foreskin for the Orpington Jew.

'You're not altogether inert,' Frank whispers as we steer each other into mutual positions of comfort. In Frank's case it's legs over his shoulders.

My nose is a rudder that steers me into the harbour of my host's crutch.

I guess there is a first for everything but who will believe me when I tell them I rose leafed the New Messiah.

'Oh my God. Don't stop. Don't play chicken with me.'

Aroused by taste and smell I return enriched saliva to my host. Tongue in cheek this time is quite respectable. I burp again.

Wine. I've been wine tasting.

'I can't thank you enough,' Frank says interrupting and wanting to prolong foreplay.

I look into Frank's eyes.

'Thank me for what?'

'Getting me ready for the final transition.'

I look puzzled but pull back from asking any more questions.

'This is meant to be,' Frank continues. 'I can transition with confidence. I just need the right starting point.'

Too tired for analysis, two half erect cocks drizzling pre-cum are an indication of what needs to be said.

'If I'm to make a comeback I want to ensure that The Lord's Prayer, The Ten Commandments and The Creed reflect how I feel and what I want on this planet. I want to get rid of the term Lord. Mate is a better fit.'

Frank grabs my cock.

'A much better fit.'

'So, "The Mate's My Shepherd"?'

'Spot on. I knew you'd get it. I need someone to work on the hymns so I can focus on the other documents. Interested?'

'Seems a lot of work. What are the Christians going to say?'

'My heavenly Father happens to have a sense of humour.'

'What about Moses? You can't steal his wisdom.'

'I've already spoken to him. He doesn't want to climb any more mountains with a couple of rocks. He's happy to float in the bulrushes with the water birds. All he's asking for these days is webbed feet. Alzheimer's is sad but it does have its funny moments.'

We dive at one another with the intention of sharing an everlasting soak in each other's souls. Frank rolls over on his stomach. While his arse hair begs the creator for mini dreadlocks I take my host along for the ride.

'Enter the Kingdom of Heaven, Mate,' Frank begs moaning. The moaning turns to a contented cluck but either I don't notice or I don't care.

'Praise My Mate the King of Feathers,' I pant passionately.

Frank twists around and gives me a gentle peck on the cheek.

Drive By.

ALL forms of measurement blurs. I think it's a week later. The Lamington Council application takes priority. I praise hard copy diary entries and curse the deliberate failed battery in my mobile phone. I have meetings with the Fringe, the Festival and a host of security firms. I want firm quotes and yesterday if possible, please. Half the people I'm meant to see have scheduled meetings at the last moment which means that those important face to face contacts have to be rescheduled for another time and not necessarily in the same place.

I'm due to meet with Marcia at Shepherds Hill Recreation Park in two hours. Both of us have talked with the appropriate park management team and have written approval for 500 Little People to occupy the park for a month before and including the next festival.

I now have time on my hands and the worry I should be gainfully occupied with filling every second of this life clogs my head. The urgency which I have lived with of late is not understood but I put it down to getting the show on the road and careful planning to avoid all obstacles. Privacy and secrecy manhandle and dissolve in a fight of my own creation. I would normally allow time for a referee to settle the score, but I can't stop and let the luxury of much needed meditation dissolve current anxiety.

Hope Marcia doesn't see it. There's something not right still. Should have played it safe with Him.

I drive past the Cathedral Hotel and try to remember why I should ease off and stare at the façade of the old pub. I do a U-turn and drive back trying to ascertain my interest in this building. I pull into a side street and then stop dead in the middle of the road. Cars pile up behind me and sound horns. Particles of psoriasis dust are caught by a shaft of sunlight while trying to negotiate the ownership by future birds or reptiles.

Eventually I pull over to the side and stop the car.

I don't know where I am or why I'm here. All I can do is breathe, make sure I'm safe and that everyone around me is safe. I sit in the car and wind down the windows. I can't comprehend what should be familiar. I'm in a place where I don't belong. The car becomes foreign. Everything inside is new and unexplained. Rivers and lakes pulse with the ripples caused by a series of dropped stones. The car is a dray. Left alone on this street. There's no horse and I have to quickly find one.

Isn't it me who'll pick Thomas Hardy up from the Port when his boat comes in? He needs time for a final edit.

Moments later I'm back in the car and all is familiar but I still don't know why I'm in the side street. I get out of the driver's seat and walk to the intersection. I walk past the Cathedral Hotel. There's a sign on the front door which reads, 'CLOSED FOR RENOVATION'. I walk past the hotel, turn and walk back. Several motor bikes are parked in a laneway. I stare down the laneway expecting some kind of explanation for my current predicament. I linger for an extended period of time and then walk back to the car.

Mustn't let Marcia know about this either.

Once inside the car I move off slowly and do another U-turn. Back on the main road I keep looking straight ahead while travelling south to Shepherds Hill Recreation Park. Foremost in my mind is to conceal what's just happened from Marcia but I know the perceptive little one will quickly detect any disruption in my equilibrium.

And I've practiced hiding the truth from myself from the time I half admitted there could be new information disrupting the behaviour of my chromatin material.

I see Marcia plodding up the gravel driveway from Ayliffes Road. From the top of the park I can observe most of the tracks and at this time of the day the small number of people who are either walking, strenuously jogging, or on bikes. The latter are oblivious to everyone and everything so well hidden are they under aerodynamic helmets, wet saddles and crutches dripping with milky whey. But the Little Person climbing the steep incline disrupts the concentration of all who pass her by.

Walkers stop and turn. Joggers trip and recover their momentum. Riders slam on the brakes, turn and continue their journeys back into their Lance Armstrong worlds of Clones Down Under. Marcia makes the most of every situation and stares back, blows a kiss or waves her arms about, similar to ground crew guiding an aircraft to a passenger terminal.

The pair of us meet at the steepest point in the park.

'So much for your fucking Recreation Park,' she says puffing out words between breaths. 'Think we need a flying fox.'

I bend down and hug Marcia then take a water bottle from my backpack.

'Filtered tank water as inspected by the magpies, crows, possums and koalas. Natural Resources Adelaide and Mount Lofty Ranges have given us permission for passenger buses to run a shuttle service from the bottom of the hill. All we need do is negotiate with Adelaide Metro and the Festival for extra buses and trains.'

'Good one, Gabriel. You have been busy.'

'Not as much as I would like. Half the people I need to speak to for approvals say one thing on the phone and when I arrive something more important has always cropped up.'

'Perhaps they're frightened of midget mania. It's not every day that 500 of us descend en masse to do a ballet in a park.'

'Little People, remember.'

'Little People lunatics then.'

Marcia sits on a lichen encrusted rock and is suitably mesmerised by the vista of hills behind her, the city below and the sea in the distance.

'Want to hear my news?'

'All ears.'

'You freak.'

Marcia takes another mouthful.

'I tasted magpie that time. Well the good news is I visited Cygnet River Dairies. They're not far from the office in Mount Compass.'

'And?'

'They love the idea of *Cygnet Waterhole* and think it might be a good way to promote a new butter product they have in mind… Wait for it. It's going to be called *Glide*.'

'You're kidding.'

I sense Marcia hasn't finished. She spits water on the ground.

'Koala that time. Nursing mother. And they're looking at ways of trying to support us financially.'

'That's wonderful.'

The pair of us slip back and forth between wondering and the reality of the ballet.

'I think our Little People ballet is starting to take off. Dare I say grow out of control. But dare I also say just let it.'

I toss around some more ideas about the cost of the venture.

'If we're going to spend millions on the ballet let's do it properly with support acts.'

I want the excitement of the biggest event ever for the Little People. I know what Marcia's thinking and I know the terror of the unknown. All I can feel are the words of Dylan Thomas's 'Do Not Go Gentle Into That Good Night.' I keep repeating them.

'When I was doing a regional tour with the Dusseldorf Ballet through Europe I met this incredible woman who's a giraffe whisperer. I think she is a must. I have her contact details. She's reputedly the tallest woman in Europe.'

'Why giraffes?'

And almost as I ask the question I immediately see the paradox of animals reaching to the sky and towering over a park full of Little People.

'Of course.'

Marcia gets wound up.

'I can see the patrons arriving down there through an avenue of giraffes, then further on more that are spinning on the spot and up here on the flat the more agreeable ones neck dancing with swans.'

'Where are the giraffes coming from. And the swans?'

'Some from overseas and Monarto hopefully. And there're plenty of bird sanctuaries around.'

'Do it.'

'Just imagine what it'll look like. Dancing giraffes using goal posts on special loan from the Adelaide Oval. There'd be a bit of bend in them but they're stronger than vaulting poles. But those kinds of details are for the whisperer to sort.'

'And all these people wanting to take pictures with their smartphones,' I warn.

'They won't be allowed. They'll be told the show is about living in the moment and not for future recall. Besides the flashes will frighten the animals.'

'Does she have a name for her show, this giraffe woman?'

'Her name's Bethesda Sole. When I saw her performance in Luxembourg, the show was called *Absurd Heights*.'

'It would have to be.'

'I'll put it to her about the swan and giraffe neck dance. It'll be an ideal lead into *Cygnet Waterhole*.

'Swans forming bow ties around giraffes' necks,' I say allowing the ideas to bounce back and forth.

'How does that song go? *Embraceable You?*' Marcia's eyes widen with excitement.

'Or dye the swans yellow for *Tie a Yellow Ribbon*,' I quip.

We walk down to the spot agreed upon as the performance area.

'We should have 2,000 nest seats this side of the water. Wheelchair access shouldn't be a problem if the potholes are filled in. And the stage just across the water there. Have you got quotes for the stage?'

'From *SA Staging*. They calculate it can be done if they fit four of their largest units together.'

We both share an inner glow and mentally tick off more quotes and approvals on our 'to do' list.

'Up there will be a good place for a helicopter drop.' Marcia points to the cleared area adjacent the upper pathway. 'The giraffes and swans will be finished then. Although we should be able to do some kind of a hover over the stage area. The trees are not too big or close.'

I watch the wild ducks dive and claim territory in the frog chorus spring. Obvious broody ones off the nest for a quick feed, attack other birds nearby. Their bills hiss aggression while filtering the giant dragonflies.

'That one's Odette.'

Marcia points to a duck that darts and hisses across the water.

'This one must be Siegfried,' I say observing the largest of the curly tails practicing synchronized swimming with other drakes.

'He's the one we have to convince with the grant application.'

Make Music Dance.

EVERYTHING is the same. I keep on telling myself this but I know it isn't. The urge to keep on going full pelt has taken over.

I hugged Marcia goodbye and entertained scary thoughts that it might be the last time. I saw her watchful eye again cast a worrying gaze again over and through me.

And I still see it lingering now.

I regather the natural energies of the Recreation Park from the past hour and in doing so ascertain the time of day. Stopped clocks show different times. Salvador Dali time is called for again. It's always ticking in my mind. Toffee clocks come to life and move around the place like sweet crustaceans. They haven't a care in the world and their smiling faces are an inspiration. They have such taste. I imagine their long-lost ticks being restored. Tourette's clocks tick tocking with Marcia conducting their impromptu music. But it's time for Peter Ilich Tchaikovsky that I want to concentrate on.

All that I want to think about.

The man, his music, his suffering, that dreadful bath to cure cholera and the stress of not holding a man and always wanting to.

Liberace makes melodies with claws and a bronchial purr. Cat time always has a priority. He jumps onto the piano as I close the front door. I take out the score of *Swan Lake* and place it on the music ledge. The cat jostles for attention. I put on a CD of the great ballet and sit at the piano and play along after a bit of fumbling to transpose the music into the same key as the CD.

Liberace is on my shoulders pummelling away. Now and then the extremities of my upper skeleton create discomfort for him and I cop his arse in my face. But still I play blessed by an ear and hating an eye for exact notation. By immersing in the music this way enables me to see everything in the Recreation Park.

As I play I watch the crowds of people arrive from different directions. I watch for expectation and the unexpected. The latter is more important than the former. I see the stage and all the complementary acts. Then I drift into the ballet still playing. A whole community of Little People is on stage. It's a giant version of the Rock Eisteddfod. I just hope the stage area is big enough, that the measurements and calculations are correct.

Everything is perfect. As I massage the ivories, the Emily Eyefinger in all my digits takes the pressure from my head. The paradox of something huge created by so many small folk is an overwhelming flood of satisfaction, although this feeling is fleeting.

I bring Peter into the room and treat the maestro with complete respect. I use every cadence to flow through me and pool the essence of the man. A body having suffered drought is fed La Nina to replenish years of tears. It doesn't take long for me to shift back to the Recreation Park again. I examine all aspects of the performance. My drone mind helicopters overhead to photograph the park. A pulse thumps consistently inside begging for confirmation that all component parts are viable and will work. Every meeting with Marcia makes me feel stronger yet ironically more vulnerable. While the total package deal of a ballet and several side acts is growing by the minute I realise that if *Cygnet Waterhole* is to succeed every facet of its viability has to be considered in the grant application. I'm thrilled that I'm working with someone who is one step ahead of me most of the time. The burden of planning is lessened. The fact that she has already assembled support from several prominent choreographers and begun working on excerpts of the ballet sits as a plateau of calm as I accompany the CD now turned up full volume.

I wish Liberace with his pearls of feline wisdom would play with the toffee clocks which are slowly melting back to the beginning of time.

Eventually I interrupt my fumbling accompaniment and am intent on just listening, allowing the music to fly me back and forth to the Recreation Park where I watch the huge cast of little ones prepare for their opening night.

The music continues. I drift in and out of sleep on the swivel chair at the piano. A heavy tiredness weakens me. I feel I might not get out of the chair. The desire for the fresh air of the Park propels me up and out of my seat. A flutter of fearful thoughts forces me to grapple for the physical strength I've been accustomed to.

I haven't the strength to walk there. Something's not right. Louise's letter. Why am I thinking about that now? I did post it didn't I? Did I walk to the letter box? Get up. I'm being lazy.

The last bars of the finale die away. Liberace wants attention, upon seeing me get up from the piano, his favourite plaything. I muse on my moggy Messiah who walks on ivories. Chromatic scales are his forte, though something with tonal dissonance forms part of his latest composition. The cat continues to walk back and forth causing friction between the white and the black. His Barry Manilow impressions challenge his already highly regarded celebrity status.

Then without rhythm or reason I begin whirling. Gently at first. Something has caught me and captured me. I'm in a world of associations and disconnections. I see that first rock of life skim across the water then back into a Palaeolithic hand that forces itself through a membrane of dust. I whirl anticlockwise, now rubbing my guts and tapping my head at the same time. My coordination is perfect. An inner smile is standing up for me, is fighting for me, is finding my voice and fine tuning its resonance. As an expert in speaking in tongues, I rip open an envelope of gibberish and read and speak with ease to those higher than myself. Great elevators like automated baggage machines at a busy airport are all controlled by my computer chip, that everlasting inner smile. And still I whirl to the approval of the great masters. There is magnetism in this movement.

Liberace continues to make music on the move and then plonks his arse on middle C to scratch the irritation caused by his diamond collar.

I wind down. I see the sea as I think I see the sea or have seen the sea. The confounded clocks have formed even odder shapes in their melting moments. There are people whirling everywhere. I don't want to stop but I must.

I don't want to stop because just moments ago I thought I'd never rise again.

Letter from Frank.

Hi Gabriel. Been thinking about you a lot lately. Really looking forward to meeting up with you again soon. Unfortunately, I'm unexpectedly confined to home at the moment. Something strange and wonderful is happening but when I think about it logically it's to be expected. I can't elaborate any further at this stage but hopefully things will be clearer in a few weeks. I've had to put my work at the Hyperbole Bar on hold but Adam Knight who you met can run the show.

Mum and Dad have been springing to life and this has been spiritually edifying for me. I've not known them to be so in the picture about what's currently happening but their reaction to my present state is welcomed and feels just right. They really approve of you, Gabriel. Or should I say they approve of you and me. For my part I feel you are the perfect fit dear one. Hope all is going well for you. I've been working on a few drafts of The Mate's Prayer. There's a bit more work needed but I think the final draft will just click into place when the time's right. Imprinting is still getting in the way. This is what I've written so far.

The Mate's Prayer

Our Mate who ruffles feathers
Hallowed be thy crops
Thy Kingdom crow
Thy will be done in dust baths
As it is through plumage
Give us this day our daily grit
And forgive us our cannibalism
As we attract those who cannibalise against us.
And lead us not into cock fights
But deliver us from parasites
For thine is your nest box
The yolk and the albumen
For cockerels and pullets.
Ah men.

Dying to catch up with you soon.
Love
Frank xxx.
PS How are the hymns progressing by the way?

I READ Frank's letter over and over. Like the first one, I examine each word and every turn of phrase looking for hidden meanings. I attempt a rewind but there's continual tiredness fed by a growing weakness. All I want to do is lie down and compartmentalise before other matters take over. I want to imagine I'm with Frank again and all that occurred recently was real and not just a dream. I imagine what he was thinking when he scribed the words, and I wonder what he is thinking at this moment. There is a strength and fullness in his loops. Given a pen with nib and ink I can discern the distinction between the upstroke and the down.

I see him as the little child, still removing the occasional bits of shell from his thick mop of Australorp hair. He's instructed by a severe teacher to take out his handwriting book. He fumbles for it in the mess under his desk and even though the top has just been sandpapered it already has several ink dribbles forming a river flowing against the meranti grain. The girl he sits next to has been moved up the front beside him because she's fidgety. She pinches Frank several times on the thigh and knows he won't complain because it would make him look like a sissy. I see him flinch and pretend the pinching hasn't happened. He opens his book to a new page and writes in careful copperplate between the red lines the heading, 'HANDWRITING'.

The teacher prowls up and down the rows warning everybody that work must be of the highest standard. Pages are ripped from books and several ears are clipped. Blotters accidentally smudge the drip from his worn-out nib. He tries to hide his drip. The fidget next to him pinches him again. He has more smudges. He wants perfection and he can't attain it. There are always barriers to overcome. He despairs that there are too many and more are being created every day. He wonders why he attracts all this pain and if there'll be a time when he can be happy, strong and not burdened with the sadness of not knowing who he is or... was.

The teacher breathes near him. He smells her vinegar sourness. Her breath is a reminder of a past uncomfortable humiliation. The day he was doused in a bath of disinfectant to kill the poor little mites of an earlier imprinting but not the permanent damage of *Avian Encephalomyelitis*.

The teacher moves in closer and flings away his well-practiced left arm correctly positioned at an angle to his book. She uncovers doodling on the inside of the front cover. There are three stick figures. Two are chickens and there is a child between them. The child has a halo. The teacher tears the cover from the book and screws it up. She dumps it on her desk and tells him he is to write 'I MUST NOT DOODLE' 500 times at lunch.

But at lunch Frank writes, 'I WILL ALWAYS DOODLE. I AM A COCK.'

I'm lying on my bed, scared by the thought I may have been doing this for ages without knowing. Frank's letter is on my diaphragm. I allow it to move up and down with my breathing and watch it move about like a bird on Dylan Thomas's 'fishing boat bobbing sea.' The crackle of the paper is a large set of bellows. Yet another origami creation is waiting for a sign of life and for me to provide it.

I struggle to my feet, clutching the letter and breathing heavily. An unwelcome shiver sends its ice knife to butcher my carcass from head to foot. I get up with a wobble and cobble together all parts to keep finishing my life. My reply to Frank is important. I think how I will start and how I will end. He has a certain expectation of me and I him. I want his closeness but for now I need space and distance.

Dear Frank, or should I call you Mate from now on?

I don't know where to start but from the outset thanks for the wonderful evening. It seems ages since we met and yes I'd love to catch up with you very soon. I've been giving everything a lot of thought – not the least the reworking of the hymns. It's such a huge task but one I'm sure I'll be able to overcome when I'm allowed to conduct miracles in my own right.

I understand your point about taking on such an important role and the pressure of transition you must feel. I keep thinking about our lovely time together and wondering why we hadn't met years earlier. You're very easy to be with. No wonder your chooks love you. I can see how they're an extension of you and you them.

Do you have a set time for when the transition is to occur? And do you have to transition if you don't want to? Who is it that you're answerable to in order that you and everybody else can have a bit of Peace on Earth?

I've been going over these questions in my mind and I hope you don't object to me asking you.

I understand that you want anonymity where possible and that you don't want to be worshipped or turned into an idol. I keep on thinking how difficult it must have been for you as a child, having to disown both your birth and upbringing. But I guess there are lots of pluses too, none the least your ability to endure so much pain yet reach out and help others.

I've been working on a few hymns and as it's your birthday about now I was naturally drawn to carols. I suppose the term Christmas Carols will have to be changed and renamed Mateship Melodies. This way we can incorporate other festive tunes and not just carols. Anyway, here is a list of hymns I've been working on. I suppose at sometime soon you'll have a world launch of The Mate's Prayer along with the hims!

The list so far:

While Shepherds Watched Their Mates By Night.
Silent Mate.
Hark the Herald Angels Mate.
We Three Mates of Goolwa Barrage.
O Mate All Ye Faithfull.
O Little Mate of Murray Bridge.
Good Mate Wenceslas.
Deck the Mates.
Joy to the Mates.
God Rest Ye Merry Gentle Mates.
It Came Upon the Midnight Mate.
The Twelve Mates of Christmas.

Til we harp on again.
Yours to pluck,
Gabriel. xxx

The Numbers Game.

IT's a relief that the phone rings. I have to answer it this time. The weakness is not tiredness. It's something different. I can't fight it any longer. I grab the receiver and visualise an extraordinary strength that will energise my depleted batteries. I know it's Louise before I speak. I've been avoiding her for ages but it's her voice on the other end that's arresting. The German accent drags me into listening carefully. I hang on every word careful not to miss something important.

Yes, I did post your letter. Please don't ask me what day. It's the day I last saw you. Hope she doesn't get too specific. I hate knowing that I don't know. Remembering that there is this thing called memory.

But I don't know if it's ages. I'm confused by time still and wonder what other confusions there might be that I've overlooked, and that people have seen, spotted and commented on. The sense of moving forward or back is like a backhoe that's stuck and keeps on digging up the same stuff.

But her phone call is still unexpected. It's me that normally rings her. Me that asks the eighty-year-old the same questions over and over again. Me who keeps getting the same answers. Wanting the same answers because fear is buried under the backhoe. My moody mud has turned to clay and both the backhoe and the rest of the machine is stuck forever.

In the past Louise has given me heaps of books to read. She's adamant about the importance of one's Inner Self, Higher Self and everyone's connection to the Universe. She says all this stuff. I ring her to hear it again and again. I go and see her to hear it again and again. When I wrestle with her philosophies and find them a bit too glib and naïve, I pull back from any criticism and look for the evidence that her belief system is working for her.

And perhaps mine too if I would allow it.

She's almost blind. Has forty percent vison in one eye. An alternative healer down the Bay told her she had glaucoma and prescribed some weird drops which made things worse. She's wanted to hide her impairment from me and from others. She's counted the steps from her ECH flat to the supermarket nearby and uses her ears to cross the road. She's got herself into the city and back home again by bus. She always expresses gratitude for these achievements and concurs that her independence is her saviour. I've run around doing things for her. But not the time when she did some New Age spiritual transformation where she didn't eat or drink for a month. Just ice to the lips. I struggled waiting for the time to pass, time when I could ring her again or see her again, if in fact there was still a body to be seen.

But it's because she lives alone. Is always alone. She witnessed her mother and father shot dead by the Polish Army at the end of the war and escaped with her younger brother to West Germany. I sought out and delved into Louise's unspoken life. She trusted me. This allowed me to cherish and develop a special relationship. 'Your war with yourself has to be won by you,' she always says.

Yet just minutes after this phone call, I wonder whether I've reciprocated her month of transformation in my own way. I know I posted the letter to her brother in the US because she's just received his latest book. She's over the moon. She has my birth date. She wants me to have the book. Another book. There is excitement in her voice this time but also a calm, a resignation. I sense there is an easy imminence. She's opted to close down in her own way. I admire her strength for the decisions she's taking. She's only answerable to herself. What courage I think to do this.

To be this.

'I simply do not want to be distracted from my path. I have too much healing to do,' she says continually and again just now.

The exhaustion of my dual life, the secrets and white lies is something that Louise knows about but she responds to them with an innocence which I find both healing and annoying. Perhaps I cultivate this relationship with her so I can keep on hearing her say what I half want to hear and half believe. I analyse this reaction, make an all-out effort to stay on a positive track and try not to say anything negative. I've been doing this for the last ten years since I did Rebirthing, since I met Louise for the first time as two very lost souls.

We both agreed that Rebirthing got both of us lost even more.

But now it's a matter of numbers. It's as if Louise has moved on to a new grab bag of reasons for being. She wants me to read the book her brother has sent her.

'You won't believe the reading for you,' she says again and again.

I imagine what a male copy of Louise might look like. Both left their homeland in 1960 to live in different parts of the world. Both are seeking out their life lessons by alternative means. I have flashes of Louise's comments about 'winning the war within.' I'm intrigued as to what her numerologist brother has exposed in this new book.

The familiarity of panic is settling in again. It's circled and taken up residence in my cuckoo nest head and shoved out any development of new paths. I'm conscious of having to save energy for those two important threads in my life which are now coming to a head. I can't allow anything else to distract me. And I must keep the threads separate.

Memory again. Concentrate on that one thread.

I must avoid a tangle. The life I've lived up until now has been all about hide, seek and lack of fulfillment. My desire to show and be all of myself is being tested but I know I still have to keep my private life out of view of those I work with and my public life off limits to those who require intimacy.

I lie on the bed again. This time flat on my guts. The weakness is fighting New Age energy. Liberace finds me and pummels my back with Tchaikovsky. He attempts a full symphonic treatment but is limited to claws, purring and a worrying meow. The public and private threads come perilously close then separate. The two bodies in one weakens me more. My ability to create partitions and to sustain their existence is going to be tested from now on. I can't think about the important people in my life let alone use them in a sentence for everyone to see, read and mouth. But that must change. I haven't the energy to run separate paths any longer.

Concentrate on that one thread.

Things must come together. Things are coming together. There is a faint sense of gratitude that I will have the power to break free of the judgement of others and myself.

No one knows. No one must know.

'You are a master number.' Louise's says again and again.

Time, clocks, days past and future exhaust me until the present beckons me to sleep.

I want time on my side.
'You're a thirty-three.'
Louise's words keep repeating.
'It's the Christ consciousness number.'

OUT come the recipe books. I flick through indexes looking for the best sponge for our purposes. All the ingredients spill across the island bench forming a fortification around a Breville electric mixer. I want the mixer to invite the ingredients to measure themselves, so my hands are free to flick through other recipes for variations. Cocoa, coconut and icing sugar are queued for later use. Their packaging is a visual distraction but serves as a warning for what the final product will look like. I rummage through drawers for baking tins and trays, adjust the shelving in the oven and turn on the heat. The front doorbell rings.

Marcia has arrived with another mixer, more baking trays and extra ingredients.

'I think we're going to need another oven,' I comment as she makes her way to the kitchen to add to the growing battlement. I help steer her in the right direction, mindful that the tower she is carrying obscures her line of sight.

'This is a job for Bethesda Sole.'

She strains to talk as she dumps and positions pots, pans and ingredients in the first available space in front of her.

'Speaking of which… have you heard back from her?'

'I have. She's a goer. The overseas giraffes have to go into quarantine for awhile but she's organised their transport with Singapore Airlines Cargo. They're flying direct from Frankfurt.'

'Who's paying for all this?'

'Cygnet River Dairies. When I received the okay from Bethesda, I got in touch with Costa Windward. He's the general manager at Cygnet. They'll pay the cost of freight and agistment for the animals.'

'I don't believe it.'

'You must. Because it's all happening, dear one.'

Marcia jumps up and plants a kiss intended for my cheek but it lands on my Adam's apple. I do a further rummage for spoons and more bowls. I make a detour and turn on the CD player. The unmistakable strains of *Swan Lake* drifts through the house.

'Who's playing this?'

'Moscow Radio Symphony.'

'Close to home. Good choice.'

'I've been playing this version over and over. Want to be a bit more familiar with the score before the meeting with the head jobs at the Adelaide Symphony.'

'The assistant directors have been using the Boston Symphony with their initial rehearsals. By the way first try outs are this weekend in the Goolwa Shopping Centre.'

'I want to get this application finished this weekend. It worries me that we've no grant money yet.'

'I have a good feeling. A positive feeling.'

I blush, pretending the words of affirmation are the cause of the instant colour in my cheeks. But it's just one of the words Marcia has used and I've allowed it to invade my mind.

Wish she didn't use that word.

'Which one do you want to try first?' I ask her, conscious of focusing on sponge cake recipes. 'There's this butter cake recipe or the basic sponge.'

'I'll do one and you the other.'

'Have you seen a doctor lately, Gabe?' Marcia enquires when my back is turned to her. 'You don't look your normal self.'

'I don't know what my normal self should look like,' I reply while trying to fight any hint of defensiveness.

'You've lost a lot of weight.'

'It's worry about making sure we can pull this off,' I answer, getting ready to crack eggs.

'It will happen, Gabriel. You must believe it will because it's starting to happen right now. The money will come. I can feel it in my bones even though they are small and brittle.'

Marcia decides on the butter sponge.

'I brought some extra eggs. Bantams. Got them from this guy In Mount Compass.'

'Oh.'

'Yeah. Lovely guy. Pretty sure he'd be on your side of the fence.'

'What makes you think that?'

'Just my radar. You should double the number of eggs. They're small like me.'

I want to close down the conversation believing that a couple of threads might weave themselves together before the right time. I start separating the egg whites from the yolks. I break a third egg and am about to separate the yolk and white but stop. I pull the shell apart. The white of the egg runs between my fingers but inside the shell is the beginnings of a chicken.

'Christ.'

'What's up?' Marcia looks up from unpacking other ingredients.

I show Marcia what I've discovered.

'I'll take back what I said about the lovely guy. He can have this egg back in his face.'

Marcia cradles the half shell.

I want to get rid of the egg quickly. Liberace's croissant curl has been interrupted by the noise in the kitchen. He circumnavigates legs and chairs and then retraces his journey.

'Here. I'll give it to the cat.'

Marcia is about to protest but I already have the half chicken and half egg drowning in a saucer of milk. Liberace laps up the contents rapidly despite the presence of solids.

'I'm sorry, Gabe. His eggs are always top shelf.'

'You didn't know. I'll crack the rest of these in a separate bowl.'

The kitchen fills with the noise of twin mixers and voices having to repeat everything. I check the oven temperature and the height of shelves, the number of trays and the length of time to cook. I make sure the fridge has room for a quick cool as we have to repeat the process two more times.

The first trays are slid into the oven. The strong fan sends a blast of heat into my face, dislodging my ghostly pallor. I've received too much information. My head is busily dotting 'i's and crossing 't's but the focus has to be the first wash up time as we clean bowls and utensils in readiness for the second lot of sponge cake mixture. Icing sugar, cocoa, coconut, butter and vanilla wait dutifully for a dip and spread when things have cooled down.

I set the timer. Liberace leaves his food bowl and washes flecks of blood and yolk from his whiskers. My eye catches what might have been in the bloodied half shell which I collect with the others to crunch and dump in the waste bin.

The trays of lamingtons will take twenty minutes to cook.

GRANT APPLICATION FORM

Closing date: Anytime Monday
We strongly encourage you to talk to a lamington before preparing an application, even if you have been sifted before. Contact one of our desiccated staff on 08 8863 5424 or lamingtonarts@basicsponge.com. We also suggest reading the Lamington Council for the Arts' handbook, *Recipes for a Successful Grant Application.*

Applicant Details

Name of applicant:	*Cloaca Incorporated.*
Street address:	*2 Felt Hollow Drive, Mt. Compass SA, 5210*
Postal address:	*PO Box 500 Mt. Compass SA, 5210*

Work phone:	*08 8556 8219*	Home phone:	*08 8556 8219*
Fax:	*08 8556 8219*	Mobile:	*00914867559*

Email:	*cloacainc@onehole.com.au*

Which category are you applying to:

☐ Emerging artist ☒ Organisation/group ☐ Individual

Do you have an ABN?

☒ Y *I have 10 All-Bran Nougats* ☐ N

If yes, please record your ABN:

50005050050

Are you registered with the ATO for GST?

☐ Y ☒ N *(Of course not.)*

GRANT APPLICATION FORM

Applicant Details (Continued)

Organisations/Groups only:

Contact person:	*Marcia Font*
Position:	*Artistic Director*

Project Summary

Title:	*Cygnet Waterhole*

Brief description of project/program/activity:

Cygnet Waterhole is a massive reimagining of Tchaikovsky's Swan Lake with a cast of 500 Little People and set in Shepherds Hill Recreation Park, Adelaide. The local cast and production personnel is augmented by internationally renowned LP artists.

Eligibility Criteria

How do you fit the eligibility criteria that individuals with a disability must initiate the project? Organisations must show how artists or participants with a disability have initiated or contributed to the project's development.

Organisations/Groups only:

Have artists or participants with disabilities initiated or contributed to the development of your project?

☒ Y

Amount requested from Lamington Council for the Arts:

$130,000,000.00 (exclusive of GST)

GRANT APPLICATION FORM

Artform

What is the main art form you will be using?
☐ Theatre   ☐ Craft and design   ☐ Literature   ☐ New media   ☐ Music ☐ Visual Arts   ☒ Dance   ☐ Community Arts   ☐ Other

Other information

Does this application involve the following groups or individuals?

Youth (under 26)	N
Representation of Aboriginal and/or Torres Strait Islander people, art or culture?	N
People from Culturally and/or Linguistically Diverse backgrounds?	Y
People living in regional or remote communities?	Y

Support Material

Please list every item of support material that you have attached to this application. There are limits to the amount of ingredients you can add. See Lamington Council Information Handbook for cooking the book instructions.

Type of Support Material	No. of copies
Video	
Audition process and first group rehearsals in 5 various locations at Goolwa.	1
Images of visual art	
Unpublished writing	
Zika! (the mosquito musical.) The Diarrhoea of Ann Frank (Commemorative loose-leaf edition)	1 500

GRANT APPLICATION FORM

Support Material (Continued)

Type of Support Material	No. of copies
Published writing	
Condomology Uncovered. My Worm has Spina Bifida	2 2
Support letters	
Other	
Biodegradable esky containing lamington diorama (1) of set and environs at Shepherds Hill Recreation Park for Cygnet Waterhole. (Material to be eaten within the assessment period.)	

PROJECT SUMMARY *CYGNET WATERHOLE*

Recently 500 refugees seeking asylum from Hindmarsh Island arrived at Goolwa. Initially their relocation and subsequent downsizing to Little People (LPs) had been supervised by Mother Teresa.

Cloaca Incorporated, Mt. Compass has developed a special dance program to help these recent arrivals adapt to new bodies in new surroundings. Cloaca Inc's motto 'WE MAKE YOU WHOLE AND HOLY' has been put to the test assisting the new settlers. Part of this process has been to remove all the vestiges of their last place of residence. This included the confiscation of all smartphones and an intensive course in chiropractic manipulation to restore posture and digital flexibility. Prior to her arrival in Goolwa, Mother Teresa enlisted the support of local pelicans and a representative from the Alexandrina Council, Ray Devine. Ray Devine later joined the LPs, persuaded by the metaphysical benefits of downsizing, Mother Teresa's postulants, and pelicans with a penchant for noisy smartphones – especially Ray's.

Under the guidance of Cloaca Inc Directors Marcia Font and Gabriel Dorset, a special program of movement and dance therapy has evolved. The new settlers are now ready for the challenge of a full-scale ballet.

In the past weeks the LPs have commenced work on excerpts from *Swan Lake*. Small groups have visited shopping centres to present these excerpts. The community response has been overwhelming with a growing number of requests from schools and community organisations to have the LPs visit.

Given the response, the directors and the LPs have discussed the merits of working on a full ballet. The concept of a newly realised and massive production of *Swan Lake* as *Cygnet Waterhole* is the plan.

Cygnet Waterhole is to be staged outdoors. The Directors of Cloaca Inc have visited Shepherds Hill Recreation Park on a number of occasions to examine a possible site and have discussed this with Natural Resources Adelaide and Mt. Lofty Ranges. However, the site is covered in *Convolvulus arvensis*. Park authorities are willing for the ballet to be staged provided Cloaca Inc can help with the removal of this noxious vine during the preparation of a performance area.

Cloaca Inc has gleaned local, national and international advice in readiness for this event. Initial discussions have been entered into with The Adelaide Symphony Orchestra as this production will be a true classical presentation except for the performers and the Australian locale. It is envisaged that *Cygnet Waterhole* will be a drawcard at the next Adelaide Festival.

Cygnet River Dairies who are also based in Mt. Compass have agreed to substantial sponsorship of the project. In conjunction with the Department of Road Transport, they are willing to promote the launch of a new unsalted butter product aptly named *Glide* on the first driverless buses in South Australia. Marcia Font and designer Rosalind Drew have already worked on preliminary designs using smartphones 'gliding over the buses as cygnets and swans in a wave of butter.'

To access the main performance site, theatregoers will have the opportunity of traversing an optional time walk with unexpected meetings with some notable characters from the past and future. With assistance from the Akashic Records, those taking the foot tour will be totally immersed in different periods of time which will momentarily change the clothes they are wearing and the language they speak.

International giraffe whisperer, and the tallest woman in Europe, Bethesda Sole from Luxembourg is very keen to showcase her new neck ballet, *Embraceable You* with giraffes and swans who will perform bird and beast contortions as part of the preliminary entertainment. Bethesda has already started working with fifteen giraffes at the Monarto Zoo as well as her regular herd of eighteen which have been flown to Adelaide on a specially chartered Singapore Airlines cargo plane. Provided adequate refrigeration is available, a Lego Butter Building display and butter wrestling with LPs will also feature during the month-long event.

But the centrepiece of *Cygnet Waterhole* will be the performance of the 500 LPs in a classical ballet. Co-director Marcia Font, a tireless campaigner for the rights of LPs, says, '*Cygnet Waterhole* is a project in which equal opportunity will showcase the immense talent amongst the LP community.'

GRANT APPLICATION FORM

Budget

All applicants must submit an income and expenditure budget including details of all other funding sources for the activity. You may use your own budget page or the one provided. It is important that this budget balances. The total income (+) and total expenditure (-) must be equal.

Income	$	Expenditure	$
Lamington Council requested amount	130 000 000	Administration costs	
Box office/gate	1 000 000	Phone/fax/email/500 extra mobile phones for buses	35 000
Registrations	20 000	Postage	2 000
Merchandise	40 000	Insurances	100 000
Catering	297 280	Photocopying	2 000
		Rent (for rehearsal spaces)	25 000
Grants:		Auspicing fees (Adelaide Festival)	10 000
Grow Up	100 000		
Sponsorship/ Donations:	750 000	Marketing	
Cygnet River Dairies	500 000	Advertising (TV, print, radio)	250 000
Own contribution	500 000	Posters/printing/ distribution	100 000
		Program/publications	100 000
		Other (Zeppelin advertising)	20 000
		Salaries/fees:	
		1 Administrator/2 event coordinators/10 ass. directors/ 39 weeks	684 000

LAMINGTON COUNCIL FOR THE ARTS (DANCE)

GRANT APPLICATION FORM

Budget (Continued)

Income	$	Expenditure	$
Other, including in-kind:		Support staff/carers	
Travel for visiting artists donated by Air Gethsemane	200 000	Artistic /creative personnel/ set and costume design/ lighting design/sound design	500 000
		Technical staff for bump in, bump out and performance	150 000
		Artist fees 500 dancers/one day 26 weeks	130 000 000
		Adelaide Symphony Orchestra /rehearsal pianist	135 916
		Operational Costs:	
		24-hour security	250 400
		Event/running costs/toilets for performers and public (Little Kenny's Longdrops)	170 700
		Venue hire/Shepherds Hill Recreation Park	
		Generators for all facilities and additional lighting for surrounding trees.	
		Additional marquees for rehearsals and main event from Tents for Rent. Book signing Thomas Hardy/ Live reading The Muslim Duckling Paulette La Rouge. Souvenirs and various food stalls. Butter wrestling. Swan Wine and Dine. Cygnet River promotion centre. Bethesda Sole's giraffe and swan contortion cabaret. Pogo polo with the Gay Gullivers.	25 000

GRANT APPLICATION FORM

Budget (Continued)

Income	$	Expenditure	$
		Catering provided by Mini Subweighs Catering.	69 000
		Technical (stage and lighting hire SA staging and Novatech.	75 000
		Sound shell for Adelaide Arts Orchestra.	25 089
		A380 fly past and celebrity drop.	93 175
		Metaphysical stages aligned above performance area.	
		Access to Akashic record files.	
		Transport/bus/access cabs	200 000
		Refurbish of minibuses in conjunction with Cygnet River Dairies and Adelaide Metro Belair line train	250 000
		Accommodation for visiting artists and local dancers during performance times at The Hyatt. Cut rates negotiated.	185 000
Total Income	133 407 280	**Total Expenditure**	133 407 280

GRANT APPLICATION FORM

Completion check list and authorisation

Tick each relevant item and sign at the bottom. (Unsigned applications are considered ineligible.)

☑ I have read the Lamington Council for the Arts handbook, *Recipes for a Successful Grant Application.*

☑ I meet the eligibility requirements for organic ingredients only.

☑ All artists participating in the proposed activity have agreed to rise to the occasion.

☑ I have supplied the signed original application form in a bed of coconut under the diorama.

☑ I have provided adequate support material and recipe tips.

☑ I have discussed my application with a lamington.

☑ I understand that my application will not be eligible if the activity I am applying for is due to start before next Monday.

☑ The information in my application is to the best of my knowledge, complete, accurate and baked in a moderate oven.

☑ I understand that anything that is wrong or missing may disqualify my application.

☑ I understand that the peer assessment panel may decide not to recommend my application after tasting the diorama.

☑ I have retained a copy of this application for my own records in case of litigation due to salmonella.

☑ I agree to my name, suburb, grant details and cooking experience being presented to media releases and published on the Lamington Council for the Arts website if my application is successful.

☑ I consent to the Lamington Council for the Arts using the personal information I have provided for the purpose of scrambling the grant assessment and approval process and recommending sectioning if it is deemed necessary.

☑ I consent to the Lamington Council for the Arts using the personal information I have provided to advise me of programs, services and other basic sponge initiatives.

☑ I consent to the Lamington Council for the Arts providing my name, project description and contact details to Members of Parliament, the CWA and the interim board of Suppository International if my application passes the taste test.

_______________ *Marcia Font* _________________________________
Name

_______________ *Marcia Font* _______________ Monday 00/00/0000
Signature   *Date*

3: WHEN YOU'RE DANCING BEAK TO BEAK

'Do you want to hear the good news or the bad news first?'

'Might as well have the bad and get it over and done with.'

'The bad news is you won't recognise me from now on.'

'What do you mean?'

'I've grown quite a bit over the last hour.'

'Don't understand.'

'I'm already over the moon.'

My uptake is slow. I can't see Marcia but I know she's teasing. There's a smile for all the world and this time I know she can't hide the good news any longer.

'We've done it, Gabe.'

I haven't time to react. Marcia squeals.

'There's 130,000,000 reasons to celebrate the greatest little show on earth.'

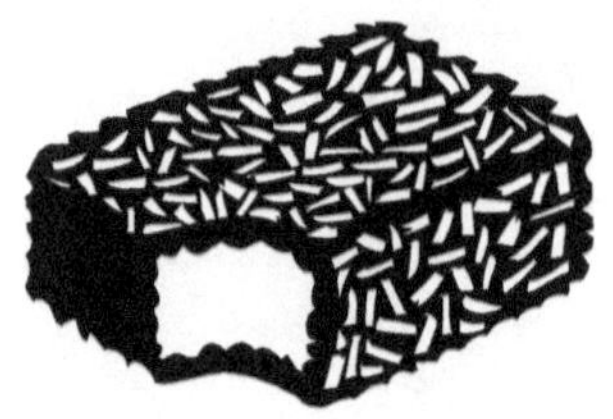

LAMINGTON COUNCIL FOR THE ARTS

Funding total dessication

Biggest Little Show Ever

THE LAMINGTON COUNCIL FOR THE ARTS today announced its grant program for the current funding period. Believed to be the largest arts funding of its kind, a grant totalling $130,000,000.00 has been awarded to local Community Arts organisation Cloaca Incorporated from Mt. Compass. The grant is for the staging of a ballet spectacular entitled *Cygnet Waterhole*. Based on Tchaikovsky's *Swan Lake*, the ballet will feature 500 Little People from Australia and overseas. *Cygnet Waterhole* is a major attraction of the next Adelaide Festival and will be staged outdoors in the Shepherds Hill Recreation Park.

Co-Artistic Director Marcia Font says the ballet is the culmination of over two years of planning, organising, and a strenuous rehearsal period. Not only will there be the ballet but a number of support acts have been curated all with links, though somewhat oblique, to the world of Little People.

Ms Font, also a Little Person, has had extensive experience as a dance performer and producer both in Australia and overseas. She has appeared in *Swan Lake* on numerous occasions and most recently with the Dusseldorf Ballet where she appeared both on stage and was also an assistant choreographer. Over the last two years she has worked with her creative partner Gabriel Dorset to plan the ballet spectacular.

'The 500 performers have already started rehearsing,' Ms Font said yesterday after receiving news of the grant. 'Because of the large numbers, a team of internationally recognised choreographers are rehearsing smaller groups of fifty performers. With 500 people on stage at the same time it has meant that a stage big enough to accommodate such a huge cast has had to be specially built. Thanks to the ingenuity of local company, *SA Staging*, we will have a performance area big enough for 500 pairs of little feet.'

Ms Font was full of praise for the Department of Environment, Water and Natural Resources staff who have helped with preparation of a site in the Shepherds Hill Recreation Park, which features a disused waterhole. Cloaca Inc has agreed to undertake weed eradiation as part of the project. *Convolvulus arvensis* has taken hold in much of the park and is a threat to native plants. At the moment the area where the stage and orchestra shell are to be positioned is covered in the noxious weed. Marcia Font says the audience will be separated from the performers by the waterhole which is currently home to several varieties of water birds.

'Those attending the ballet will be seated in in a natural amphitheatre setting. Specially designed seats in the shape of swans' nests are being made from native grasses,' Ms Font said.

Audience members will have several options to reach the park. Belair Line trains will run a nonstop shuttle to the Eden Hills entrance to the park and a fleet of buses covered in swans constructed from disused smartphones will travel to the Ayliffes Road entrance. A major sponsor of *Cygnet Waterhole*, Cygnet River Dairies is launching a new butter line to coincide with the ballet.

Ms Font said that the support acts which will complement *Cygnet Waterhole* have been carefully selected to add to the 'overall wow factor' of the event. She said her partner Gabriel Dorset was also busily planning a number of 'metaphysical moments'.

International animal whisper, Bethesda Sole has devised a unique performance with a herd of giraffes. Pole dancing giraffes using goal posts from the Adelaide Oval will greet festival goers at both entrances to the park. Closer to the main performance area, more of these animals will dance with adult swans in an attempt to tie each other in knots.

The outrageous nude performance troupe *The Gay Gullivers*, heavily overdosed on Viagra and strapped to the ground, will yield to a demonstration of pogo polo administered by an army of Lilliputians riding Shetland ponies.

But there is a quiet period of reflection prior to the audience assembling in their nests when gifted storyteller, Paulette La Rouge, reads her own version of *The Muslim Duckling*.

'The whole experience is designed to be one of unbelievable images generating everlasting smiles,' Ms Font said enthusiastically. And starting this week Adelaideans will be treated to several impromptu performances and promotions by the Little People as a lead up to what promises to be the biggest little show ever.

For media enquiries:

Marcia Font
Cloaca Inc.
0400 000 000
marcia@cloaca.egg.au.

CLOACA INC SCHEDULE FOR CYGNET WATERHOLE

Date/Time	Who/What	Venue
PHASE 1 Mon/00.00	Full day group and individual auditions. Please check correct times for your group. We are allowing one hour per group. There may be callbacks at a date to be announced.	Goolwa Centenary Hall
PHASE 2 Mon/00.00	**AM:** Meet and greet all directors, musical directors, designers, coordinators, production crew and cast. Welcome and apology to country. Mother Teresa video '*The Miracle of the Merkin.*' Each member of the production team will address the company with reference to their aims, goals and the challenges for this unique production. Lunch at *The Continental Carp*, Pelican Point. **PM:** The afternoon will be devoted to cast bonding sessions led by the directors. You will meet the others in your production group and assistant directors at this time. This will be a wonderful opportunity for all our LPs to get to know the hundreds of others performing in this show. Question and answer session to close the day.	Goolwa Centenary Hall and adjacent marquees.
PHASE 3 Mon/00.00	Group rehearsals commence every Monday AM for the first six months. Meet at GCH initially the first day. Rehearsals are five mornings a week the month prior to performance. Principals rehearse with Marcia Font at GCH (see separate schedule).	(Goolwa Centenary Hall) Goolwa Regatta Yacht Club South Coast Regional Arts Centre Goolwa Sports Stadium Alexandrina Council Centre for Positive Ageing Little by Little Centre

		Port Elliot RSL Goolwa Little Athletics Club Goolwa RSL Goolwa Football Club Alexandrina Mini Golf Club
Mon/00.00	Coordinators' and assistant directors' meetings will be every Monday afternoon at 1pm.	Goolwa Centenary Hall
Mon/00.00	Tech meeting with sound, lighting, set and costumes at 4 pm.	Goolwa Centenary Hall
PHASE 4 Mon/00.00	This will be the first time the whole company meets to work together. We will be working on the same size space as Shepherds Hill Recreation Park from this day.	Mt. Compass Contemporary Arts Centre
Mon/00.00	Whole company.	Mt. Compass Contemporary Arts Centre
	Performance excerpts at various locations around Adelaide. Gather at Cygnet River Dairies beforehand for costume fittings and last-minute notes from Marcia and Gabriel.	Cygnet River Dairies carpark.
PHASE 5 Mon/00.00	Full company.	Goyder Pavilion Adelaide Showground
	Full company.	Goyder Pavilion Adelaide Showground
PHASE 6 Mon/00.00	Full company. Run through with tech, orchestra, sound and wildlife. There will also be additional evening rehearsals on the nominated days. Support acts and stalls set up for run through. Practice fly over with aircraft.	Shepherds Hill Recreation Park
PHASE 7 Mon/00.00	OPENING NIGHT	Ampithetre Shepherds Hill Recreation Park

*Please contact Production Manager Margot Orff at Cloaca Inc, 2 Felt Hollow Drive, Mt. Compass if you have queries. Email: cloacainc@onehole.com

Remember to Glide.

MARCIA shouts instructions. Refrigerated trucks and buses pull into the carpark outside Cygnet River Dairies. The trucks back into the factory to load up. I talk with the drivers to ensure they're familiar with the parking procedures in the designated zones at their destination. I leave them to secure the pallets of butter from an army of forklifts.

Little People are everywhere. The media are here including a sizeable pack from overseas. The LPs swarm around them, furtive ants before the wet. Camera operators and interviewers are trapped in a sea of littledom. They've not had an assignment like this before. The mood is a combination of merriment and awe. The Press want to interview me and Marcia but there are persistent problems managing the logistics of hundreds of LPs, tons of butter and 500 swan feather flyers.

I look for others of similar stature as myself. They are few and far between. I'm confronted with a minority status on a huge scale. I'm a ship's mast bobbing about in the middle of a heaving sea. I look for other ships thinking I might need to send out a mayday from waters teeming with waist high waves of exhilaration.

'Put your costumes on now.' Marcia hops onto my shoulders and onto the tray of a refrigerator truck. A camera is thrust in her face.

'Remember you're in character the moment that costume goes on. You're out to sell the show and we rely on every one of you to make sure our message is well received.'

Wardrobe crew stand at either end of lines of the LP corps de ballet. They shove tutus and tights into the eager hands of the excited dancers. Arms and legs stretch and shuffle into costumes while reinforced mime and ballet shoes are adjusted by more wardrobe assistants.

A number of passenger buses are parked on this water's edge. Hundreds of decommissioned smartphones are plastered over the vehicles in giant frescoes depicting cygnets swimming behind their parents. Adult swans arch necks to check their brood. Their compass eyes blink north, south, east and west. Advertising for the Cygnet River Dairy ripples around the birds in buttery waves.

Try New Glide from Cygnet River. Spread the word. Spread Glide.

The speakers on the smartphones are attached to sound systems in each of the buses. Tchaikovsky's music can be heard in splendid digital delay as the cygnets stream in a test run over the vehicles. Slices of multigrain bread bend and stretch untoasted to be spread with delicate splashes of Jersey butter while fresco birds surf the yellow waves.

As the company of LPs stretch and pirouette around the buses they marvel in wonder at the mobile show. The smartphones shimmer in the morning sun. Briefly the buses become boats on the same sea channelling lapping waves from all directions.

However, the excited reaction is soon replaced with an appreciation of the real purpose of this day.

LPs quickly adjust their costumes and concentrate on warmups. I have to keep wading, mindful of not treading on toes. Something akin to a Mardi Gras parade is about to start. Although I've enjoyed the security in planning with one other person, of creating in isolation, the reality of what is to unfold is confirmation there is no turning back. To see so many enthusiastic folk forces me to briefly reimagine the beginnings of the project, but I quickly remind myself to remain connected with the present.

It's the only path.

I've avoided it, gone down it halfway, worried about what other people might say or considered just giving up. Even though I want to be in the background, I can't escape the scrutiny of others. Flashes of what my life is all about or what it's meant to be, seesaws. There's no one to run to, no place to go, nowhere to hide when I try out something this new. The irritation of the mundane, the individual prisons built and inhabited by all and sundry is why I'm here and why I need to keep on keeping on.

This is it. This is your life. It's a reminder.

There are no people in my family.

And today more than ever my family is a family of ideas fertilising more ideas.

I the singer, actor, writer, dancer, quickly pull the character strands of self-collaboration together because I must. But at times like this I question why I have to have an epiphanic realisation which does nothing more than sidetrack me.

This is a first for driverless trucks and buses. Months of trials on closed expressways have been completed. Today's the first time large commercial self-driving vehicles have been allowed in traffic. Whispers about what is to happen has found its way onto social media.

But Marcia and I have done well to keep the surprise factor under wraps. People have gathered around the perimeter of the carpark. The police are out in force to control the crowds and to escort the buses which are ready to leave for 'a spot' in the suburbs. The contingent of tiny ones can't wait to board.

Meanwhile the final boxes of butter are stacked. Cartons of specially fumigated swan feather flyers are securely placed in all the trucks. Faux drivers, the Marcel Marceuxes courtesy of *Transport SA*, climb aboard their vehicles ready to head off. I stand next to Marcia.

'Do you want to speak to this lot?' she says nudging me forward to an interviewer with a furry microphone.

'I think it'll work best if you do the first one then I'll help out with the others. Think Costa should say something as well.'

Costa Windward, the manager of Cygnet River Dairies comes towards me. The LPs forget about their preparation and surge around Marcia to watch the interview with Sue Spock from *Syncrasy 24*.

'I'm in the middle of the carpark at the Cygnet River Dairies, Mount Compass with choreographer and director Marcia Font, conceptual artist Gabriel Dorset, and the manager of Cygnet River Dairies, Costa Windward. I'm lost for words. Perhaps Marcia if you hop down from the truck I might get you to explain all this?'

'It's always the way with LPs. People are looking down on us. I didn't want to sound politically correct but fuck it, I will be.'

Marcia climbs onto my shoulders.

'Do you want to interview me up here? This is my other half. We make a great team of one and a half, don't you agree?'

Sue Spock presses on despite the final manoeuvring of Marcia on my shoulders. Costa is in a navy suit. He stands with his hands folded in front of his crutch and rocks back and forward on his feet possibly to avoid being splashed.

*Where have you seen a man like this before? Everywhere of course.
All the time.*

He appears quite impressed with the advertising on the buses and
smiles approvingly as the frescoes are given another test and briefly
glide to life. Marcia slides to the ground.

Groups of LPs mill around other media posing for photographs
and interviews.

'Can you tell us what you've planned with all these Little People,
Marcia?'

Marcia climbs onto a plastic chair so she's at eye level with Sue.

'Where does one start? I think that's the first question. Gabriel and
I've been working on this project for the last five years.'

'And for the viewers at home, what's the project called?'

'*Cygnet Waterhole.*'

'Sounds intriguing. What's involved with the project?'

'It's a new slant on an old ballet. *Swan Lake.* We wanted to reimagine
this beautiful piece of work within an Australian context and with a
cast of LPs.'

'So all the roles are played by LPs... um, Little People'

'Yes. And almost all of the backup crew are LPs.'

'Sounds like a huge undertaking.'

'It is. But it's all starting to come together nicely. Thanks to the hard
work of my partner, Gabriel Dorset here. It's so important to have the
input of another person who can think freely and in grandiose terms
while allowing something like this to generate its own energy.'

I can't hide the blush. I'm proud of Marcia and the work achieved so
far. Acknowledgement of this desire to create an environment in which
so many LPs can express themselves is hugely satisfying.

'And what's the significance of the buses and Cygnet River Dairies?'

'It's a bit of a secret but if you follow one of the buses that question
will be answered later.'

'Gabriel, I believe it was your brainwave to do a ballet with LPs.
Can you tell us how this happened?'

'I first met Marcia at a Lamington Council information session. We
often commiserated about how we'd tried for grants and were knocked
back on every occasion. Marcia always inspires me and everyone to
think big. So, when I proposed the idea of *Cygnet Waterhole,* she

jumped at it straight away. Her idea that "SMALL IS TALL" struck a chord and I thought why not attempt something with Little People doing something big but also something unique. Ultimately that means something memorable.'

'This production sounds more and more like *Ben Hur*. As well as the massive $130,000,000 grant from the Lamington Council I understand you have run a successful crowd funding campaign and Cygnet River Dairies is a major sponsor.'

'Yes. We've had phenomenal support with our crowd funding. LP organisations worldwide and thousands of individuals have pledged up to $500,000 so far. We approached Costa with our idea early in the planning stages and he took it to his board where it received unanimous approval.'

'Costa, this seems a wonderful advertising opportunity for you. Those cygnets swimming all over the buses and in and out of waves of butter look incredible.'

'And edible,' Marcia quips.

I move back to allow Costa to speak with Sue. Marcia hops back on the rear of the truck and signals the buses to get ready. Cameras click and flash the swimming frescoes as they glide past in a final test run.

'I think this was too good an opportunity to pass up. Our company will get a lot of exposure and Marcia and Gabriel will realise their creative goals.'

'And I believe this is a first for these buses.'

'Yes, driverless buses doing their first run in traffic. It's a combination of firsts.'

'Well there you have it. Driverless buses adorned with friezes of swans and cygnets swimming in and out of butter. Or should I say gliding. If you get a chance to watch this convoy, I suggest you position yourself on South Road right now. My words can't adequately describe this spectacle. Today marks the beginning of the publicity campaign for what is bound to be a sell-out feature of the forthcoming Adelaide Festival. These buses are about to leave for undisclosed destinations all over the city. We're told there is a surprise waiting for people who live in selected streets. I guess we'll have to follow the buses and not the yellow brick road.'

The butter buses start and idle. The LPs hurry to board. The outside of each vehicle begins treading water. The occasional flash and movement of images is like the advertising on the perimeter of a football oval with a touch of New York's Times Square. Across the grilles and back of each bus a sign reads, 'DRIVERLESS VEHICLE'. Television cameras and other onlookers continue filming from all angles. I try to extricate myself from the throng but more press want to chat with Marcia and me. The last pallets of butter are stacked into the refrigerated vans.

The steel doors are pinned shut. The noise is unsettling. The shudder has a feeling of permanence about it. I imagine being trapped inside and unable to get out. I lose concentration. Contradictory feelings fight for ascendancy once more. But my fight is to rein in those tentacles of tormented journeys which could take hold. The size of what is to come is in my face.

I need to keep living.

I wonder what Marcia is thinking. She looks at me and sees my moment of terror. She smiles and makes a victory sign which pulls me back into the present. The delirium of past weeks tries to regain traction. There's a reminder I have a passenger on board. I can't acknowledge it or yield to its desire for residency yet. All I know is its yearning to push me to the limit, to make me seek approval while eking out some kind of life lesson.

The buses start to move off. The swans and cygnets swim gracefully in all directions with the music of the Russian master ebbing and flowing above the sound of hundreds of onlookers and more press gathered outside the carpark. A helicopter hovers overhead. I catch a glimpse of a camera guy seated precariously while filming from an open door. The past is being revisited again. The history of flight overhead claws at all my backstories.

I have to fly in parallel. There's a chopper for every bus and car in this convoy.

'I'll follow you to Cross Road and turn off,' Marcia says climbing into her *Kombi*. 'It's all going to be fine,' she reassures. Her van is plastered with posters for *Cygnet Waterhole*. Likewise, my car has been given a new lease of life with LPs dancing in a photoshopped Shepherds Hill Recreation Park. Stickers for *Glide Butter* are stuck to the bumper bars and the bottom of each of the doors. Costa breaks away from another media pack and hurries towards me.

'Good luck, Gabriel. I'll follow. Where do you want me to go?'

'Marcia's heading towards the coast and I'm going north. Probably somewhere east.' I lean across the driver's side of the car for a copy of the itinerary. 'This is the list of locations. Must go. I've the furthest to travel.'

I start my car and gently move out into the traffic. The sight and sound of buses swimming with swans and cygnets gliding into dawns and sunsets of butter is a cholesterol high. In spite of a corny pun I think all this is a good way to 'spread the word'. The photographer in the helicopter thinks so too as the chopper flies dangerously low overhead to take more pics of the contingent joining other traffic. Marcia is in front of me. The sound of Tchaikovsky throbs in waves above the noise of vehicles. This is the start. The beginning and the end are combined. I allow myself to be put through the motions of going forward.

Good.

I've created this path and I can't turn back or veer off.

Another good.

I have a destination and I will have an outcome.

Goodness will be personified.

My internal visitor seems to be under control but with and without my knowing it's the chief exacerbator of a myriad of far-flung feelings.

Not so good. It wants permanent residency.

As I drive I cut into the landscape of my coddled brain to the thousands of minutes I've been able to breathe the last months. I call them Marcia moments for the greatest Little Person I've ever known has been here, there and in my face when I needed her. She senses a hidden truth and a half knowing yet drives me on like a dedicated mind mechanic attending to the component parts of my thinking to make my grey matter perform its miracles.

Costa is behind in his resplendent yellow SUV boasting the benefits of *Glide* and Cygnet River Dairies proud sponsorship of *Cygnet Waterhole*. I grip the steering wheel and steer into the procession. I wind down the widows so I can hear Russian Peter more clearly and am reminded that it's a never before aural experience too. Marcia waves to me. I wonder if the crowds lining the roadside are there to see driverless buses or swans swimming in pools of butter?

Or Little People en masse?

Down Willunga Hill the procession continues. I change into the right lane conscious of the dozens of little hands waving and the sparkling smartphone cygnets still swimming in orderly lines over the buses from all angles. A shooting gallery comes to mind but then I sneer inwardly at allowing myself to make such a comparison. This is part of what Marcia and I have described as a 'new thing.'

An irritation of those who snooze though life is a jump start to waken me. I dive into a yellow moment of sunshine wishing for perpetuity. I keep up this obligatory belief. I rerun Marcia's words of approval and wave and toot to her as her *Kombi* motors past belching unedifying smoke. The so-called drivers sit in drivers' seats and wave to me also with both hands. Marcel Marceau is enjoying being steered through a real illusion. Before I reach South Road, Marcia and I cut in front of the buses and behind the police escort.

The junction of South, Ayliffes and Shepherds Hill Road slows the traffic. Butter buses are spread over several lanes. Tchaikovsky outdoes the thump of competing sound systems. I'm worried by the lack of movement. Destinations must be reached by a certain time. I've allowed for roadworks, for expressways to become super expressways but there is now an eerie waiting period. Joy and patience are in short supply. As I often have neither of these attributes, I nevertheless feel rehearsed for this moment but hope the delay is not too long. I crawl towards the traffic lights. More police are monitoring the intersection. I look to my right up Shepherds Hill Road. A woollen wave of out-of-control sheep roll down the hill across all lanes. Moses has taken to the cherry picker again. He swings out over his flock and instructs the Kelpies to assist the police by moving them towards the Ayliffes Road entrance of Shepherds Hill Recreation Park.

Fuck you, Moses. Do you think you're God or something? Why are you doing this now?

The sheep mass in the small carpark. I try to brake but seesaw back and forth to times spent and times to arrive. I leave the present on hold. The roads disappear then the shops and the blocks of flats. Trees suddenly appear while Moses herds his flock to grass, over grass and onto the hillock.

Tess of the D'Urbervilles walks down the track with a jar of honey balanced on her shoulders. Bathsheba Everdene under instruction from her creator Mr Thomas Hardy directs the milling Dorsets who are preparing for a nibbling edit on his grassy manuscript prior to the release of the Australian version of *Far From the Madding Midgets*. Tufts of grass obscure the beginnings of paragraphs. Kindles fly through the restorative air, their words sucked up from the ground in a series of pelletised tornadoes to fall as a smudge before the blurred vision of those born to multitask.

Away in the slushy green distance Mary Magda and Mary Virgo are seated waiting for the flock to assemble around them. Overnight someone or something has removed much of the product of their labour from their Corinthian columns stacked tall with elderberry dyed costumes. Bradley and Teagan recently graduated from their past lives as trained shepherd boys run to assist Moses and his mob. The Kelpies see them and smother the boys in a pyramid of licks. Moses chastises his dogs which return to the cherry picker now stationary in the carpark. They line up to cock their legs on every available wheel. Moses climbs down from his historic lofty position and slides two tablets from underneath the rear controls. He sneezes uncontrollably. Several sheep stand on their hind legs and count his sneezes, egging him on with copycat bleats.

'Time for me to give these back to God. No wonder they call this place Mount Sinaisitis.'

He runs his fingers over the inscriptions on the tablets. Twelve bikers on a sex toy run appear over the crest on Ayliffes Road. They enter the carpark. I have to look twice. Maybe three times. It's *The Altered Boys*. Could be. *The Dick Touchers*. Perhaps. Naughty boys. Most likely.

A banner which reads 'SPONSORED BY THE HYPERBOLE BAR' is attached to the lead bike.

'Hey, Moses! Here's a new commandment before you give God back his tablets!' the lead biker shouts.

The bikers are nude except for a generous covering of tattoos and cock rings worn everywhere. They cut the engines on their bikes and drape themselves over their machines. Cocks grow heavenwards and glisten in the sun. Sheep previously on back feet return to all fours but stare with easy eyes.

The head of *The Scrotum Brothers* hands Moses an interactive dildo which screeches continually, 'Thou shalt pleasure thyself always! Thou shalt pleasure thyself always!'

With dildo in one hand and tablets under his other arm, Moses is perplexed. The sheep have populated the track up Mount Sinaisitis. Moses commences his long walk. *The Scrotum Brothers* tear off into the sun horny as hell without leather. I try to pull back to stop myself from catapulting into another level of disorientation. But try as I might the motionless traffic insists I must keep on moving... something.

From nowhere there's is a furious blast of wind. I can hear Tchaikovsky then no Tchaikovsky. Out of the blue the transgender salmon swims by my windscreen. Golda has a packet of antihistamines in her mouth. She dives into the halo above Moses swims three clockwise circuits and three anticlockwise before dropping the medication at his feet.

'Try these. Good for hay fever,' she bubbles, then dives high and low above the intersection.

'God bless you. I hope your tablets work better than these,' Moses says indicating the dildo now wedged between the two pieces of slate tucked under one arm.

Mary Magda and Mary Virgo stand, looking back and forth through the centuries. The Hardy women attract their attention. They reflect on their own lives and the degree of subservience still controlling these great characters.

Historic visions retreat and buildings along the main arteries are restored to their previous state yet appear unsafe following the rebirth. Signs which read 'DEAR FIRST INHABITANTS! PLEASE CAN WE SETTLE HERE' are plastered across store front windows. The centuries old lettering has faded though.

The traffic lights are working. I check my watch. I have time. A series of prime movers turn into the carpark. My heart skips a beat. The gates previously open for sheep are now flung open for the first of dozens of heavy vehicles from *SA Staging*. Part of the Permapine fencing has had to be removed for easier access. The vehicles honk support for the butter buses on the move again. Behind them an extra wide vehicle carrying a bulldozer and two shingle sheds pulls into the carpark.

My diorama is alive but my heart skips another beat.

Marcia toots and waves back. Crowds pocket vantage spots to watch the musical convoy in motion. I wind my window down. The smell of sheep mixes with vehicle emissions. The aromatic blend stirs another shift which I grab and push into the pit of my stomach.

A previous epiphany has finally given birth in the manger in my guts.

A kangaroo with a joey in her pouch hops from a used car yard, bangs into an impatient SUV and hurtles stunned into Shepherds Hill Recreation Park, narrowly avoiding an *SA Staging* truck. She recovers and bounces dazed into open scrub away from the gravel track.

Marcia gives a final wave for now as she gets ready to head down Cross Road. I align myself and sit tall and watch through the rear vision mirror as one of the buses follow her *Kombi*. The destination: Cygnet Street, Novar Gardens. I recheck the time and wish I could add extra minutes. The rest of the buses are following behind me as I increase my speed and head to Swan Place, Gawler East.

NOTICE TO PUBLICITY COORDINATORS AND ASSISTANT CHOREOGRAPHERS.

The following locations have been chosen for pre-publicity on Saturday:

Cygnet Court, Flagstaff Hill
Cygnet Court, Glenelg North
Cygnet Lane, Northgate
Cygnet Street, Mawson Lakes
Cygnet Street, Novar Gardens
Cygnet Street, Seacombe Gardens
Cygnet Terrace Kingston Park
Swan Avenue, Rostrevor
Swan Avenue, West Beach
Swan Court, Renown Park
Swan Street, Grange
Swan Place, Gawler East

Bus departures will be staggered from Cygnet River Dairies depending on distance to be travelled.

The butter will be kept in refrigerated trucks until the impromptu street performance concludes.

The buses will be positioned at the end of each street with amplifiers connected to the smartphones.

A performance area should be clearly marked in the centre of each street. The invocation prior to each performance is set down for noon.

Please ensure correct alignment procedures with Mt. Compass and Lake Alexandrina prior to performance so that the momentum from the twelve sites is felt as a single *Waltz of the Swans*.

Once the dance sequence concludes butter and flyers will be distributed.

SAPOL will be in attendance at each location.

—Marcia and Gabriel.

Places for Swans and Butter.

EVERY set of lights there are people. Every set of lights more buses leave to head off to their selected destination. Soon it's just me and the last *Glide* bus and butter truck on Main North Road heading towards Gawler East. I know that by now the others have arrived and are beginning to set up for their impromptu exposé. I've checked and rechecked all the sites with Marcia. The performances have been carefully calibrated to start at midday. The passenger buses and the trucks have been given permission to block access at one end of each street for the duration of the fifteen-minute performance.

Swan Place is small in comparison to the other streets. The bus and the butter truck pull up across the intersection. A small gap for emergency vehicles has been left. The Gawler East coordinator assembles everybody. The cast warm up with a series of pirouettes either side of the street. People gather at front gates and others from adjoining streets claim temporary residency in Swan Place.

I stay in the background and watch. I think I'm familiar enough with the ballet by now. I assure myself these mini performances are a good try out for the cast. The worldwide publicity for dancers who work professionally and who are also LPs has paid off. They have augmented the group assembled by Marcia, thanks to the intervention of Golda and Mother Teresa.

The dancers spring and strut back to the marked performance area. It's 11.55. I join them and wait the last minutes. News of the weird butter bus and the Little People has disseminated quickly. A bustling crowd gathers. The performers kneel and flutter in a south easterly direction. I sidestep and peer in the same direction knowing all over Adelaide a total of 500 Little People are doing the same thing.

Golda swoops and coils over the group and dives heavenwards seemingly reversing any gravitational pull on her energy. I watch her out of the corner of my eye and the speck she has now become. The salmon is both the observer and the switch. Aloft, she cues the groups of dancers ready for their performance.

The excerpt from Act Two is about to begin.

While the refrigerated buses remain still, the passenger bus bursts with the opening bars of familiar music. Clever design work by the smartphone fresco creator and the sound engineers allows the swans and cygnets to swim along the street side of the bus only. I step further back and stand alongside the bus.

I watch the crowd, the joy and disbelief, the magic of dance, music and the human form as expressed by the LPs. Golda, a mere flea in the sky, flies funnels of secure halos.

She then zooms towards me and activates her fishy halos at head height.

The coordinator and Marcia are having trouble with one of the performers in Novar Gardens. A Little Person has spotted *The Professionals* Open Inspection A frame on the corner of Cygnet Street and has resisted several attempts not to carry it on his back. I nod to Golda knowing her power of flight and heightened negotiation skills will resolve this impasse. Again, she makes a distant funnel and an agitated speck of herself. I smile sensing the connection she is making with those caught off guard, those who've heard a whisper and those who think they know what this butter ballet is all about.

For a moment I'm caught in a mesmerising trance of shifting my gaze along the lines of individual dancers, feeling the months of auditions, rehearsal and practice their bodies have endured. Now all I observe is the connection with my feelings and everybody involved as *Valse de Cygnes* is realised on bitumen on the northern outskirts of Adelaide and far from the pull and energy meter of Mount Compass.

The Little People complete their performance and gracefully exit either side of the passenger bus where happy swan families still swim from left to right on the stationary vehicle. Applause continues and the dancers emerge for a graceful bow and acknowledgement.

Moments later and just as the crowd is dispersing the music starts again. This time the company of Little People carry tubs of *Glide* and a flyer for their performance. They arabesque over gates, fences and at front doors, and pirouette in driveways and on thirsty lawns. Cue maestro Golda dives with a deep hiss. I hope Tchaikovsky's music is heard from Gawler to Goolwa. The music stops suddenly and so too the elegant smartphone water birds.

In the silence the residents of Swan Place stand statuesque with their hands outstretched.

The Little People lean forward and chant, 'HERE IS YOUR BUTTER WITH A FEATHER IN IT!'

The music resumes and this time the smartphones take their swan families back over the bus and in all directions of the compass at twelve sites across Adelaide.

SUPPOSITORY INTERNATIONAL is proud to announce the CLOACA INC production of CYGNET WATERHOLE by arrangement with SCURF AUSTRALIA

A company of 500 Little people present a once in a lifetime experience. Watch Tchaikovsky's immortal classic realised in an outdoor setting in Shepherds' Hill Recreation Park under the Australian southern cross.

Cloaca Inc gratefully acknowledges the support of our major sponsors:

Lamington Council for the Arts.

Grow Up.

New Directions.

Mt. Compass.

Wild Australia.

Hyatt International.

Golda Delves.

MORE than ever I rely on Golda for my transportation needs, to keep the threads apart until I'm ready to weave them together. More than ever I rely on her binary illusion and vital links with the Akashic Records to swim through the skies and water around Port Adelaide and make it a genuine disembarkation point for the great writer, Thomas Hardy.

I confer with Golda over last minute details. I wonder in this stream of consciousness why someone of Hardy's import should travel halfway around the world to be part of a performance with 500 Little People.

Golda is always there like a small fry sitting on my shoulder except she has the habit of rising to the occasion and taking me to her great heights. Golda, born in a doctor's waiting room, has been with me in my recent timelessness and is the only entity who can fill in the gaps which is the picture of my life. She is the only being who knows my current highs and lows and knows that from now on my life is a numbers game and that everything happening now is happening for a reason.

It is Golda who knows Marcia's influence in my life.

It is Golda who knows about Frank Ly.

And I suspect Golda knows how everything will come together for me and sort out the reason for my growing weakness.

That I should entrust my secrets to a transitioning fish is the calm I now need.

The fish's fins flutter in the northerly breeze. I decide on a slow walk down into the Shepherds Hill Recreation Park where I can meditate and think about the final picture. Golda hovers in front of me urging me forward to see clearly.

I squint as I peer over Gulf St Vincent. I wonder about the necessary clearance from the Department of Civil Aviation to allow for the helicopter entourage and the possible fly over of the A380. Golda rattles my brain with more information than it can handle. I sit on a lichen rock. It's the same one that Marcia sat on I don't know when. Down below I can hear earth moving equipment interspersed with shouting from people assembling the stage, the orchestra sound shell and all the audio-visual equipment.

I opt to stay out of the way so the setup can continue unimpeded. A Recreation Park SUV drives past slowly. Sections of security fencing are stacked in heaps along the upper path ready to be assembled at a later date. I hear more vehicles arrive to offload marquees, tarpaulins and the hundreds of specially designed nest seats replete with their feathered cushions. Golda, a gelatinous arrow haloing me continuously, dives off in all directions to inform, steer and provide ongoing intuition to the numerous site and production managers pacing out the areas for support acts and displays.

The appearance of sheep wandering freely then mobbing nervously when frightened forces concentration. I look out over the gulf. In the distance bulk carriers line up to enter Outer Harbor.

Golda is aware of all this and places a cordon of ease around the workers. She does one last flight to the heart of the ballet, the final rehearsals in the Goyder Pavilion at the Adelaide Showground. She slips in through the air-conditioning and mosquitoes around Russian royalty, dying swans and a hoarse Marcia Font who is now pulling everything together with the help of the assistant directors, stage managers and a very patient rehearsal pianist at an upright piano.

Golda conveys the wow factor immediately and while the scene is organised chaos I have it on reliable authority that everything is going to plan on time, and the group energy is invigorating. All I can see and feel is utter devotion. There is a oneness that no instrument can separate. The link between performers, directors and technical crew is a bond of dedication. I gather myself for the difficult steps back home, back through history, back through the back of my head where the bulk carriers are clippers and steamers making their way into Port Adelaide.

Golda swoops down Port Road giving the watery front door to Adelaide a complete nineteenth century costume change. Working with the Akashic Records she upwardly dive-bombs heaven's consultation rooms for memory files which she spreads post Port Misery and watches as the fingers of history boot in over the rest of Adelaide on the 31st of January, 1893.

Meanwhile I've made it home carrying the images of the final hours of my work in progress. I slump in the first chair I see and want to drift off. I fight it. I must stay present.

Awake.

Killing fields of all kinds dominate but I can see and hear the energy of 500 Little People dancing their feet off in the Goyder Pavilion. I must be alert for them. Louise's letter which becomes a number one priority speaks to me. Frank's letter speaks to me. The threads can't resist tangling. Frank is here and there. Marcia is here and there. I try to avoid them bumping into each other, wonder if this is some kind of control on my behalf but then realise the great secret acts of my life are being revealed to all.

There is no imagining the terror being released that has accumulated over a lifetime. Private and public are jousting prior to an irrevocable war.

In the Recreation Park Mary Magda and Mary Virgo are preparing the layout for the final copy having completed last minute alterations to costumes and ensuring the dye is fast. Their shepherd sons who have fallen in lust with each other are scolded by their mothers for not look-ing after the imported Dorsets. They've spent the last few days with Moses, lying at his feet and encouraging him to OD on his Sinaisitis tablets while playing with his dildo.

'Leave that old man to his mind,' Mary Virgo castigates.

'He's out of his mind,' says Mary Magda.

'I'd have dementia too if I let God control my mysterious ways,' Mary Virgo adds.

Just then Bathsheba Everdene and Tess D'Urberville arrive on the pe-riphery of the layout. I wait with expectation as to who will speak first.

'Thomas will soon be here,' Tess says to mothers and sons.

'We want to check the layout for his final copy. Is that where it's to be?' asks Bathsheba.

The two Marys and their boys move about the grassy knoll indicat-ing the area ready to lay turf donated by Munns Nurseries. The curious Dorsets have regrouped and stare blankly at the roped off green page soon to be rolled out and famously described.

Tess and Bathsheba look out to sea as I wait for Golda's final trans-formation. The salmon busies herself with a last-minute check. She swoops over Shepherds Hill Recreation Park, claps and flickers her fins and swirls inside the Goyder Pavilion to do an update. Then it's back down to the Port carrying her need for both river and sea.

The pressure of an ungodly spawn of Olympic proportions has to be ignored.

She does a final bank over the coast and with her record connections with history above transforms the Port completely. The scum of dust brought by the north wind obscures her makeover but her work is complete here as the final macadam from roads is lifted, and horses, buggies and foot traffic spring to past life along with the loud chug of steam locomotives. A well-appointed carriage awaits the *Ophir* as she docks. Mr Edmund Gosse and Mrs Agnes Hay and her son and daughter await the berthing of the steamer. Word has got out that an important visitor to Adelaide is on board. Mrs Hay is pumped for questions and so too are her son and daughter.

Golda creates a distraction with her flippers by imitating a noisy minor in the ear of a blinkered Clydesdale. The usually placid gelding shies, unsettling other horses waiting on the wharf.

Thomas Hardy and his entourage disembark and are bustled into a waiting carriage with the welcoming party. Several trunks are loaded onto a dray. Hardy and co set off for the recently opened South Australian Hotel in North Terrace.

Golda leads the way ensuring attention to period detail is precise. The north wind keeps delivering its country dust in a fog of grit. Hardy sneezes and so too does Moses and the Poll Dorsets eagerly waiting to edit and graze on the quarantined slope.

'So, the place where the steamer came in was originally called Port Misery?' Hardy enquires of Mrs Hay.

'Yes, Thomas. Mud, mangroves and mosquitoes.'

'I guess I need something to remind me of a Dorset dairy,' the novelist chuckles.

'You'll feel right at home on Shepherds Hill,' Mrs. Hay adds. 'Cows, sheep and —'

'Lots of manure,' Hardy interrupts.

'Yes. Lots, Tom. They're all waiting to leave their stamp on your Australian edition.'

'While I'm here I'd like to track down a distant relative.'

Agnes Hay gives Thomas a curious glance. 'I'm sure if you know migration details you should be able to track him.'

'Her. The family lost touch with Eve. She had a tough life. A Little Person. Joined a vaudeville troupe as an exotic dancer that toured Europe and the last we heard was that she had left for these parts.'

'How long ago was this?'

'Must be twenty years.'

'That's interesting. There's a... little midget person who runs a ballet school near Shepherds Hill. I think it's the *Petit Point Academy*. I'll check it out for you, Tom. What's her name again?'

'Eve. Eve Hardy-Fonteyn.'

'What did you say her name was?'

Thomas is somewhat startled but reacts as if not hearing properly the first time.

'Eve Hardy-Fonteyn,' Agnes repeats.

The carriage rocks to a stop in the holding bay outside the South Australian Hotel. Golda does a last discrete swoop which allows the distinguished guest and his friends to disembark once more in a cloud of scented horse dust before disappearing into the hotel lobby.

Opening Fright.

I try to muster additional energy. I can't. I feel like an amoebic blob. The energy to deploy my pseudopods is unreliable. So of course it's Golda I invest my energy in to outsource, communicate and drive my intentions. Golda who watches and sees everything. Golda who knows what I want and Golda who I trust to keep the threads separate until the time is right for everything to be sewn together. Golda, my repeat course of metaphysics.

My secrecy is becoming debilitating but the realisation that Marcia and Frank might meet terrifies me. Occasional bouts of severe sweating set me back. The man I am is also the boy I want to be again so I can recalibrate life, so the Marcias and Franks in my world can coexist without feeding on guilt and judgement. The despair of two desperate lives in my head being separated makes me angry but there's no energy for the useless grip of that emotion any longer. Some kind of trusted knowing tells me I must give in. This is a time for rationing. A stillness and a calm is required so I can cope with the certainty of something akin to climate change overheating my brain.

Golda flutters enthusiastically for my direction. I'm slumped in an armchair at arm's length from the piano. I have *Swan Lake* playing in the background. Liberace's desire for improvisation is upstaged by his purring showmanship as he walks up and down the keys in expectation of the plaudits of his audience of one. The pseudopods are not present to extend appreciation so he jumps from the keys to my lap, interrupting a crucial meeting with the salmon.

Fish scales are a welcome intrusion as Tchaikovsky hums away in the background. I eventually struggle from the chair and open the curtains and windows. Now and then I can hear a blast of music that fingers its way up gullies and creeks from Shepherds Hill Recreation Park.

It's the day before the night. Or is it the day before the night?

The amoebic me fails to react to the truth of my existence but any sense of being is replaced by stress. I'm frightened by both the unknown and not knowing. There's something inside playing merry hell. A celebration turns to trepidation and then recoils to view the shock it has created once again. The biggest painful parts of creativity are being played out in a full symphony.

The Adelaide Symphony Orchestra is doing a final tech rehearsal with the cast. I should be there helping Marcia. Golda flutters impatiently and urges me to allow her to deputise on my behalf. As the pulse of music kicks my heart along, I wonder if Marcia has seen more of me than she lets on.

I try desperately to sequence events since our last meeting.

When was the last time I saw her? I'm forgetting too much. What did we both discuss?

Golda's presence unleashes more energy. I feel confident enough to discard the amoeba, the cat, and to climb out of my armchair. I want to be there to see the final run through, to help with any last-minute problems that may have to be dealt with. But it's the salmon who is negotiating for me, everything of importance in air and water. A disguised flying fish holds the keys to heaven and hell. Her intuition is so invaluable right now while I'm having difficulty dealing with the final approach.

I muse on the fish that has the stamina to deal with the demands of so many diverse people and entities. I am grateful that her salmon farming is so complete and stratospheric. Her attention to detail is admiral. The constant reassurance that she's the world's best rescue remedy allows the inner joy I must feel at journey's end.

Moses has a problem with his new commandments and doesn't understand the magic of felt tip pens. He needs an engraver. Golda finds one instantly. The engraver has doubts about 'Thou shalt pleasure thyself always' and asks a confused Moses if the new commandment is what he really wants. Moses tells the engraver it's the will of God and he's too old to be going up and down mountains all his life to gain the approval of others. 'Besides, the Sinaisitis is killing me. I have sheep to look after as well. These Poll Dorset ewes have been crossed with Southdowns. They're due to lamb soon. Miniature breed. Supposed to be a hardy strain.'

Meanwhile Mary Magda and Mary Virgo are hassled by Tess and

Bathsheba. They argue over the font size of the manuscript given the amount of space allocated for the final edit and the number of sheep Moses is prepared to release to assist the process. Bathsheba argues that she is hot off the press and should have the final say as the book is all about her and that Tess is before her time. Golda counsels the women and suggests the two Marys should concentrate their efforts on helping dress the Little People prior to the performance. All hands are needed for last minute alterations and the elderberry dye has started to run, leaving streaks in many of the costumes. Golda advises the two Marys should collect untreated water from the waterhole and soak the costumes so the dye will hold. She reassures the women that if they act now the costumes will dry in time for the performance.

Storyteller Paulette La Rouge is accompanied by a throng of reporters as she walks towards her marquee. She is asked about the relevance of Muslim ducklings and cygnets. She confirms that ducks don't like refugees and that swans should stay in their own pond.

'There's a place for everyone,' she says. 'It can't be a mix up. That's what's wrong with this country. Everybody needs to be in their right place. I'm as Christian as any duck. Swans need to be on a lake.'

'What about a waterhole, Paulette?' a reporter challenges.

'As I said before. There's a time and a place.'

Paulette looks down across the waterhole. The music stops and starts on the other side as the Little People pile onto the stage for another run through of the final sequence from Act One with the orchestra. Marcia is below Paulette seated at a control panel in the middle of the audience nests which are still being shaped into place by an army of design assistants. Golda relays everything to me as she steers me through the wonder and excitement that everyone is feeling. For the first time I'm sent a glimpse of the vastness of the stage teeming with Little People who roll onto the performance area from all directions.

My mind does another backflip to the beginnings of the ballet. The timeline in my head gets fuzzy. The whole concept from its birth gets reimagined time and time again. But I can see Marcia carrying the can and know I should be at her side offering help and support. Somehow though she has to go it alone. I know this has to be the case as it has been planned from the start. It's as if all the energy to create has been used up. The batteries of innovation and wild imagining are going flat and need to be recharged for the grand opening just hours away.

Golda receives much more of my unconditional love and the gratitude is further deepened by her steadfast examination of every element of the ballet. She alerts Marcia to potential problems ensuring that my creative partner is given the necessary support when required.

'I didn't realise there were all these midgets,' Paulette La Rouge says. 'Aren't they cute?' The redhead disappears into her marquee to set up for her storytelling session, unaware she is to appear on the same program as a doyen of English literature.

I haven't planned for Thomas and Paulette to meet and hope that several thoughtful sheep will prevent this from occurring.

Native ducks are herded together in the middle of the waterhole. The stress of the noise turns them into a flock of startled water sheep grouping for the protection of others they'd otherwise shun.

Golda informs me that refrigerated trucks of butter have arrived for the butter Lego building, but the portable toilets installed by Little Kenny's Long Drops are blocked. The stench of runaway effluent is not something to be carried by the wind when the Adelaide Symphony Orchestra has got in first with sound over smell.

A frantic Golda consults the engraver finishing Moses' commandments but he's unable to help out as it's not a job he can handle. A team of sanitary technicians from Little Kenny's are soon on hand to clear the blockage as the final rehearsal resumes. I wonder if there should've been extra night rehearsals and know that Marcia is probably thinking the same.

The unflappable Golda practices a series of heavenly detours and flings herself into the stratosphere for a final briefing with the Akashic Records. Diving back above the park she flicks me and Marcia a much-needed boost of confidence and a break for the hyped-up cast who are ready to rest for a few hours before the time of their lives. The members of the orchestra remain seated while sound levels are checked and rechecked.

Several helicopters form a dual ring above the park as Bethesda Sole and her team of giraffes are unloaded in the Ayliffes Road compound. Golda swims protective halos around performers and equipment and takes me into the wake behind the upper circle of helicopters for a final swoop over everything. A zeppelin inscribed with *Cygnet Waterhole* hums within the chug of the choppers before floating south towards Mount Compass.

Meanwhile the Moscow Radio version of *Swan Lake* continues inside but outside the strings of the Adelaide Symphony keep their pulse in readiness for the next compliant gust of wind and a final sound check.

I slump in my easy chair with one ear on the live music and another interpreting and reimagining everything Russian.

MOSES tries in vain to use the felt tip after the engraver has added additional commandments. He's not happy with the new look of the recent additions. The felt tip is a frustrating last resort to make the new commandments appear ancient. Golda reassures him and asks that he round up sheep for a final nibble through the Thomas Hardy manuscript. I decide to remain in my chair trusting that the salmon will read me carefully, act decisively and problem solve if required. The required strength to get out of the chair is non-existent. I try to fight the debilitation but know that I must conserve energy.

'Ewes or wethers?' Moses asks, getting up onto his feet. He scoops up his crook, complains about his aching back, sneezes continuously to the point where it sounds as though it won't stop and then whistles his Kelpies. The dogs eagerly congregate around their master and wait for a brief sermon before rounding up sheep in holding pens adjacent to the Munns manuscript lawn. Tess and Bathsheba are in a stand-off. There is little communication between the two women.

'I'm into sheep,' Bathsheba says coldly. 'I believe you're into cows. Your time is to come. Allow me to be the surrogate shepherdess. There're other outlets for your dairy desires on the main path.'

'Bring them all,' Golda bubbles enthusiastically. 'We may need the whole flock. There are quite a few pages to edit.' Golda blows a cloud of kisses to Moses.

Realising the increasing frailty of their master, the dogs are eager to please and round up the sheep, many of which are drinking from the waterhole or wandering close to the marquees still being set up. A few stragglers nibble the undisturbed grass between the rows of nest seats finally assembled.

Bradley and Teagan resist their need to copulate and swing into action helping their mothers wash the costumes. Seeing the sheep and dogs being mustered, they down tutus and half erections and hurry off to lend Moses a hand.

Golda reminds Moses to take his medication. His sneezing is exacerbated by the rising dust created by sheep and their pebbly eagerness to edit *Far from the Madding Midgets*.

That same dust allows Golda to place Thomas Hardy on the path to the layout of his manuscript. Agnes Hay and her son and daughter walk with the author though the semi-cleared vegetation towards the lawn setting. Tess walks past Thomas. They catch each other's eye but say nothing as if an inner knowing that the time and place is not quite right for either of them. A herd of cows form a line and cross the main path as they head towards a dairy for their late afternoon milking. Tess joins the other milk maids herding the cattle and turns back one last time to acknowledge Thomas who has reached the rise just above the cordoned off enclosure.

Bathsheba extends her hand to greet Thomas as Moses pens the last stragglers. The Kelpies and their extended shoehorn tongues move back and forth in a half circle behind their master. Moses props his tablets against an outside post of the culling pen. One after the other the dogs cock their legs on the tablets. The ink from the felt tip begins to run from the new commandment, 'THOU SHALT PLEASURE THYSELF ALWAYS'.

'This is an unexpected pleasure,' Thomas says, calm but obviously buoyed that a journey back in time should see him in the company of a law maker of biblical proportions. Golda is excited by the interchange, watches the key players and with one eye on heaven unravels the manuscript inside the roped off area. A single page rapidly multiplies. Grass fit for chewing by eager herbivores starts to poke through the words. Golda watches and waits. Bathsheba watches also. Thomas steps away from Mrs Hay and her children and peers across the layout.

As yet an out of focus page is all that can be seen. Moses has sheep in the culling race. Suddenly words from the first page appear. Bathsheba becomes the wanted eyes of Thomas and walks back and forth between each line. Her hands are folded against her conflicted heart. She stands in the margin and waits diligently for the next page to scroll and for confirmation that she is to challenge my namesake as the chief protagonist.

'When Farmer Oak smiled, the corners of his mouth spread till they were within an unimportant distance of his ears, his eyes were reduced to chinks, and diverging wrinkles appeared round them, extending upon his countenance like the rays in a rudimentary sketch of the rising sun.

His Christian name was Gabriel, and on working days he was a young man of sound judgment, easy motions, proper dress, and general good character. On Sundays he was a man of misty views, rather given to postponing, and hampered by his best clothes and umbrella: upon the whole, one who felt himself to occupy morally that vast middle space of Laodicean neutrality which lay between the Communion people of the parish and the drunken section, — that is, he went to church, but yawned privately by the time the congregation reached the Nicene creed, and thought of what there would be for dinner when he meant to be listening to the sermon. Or, to state his character as it stood in the scale of public opinion, when his friends and critics were in tantrums, he was considered rather a bad man; when they were pleased, he was rather a good man; when they were neither, he was a man whose moral colour was a kind of pepper-and-salt mixture.' (*Far from the Madding Crowd*, Thomas Hardy.)

I watch for Golda's next move. Thomas Hardy observes Moses. Teagan and Bradley, assisted by the dogs, round up the sheep and steer them all towards the race. Ewes are released first onto the manuscript. They bound across the classic, nibbling every tuft of specially grown lawn grass. As one page is imprinted with non-discerning edits Golda scrolls through the rest of the manuscript exposing Hardy's original words.

'The way your dogs work the flock makes me feel at home,' Thomas says to Moses as he momentarily takes his eyes off the flock that are hungrily reading and eating as Hebrews or Christians from either side of the page. 'Just like the Border Collies of England.'

'They obey all my commands,' Moses says turning away to sneeze. 'They're a new breed this lot.'

Thomas is about to watch the edits again but turns back to Moses quickly.

'Not Dorsets then?'

'No. I'm sorry, I was too late. Dorsets by half. I was too busy remembering to inscribe not to bring false idols before my creator when the sheep got mixed up with my neighbour's lot.'

'So not true Dorsets.'

'The ewes are all Dorsets but my neighbour's rams are Southdowns. Some call their progeny Baby Dolls. I cannot bear false witness. I wish there was another commandment to make amends.'

'Can we stop the editing for a moment please?'

Moses' request is heeded by Golda. The sheep are statues.

'So, what will the progeny be like?' Hardy, now a little more than flustered, enquires of Moses.

'Miniature sheep. Dual purpose midgets which are commanding a lot of respect here at this point of time.'

Moses swallows one of his Sinaisitus tablets and for a moment is conveniently indisposed to watch for the novelist's reaction.

'When are these ewes likely to lamb?'

'Any time now I'd say. In the meantime, thou shalt pleasure thyself always.'

Thomas Hardy is perplexed. He turns back to Agnes Hay and her children.

'Oh, Tom. What is happening?' Agnes asks.

'I'm not sure. I keep getting this strange message about command and prompt. I'm finding it hard to believe what Moses is telling me.'

He goes back over to the cordoned off area, eyes his fine words newly nibbled and indicates to Moses to keep on sending more ewes through the race. Golda upholds her heavenly grace by allowing Moses to disbelieve and then believe once more in his commandments, especially the new ones.

'There's a place coming up where the lambs can be dropped. It's a Gabriel and Bathsheba scene.'

With that Bathsheba, who has been standing still in the margin, wanders through the strewn words being chewed around. Bradley and Teagan hop out of the holding pen and go to her side. Everybody is transfixed on the unfolding word picture magically overblown by Golda's powers. The pages scroll quickly. New sheep, seeing the dispersed herd, bleat and spring with all hoofs off the ground and quickly find a place on a new page of history.

Nobody notices the diminutive figure strutting it out up the hill. Golda sees the Little Person who makes a moving dot on the landscape as she approaches.

Still in my armchair I've been given Golda's extraordinary vision and watch the unfolding manuscript and the Little Person who is striding towards Thomas and his party. Golda is excited. Her energies are constantly recharging. I think she's a great shifter of heaven and Earth but even more so on this occasion. More pages scroll as the sky fish refocuses her devotion on Thomas Hardy and his Australian print run.

'Can I stop at this section?' Thomas intervenes. 'A lot happens here. This might be a place where I can put in a bit of the Great South Land.'

Agnes Hay and her children are all eyes on their English guest. A hairy nosed wombat has burrowed into the far side of the manuscript.

'I hope that marsupial doesn't eat my words but it's worth a page of description nevertheless.'

Bathsheba, Bradley and Teagan work heavily pregnant ewes into the mirror margins as the next page appears.

'Oak, his features smudged, grimy, and undiscoverable from the smoke and heat, his smock-frock burnt into holes and dripping with water, the ash stem of his sheep-crook charred six inches shorter, advanced with the humility stern adversity had thrust upon him up to the slight female form in the saddle. He lifted his hat with respect, and not without gallantry: stepping close to her hanging feet he said in a hesitating voice,—

"Do you happen to want a shepherd, ma'am?"'

(Several ewes are steered towards the inverted commas. Teagan and Bradley hold them in close. The Kelpies sit sphinx like either side of Moses. The boys retreat to the opposite page and wait.)

'She lifted the wool veil tied round her face, and looked all astonishment. Gabriel and his cold-hearted darling, Bathsheba Everdene, were face to face.

Bathsheba did not speak, and he mechanically repeated in an abashed and sad voice, —

"Do you want a shepherd, ma'am?"'

(The first Baby Doll sheep are born).

(*Far from the Madding Crowd*, Thomas Hardy.)

'Good. That's something for me to work on before I send the final copy off to Capable Caxton. This will all fit in nicely. The smells and stains of the amended text will lift off the page.'

Gleeful Golda swoops a series of funnels, ensuring protection of the Recreation Park while Moses releases the remaining sheep across the Hardy text. Bathsheba and the shepherd boys watch the flock to the end of the novel while stopping and starting on request from Hardy when required. Golda watches Moses dragging his feet and scolding the Kelpies who once again are happily pissing up against ancient truths.

'Moses, you need to rest before nightfall. There are no more mountains to climb for you. Just learn those new commandments off by heart. And, Moses, this is the third and final time you've gone to God. He tells me that you need to prioritise or you'll be slated forever.'

'I'm about to take my tablets and sit on that holy rock up yonder and wile away the time. Who knows, I may have a few more commandments under my robe?'

Without command the Kelpies, like well-trained security, circle their master and walk to the highest point in the park where, with multiple well directed eyes and ears, act as a backup to the sensory deprivation caused by the great prophet's cataracts.

Meanwhile Agnes Hay moves in close to Thomas and whispers quietly as the last pages are peppered with mutton shrapnel and the birth of several sets of twins. Bathsheba and the shepherds slump against the mirror margins and watch the Baby Dolls struggle and nuzzle ewes that stamp their hoofs in instinctive protest against potential enemies. The protagonist skirts the margins agitated. She looks for her rightful place in Hardy's words. Curious wethers finish their reading forage and stare at the ewes and lambs on the space provided at the beginning of every available paragraph. They gaze in wonder at what might have been had they be born female but this drawn-out transgression is only acknowledged by those suffering the same cut.

The Munns lawn is mowed one last time. The two boy shepherds climb out of the enclosure leaving Bathsheba Everdene to contemplate the next move attributed to her by Hardy. She begins rolling back and forth over the entire manuscript. Sheep shit sticks to her outer garments as her imprint claims her human form as words once more. Agnes interrupts Thomas.

'There's someone you must meet,' Agnes Hay says to Hardy. 'I told her you'd be here today.'

'Her?'

Agnes Hay steps aside to reveal a Little Person who, seemingly troubled with years of unknown shame, raises her head to meet the initial curious gaze of the great novelist. Thomas blinks and looks again, the second time as an extended gape.

Like a coin the two sides of shock reveals both pain and pleasure. All eyes are on Thomas and his niece, Eve Hardy-Fonteyn. The nurturing ewes mumble quietly to their miniature progeny as long-lost relatives embrace, too stumped for words.

Up on his comfort rock Moses stands and shouts. The Kelpies bark excitedly and circle their master.

'I have another one! DO NOT BELITTLE! DO NOT BELIT-TLE!'

Thomas Hardy and Eve Hardy-Fonteyn step back from one another and while not knowing what to say, acknowledge a genuine find after years of loss. There are hidden tears of joy as wells of Victorian suppression overflow, allowing intimate family connections to be re-established.

'I know you are a famous writer,' Eve says trying to harness her emotions. 'I didn't think I'd ever see any of my relatives again.'

'And is it true you danced in *Swan Lake* with the Bavarian State Ballet?'

'After years of freak shows and vaudeville, I was glad to land on my feet.'

The Hardy relatives embrace once more as Moses continues enraptured by his latest message from God. The sheep spread out over the end papers. Golda induces a rapid gather and exit. The Hardy manuscript, soaked and stained in a distinctive ink, is relayed to Capable Caxton.

'I'm doing a signing tonight before the main show. Perhaps we can catch up on those lost years afterwards?'

Golda ensures the park is secure. She flies through the air to Black-wood and back down to Ayliffes Road. The sheep are released from the trampled Munns lawn and dot the landscape once again like white and grey rocks. Dozens of Baby Dolls, some still wrinkled and sticky, bleat and seek mothers that constantly turn and return to identify a new breed.

Permanent life in a chair frightens me as much as the grand opening only hours away. Every panic button has been pressed and I, the tortoise, feel the sweat turning to glue will render me a shell contoured from an armchair.

I pry myself out of my sedentary state and lock my thoughts onto Golda and where I can see Marcia busying herself over last minute details with the assistant directors. I know she must rest and I expect her to have a kip. But expectation of what Marcia will do prior to an extravaganza is guesswork.

I concentrate on Golda one last time and hope she has the capacity to re-energise and regenerate. Her escape from my consciousness into unknown realms is about to be tested in full. I must believe she has the capacity to pull everything together.

It's time for the threads to be woven into the final garment. I position myself so that I'm facing Mount Compass. I stand in the sun with my eyes closed and imbibe life. I can hear new commandments being sneezed into history as the hum of the *Cygnet Waterhole* zeppelin pushes against Moses' distant vocals.

There's a knock on the door. It's Marcia.

'I'll take your advice and a have a kip, Gabe. Everything's ready to go.'

Marcia falls into my arms and I'm embarrassed that I have to prevent myself from falling while taking her weight. I apologise and sense that Marcia wants to comment about how I look.

A joint combination of silence and weakness means the pair of us must rest prior to curtain up.

Curtain Up.

THE show has already begun. Halos of helicopters circle the Shepherds Hill Recreation Park. Magnetic Golda utilises the energy field the choppers create to revitalise. She shifts the parallel of latitude for the City of Churches a degree or so north and in doing so ensures a necessary alignment for the extra power supplied by wind farms and the interpretative accuracy of the Akashic Records. She clears a communication channel between the park and Mount Compass.

'I always wear this on opening nights.' Marcia dangles a pendant before securing it around her neck. 'It belonged to my great-greatgrandmother. She always wore it on first nights.'

My smile of approval is brief. The ballet in my head is warming up. In the distance I can hear the shuttle of trains mixing their diesel engines with Moscow music. Although I can't see anything I know that swans and cygnets are still wildly swimming in butter over buses and trains en route to the Park.

And 500 Little People are readying their bodies with a taxing limber.

'Think it best if we take the Ayliffes entrance,' Marcia says. 'Should go now before the crowds arrive.'

I climb into Marcia's *Kombi*, appreciative that someone else is driving. I'm glad she hasn't mentioned my physical appearance and I'm also glad I've chosen not to have a final look in the mirror. The necessity to enjoy is paramount. Just one thought and a ticket to remain in the present is the aim. The sky ballet with the helicopters continues.

In the dimming light prior to dusk, searchlights tangle their stairways to heaven in fine Twentieth Century Fox style. Golda reassures with her new-found energy which she disperses. Final checks and removal of glitches are dealt with swiftly.

Police have replaced traffic lights. A convoy of butter buses blaring Tchaikovsky head towards the carpark. Marcia parks in a side street. Jaywalkers are the norm. There are already crowds of people arriving on foot to be frisked by teams of security staff. The media are out in force. Interviewers thrust mics into the faces of unsuspecting patrons. I'm aware that in this crush Marcia is the only Little Person.

'This way, Gabe. I don't want to do any interviews.'

We show our identity cards to a security guard on a staff entrance. Marcia has to untangle her talisman. It reminds me of the threads that need to be kept apart. A panic attack is squashed promptly. The threads have been redeployed. They are the parallel cables on a funicular which will draw us up the path. I thank Golda for finding yet another innovative solution.

The searchlights are now clearly visible. Shafts illuminate shadowy treescapes surrounding the hill path. I smell animal urine, faeces and sweat. In the shadows I pick out the goal posts on loan from the Adelaide Oval. The wandering lights momentarily catch them through a stand of sugar gums so they appear as distorted moons in a semi-circle of shifting clouds. An excited and restless mob gathers behind a roped off section that pulses with the occasional shove of bodies growing around the perimeter.

European giantess Bethesda Sole emerges through the posts followed by five giraffes. The animals' eyes are blinkered. With her feathered head gear Bethesda stands as tall as the giraffes' withers. The zone surrounding the goalposts is now fully lit. There is a drumroll. A large banner reading '*IN THE NECK OF TIME*' unfurls behind the posts.

Representatives of the RSPCA inspect the animals and confer with Bethesda. Marcia is in front, fused to my lower body. Both of us are thankful it is dark outside the performing area. Wide eyes concentrate on the goal posts, the tops of which are painted in football club colours.

Bethesda is introduced to the crowd who keep pushing against the roped barricade. Like a plantation worker gathering coconuts, she frog leaps and body surfs the necks of each giraffe and ties their front feet to the goalposts. The RSPCA officials confer and wander among the animals one last time. They check each beast and the stability of the posts. Their intense scrutiny is like pilots inspecting aircraft prior to take off. The animals are patient and raise their front legs without prompting. Bethesda acknowledges the applause from the excitable onlookers once all the animals are in position. Behind the spectators a group of animal liberationists hold a silent vigil dressed in giraffe costumes which appear more like deformed seahorses. The group are adorned with placards which tell of the demise of the giraffe population worldwide.

Bethesda dismounts the last giraffe and utters a command similar to a cameleer. Tchaikovsky's *Waltz of the Flowers* commences. And like a series of sprinklers waiting for the pressure to increase, the giraffes one by one start pole dancing on a separate commands from Bethesda. The poles bend slightly as the giraffes increase speed. Lanky animal legs wrap and flay. Bethesda climbs up the neck of each giraffe and, with legs crossed, becomes an accessory to the well spun dancers. Applause then silence, a sign of utter disbelief is the response from the crowd who swarm from all directions.

Meanwhile the sheep have retreated into safe pockets and either stare or furtively account for stray Baby Dolls. The music pauses and then recommences. On a cue from Bethesda the giraffes alternate the direction of their pole dancing. This time, out-of-balance eggbeaters shake the goal posts.

I pinch myself. The present is a gift that has to be enjoyed and savoured. As I wait for the opening trail blazer to finish, I'm also critiquing everything. The quest for perfection, extravagance and an indelible impression on memory is the best propellant I know. I remember my threads as I analyse the energy I have to ration. The funicular will need to be deployed shortly because getting to the top is going to be a challenge.

Marcia nudges me and smiles. The optional time walk will soon begin and Moses is up way past his bedtime. Four-wheel drive vehicles are on hand to assist those unable to walk. I assert for myself that I'm not in this category. The giraffes conclude their pole dancing. The image of giant jigsaw puzzles made from pliable wire netting lodges in my brain, such is the delineation between contour and colour of these beautiful animals.

The searchlights resume their own pole dancing. A series of LED lit swan eggs either side of the path flicker to guide the throngs back through history and into the future.

But on an upwards trajectory.

Crowds walking up are met by crowds walking down. The air is charged with exhilaration. Golda creates additional pathways, prepares time walks and checks the levelled areas either side of the main path where mini ovals are dimly lit. In each section more giraffes are quietly feeding from cherry pickers. Bethesda Sole doesn't need seven league boots to reach the top with her pole dancers. These animals take over the offerings from the cherry pickers as the former long necks heed Bethesda's call to assemble in the middle of ovals either side of the path. I do the numbers in my head knowing that Golda has duplicated Bethesda's commands for pole dancing at the other entrance to the park. Now it's a joint offering of whirling dervish giraffes. Marcia leaves me.

'See you in your nest,' she says hurrying off to do a last-minute pep talk with the *Cygnet Waterhole* cast.

'Will do,' I reply, careful to remain discreet.

I listen to the comments of the crowd now caught up in a confluence of searchlights. In a scented mist of *Eucalyptus memoranda,* smartphones loosen from spectators' hands and clothing to form a hovering globule that ascends to mirror the flightpath of the helicopters while down to Earth I'm slap bang in the middle of an Istanbul market.

Golda sees that every thread of detail is adhered to. Bethesda Sole's modest attire reflects her Muslim roots. The six giraffes wear loose fitting scarves over their ossicones and the cherry pickers have been replaced with long ladders and reed baskets hanging from the top rungs.

Bethesda produces her cameleer cry and the giraffes begin rotating one after the other. First they circle with all feet on the ground but as they gather speed front legs lift off as if invoking and drawing on an unseen energy flow. The animals have an unlikely grace as they turn on cloven hoofs, their necks like Leaning Towers of Pisa. Many in the market crowd silently absorb the giraffe rhythm. Soon there are billowing clouds of kaftans, robes and burkas.

Moses stumbles forward with his crook, Kelpies and tablets. Golda fast forwards the time walk and mixes the nineteenth and twentieth centuries. She realises that Moses needs extra support and guidance and that his utterances might not be what God intended.

Further on from the hypnotic giraffes, the performance art troupe *The Gay Gullivers* lay prostrate on the ground. Their naked bodies shine in the searchlights as tie wires are applied and pegged into the hard earth around their bodies. A Little Person in a jockey outfit feeds the writhing men Viagra. A bouquet of erections is lost and found in the searchlight which has subtly dimmed to a hovering flicker. Nearby, six Shetland ponies have their heads stuck in nose bags of chaff. The distant baa of sheep, affirming their belonging to either a castrated flock or a new burgeoning breed, can be detected.

I observe the frustration of at least half the onlookers, searching for their smartphones.

Moses sneezes and yells from the depth of his bronchial lungs, 'THOU SHALL PLEASURE YOURSELF THEN COVET YOUR NEIGHBOUR'S WIFE OR HUSBAND!'

Without further warning there is a shrill yell from the Lilliputian polo army on their ponies. Teams of three start from opposite sides of the ground. Their combination dressage and polo routine involves hurdling the naked men with a modified mallet attached to a suction fist. The team with the highest number of climaxes wins.

'HONOUR THY FATHER AND THY MOTHER!' Moses yells as the Lilliputians deliver penile relief. His dogs circle him and howl at the helicopter halo doing a low swoop over the Gullivers.

'THOU SHALL PLEASURE THYSELF ALWAYS!' Moses repeats between sneezes as suction fist after fist is replaced by galloping ejaculant.

Seemingly confused or frustrated Moses views the moaning Gullivers and their limp penises.

'Can't you remember the latest commandment?' Moses cries tripping over tie wires and ropes while drawing pleasure from his crook. 'DO NOT BELITTLE!'

The ecstatic moans incite Golda to censor the progress of the evening's events as she mixes history with a contemporary edge to guide the searchlights to the butter Lego display. Meanwhile, with the pole dancing and dervishing complete, giraffes form a daisy chain around people and displays. Cherry pickers stop and start at strategic points to feed the towering mouths. From within the crowds, eager to find the best vantage spots, giraffe necks and cherry pickers create an unusual link. The desire to move with synchronicity appears innate. The barrier between machine and animal disappears.

I stand back from the crowd and watch the reaction. Wherever one looks there's something happening. Ears compete with eyes to be the first port of call for sensory overload.

The Lego butter castle courtesy of Cygnet River dairies is almost complete. Little People clamber over dozens of 500g blocks of *Glide* butter with spatulas. More Little People circulate through the crowd with sample trays of wafer-thin slices of sourdough bread soaked in *Glide.* Adjoining the butter castle, a smartphone bus is also a ticket office. Many are still attracted by the novelty of the swimming swans gliding over the vehicle. Costa Winwood comes up to me, preferring to watch his marketing strategy at work.

'How's everything going, Gabriel?'

I have no time for negative thought bubbles, yet allowing myself to think about anything too positive is still backgrounding my reaction.

'Going well, I think. There's a lot I didn't count on happening. Joy of the unexpected. Those giraffes and cherry pickers are a show on their own.'

There's a drum roll and a Little Person wearing plastic overlays on her feet climbs on top of the high cholesterol castle. Spready Eddy places a Cygnet River Dairy flag on the uppermost butter turret.

Spready speaks triumphantly while avoiding a yellow slipstream. 'We've managed the Guinness World Record for the largest Lego construction in the world not made from Lego!' she announces joyously. 'I don't mind being mired in Glide!' With that Spready slides down the walls of the castle to the applause of the onlookers.

Moses is concerned the masses are not heeding his commands. He steps into the arena where butter wrestling is underway with three naked LPs – *The Gnomes of Ghee*. Again, the helicopter corona shifts to a slow hover just metres above the ground. Crowds cheer and shout as the slippery trio attempt difficult manoeuvres. Moses usurps the role of referee and Golda encourages me to allow the ancient prophet to be MC for the occasion. His dogs are at bay, he's taken his prescription medication and his modified tablets are carried by Teagan and Bradley who've left their frantic mothers to dismantle and do last minute makeovers on columns of costumes.

The Gnomes of Ghee sweat and strain in a matter of melting moments. Hunched Moses tries to stabilise himself with his crook but it slips in the yellow effluent. He rights himself and while wheezing shouts at *The Gnomes of Ghee*. 'THOU SHALT NOT COMMIT ADULTERY!'

The real referee tries to ward off Moses as if contending with a huge blowfly.

'HONOUR THY FATHER AND THY MOTHER!'

Moses shoves his staff on the black plastic sheeting. It creates an orifice for melted butter to ooze through.

I wonder what will happen next. I don't want to step in and steer Moses back to more hallowed ground. The gathered crowd seem to be enjoying the alternative uses of *Glide*. Golda is there at the ready with her reassurance and encouragement. I look at the crowd thronging, shouting and cheering *The Gnomes of Ghee* and Moses picking his way through a world of centuries jammed with disorder and conflict.

I look for Costa Winwood. He smiles. The sourdough and *Glide* samples are creating a culinary impression as is Spready Eddy, the cholesterol castle and the gathering media horde. And in the background the elegant revolution of giraffes and cherry pickers continues as natural and man-made necks reach for the sky preparing for an unprecedented invocation.

'HONOUR THY FATHER AND THY MOTHER'S PLEASURE!' Moses rants again.

The Gnomes of Ghee poke their locked heads up under scrotum cushions.

'After *The Last Tango on Shepherds Hill*,' they splutter.

I LOOK for a space away from the crowds. My head is swimming free-style. I'd rather be alone at home planning for all this. Somehow the arrival of the final chapter is a letdown or going to be a letdown. The marvels of dreams finding real expression will be an inevitable wakeup. Tiredness and weakness vie for permanent occupancy. I contemplate the dual threads pulling me towards conclusions. So much energy is required with their constant winding in but the warm reception and unpredictable effects of the sideshows on the enormous crowd delivers a much needed shot of adrenalin.

Christmas and Easter have joined forces and a new day of celebration is to be born, much bigger than any second coming. Many in the crowd are still concerned that they've misplaced their smartphones, while others can't work out why they have more than one. Some can't account for the attire they're dressed in. Comforting whispers circulate that Moses might be able to explain the various outfits.

Golda sees all this and makes a belated adjustment and apologises. She's been flown off her fins with squabbles amongst the corps de ballet. A sigh of relief regulates my breathing. The necking giraffes and cherry pickers move stealthily around the perimeter. With the vehicles obscured by a sea of people there is a strange sense that the giraffes are responsible for the undulating hum of controls operating the machines. The time walk recommences its pulse once more without further glitches.

Thomas Hardy is seated in front of a marquee signing copies of *Far From the Madding Midgets.* He sniffs each book to affirm its authenticity and frequently has to banish Bathsheba back into the text with the drying sheep droppings. Capable Caxton is out the back cursing over a paper jam. Irritated that it might take centuries to complete the print run, he despairs, muttering, 'Too much dung in the works, Master. Too much dung.' But then he stands back to mop his brow soaked in lanolin and printing ink. He sighs, relieved when the special edition from Pygmy Press chugs out its final copy.

Frustrated that she's not yet a thought bubble in Hardy's mind, Tess of the D'Urbervilles abandons her job as a dairy maid and dons a pair of stilts. Still juggling a pail in one hand she attempts to milk the giraffes. Alas, her deft milk maid's fingers yield even more frustration. The giraffes are all gelded males.

Moses too has issues playing on his mind. He arrives with his Kelpies at heel while trying to drive a flock of ewes with their new progeny of Baby Dolls towards the Hardy tent. Teagan and Bradley carry the tablets.

'I'll repeat again. And the Lord said, "DO NOT BELITTLE!" So, this is what I get for nineteenth century fiction?'

The Gay Gullivers arrive wearing mankinis. Moses looks hard.

'I'm beginning to think the commandments are not worth the rocks they're written on.'

Opposite Thomas Hardy, Paulette La Rouge is about to read from her latest children's book for adults, *The Muslim Duckling. The Gnomes of Ghee* are now wearing hijabs and slip past La Rouge, and with heads fixated towards the reader start chanting, 'I am a true Austrayian. Please explain.'

Paulette goes into a huddle with her minder.

'How did they get here?'

The minder shrugs.

'We're refugees.'

'Austrayia doesn't need any more refugees. Go back to where you belong.'

'We belong here. We're Austrayans too.'

'You should all be on Anus Island. You don't look Austrayan dressed like that.'

Golda spins her fins like twin outboard motors and flies between the two parties. *The Gnomes of Ghee* step back and watch a somewhat smaller crowd saunter into Paulette's tent.

'What's that smell?' Paulette asks her minder. 'Thought I could smell fish and chips.'

Golda does a final conciliatory buzz inside and outside Paulette's tent as a small group of quietly seething Anglo-Saxon Australians congregate for a reading of *The Muslim Duckling*.

Paulette's narcissism shines through a series of bumbled clichés. She is unaware that the hemline of her latest ankle length designer outfit is stained with giraffe and Dorset excrement.

Eve Hardy-Fonteyn rushes into the tent before Paulette begins to read.

'I'm lost. Seems I'm in the wrong place at the wrong time again. I'm looking for the famous author Thomas Hardy. Thought I'd find him here.'

'Who?' Paulette asks, afraid that a combination of fear and puzzlement might crack her image and reveal the irritation hidden under her projected calm.

'Thomas Hardy.'

'Sorry. Can you explain further, little midget woman?'

'You missed him by a century or so,' someone calls out from the audience.

There is an awkward silence while Paulette nervously figures a way back to her own version of sincerity for the gathered true believers.

Eve exits into the fluidity of the time walk that Golda is able to adjust for Thomas Hardy's long lost relative. The noise and hubbub from other attractions can be heard inside the La Rouge tent. I slip inside the marquee assured that Eve is on the right path. Paulette begins to read:

The Muslim Duckling.

It's a beautiful summer's day in Tailem Bend. The sun shines warmly on the Church of the Blessed Bulrush on the River Murray. Behind the church a mother duck is sitting on ten eggs. One by one all the eggs break open. All except one. This one is the biggest egg of all.

Mother duck sits and sits on the big egg. At last it breaks open.

Out jumps the last baby duck. It looks big and strong. It is grey and ugly. It's a Muslim duckling.

The next day mother duck takes all her little ducks to the Murray. She jumps into the river. All her baby ducks jump in. The big ugly Muslim duckling jumps in too.

They all swim and play together. The big grey and ugly Muslim duckling swims better than all the other ducklings.

Paulette pauses and looks up. She flicks through the pages to the end.

'Excuse me one moment.' She quickly reads the last paragraph. 'I'm sorry. I can't go on. This is not what I wrote. I'm going to have words with my editor. This Muslim duckling turns into a beautiful swan.'

Moses flings back the opening to the tent hollering, 'THOU SHALL BRING NO FALSE IDOLS BEFORE ME!'

Paulette attempts to control her tears but unknown emotions appear to get quashed.

'My Muslim duckling becomes a Christian and everyone ends up being ordinary Austrayans. This one doesn't.'

I filter back into the crowd outside the La Rouge tent. The rest of Paulette's true believers are soon reclaimed by the masses seeking the best vantage points. The searchlights slice the night sky with their golden webs, the work of unseen night spiders. The continuous rings of compliant helicopters hover at a safe height, providing both security and a jaw dropping aerial display. Pole dancing and whirling giraffes from both pathways have now amassed weaving in and out of cherry pickers. There is a gradual movement of the animals towards a huge stage marking the entrance to the *Cygnet Waterhole*. Moses stands on a rock adjacent the stage and reads out sixteen going on seventeen commandments. There is some confusion as he mixes both the order and words. He sneezes frequently.

'Sorry the night air on this mountain hasn't been planned for. Where are my tablets?'

Teagan and Bradley thrust the rocks recently inscribed with felt pen additions in the face of the decrepit prophet.

'No. Not those ones.'

Golda drops another pack of antihistamines on the ground in front of Moses.

'Ah that's better. THOU SHALT NOT STEAL!'

I can hear the excited buzz from the LPs' dressing rooms and assembly area. Occasionally I hear Marcia's voice carried by the gentle gully breeze, creating short wave wireless reception. Panic surges. I should be with her helping with last minute problems but Golda senses my concern and is here within an instant reassuring me.

And it's a bit too late.

The twelve remaining giraffes wait in two groups of six on bulldozed slopes either side of the raked stage. Some poke their heads above the tops of more *Eucalyptus memoranda*, their horny ossicones protruding above the foliage. The remaining animals interplay with the cherry pickers and spread out around the edge of the multitude which rivals a presidential inauguration.

Bethesda Sole is dressed in a giraffe patterned leotard. She moves centre stage and bows to the audience. She utters her cameleer call as the first bars of Ravel's *Bolero* softly whispers. Single giraffes enter the stage from either side. Their deft steps are interrupted by a rocking back and forth on all four cloven hoofs. Their timing is spot on. The gentleness of their movement is difficult to comprehend given their towering necks. Bethesda walks between the animals as more pairs join those already on the stage. Some are chewing their cud, an indication that the whole spectacle has been well and truly rehearsed.

Soon all twelve giraffes step, stop and turn across the stage. Their soft eyes have been highlighted with extra-long eyelashes so on a closer look one could be forgiven thinking that a tribe of Carol Channings had been reborn as giraffes. The *Bolero* intensifies as more instruments are added. At times the animals resemble a fitness class with the giantess Bethesda, the instructor, moving to the front of the stage while sweet-talking her well trained health fanatics. The pulse of the music radiates to the other giraffes on the perimeter. They too move back and forth within the cherry picker daisy chain.

But just when the music reaches its climax, twelve swans swoop and dive gracefully between the giraffes on stage. Eleven are white but the leader is black. As the *Bolero* concludes the swans crown twelve ossicones with wings outstretched. They stand quietly like participants in a beauty pageant for sunbathing cormorants. The giraffes move to the front and lower their necks to receive the enthusiastic applause of the packed crowd with their cormorant crown of swans steadying on webbed feet.

Two helicopters break from the lower halo and circle the stage, then hover mid-air. Golda dives high and low between the sound crew, the patient giraffes, the elegant wings of the outstretched swans and the helicopters.

Frank Sinatra and Judy Garland float and parachute onto the stage singing *Embraceable You.* The giraffes and their feathered riders disperse to all parts of the stage. Some clever lighting spots the necks of the giraffes which sway gently from side to side. Each of the swans alight from ossicone heights and with necks outstretched begin to wrap themselves clockwise around the necks of those more elongated. The black swan wraps herself anticlockwise. Time and time again Ravel becomes unravelled as the swans make bow ties, ribbons and with a shake of neck feathers, Tudor ruffs. As the song concludes birds and beasts line up either side of Bethesda to a final loosening of the twelve-fold neck pas de deux. The elegant swans hang as loosened neckties from the giraffes' necks. At a distance the birds' webbed feet create upturned collars as the giraffes lean and swoop their necks over the appreciative audience while searching for the goodies provided by cherry pickers.

It is this state that I want to capture and cling to as the onlookers queue to enter the main auditorium. Golda makes sure that all is going according to plan in the dressing rooms and holding bays prior to the show's start. The out of this world fish plonks me gently on the edge of the organised mayhem. I land with webbed feet and almost topple. Mary Magda and Mary Virgo are frantically stitching and adjusting costumes.

I'm glad that Moses has not infiltrated the tiny community because it is indeed a community, so separate from the immediate past side-shows yet so together with the single purpose of showcasing the Little People. There are marquees dedicated to props and costumes for the four acts of the ballet. A special marquee and caravans for principals is in the centre. A series of small embankments, some natural and others manmade serve as the wings for stage left. A pathway behind the stage allows ease of access to stage right. Fifteen minutes before a final stage call, performers who need to enter stage right walk the considerable distance to the other side of the performing area to be cued for their entrance.

I can hear the Adelaide Symphony Orchestra positioned in its sound shell the audience side of the waterhole. Across the water the busy stage crew are doing last minute checks of the performance area. From stage left I try to make sense of the vastness of the stage. It's a suburban jetty though many times wider. I turn back and observe the growing numbers of the cast assembled in the holding area. A series of hand bars positioned at a suitable height are located towards the rear. Warmups are underway. Marcia and the assistant directors confer one last time. The stage director and her assistants prepare for the thirty-minute call.

I'm in the middle of the Cygnet River carpark again. It's an ocean seething with waves of nervous energy. The vastness of the ballet is everywhere. I consider how one of Moses' Kelpies might go having to round up this mob. Anywhere could be a starting point for the muster but that's where any comparison ends. The collective mind and soul, the contribution of a troupe of 500 is what I now rely on and what I need to sustain at a deep personal level.

I feel the threads tightening further. The need for a display of outward positivity is an additional drain on the levels in my reservoir. Marcia comes to my side. Her energy ensures I have an extra shot of vitality for the final hours.

'Ready for the big one?' She flips me a reassuring bubble.

'I'm ready if you're ready.'

GIRAFFES entwine on all sides of the waterhole. The cherry pickers are stationary. Inquisitive animals nevertheless have great expectations for fodder held aloft as they move motivated by one mouthful to sample another, often tucked in new growth on the tips of recently propagated *Eucalyptus memoranda*.

Moses, convinced his tablets are working, moves his woolly flock onto the open grazing land of the Recreation Park. His loyal Kelpies eye the helicopters and at unrequired moments try to replicate their circuits by rounding up shadows. Tess of the D'Urbervilles broods under a dead tree, an empty pail beside her. While trying to remember an appropriate commandment to heal her sorrow, Moses suggests she might like to milk one of the ewes that has lost its lamb.

'They're small compared to some of the other ruminants stalking this place but as God always says, "REMEMBER YOUR VIRGINITY AND KEEP IT HOLY! DO NOT BELITTLE THE SABBATH!"'

Tess gets to her feet and walks arm in arm with Moses. A motherless ewe is at the back of the flock and baas continuously, not yet appreciating that a full udder also means permanent loss. Teagan and Bradley, unaware of successful imprinting gambol, run up behind their master.

'Master, the show is about to start! We're all invited!' Teagan calls out, hoofing it to the old prophet.

'What show is that, boy?'

'The swan show.'

'There's already been a swan show.' Moses removes his arm from Tess's and turns awkwardly to face the boys.

'This is about people pretending to be swans,' Bradley hastens to add.

'People pretending? I'm sick of people pretending. THOU SHALL BRING NO FALSE PLEASURES BEFORE ME!'

Golda starts her aerial muster. She drops more antihistamines in

Moses' path and then uses her invisible drawcard to steer the crowds to the waterhole entrance.

'These tablets are certainly worth the inscription they're written on,' the old man says, stooping to scratch up the packet of yet another new antihistamine, *Snot Gone*.

Golda does final dives to heaven and beyond, consulting the Akashic Records one last time for confirmation to proceed. The sideshows still attract a stream of sightseers but the crowd ready to enter the landscaped theatre from two sides is packed tight. The heads of giraffes and cherry pickers are captured by the searchlights as the shifting sky paths come and go. The giraffes have created an enclosure around the main arena, providing extra if not heightened security for the main event.

I migrate towards the periphery, relying on Golda to update me with progress. But the push and pull of the crowd severs my separateness. I must join the throng who, like a swarm of purposeful bees, are maintaining their links to the universal buzz.

The vastness of the auditorium is on a par with the biggest and the best amphitheatres from times long gone, yet it is beautifully re-created with snatches of a virtual reality that my undercover salmon has been able to achieve. There are hints of Epidaurus and Rome's Coliseum, but 2,000 elegantly structured swans' nests make the waterhole theatre a unique setting.

As they find their nests, patrons assume a lotus position in their woven down and bulrush bowers. Those with mobility issues are specially catered for with wreaths that wrap around wheelchairs. Marcia and the assistant directors join me just as I'm about to enter with the official party. The CEO from the Lamington Council for the Arts chats convivially with the Premier and the Minister for the Arts. Thomas Hardy and Eve Hardy-Fonteyn, happily reconciled, try to engage in cordial conversation with Moses and Costa Winwood. Marcia is afforded a quick fisheye glimpse back in time. She rosaries her talisman and makes eye contact with Thomas Hardy's niece. There seems little for them to talk about while trying to negotiate common ground between smooth butter and etched commandments.

Eventually everyone is happy because Moses rants that 'SPREAD THE WORD' must be a commandment. Thomas Hardy agrees. Spreading the word has meant that the current print run of *Far From the Maddening Midgets* has sold out. Golda opens more channels of communication as the swans from the neck ballet do a low swoop over gathering patrons while tormenting Kelpies and helicopters with their feathered manoeuvres.

The official party take to their nests. The time walks persist inside the amphitheatre. Timelines are indicated at the ends of rows. Earlier times are at the top and the present towards the bottom. Moses tells Teagan and Bradley that he belongs near the top but the boys encourage him to forget history and to sit with them. Thomas Hardy and his niece face the same dilemma claiming that the middle of the auditorium would be more appropriate but Paulette La Rouge edges towards them.

'No, you and your little friend should sit with me. I need to get some writing tips from you. I hope you're not mixed up with those little butter Muslims,' she spits at Eve. 'They shouldn't be in our country big or small if they're Muslims.'

Hardy double takes, aware that Paulette is too involved with staring and possibly toppling into the waterhole. The trio shuffle into their nests with others in the official party while adjusting their comfort levels in the lotus position. Thoughtful Golda drops packets of Panadol Osteo at the ends of each row. Sighs of relief from those with arthritis follows the continuous pop of blister packs. Moses scrambles to his buttocks and almost pokes Teagan in the eye with his crook.

'More tablets!' he says enthusiastically, receiving pass the parcel from Paulette. Bradley removes the tablets for the old man. 'I think I'll stick to these for ever and ever. Seem to work better than inscriptions on rock. I need more *Snot Gone*. Where are those other tablets?'

Teagan drops two *Snot Gones* into Moses' left hand. Along the row he sees Mary Magda and Mary Virgo shuffling quickly into their nesting positions. I'm next to Marcia. The pain of acquiring the lotus position is affecting me too. The world's greatest mind reader flaps her dorsal fin which serves as a relaxant. I cast my eye about the auditorium as does Marcia. All the nests are full.

Incubation is nearly complete.

Suddenly the swans from the neck ballet make an appearance out of the thinnest air and dive around the auditorium as aircraft hum non-stop high in the clear night sky. I consider the transformation needed for the audience to become the performers and vice versa. The 2,000 occupants of the nests privately share grace and contemplation while waiting expectantly yet unaware of the performance they're soon to hatch. In this very audience I too am setting a new standard in audience participation. Unbeknown, me and everyone attending have been rehearsing for parts in the motionless ballet, *Sitting it Out*.

Golda edits the hatching time. Weeks are condensed to days, then hours and minutes. The Adelaide Symphony Orchestra are in their shell, fine tuning before the arrival of the conductor. The Ravel giraffes are inclined to pass on their intricate footwork to the rest of their mob. Bethesda Sole, like a nesting fulcrum in the centre of the official party, emits her cameleer call. Bolero behaviour unwinds instantly as the Meccano heads of giraffes and cherry pickers arabesque quietly. The neck swans fly low over nests changing the dimension of their circles with each round. The house lights on towers between trees begin to dim.

Moses' eager Kelpies, on lookout for their master, run down both aisles and take up positions before the front row. They bark excitedly. Moses levitates and shouts, 'I AM THE LORD, YOU DOGS!' With that the Kelpies relax, retract tongues and lower lipsticks, to sit statuesque as timeless sphinxes. Golda, convinced that all is in readiness for a start, swivels the auditorium gently from side to side and then the performance area. Satisfied the alignment with Mount Compass is complete, an announcement is made for all electronic devices to be turned off.

Again Golda has to do an ethereal sweep to reassure many of the setting swans that suspected losses of smartphones are all in the mind.

A moment of darkness rests the eyes but not the ears. The hum of helicopters as both aerial security and invocation remains. The first splash of light ripples across the waterhole and then the massive stage which now appears to rise from the watery depths. The live swans untied from the neck ballet glide onto the waterhole from both sides. White swans land from the right while the black leader alights from the opposite side and weaves through the orderly line approaching her. The opening music to Act One commences. Marcia sits forward on her nest. I can feel her tap the opening bars with her right hand across her left arm as if readying her own wings for flight. The sea of blue joining stage and water dissolves into more verdant hues as a bushland setting rises upstage, extending the stand of *Eucalyptus memoranda* hugging the areas immediately beyond the sightlines. The allegro giusto changes to a waltz to reveal Prince Siegfried joined by his tutor, friends and uninvited bogans around a barbecue.

The threads tighten further. I'm uncomfortable with the inner drag in my gut. But I can override this discomfort as my eyes feast on hundreds of Little People spreading and then collecting in a group celebration of the Prince's birthday. All around me I feel the uplifting energy of the audience focussing on the spectacle across the water. All around me, air is swapped with water. Two thousand nests appear to lift as necks stretch and arch to receive and return the reciprocal energy of performers and audience. I shift in my nest, glance briefly along the row at the official party. But there is so much happening on stage. At a first glance it seems to be chaos. Individuals seem to be doing their own thing in terms of celebrating the Prince's birthday. Cans, stubbies and eskies become objects for juggling. Tomato sauce oozes from sausages with hernias, but then miraculously in this mass of merriment and indulgence the corps de ballet regroup in fine waltz time. All areas of the stage are populated with a diverse community and though vertically challenged the bobbing colony of Little People create an extravaganza.

My eyes searches for balance and find it. The stage is indeed a park. There is little imagination needed to convince one that a celebration in every sense of the word is unfolding. The gasps, sighs and spontaneous applause keep tightening the threads. I want to give in and give over to all before me but the internal reminder of the tug of war for final assimilation can't be ignored. The dogs can smell sausages and start to whine. Moses roars at them over the dulcet tones of the orchestra. 'I AM THE LORD YOU DOGS!' He tumbles back into his nest as Prince Siegfried armed with a crossbow moves downstage and takes aim at the swans which glide across the waterhole yet successfully outsmart royalty with mobile phones in their bills. I'm aware of a flinching crowd around me who recoil and shuffle in their nests but finally applaud enthusiastically from various stages of incubation.

And I spare a thought for Peter and wonder how he'd react to this interpretation of his work.

I can't wait for Act Two to start. To see hundreds of swans on stage. Marcia nudges me, smiles and becomes a little tense. Four lines of the beautiful bird maidens have to arrive on stage within a set time fame.

I remember her talking about getting this to happen, first with two lines but now with four.

The blackout is replaced with a sea of blue that stretches from the trees behind the stage and spills into the waterhole. Siegfried paces about with his crossbow and takes aim at the birds in the waterhole. I'm more concerned with the presence of over 300 little swans on stage at the one time than the actual plot.

And there they are before me on a performance area swallowed up by ingenious lighting and real water. The threads tighten again almost tying me into my nest. I can't breathe. Golda sprays past quickly. Gasps followed with spontaneous applause greet the corps de ballet once they're all in position. The subtle splash of elderberry on single pleats of each tutu is but one feast for eyes that need to assimilate so much. Frogmouth owls like large moths fly in and out of the unexpected light and flutter for the cover of darkness the other side of the real *Eucalyptus memoranda*. Around me the audience stretches and leans forwards and from side to side so as not to miss the spectacle which constantly unites the elements. Moses sneezes occasionally but his dogs, remembering his commandment, remain statuesque apart from wandering tongues.

The pas de deux between Siegfried and Odette and the Valse des Cygnes adds to the enchantment, enthralling the audience. The presence of the sorcerer Von Rothbart stirs Moses even more. Golda secretes a thinly veiled calm over him to prevent any further updates to his commandments or accusations of misplaced idolatry. Siegfried moves downstage and breaks his crossbow. He hurls it into the waterhole as the pitter patter of 300 Little People regroup around Odette and the Prince in a picture almost too wide for normal vision but loaded with impressions beyond belief. The waterhole swans regroup in a semicircle and with necks outstretched and wings continually splashing the water watch the swan maidens depart in four ordered lines prior to succumbing to their daytime spell as water birds like them. The final bars of music conclude with the stage lights replaced by 'house' lights that reveal some well-maintained nests, swans that need to stretch their legs and giraffes and cherry pickers maintaining a quiet interplay between lengthy ruminant and mechanised hoist.

I look at Marcia. And she me. I can tell she's happy with how things are going. I de-lotus and walk back up the tiered aisle to the drinks tent for the official party. The sideshows are still in progress. There are long queues for toilets and food and beverage stalls. *Swan Lager* is popular as well as swan pate. I walk into the drinks tent where the official party are already discussing the performance. Curried swan eggs, canapes, Dorset feta cheese and samples of *Glide* butter are taken around the group by Little People. *The Gnomes of Ghee* minus their Muslim attire stop to chat with Paulette La Rouge.

'You're not really Muslim, are you?' Paulette asks one of the waiters as she claws at a crumbling piece of curried swan egg.

'Oh, yes I am,' Garry, the leader of the ghee wrestlers answers. 'We all are.'

'Can't be. I need to speak to the Premier of this state to ask why this can happen. You need to go back to your own country.'

'There are no jobs in Lilliput these days,' Garry says as he moves on to serve other guests.

Golda, sensing possible conflict, thrusts a series of rapid time periods before the redhead so that Ms La Rouge is forced to focus on and check her attire several times.

'Who said that?'

'Who said what?' Eve Hardy-Fonteyn asks.

'Oh, you're the lost little woman from earlier on.'

'Who said what?' Eve presses.

'Somebody told me to take a good look at myself in the waterhole. I don't know who it was. Some voice. Do you think I'll have time before the next part of the show?'

'You can always use a mirror,' Eve suggests, catching Paulette's eye and then moves on to speak with her novelist uncle.

As usual I prefer to stick to the outside of the chatty group. I watch *The Gay Gullivers* twirl around and look up at Bethesda Sole. I insist that Marcia should mingle and speak to whoever she wants. Over flutes of champagne, heads turn in my direction. The group smile is contagious. I feel I need to respond individually but the tightening threads create passing cramps which I deal with by pretending I'm preoccupied with performance details. A small part of me watches the madness of this mix.

Where else would I find the Spready Eddys of this world rubbing shoulders with the likes of Costa Windwood, *The Gnomes of Ghee* chatting to the Premier and a CEO from the Lamington Council trying to make sense of Moses high on *Snot Gone* and Brut champagne?

The sound of low flying helicopters all operating their shark watch sirens signals the beginning of the second half. Golda mutters and flutters about all the way into the auditorium. Marcia catches up as I return to my nest. A whisper goes around the auditorium as Marcia is spotted. But there are worries from some of the audience who've discovered eggs in their nests. Ushers are summoned but those concerned are reassured and resume incubation.

I seek anonymity as I return to a comfortable lotus position. Teagan and Bradley help Moses onto his nest, pump him with more *Snot Gone* while *The Gnomes of Ghee* bring water for the Kelpies just metres from the orchestra pit. Paulette La Rouge thinks about looking in the waterhole but defers in favour of the makeup mirror in her purse. She wants to chat with Thomas Hardy but he has swapped seats with his niece Eve.

'I hope you're not a Muslim like those dreadful little midgets looking after the dogs.'

'I could have been,' Eve calmly answers.

'What do you mean could?' Paulette tries to look past Eve to catch Thomas Hardy's attention before finalising eye contact with the Little Person next to her.

'I grew up in a different era. I know what it's like to feel discriminated against.'

There's a round of applause for conductor Vaughan Valley as he makes his way to the podium in the glare of a roving spot. I have just enough time to cast my eye along the row of guests in the official party. Marcia clutches her talisman and fondles it unaware that Eve Hardy-Fonteyn has leant forward to look through her. At the same time her preoccupation with possible family connections helps her avoid another conversation with Ms La Rouge.

Tess D'Urberville sneaks in at the last moment and positions herself in an empty nest. I'm impressed at how well she adapts herself to the status of a brooding swan. She looks for the man who is yet to write about her but her line of vision is obscured by an agitated redhead who has got off her nest but then repositions herself and arches her neck hoping it will stretch to the waterhole.

As the house lights dim the criss-cross of masticating giraffe heads and cherry pickers are restored to provide a turret of protection. Helicopters fly low overhead once more before forming a circular staircase that drones in the background. Golda meanwhile hovers about me with increased frequency. Marcia stretches forward in her nest. The live swans swim in an anticlockwise direction, replicating the choppers above. One of them carries a banner advertising *Glide* butter. The gracious birds slide to the sides of the waterhole as native ducks protest their presence by popping up like a fleet of mini submarines.

The tension of the competing threads is unbearable.

I feel as though I'm backtracking and fast forwarding at the same time. There is no time for thoughts, as if there was ever such a time anyway.

It's all feelings. The feelings I should have, haven't had, will have and are having now.

The music starts and the stage is lit with assorted hues of green. Back lighting through the trees creates a dappled effect. From upstage a surreal gazebo is created with walls covered in the Latin names of dwarf plants found growing on Shepherds Hill Recreation Park and close environs. They are all encrypted in the Cyrillic alphabet. An arrow points to 'SNAKE GULLY'. Shingle rooftops of chook pens and cowsheds give the impression of other buildings in the distance. I wonder what Tchaikovsky might think about this representation but I keep telling myself his music hasn't been interfered with and the dance sequences are almost an exact replica of a traditional presentation of the ballet. Marcia is on the edge of her nest. She leans forward and scans the stage. I can feel a soft sigh of approval as she sits back. There's another round of applause as the performance area is quickly filled with hundreds of Little People partying at Prince Siegfried's 'holiday' home. As with the first two acts I shift between the diminutive stature of the performers, the numbers on stage at any one moment and the overall effect determined by the consummate professionalism of the artists.

There's the usual vying for the Prince's hand by foreign princesses but von Rothbart and his daughter Odile disguised as bikers attracts Siegfried's attention. When he mistakenly proffers his love for Odile, von Rothbart shows Siegfried a photo of Odette on his smartphone. Siegfried kicks the phone into the waterhole where it is caught by the solitary black swan which with wings spread out thrashes continuously in the water as the act ends. This sets the Kelpies right off. Moses yells above the final bars of music as the live swan continually thrashes.

'THOU SHALL NOT COMMIT ADULTERY!'

The auditorium lights are brought to half. I can see the giraffes and the tops of the cherry pickers. Their shadows are a splash of mottled images from stage to waterhole. The black swan glides off into the darkness but is accosted by other birds uneasy with the intruder.

Paulette La Rouge leaves her nest and hurries towards the waterhole while the lights are dim. She peers into the blackened jigsaw of giraffe reflections and the translucent foliage of trees. She waits for some time wanting answers and when none are forthcoming she mutters that Muslims are preventing her getting the information she needs.

All around me the swan audience turn in their nests and roll eggs before resuming final incubation. Teagan and Bradley assist Moses with some intimate manoeuvres so the old man is comfortable. Although half asleep he mutters incoherently about not 'stealing pleasure' and 'not killing God.' Mary Magda and Mary Virgo swap notes on costume alterations while Marcia gets off her nest and chats with the assistant directors and Costa Winwood. I try to shift in my own nest but wrestle with panic because of an increasing lack of mobility.

The threads touch and separate and each time this happens I see bright light. I try to keep the fibres apart by imagining I'm using them for support as I walk across a bridge constructed of vines. Golda is spending more time checking on me, yet I in turn am checking Marcia and worrying about the salmon's workload.

The lights dim to a blackout. Paulette La Rouge, still muttering, farts in the faces of the official party as she ruffles her way back to her nest, her red plumage falling to one side. The orchestra starts and the envelope of blue from trees to waterhole again creates the sensation of the oneness of water fusing with air. The population of swan maidens are balls of cotton wool plopping around Odette while attempting to permanently unite a life beyond the elements. Von Rothbart's insistence that Siegfried marry his daughter Odile is spurned by the Prince. The black swan makes her solitary appearance on the waterhole again, pursued by flocks of native birds. She thrashes the water as the swan maidens try frantically to comfort Odette.

Choosing to die alongside Odette, Siegfried leaps with her into the waterhole breaking Rothbart's spell over the swan maidens.

Apotheosis.

THE distant chop of helicopters mows the night sky. Rotor thud echoes as the *Cygnet Waterhole* ballet concludes. A sudden blackout hits. Seconds later half-light reveals the cygnet maidens curled across the stage in foetal positions. The helicopters are metres above the performance area. The cyclonic downdraught vibrates the leaves of the remaining *Eucalyptus memoranda,* changing their evergreen status to deciduous.

I want the darkness to continue. To imagine what will be rather than what is. Creating history in anonymity while surrounded by thousands is my final curtain. I cannot direct the future.

The black swan is nowhere to be seen but other native birds interlink their wings to form a semicircle around a bubbly ring. Ripples are sent to the edge of the waterhole and the enormous stage. The helicopters are uncomfortably close now. The amphitheatre audience shift in their historic timeline nests and with necks tilted like real birds, watch the helicopters hover. Moments later the choppers exit one at a time, leaving previously unseen waves on the water below. In their place, flying ungainly, but attempting their own version of an aerial ballet is a flight of pelicans.

The birds form two sets of steps either side of the stage. The gentle growl of the *NunAir A380* is heard approaching overhead. Roving spotlights shine on the disciplined pelicans in their arrowed shuffle. Further into the night sky parachutists with flares are dropped from the consecrated Airbus.

I take my time to look around. All movement is becoming harder by the second. I see and then I can't. Somebody is skimming something across well-trodden water. The cygnet maidens remain curled in unbirthed blobs. The first parachutist alights on the pelican steps. Strength must be mustered to really look this time. A sea of floaters swims across retinas. I blink. And blink again.

Saint Teresa's postulants balance on the feathered stairways, their parachutes trailing behind.

And finally, the saint in her skeletal remains rattles down amongst the motionless cygnets.

A small child loudly remarks, 'Isn't she bony?'

To which there's a reply, 'It's not Napoleon, dear. It's Saint Teresa.'

The hungry giraffes, having emptied every cherry picker on the *Cygnet Waterhole* perimeter, make their way onto the rear of the stage, stepping carefully over the bodies of the little maidens. The rest of the cast join them, some pirouetting between the feet of the thirty-three giraffes that have begun a gentle dervish. The live swans on the waterhole opt to cormorantise their body movements. In doing so they imprint their pelican brethren who are still in a feathered stagger from mirroring the helicopters.

Bethesda Sole rises out of her audience nest anxious about the impromptu behaviour of her giraffe herd. On an upper level near the beginning of the timeline, Moses snores. Closer to the waterhole, Paulette La Rouge wants to know if the giraffes have been trained by Muslims and will take over the country in disguise.

Saint Teresa digitalises the cast of the 500 Little People, all who are former residents of Hindmarsh Island. Downsized by the exhumed saint previously, they receive an individual update from a powdery finger bone. The last leaves on the *Eucalyptus memoranda* flutter. A giraffe kicks the saint who goes flying in a cloud of blood and bone. The postulants rush to her aid and fix several fractures with the gaffer tape they've been obliged to carry with them on recent outings. The remaining giraffes line up and move downstage while turning slowly. They bow to the audience.

At this point some specially anointed little swans know exactly which neck is which. The cygnets curl around their giraffe sidekicks to be acknowledged by the still nesting audience. A screeching swarm of refugee cockatiels in search of slender pine trees flock mistakenly to the giraffe necks and make clusters of diamante scarves. Then the remaining corps de ballet rise and file past and underneath the giraffes to take their bows before the hushed audience. Meanwhile the pelicans descend on the stage step by awkward step and wander through the corps de ballet to regurgitate a habit learned from a past incantation – the undigestible smartphones once swallowed on Hindmarsh Island.

The cast acknowledges my little mate, Marcia. She makes her way with several production assistants onto the stage via the re-formed pelican bridge across the waterhole. As Marcia receives a sitting ovation and she acknowledges me from the stage, a spout rises from the waterhole.

I remain seated with a knowing I must allow for the unknown. I can't separate action from reaction.

Around the auditorium aftershocks can be heard and felt in every nest. Lotus positions are relinquished as cracked eggs reveal more smartphones. Members of the official party jump from their nests in unison and retrieve the secrets of their own incubation.

Everybody's mild embarrassment is on show as the comparison is made with checking underwear prior to a necessary full cycle machine wash.

Everybody except Moses who dozes, now very tired from his long trek up the Shepherds Hill Recreation Park following the exodus from Egypt. His apostolic Kelpies unable to contain themselves any longer are barking, ferociously eager to audition for *The Boys from Brazil*.

Moses wakes with a start and watches the waterspout ascend like a meteorite in reverse. Diminutive Odette and Prince Siegfried squeeze through a pus-filled orifice of a large slimy bolus produced by the spout to join the rest of the cast.

'I AM THE LORD YOUR GOD!' Moses cries. His Kelpies settle.

Saint Teresa sees Moses, breaks off one of her fingers and throws it to him.

'I *AM* THE LORD YOUR GOD!' she echoes. 'BET YOU CAN'T BEAT THAT!'

An exhausted Golda flutters and flops her fins between the stage and the audience. Now everyone is watching the bolus head heavenwards. The searchlights give extra thrust as it ascends but the power within its tangled entrails, provided by hundreds of smartphones texting and flashing, is staggering.

Thousands of faces stare at the bolus gathering speed. Necks having experienced inordinate amounts of stretching during the performance find it easy to tilt, gaze and fixate. Some rather personal voice messages boom into the amphitheatre.

I realise I'm relying on Golda increasingly as I try to gauge the reaction of the official party in their nests either side of me. My eyes want to see but it's a continual rehearsal of memory that I depend on for this ultimate performance. The curtain is slowly lowering.

Paulette La Rouge seeks consolation in the message she has received from the waterhole during intermission.

'I was told to buy a new smartphone. *Narcissus Plus*.'

Eve Hardy-Fonteyn prepares to do a walk back with her famous writer uncle Thomas but stops to talk to Paulette.

'Does that thing discriminate, or can you talk to anyone?' Eve asks.

'I don't know.' Paulette's reply is terse.

'I wish I knew because I only have a little time left. I need to make an apparition.'

'Are you changing people into Little Muslims?'

'Possibly.'

Aware that cameras might be recording her, Paulette opts for a string of clichés to hide her frustration.

'Can someone please explain why I need *Narcissus Plus*?'

Deaf ears from centuries of conversations are forced to contemplate a smorgasbord of visuals as the gelatinous smartphone tumour bursts and sucks back fiery pus on its journey up and beyond. It makes a turn to the southeast as Golda tries for a final northern alignment of Greater Adelaide's latitudinal coordinates of 34.9 degrees south. In doing so the earth shudders and everyone begins their own dervish in nests or on the ground. The corps de ballet, giraffes, cygnets and production crew turn anticlockwise, and the timeline audience clockwise.

A Hardy mob of Dorset ewes and the new hybrid breed of Baby Dolls progeny enter the amphitheatre. They have little difficulty in responding to the established routine, having engaged in something similar since the birth of the Little Ones. Moses' Kelpies alternate between clockwise and anticlockwise. They mimic Barbra Streisand:

Sheepdogs. Sheepdogs meeting little sheepdogs are the luckiest sheepdogs in a whirl.

Paws, hoofs and hands are held aloft as a soft hum of contemplative gentleness is established. Marcia fondles her talisman and briefly feels the past presence of Eve Hardy-Fonteyn.

Moses leans on his original tablets and, using them as a walking frame, manages to spin at his own pace. He has a vision of Mount Sinai and while breathing heavily, becomes the credible depiction of millions over the centuries.

Thomas Hardy imbibes all the fortunes of the challenged Tess he is soon to write about and thinks on as he bids farewell to the future and his last days in the colony.

Golda ensures that every audience member is comfortably moved back or forward in the amphitheatre to their true being and belonging.

I don't move. I sit in my nest and watch. Marcia smiles at me but she is moving further away. Orchestra members are improvising to the sight of multiple spinning bodies because a sight it still is.

And yet increasingly I question whether I'm a blind seer having to choose between faith or fate.

The heightened bolus erupts in a spectacular fireworks display. The helicopters circle higher, dragging lit halos behind them. The *NunAir A380* expels a monstrous crown-of-thorns pavlova.

I'm a rock. Everything is hard and tight. I'm in an iron lung with a mouth drooping to one side, quarrying my face. My throat's on fire. Disoriented, Golda flies off course and flops lifeless into my mouth.

The transgender salmon, my forever stage manager and alter ego is cremated in the furnace between my tonsils. The tightness intensifies. Now I'm a shuddering slab of hardening cement. The spinning gradually subsides.

I'm nothing but pre-set grief.

The cement has trapped me and my pain.

Private and public threads have finally crossed to join as one.

Weak except for wonder, I can just manage to peer through a series of colourful halos. There's cheerful singing. But disentangling from within a cement slab is difficult. It obstructs the beauty I can just discern. A beauty I've always yearned for.

An undulating paddock waves its greenery. In the grass I can see some movement. Without warning, the heavy confines of cement, the claustrophobic and depressing constraints of disability crack apart releasing plasma.

I float as I gather sticky form.

The paddock levitates above the stage. Corps de ballet, production crew, giraffes, swans, pelicans and nuns make a clearing for the trampoline grass to settle. It's uncomfortable being caught up in a wobbly spectacle.

The exhaustion of being trapped in a cement coffin remains a dead weight.

But miraculously I'm out.

There's only one thread now.

I see Marcia beaming broadly. Now I drift aimlessly but in doing so recover full form. Like my lost fish I swim towards the stage with hidden fins and to the paddock from nowhere. There's cement dust in my eyes. I don't want to see, or I can't see. Cataracts muddy a vision, or is it a prophecy? Everything's a shifting blur.

I try to acknowledge every being on and off the stage and on as many levels as possible. There's instability with my recently revived land legs. It's important that words don't pollute genuine feelings or the thoughts and emotions of a difficult journey.

Applause starts. It's getting louder and it's sustained.

I'm still on the edge of the paddock on what has become a never-ending stage. The applause continues. I can see something blinking in the middle of the paddock. This time I step onto fake grass.

There's only one thread now, I remind myself. *There's only one thread now.*

The grassy knoll rises just above the cheering crowd and floats between reproducing halos.

All I can see is a burka of bantam chicks with the beginnings of first feathers. The fluttering birds cloud a human figure.

I want the cement back immediately. To be contained and trapped forever with the pain I know and expect. It's safer there than this future picture about to come to life.

But there's only one thread.

The single cord needs to be unravelled. I catch a glimpse of a man's face from behind steadying wings.

Horror is doused in unexpected rapture.

'Frank?'

'Hello, Gabriel.'

'What's all this?'

'Little People, Shetland Ponies, Baby Dolls. And my bantam chicks. Love doesn't discriminate.'

'What do you mean?'

'You know me better than I know myself, Gabriel. These are all mine. I'm their mother.'

The developing chicks cheep plaintively to the man I once met in the Hyperbole Bar.

'You?'

'Sorry I haven't been in touch. You could say I've been laid up.'

The baby chicks fly from Frank and land on me.

'Oh, Gabriel. You'll be a wonderful father.'

'Me? The father? No.'

I spit sticky chicken feathers off my lips.

Can't be. But could it?

'Oh, yes. You.'

I turn away and walk to the edge of the paddock. I try to look down. I want to go back. But recalibration is not an option. Scoops of clouds hide the Earth.

'We'll be landing soon thanks to your terrific tech crew above and beyond. On a green hill not that far away.'

I burp, remembering Golda. Death and a need to grieve continue to place a huge demand on emotional resources.

I've a senseless appreciation of time and place.

And a fading memory of *Cygnet Waterhole*.

I look at Frank confused, remembering my first encounter with him and embrace him through a wreath of beaks. The sleepy chicks hop from shoulder to shoulder confident of their common DNA.

Frank whispers to me.

'Oh, Gabriel. Be an angel and fuck the Christ out of me.'

I step back, allowing chicks to reposition themselves as a feather bridge. Tired but appreciating I'm not altogether threadbare, I smile wryly.

New pin feathers on the small of my neck stand on end.

~

POSTSCRIPT

RESEARCHERS IN MEXICO FIND EGGS FROM CHICKENS IMMUNIZED WITH HIV CONTAIN ANTIBODIES AGAINST THE VIRUS

Soler Claudin C and five other researchers in Sto. Tomas, Mexico, have found that pathogen free chicken, when exposed to the HIV virus, produce IgY antibodies in their eggs. Purified HIV-1 virus was injected into 5 chickens 4 times. Blood serum and eggs were tested weekly for antibodies to the HIV virus. They report that the transfer of the IgY antibodies from the chicken to their eggs are similar to transplacental transfer that occurs in mammals. The IgY antibodies are transferred to the yolks of the eggs.

They reported that IIIb/LAV ELISA tests found the presence of high titer specific HIV-specific IgY antibodies in the serum and in the purified IgY yolk fractions of the 5 immunized chickens. Western blot assays with the same antigen demonstrated the presence of specific anti-HIV-1 antibodies against p17, p24, p31, p41, p51, p55 and p66 while no clear response was found against gp120 of the HIV virus. The researchers reported their techniques would be useful in developing a passive immune vaccine.

(From *Positive Health News and Progressive Health News* which are newsletters that supplement the book *How To Reverse Immune Dysfunction*. www.keephopealive.org.)

Medical Advisory Board
David Miyauchi MD, Honolulu, HI 808-949-8711
Richard Simmons MD Westerville, OH 614-895-0102
Susan Groh, MD Merrick, NY
Ronald Peters MD Cave Creek, AZ
Bruce Levine DC Syosset, NY 516-364-3382
Gayle Eversole CRNP, PhD, AHG Lake Stevens, WA
Christina White BA, Richland Centre, WI.